THE ORDER

WORKS BY JEREMY ROBINSON

The Didymus Contingency
Raising The Past
Beneath
Antarktos Rising
Kronos
Pulse
Instinct
Threshold
Callsign: King
Callsign: Queen
Callsign: Rook
Callsign: King 2 – Underworld
Callsign: Bishop
Callsign: Knight
Callsign: Deep Blue
Callsign: King 3 – Blackout
Torment
The Sentinel
The Last Hunter – Descent
The Last Hunter – Pursuit
The Last Hunter – Ascent
The Last Hunter – Lament
The Last Hunter – Onslaught
The Last Hunter – Collected Edition
Insomnia
SecondWorld
Project Nemesis
Ragnarok
Island 731
The Raven
Nazi Hunter: Atlantis
Prime
Omega
Project Maigo
Refuge
Guardian

Xom-B
Savage
Flood Rising
Project 731
Cannibal
Endgame
MirrorWorld
Hunger
Herculean
Project Hyperion
Patriot
Apocalypse Machine
Empire
Feast
Unity
Project Legion
The Distance
The Last Valkyrie
Centurion
Infinite
Helios
Viking Tomorrow
Forbidden Island
The Divide
The Others
Space Force
Alter
Flux
Tether
Tribe
NPC
Exo-Hunter
Infinite^2
The Dark
Mind Bullet
The Order

THE
ØRDER

JEREMY ROBINSON

For the real Cassidy Rose,
For inspiring such a fun character!

PROLOGUE

When you're killing Nazis, it's tempting to let your less noble side rise to the surface like a vengeful poltergeist. Killing in a war, for the preservation of life on a grand scale, is a good thing. Enjoying it is *not*. To avoid that sinister temptation, we set standards, follow guidelines, and do no harm—except to Nazis plotting genocide.

So, when Chuy says, "I count four pint-size in the AO," things get complicated.

After months of hunting down their co-conspirators, this cell has resorted to shielding itself with children—probably their own.

"Ages?" I ask.

"I look like a pediatrician to you?" Chuy is somewhere in the forest surrounding the compound, looking down the scope of a sniper rifle. I can't see her, but I have no trouble imagining the dour look on her face. She's a fighter. A soldier. She's not a fan of children, and despite meeting our descendants in the future, a family is not on our radar at the moment.

"How tall are they?" I ask.

"Tallest is sub-four feet," she says. "Smallest is two feet."

"They are young," Cowboy says, crouched beside me. While I'm wearing tactical gear, carrying an assault rifle and enough mags to spray-and-pray John Rambo style, he's dressed like we're about to meet Billy the Kid at high noon. Even has a red bandana around his neck. He might as well be wearing a target, and I've told him several times, but I think the threat of danger heightens his reaction time.

"Hold on," Chuy says. "Movement."

"What are you seeing?" I ask.

"Man wearing a lab coat. Has a real Mengele vibe about him. Holy shit..."

"What is it?" I ask, wishing I could see through her eyes.

"Laboratory," she says. "Center of the compound. He's inside now."

We've been all around the world, taking out Nazi cells, but we've never come across a laboratory in which a plague could be created. In my original timeline, white supremacy blossomed into full-on, old-school Nazism in the not-so-distant future. The result was a manufactured plague that targeted a specific, but vast, group of people: anyone with more than a dash of melanin in their skin. The result was a 'purified' nightmare future, and I've been sent back to this time to stop the outbreak before it leaves the test tube. If there's a lab here, this might be ground zero for the virus.

"Where are the kids?" I ask.

"Three of them are in the southeast Quonset hut," she says. "Fourth is...strapped to a woman. North end of the compound."

"How many hostiles?"

"I've counted twenty-two. Could be more inside the buildings."

The compound is spread out over several acres of Washington State forest. Built around the trees, it's nearly impossible to see from above. A mix of trailer homes, metal Quonset huts, shipping crates, and apparently a lab of some kind.

"What's the mood?" I ask.

Cowboy gives me a side-long glance. We've been working together for a while now, but he's still getting used to the rapport Chuy and I share, not only because we're a couple, but because we've been operating in various hells on Earth—and throughout the universe—for a long time.

Back in the 80s, when Uzis were all the rage, and the Soviets were the bad guys, we served the good ol' US of A as part of a Marine Rapid Reaction Force. That's how we ended up in Antarctica, sent to secure a strategic site containing an artifact that sent us a thousand years forward in time. We worked there as Exo-Hunters, scouring the universe for habitable planets—and our missing teammates—and we ultimately led a rebellion against the Union, an evil Fourth Reich empire. Doesn't sound like the backdrop for romance to blossom, I know, but here we are, back in the past, going strong. And Chuy knows as well as I do that the enemy's emotional state can make or break a mission.

Maybe not for someone like Cowboy, who can empty both revolvers faster than I can raise my rifle. But for us mortals, exploiting our enemies' weaknesses—physical, psychological, or emotional—can help keep us alive.

"On guard, but melancholy," she says.

Word got out, I think. *They know we're coming for them.* And if that's true, they're probably working double-time to create and release the plague that bleaches the future.

"How many on the perimeter?" I ask.

"Eight," Chuy says. In the distance, I hear a subtle pop. "Seven."

I smile. "Slick."

"You know it, pollito."

"Small...chicken?" I ask, curious about the new pet name.

"Would you prefer polla over pollo?"

Small...rooster?

Ahh. Small cock.

"No me gusta. Pollito it is." I motion to Cowboy's revolvers. "Any chance you'll let me slap some sound suppressors on those bad boys?" He carries two Smith and Wesson special edition revolvers that fire .38 Super ammunition capable of juicing a watermelon—or a head. When he unleashes a rapid-fire stream of bullets, it sounds like thunder. Shakes the air from your damn lungs if you're close enough.

"Are revolvers," Cowboy says, holding his pistols up and shaking his head at me. "Silence comes after I shoot."

"Because you're deaf?"

He scrunches up his face, holstering the weapons. "Because dead people don't—"

"I know, I know. Just... Take the Quonset huts. Keep the kids safe. Try not to fire those things until an alarm is sounded."

He tilts the brim of his Stetson at me like he's greeting a fair lady in a rough, 1800s Western town.

"You good to rotate solo?" I ask. We have enough personal slew drives—PSDs for short—for each member of the team. They're future tech that opens a rift to the fourth dimension, where time and space work... differently. Moving just a hair in the fourth dimension might take you a mile in the third. It can be disorienting at first, but eventually it becomes instinctual—though it's not without its risks. Emerging inside another person, for example, would be deadly for the person on the receiving end—and really gross for the person rotating. Luckily, we have safeguards built into the PSDs that help prevent mishaps like that. Up until today, Cowboy hasn't been comfortable using the devices, despite the fact that he's traveled between dimensions of reality using older Nazi tech—a giant bell, aka *Die Glocke*—from his home dimension. Something about moving through the fourth dimension's white void doesn't agree with him. The first time he tried, he attempted to rotate just ten feet, but ended up in a vineyard in France. He usually holds on to my waist like a dance partner, and we rotate together. A little awkward, but we get the job done.

He nods. "Hildy is good teacher."

Another pop, followed by Chuy's voice. "Six. Are you two going to get things done or is foreplay the only thing you have scheduled for today?"

"That's our cue," I say. I slide my black facemask down, keenly aware that I now look a lot like one of the brutal Overseers from the future, sans the pregnant belly. Overseers were...security guards in the Union's capital planet, dressed like dominatrices, but in various stages of childbearing—in part because they were the epitome of the Fourth Reich ideal—powerful, ruthless, beautiful—but also because *who would fight a pregnant woman?* Thinking about them makes me cringe every time. Cowboy pulls his bandana up over his nose and mouth, like he's a bandit.

"I got your six," Chuy says.

I hold my hand on the slew drive attached to my hip. "Three, two..."

Cowboy and I activate our PSDs, slide into the bright white gaps in reality, and travel the short distance from the forest to the compound.

I emerge on the north side of the compound. If Cowboy was right about Hildy's lessons, he'll be southwest. And everyone in between us is about to meet God.

I emerge in a clearing that smells like shit—because there are three open-pit outhouses behind me. Had I stepped out of the fourth dimension five feet back, I'd have fallen into a feces-flavored Chunky soup.

Instinct guides me, my weapon coming up toward a man with a swastika tattooed on his forehead, struggling to overcome his surprise at my sudden arrival. He reaches for a handgun on his hip, but he never gets to draw it. I put two sound-suppressed rounds in his chest and a third in his head.

His body hits the ground in unison with a second man to my left, who's missing part of his head.

"Thanks, Hun."

"Contact right," Chuy says.

I snap right, weapon raised, trigger finger ready to pull.

Years of training keeps me from firing.

Not because the target is a woman, but because she's got a baby strapped to her chest. Details leap out at me. Bruises on her cheeks. Red swollen eyes from crying. Raw wrists from being tied up. I lift up my mask so she can see the sympathy in my eyes. "You don't want to be here."

She nods, sniffing back tears. "Got someplace you can go?"

She shakes her head, no. "M-my family is in Nova Scotia."

I crouch by the man I shot. Dig his phone out of his pocket. "Know their number?"

She nods.

"Great," I say, and I close the distance between us. She starts to pull away, but I'm too fast and too strong. I pull her into the fourth dimension, slide a bit to the side and step out into a green field thirty feet from a road sign.

She staggers, confused. Nauseated.

I hold her upright and waggle the phone in front of her face. "Call your family."

"But...what... Where are we?" she asks, eyes wide, taking in our dramatically different surroundings.

"Welcome to Nova Scotia," I say. I place the phone in her hand, give her a wink, and then rotate back to the continent's far side.

I step back into the compound in time to hear Chuy calmly say, "Two."

"Geez, woman," I say, lowering my mask and lifting my assault rifle before moving quickly south toward the lab. "Cowboy, sitrep on the kids?"

"Young ones are secure," he says.

Good, I think. Means I don't need to hesitate. Anything between me and the lab is a target. I move through a maze of cargo crates, catching two men off guard. Two bursts of three rounds drop both.

"Hey! Who are y—"

I snap left. Pull the trigger. The man flails backward, tossing his hot coffee onto a woman with a shotgun, emerging to see what all the fuss is about. Before she finishes registering the scalding liquid, I put her out of her misery.

Catching up to Chuy now.

"Perimeter is clear," she says.

Damnit.

I spot the lab ahead. It's a portable affair—white plastic stretched over a metal framework. One guard by the door.

Three bullets later, the doorway is clear, and the white exterior is marred by a spritz of dark red.

The door opens silently. Inside is a modern, decked out laboratory. A man in a lab coat sits with his back to me, tapping away on a keyboard.

I throw on a Southern accent, which is horrible of me. I have no idea where these Nazis hail from. Could all be locals. Not all racists are from the South. But I've already committed. "Hey, how much longer until that virus is ready to go? Can't wait until all them colored people are rotting in the ground."

"Two more weeks," he says, revealing how much faster the pathogen was developed, as a result of us taking action against them. By trying to stop the Fourth Reich's rise, we lit a fire under their asses.

Time to put it out.

For good.

I step farther into the lab. "The Mexicans. The Africans. The Puerto Ricans. The Italians. Do Italians count? I mean, some of them can be pretty brown in the sun, right? Hey, what if *I* tan?"

The man stops working.

Slowly turns around, eyes widening.

I look down the barrel of my rifle, say, "Howdy," and pull the trigger.

The door opens behind me. I spin around and—hold my fire.

Chuy.

"Rest of the compound is clear," she says.

"What? I just... C'mon. You're making me look bad." I hand her an incendiary charge, and we place them around the lab, setting short timers. As we step back outside, the lab goes up in a blaze of glory. I feel bad about setting the fire, but the lush, damp forest lowers the risk of causing a true forest fire. And we can't risk anything inside that lab surviving. The future depends on it.

"You seen Cowboy?" Chuy asks.

I shake my head. "Cowboy, you read?"

Silence.

We rush through the compound, encountering zero hostiles as we head for the Quonset huts. All but one are open. After quickly clearing two, we head for the third. I count down to three, and Chuy opens the door. We charge in together, weapons raised to find...

Cowboy sitting on a cot. Two kids lie beside him, sound asleep. The third has her head on his lap, nearly asleep as well. "'Goodnight noises everywhere,'" he says. Then he looks up from a worn copy of *Goodnight Moon,* and shushes us.

1

Two Weeks Later

"This isn't new," I say, leaning back in my recliner, eyes closed, listening to the rich voice of Nina Simone. "'Feeling Good' was released in '65."

"Keep listening," Hildy says. The combination of her faux German accent and her sweet voice is adorable. She's perched on the edge of a footrest, bouncing with excitement, her curly blonde hair somehow defying gravity as it bobbles around her head.

Nobody delights in music more than me, except for maybe Hildy— and her taste is impeccable.

I missed nearly forty years of...well, *everything,* and she loves exposing me to tunes I haven't heard yet. It's our Sunday afternoon tradition. Just the two of us. A couple of beers. Speakers turned up. Turntable spinning—usually. But not today. Hildy is playing her first track straight from YouTube...which is one of the weirder things about the twenty-first century. Not the technology, but what people are willing to upload for the world to see. You can watch twenty-four hours of a Pop-Tart cat, rainbow flowing from its backside, flying through space to an admittedly catchy tune. Fun for a few minutes, but I think the twenty-four-hour track was created to help black op interrogators break down prisoners.

"They don't ruin 'Feeling Good,' do they?" I ask, nervous about what kind of abomination Hildy might have dug up on online.

Hildy leans in close. "Shut. Up."

The bass kicks in, the familiar tune bringing a smile to my face. Haven't heard this song in a long time. The music builds toward a crescendo, but there's something different about it. A snare drum, tapping to a fast tempo.

I squint, unsure about what to expect.

Hildy's smile spreads. Her eyes flare wide.

And then...

...it happens.

The bass drops and I'm surrounded by a cascade of sound that projects all of the original song's chutzpah, but it's intensified by a mixture of electronic instruments and modulation that perks me up out of my seat.

Hildy laughs with delight, but I can't hear her. I'm focused. I'm in love. The music transforms my lazy Sunday in an instant, making me feel like a god-damned bad bitch—the good kind. I'm ready to slap the universe's ass—*whapish*—and shout, 'Giddyup, Flamingo!'

Flamingo being the name of my fictitious horse. Maybe it's a white horse that's been eating too much red algae, like those freaky-ass pink dolphins that live in the Amazon, that can turn their heads and look at you the way dolphins do when...

Thinking of dolphins reminds me of BigApe's situation, and the subject nearly squashes my music-high. He was taken to the future like the rest of us, but something went wrong. He found himself merged with one of the Russians that made the trip with us, his face fused to the man's well-forested chest. It was a nightmare existence that ended when we returned to the past. He was made whole again...but his body... His mind... I shake my head. Nina's voice beats back my woes.

For a moment, I'm lost, just feeling the ebb and flow.

Then my thoughts drift to the future. A thousand years forward to a timeline that no longer exists, controlled by the Union, where self-expression was forbidden, and the past had been erased.

Tears well up in my eyes like a damn anime character.

This is my favorite kind of music. Not the instruments. Or the voice. Or the creativity. It's the transformative nature of it. Sound captured, shoved into the chrysalis that is the human mind, and emerging as emotion.

Hildy leans away from me. Looks a little confused. Points to her eyes, and I understand.

I've got an alien lifeform living in me. A blue Europhid from the future. They normally look like erect, blue, bioluminescent cucumbers, but this one...is inside me—a phrase I will never say aloud. It makes my eyes glow blue when its experience of the world, through me, becomes intense. Good or bad. Chuy was the first to notice the phenomenon... while we were dry humping on the couch, too lazy to move things to the bedroom. Killed the mood—who wants an alien creeping from inside their boyfriend's eyeballs—but she's gotten used to it. The Europhid and I are kind of one and the same now.

That's what I tell myself.

It's less mind-blowingly freaky that way.

Apparently, Garfunkel likes this rendition of 'Feeling Good' as much as I do.

Yeah, I named the ancient, super intelligence living inside of me after the lesser half of Simon and Garfunkel. Reminds me that my existence will continue even if the Europhid decides to someday seep out of my pores. And that I'm the one in control. Not the Europhid.

Totally in control.

Nothing to worry about...

I bask in the cacophony of sound washing over me, head bopping, foot tapping, relaxing as it winds down to a heavy beat over the original piano and horns.

My recliner shakes as I plop back down. "I need a cigarette."

"Right?" Hildy says. "It's like an orgasm in my ears."

"Don't need to know that," I say. "Any information you have about orgasms can be—"

"Burn says I'm good," she says, beaming with pride, like I'm going to say, 'Way to go, kiddo.'

Instead, I say, "Really don't need to hear that. And I'm pretty sure Burn is not qualified to judge. His experience before you was a worn out pillow."

"Stella Vermillion."

"Stella Ver-what now?"

"The pillow is named Stella Vermillion."

"Is that like a back-alley strumpet or something?"

"Strumpet?"

"A hooker."

"Ohh, a prostitute. No. He said something about 'waifu,' but I don't know what that is."

"That man's a mystery. Back to the song. What's it called?"

"Well, you were right about Nina Simone," she says, "but they call that a 'remix.' That one was by Bassnectar."

"Bass...nectar?"

"Like a bass drum, and the stuff that bees collect."

"To make sweet, sweet ear honey," I say. "I like it."

"Ear...honey?"

"Not a real thing," I say. "Made it up."

Hildy was far more aware of Earth's history and culture than the average Union member in the future, in part because her job was suppressing it, but also because she sneaked a lot of movies, TV shows, and music while working. The result is that she knows a lot more about current pop culture than I do, but she doesn't have an accurate grasp of the real world. She's honest and naïve. Like Burnett, she escaped a future steeped in hatred, and came out innocent.

Says a lot about who they are.

Also means the life lessons are coming hard and fast.

In my head, Drago says, 'That's what she said,' and then bellows his big Russian laugh. Upon returning to the past, thirty-seven years after we left, he drowned his sorrows in vodka and countless episodes of *The Office*. For three months, 'That's what she said' jokes flowed like Niagara Falls. Then he went home to reconnect with his family. He'll probably end up marrying a niece or something. I didn't think I'd miss him, but we went through a lot together.

At least the house smells nicer now.

Hildy leans back in her chair, smug smile on her face. She's set the bar high, but I've got some good picks.

I'm about to get up and turn on the record player, when I notice a subtle downturn of Hildy's lips. It's not much, but she's generally more positive than an old school Catholic's pregnancy test.

"Speak," I say.

She crosses her arms and sighs. "You need to work on your people skills."

"I kill people for a living," I point out. It's not entirely accurate. I save people for a living. Billions of them. I just killed a bunch to get it done. And it is done. Present day Nazis? Not really what I expected. All bluster and not a lot of good old fashioned, crystal meth-fueled blitzkrieg.

"Mmm," she says. "We defeated the Union..."

"Check," I say, checking off an imaginary list with my hand.

"We traveled to the past."

"Check."

"And we stopped the people planning to unleash a doomsday virus that would have killed billions of people."

"Check, and motherfucking check." I give her a sidelong glance. "All I'm hearing is good news."

"Well," she says. "What now?"

"You mean like, other than kicking back, listening to music, and reminiscing about how we saved the world? Twice."

She gets serious. "Yeah."

"Oh." I sometimes forget that while I've had a long career, first in the U.S. military and then as an exo-hunter turned pirate turned leader of a rebellion, Hildy spent nearly her whole life in the confines of a single building, staring at the same screen every day. She's never had an actual job, and she only got to be a pirate for a short time.

Her role here, tracking down and dealing with the fledgling Union, has been minimal. Most of our leads were fed to us by a woman named Wini. Haven't seen her since the day she showed up in a helicopter, but I was able to explain who we are and what we're doing here via e-mail. Apparently, she believed me, because she's been feeding us information ever since, up until two weeks ago when we took out the lab in Washington state. She sent a message that said, 'Congrats' in the subject line, and 'For a job well done,' in the body. With her help, and Cowboy's, zipping around the globe, taking out cells and preventing genocide didn't require a whole lot of help from the others.

Aside from Chuy and myself, the crew of the *Bitch'n*—our former salvage ship turned battleship, still in orbit behind the moon—hasn't had much to do for the last six months.

And being pirate rebels at heart, inaction isn't easy.

"I hear you," I say.

"I...haven't really said anything yet."

"People skills." I give her a wink, and she rolls her eyes. "We need a mission, right? A cause. Something to fight for."

She's smiling again.

"How about this? For now, we train."

"Chuy has been training me for six months."

"Six months is a good start," I say. "People like Cowboy and me—"

"Nobody trained Cowboy. He's just obsessed with 'being gunslinger' and hunting down Nazis. What's he going to do now that they're all kaput?"

"Kaput?"

"Is it the wrong word?"

"Just a weird word to choose. But not wrong." I lean forward, elbows on knees. "Look, when you're a soldier, or a pirate, or an exo-hunter, most of your time is spent preparing for the few insane moments things go sideways. That's how you succeed and survive. Rush it, and it's like jumping into a pool before putting in the water."

"Why would anyone—"

"Never mind. I'm working on my metaphors. Point is, until we find a cause worth fighting for, we need to prepare for that fight."

"What if it never comes?"

"Hildy, the human race has never not needed saving. We just need to—"

I'm interrupted by a knock on the door.

Hildy and I look at each other.

"Burnett went to visit BigApe," she says.

"Chuy's in lunar orbit." I roll my eyes. "Alone time."

"Cowboy?" she says.

"Who knows? But he has a key."

Hildy gets a suspicious look in her blue eyes. "We *all* have keys."

We head for the door together. I'm unarmed, but we both have PSDs on our hips. We can rotate away at the first sign of trouble.

I flinch when the knock repeats. It's followed by a muffled sassy voice. "C'mon, hurry up. I've got enough wrinkles as it is. Don't need to stand in the sun all damn day."

I open the door, revealing the mysterious old woman I know only as Wini, dressed in a leopard print skirt and silk blouse.

"Thank the good Lord," she says, and she struts inside between Hildy and me.

"Umm, can I help you?" I ask.

"Better not be reluctance in your voice," she says. "Not after all I've done for you."

"Never asked for your help," I say.

"Well, you sure did need it, didn't you? Crisis averted. Bad guys defeated."

She's getting to a point, but I don't see it yet. "Yeah..."

"Wrong," she says. "Not all of them."

"But your e-mail—"

"Was about Nazis. The Union. Whatever you future-past people call them." She looks me dead in the eyes, no trace of humor, and says, "We got bigger problems."

"The Union killed billions of—"

She waves me off. "I'm sure it was all very dramatic, but it's not going to happen now, right?"

"Right..."

"Ipso facto, not a problem anymore, which makes my nagging hang-nail a bigger issue than your big, scary Union."

I cross my arms. "If you need nail clippers and rubbing alcohol, there's a CVS in town."

She squints at me, the fires of Hades flaring in her eyes. "What I need is someone experienced with a particular kind of problem."

Hildy claps her hands. "Do you need a pirate? Are we pirating?"

Wini slow-turns to Hildy with an astonished look on her face, then slow-turns back to me.

"What's the problem?" I ask.

She takes a deep breath and lets out a sigh like she's exasperated by what she says next. "Aliens."

2

"Okay," I say. "What kind of alien? Whatever it is, it can't be as bad as puddle jumpers or Beatrice."

"My best friend growing up was Beatrice," Wini says. "And she died twenty years ago, when an elephant sat on her. Circus hand. Funny story. Another time."

"Well, this Beatrice was a..." I turn to Hildy. "What do people call them these days?"

"Kaiju," she says.

"Right. Kaiju."

"Like that Nemesis TV series?" Wini shakes her head. "I'll never understand why a show about a giant monster won so many Emmys."

Hildy is aghast.

She loves the show. Made me watch all four seasons that have been released.

"Because at the monster's core was the soul of a murdered little girl, twisted by the ruthless nature of the Goddess of Vengeance. It elevates the genre and is profound compared to—"

I clear my throat. "Ahem."

Wini's in a feisty mood. From what little I know of her, she's always in a feisty mood. This could turn into a long argument. "You were talking about aliens."

Wini straightens her dress like she's just taken part in a brawl, and she lifts her chin a bit. "Yes. Well, in a manner of speaking."

"You can't be an alien and not an alien at the same time," I say.

She looks me square in the eyes, so incredulous that words don't need to be spoken.

"Aside from me. I'm different."

"That's what every man likes to think." She takes a seat and slowly crosses her legs in a suggestive manner.

Hildy observes all this and gasps. "That was like Basic Instinct." She turns to me. "I think she wants to have sex with you."

Wini raises an eyebrow. "Honey, I may not look it, but I'm at my sexual peak. Spry enough to gyrate and old enough to not require—"

"Holy shit," I say, "let's just...stay on topic and try to be a little less ADD."

Wini gives me a smirk. She enjoys getting people riled up. She's really good at it too. "Aliens."

"Please, good God, yes."

"But not aliens."

"I'll take your word for it."

"Yes..." She leans forward, clasped hands on her knees. "You will."

She then proceeds to tell me a story about her and her boss, Dan Delgado, and a strange cast of characters uncovering a child abduction ring between a Mormon fundamentalist cult and little gray aliens. They turned out to be automatons—several of which were destroyed in a brothel—serving a pre-human, intelligent species that evolved on Earth called 'cryptoterrestrials,' also known as The Others. Now Wini and their people scour the planet for threats of the weird, using some kind of nano-tech inside Delgado, giving him access to basically all things electronic. He's a living ghost in the machine. That's how they found us, and apparently other people, too, including a town that traveled back in time, and some folks with superhuman abilities—though she has yet to make contact with them.

"So, you're part of a non-government, secret organization that protects the world from aliens-not-aliens and other weirdness, including, through us, future-Nazis."

Wini gives a slow nod. "Yes."

"Have a name?" I ask.

"Delgado Investigations," she says.

"Delgado... Seriously? Sounds like a P.I. business run out of a strip mall."

"That's exactly what we were," she says. "I answered the phones. Phone. Just one. We maintain the business—"

"As a front," Hildy says, "right?"

"As a trap," she says. "For anyone who might come looking for us."

It's a fantastic story, and I can't really complain about the more ridiculous sounding elements—not after what I experienced in the future, but why send Blanche Devereaux to recruit us?

Something feels off, even if every single lead Wini sent my way panned out and saved us years of work.

"Where do you operate out of now?" I ask.

"Wherever I want. And that's why I'm here," she says. "Time to go on a little trip."

"Didn't hear your helicopter," I say.

"Didn't bring it this time," she says. "We'll be flying in style."

I shake my head. "Yeah, I don't think so."

Wini's gaze doesn't break. She's not accustomed to hearing 'no.' Not afraid to show her displeasure, either. "Have either of you ever had a dream about penises?"

The question is meant to disarm me. Make me laugh. Or make me confused.

I'm not falling for it, though.

Hildy bites like Beatrice on a bender. "All. The. Time."

Wini blinks in surprise. "Do tell."

"Well, sometimes, they're, you know—"

"Sex dreams," Wini says. "Oh, I know. What about the ones that aren't?"

"Sometimes, they're just like, floating through space. Like spaceships, you know, but like flopping around."

"Flaccid," Wini says.

Hildy nods, her hair bouncing. "Exactly. But other times, they're weird."

"Weirder than flaccid space penises?" I ask.

"Yeah, like penises on a stick," she says. "Like corn dogs, but they're fed to pigs."

I wince. "Hildy...what the f—"

"What about detachable penises?" Wini turns to me. "And I'm not talking about the song."

"There's a song about detachable penises?" I say, unsure of how I should feel about that factoid.

"By King Missile," Hildy says. "Released in '92, just after your time."

"What about in a bag?" Wini asks, taking this conversation to places I've never been, even as an exo-hunter traveling the universe.

Hildy thinks on it. Then her eyes flare. "Once. Yeah. I was...carrying it."

"Any idea what it means?" Wini asks. "What it represents?"

"Well," Hildy says, "I came from a future where women with desirable features were forced into breeding programs. If Moses hadn't saved me when he did, I'd have eventually been raped and would have given birth to children I'd never see again. So, it probably represented my feelings about the patriarchy I lived in at the time."

"Oh..." Wini looks genuinely caught off guard and more than a little sad.

"There's a lot you don't know about us," I say, "and I'm not really comfortable with demands from people I don't know or trust."

Wini tilts her head. Someone's talking in her ear. Probably that Delgado guy.

Knowing he can hear me just as well as she can, I say, "I'm going to talk with my people. I'll let you know if and when we're ready to hear the sales pitch."

"I would kind of like to hear the sales pitch now," Hildy says.

I give her a flaming hot stink eye, and she nods an apology.

"Where the hell is Cowboy?" I ask.

A hand snaps up from a recliner on the living room's far side, positioned to admire the St. Augustine ocean view. "Am here," he says, standing up. When he sees my incredulous look, he adds, "I enjoy sneaky music time."

"*Sneaky* music time? How the hell did you get in here without us knowing?" I ask.

He shrugs and places his Stetson atop his head. "Am Cowboy?"

"Cowboys are not known for their subtlety," I grumble, and I motion to his feet. "And you're wearing boots! Hold on...how many *sneaky music times* have you attended?"

He counts on his fingers. "Nine."

"*Nine?* That's one more than me."

"Well, there was that time you and Chuy had to—"

I cut Hildy off with a gasp. "You did music time with someone else?"

"Are you sure?" Wini whispers, speaking to the voice on the other end of her comms. "These people are kind of—"

I switch to my commanding voice. "Hildy, Cowboy: Bitch'n, on my mark."

That catches Wini's attention. She opens her mouth to speak, but I beat her to the punch. "Rotate."

Glowing white slivers in space-time, granting us access to the fourth dimension of reality, where distance is mostly irrelevant, open beside Cowboy, Hildy, and myself. I watch the two of them rotate out of the living room. Then I give Wini a wink and follow them into the light, leaving a jaw-dropped old lady to listen to music on her own.

3

Seconds later, we slide out of the fourth dimension, onto the *Bitch'n's* bridge, two hundred forty thousand miles away from Wini.

"Hijo de las mil putas!" Chuy shouts behind me.

I spin around to find her sitting in my chair, topless and doing nothing to hide it.

"Ach jo," Cowboy says, turning away and shielding his eyes with his Stetson.

Hildy just stares, wide-eyed. "Wow. You have nice—"

"A little warning next time," Chuy says, pulling on her shirt—her tight, bra-less shirt which somehow makes her look even sexier.

She snaps her fingers in my face. "What are you doing here, Moses?"

"Why were you topless?" I ask.

"I was letting the girls air out," she says. "Because I was supposed to be alone. And that's what women do when they're alone. You're lucky I wasn't letting the cooch breathe."

"What's a cooch?" Hildy asks.

"And what is strange cartoon?" Cowboy asks.

I turn around and I'm greeted by a paused animated freakshow featuring an anime dude whose arm looks like stretched-out worms with eyeballs and big blades at the end. "Okay, seriously. Who are you, and what did you do with Chuy?"

Hildy looks at the screen and recognition flashes across her face. "Parasyte!"

"I'm lost," I say.

"Is anime," Cowboy says.

"Burnett recommended it," Chuy admits. "It's actually pretty great."

"Is there anyone on the team not currently watching anime?" I ask.

Even I'm guilty of watching anime, which I still believe peaked in the '80s with *Ghost in the Shell* and *Akira*, but Burnett's incessant recommendations have us all intrigued.

"Well, I doubt BigApe is watching anything," Hildy says. "The glass wall would distort the image and all that water would muffle the audio."

A moment of silence descends on us as we reflect on BigApe's fate. I'm not sure if it's better or worse than being grafted to a hairy Russian's chest, like he was in the future, but at least he's alive.

"So, why the hell are you all here, ruining my alone time?" Chuy asks.

"Was Dark Horse's order," Cowboy says, hiding his smirk from Chuy. He's busting my balls, trying to rile Chuy up and send her in my direction. "Is running away from old woman."

Hildy laughs. "Pfff," and in her best movie announcer voice says, "Dark Horse, the man from the past, who went to the future and then back to the past a little later than he left, encounters his greatest threat yet: an old lady in a tight dress."

Cowboy keeps quiet, but his shoulders are bouncing.

"Look," I say, "I know she's not intimidating to look at, but the organization she represents was able to locate every single Nazi cell we took out. These are powerful people, and I wanted to get everyone's input before being harangued into a meeting with this Delgado guy."

"Why *wouldn't* you meet them?" Chuy asks.

"They could be dangerous."

She shrugs. "If they were dangerous the way that you and I are—"

"Hey, I'm dangerous, too," Hildy says.

Cowboy raises his hand. "Most dangerous."

"—they wouldn't have outsourced saving the future to us. They might have knowledge and access, but they don't have teeth."

A loud beep fills the bridge.

"What is beeping?" Cowboy asks.

"That's an incoming transmission," Hildy says.

"We're on the far side of the moon," I point out. "We can't get transmissions here."

Hildy's mouth drops open for a moment. "Unless it's not from Earth." She sits down at a console. Starts working the keys.

"What are you doing?" I ask.

"Connecting us," she says. "Duh. It's audio only, but the signal is active. No way it's from deep space, and it's definitely not a recording."

"Let me hear it before you accidentally connect us to a 900 number."

"Those aren't a thing anymore, baby," Chuy says. "I know you miss them."

"Receiving...now." Hildy taps a key.

A familiar voice fills the bridge. "Helloooo. Yoohooo."

My sigh draws Chuy's attention. "You know who this is?"

"The old lady in the tight skirt," I say, taking a seat. "Wini." I turn to Hildy, my only resident nerd. "How is she doing this? Redirecting the signal from a satellite outside the moon's orbit?"

"I don't think that's—"

An alarm sounds. Red, blinking lights flash on the futuristic, but somehow still old school, control panels.

"What is new sound?" Cowboy asks.

"Proximity alarm," I say, bringing up my personal data screen. "We have company." To Hildy, I say, "Show me what's in front of us."

The new, curved 4K screen installed by Burnett, displays a view of what should be open space. Instead, there's an honest to goodness, flying saucer filling my view. It's closer in size to *Lil' Bitch'n*, our landing craft, but it shouldn't exist. Not here. Not in this time.

The front of the dome at the top of the craft is translucent. Inside? Wini waving at us, and she's framed by two of the classic 'Gray' aliens I've always assumed were fiction because I've visited a lot of the universe, and these guys weren't in it.

I lean back in my chair. "What..."

Chuy stands up. "...the hell?"

We've seen a lot of weird shit. Traveled the stars. Orbited more planets than Captain Kirk. But we've never seen anything like this. The UFO is sleek, like the newest iPhone, if the *Bitch'n* were an old rotary. No way to know if it packs the same firepower as *Bitch'n* or the ability to travel far beyond the moon, but I'm a little jealous. I'm a teenager again, driving a rusted-out Pinto, looking at Sonny Crockett's Ferrari Daytona Spyder 365 with envious eyes.

Except Sonny is old enough to be my mother.

"Hellooo," Wini says. "I know you can see me."

"Connect us," I say, and a moment later, the viewscreen displays a closer view of Wini and her Gray friends.

She twiddles her fingers at me. "You're going to have to go farther than the moon to get away from me."

"Listen, Pepé Le Pew, I don't... I just... Okay, what are those things with you?"

She motions to the two egg-headed, black-eyed aliens framing her. "This is Hans, and this is Franz. They're my pilots. Assistants. Whatever I want them to be."

The duo isn't fun to look at, but they're a good six inches shorter than Wini and skinny enough to look frail. "These aren't the..."

"Aliens?" she says. "Heavens, no. They're not even alive."

"Look alive to me," Cowboy says.

"They're... What's the word...automatons? Mostly full of gelatinous purple goo. Intelligent, but not self-aware, and not organic."

"And your people made them?" I ask.

She shakes her head, answering all of my questions without hesitation or apparent attempts at deception. "The spoils of war. They were created by the cryptoterrestrial."

"The Other," I say.

"The *what?*" Chuy asks.

"You missed a bit," I say. "I'll catch you up later." And then to Wini, I say, "It was using these guys to abduct people?"

"A lot of people over a lot of time, including Delgado's son."

"Oh," I say. That adds a dimension to the mysterious Delgado that I had yet to hear. "Sorry to hear that."

"Don't look so sad about it," she says. "We got him back before he could be incorporated into the Other's body."

"I'm sorry," I say. "Did you say 'incorporated?'"

"Into its body," she says. "It's as revolting as it sounds. I'm going to send you some coordinates in good faith. Then I'll let you all have your little pow-wow, and when you ultimately decide to trust me, you can beam down—or whatever you call it—and say hello. Okay? Great. Toodles."

The connection is broken and our view returns to the exterior of the UFO. Wini, Hans, and Franz are still visible, all three of them waving like pageant queens as they descend out of sight.

"She's a handful," Chuy says.

I thrust my hands toward the viewscreen. "You see?"

"What does she want to talk to us about?" she asks.

"Something about aliens," I say. "That's all I know."

Chuy mulls everything over for a moment. "Any reason we shouldn't trust her?"

I look from Cowboy to Hildy. They've got nothing.

"Okay," I say. "Well... I guess we should go say hello."

Hildy taps a few keys and buttons. "Coordinates received and forwarded to your slews."

"On my mark," I say, and before I can speak the word, Chuy activates her slew drive and rotates out of *Bitch'n*. Following her lead, Cowboy and Hildy rotate away, leaving me standing alone on the bridge.

I sigh, say, "Mark," and then rotate after them.

4

I leave the fourth dimension and step atop a mesa somewhere in the American Southwest. The view commands my attention, rugged terrain in hues of brown and dark green stretching out around us in every direction. Far below, a town. It appears small, but it's also bustling.

"This doesn't look like a secret base or whatever," Hildy says.

"Is secret base," Cowboy says, his expression grim, hands down by his twin revolvers.

"You've been here?" I ask. It seems unlikely. Cowboy claims to be an interdimensional traveler using a device he calls 'bell,' which I have never seen. His story is outlandish—starting with Nazis plotting to take over the world in his home dimension and ending with a real life encounter with Nemesis, who is real in that dimension, but fictional in ours. According to him, he appears in season five, which has yet to air. We'll see. There was a time in my life when I would have dismissed him as a lunatic, but we just rotated through the fourth dimension to meet an old lady in a UFO. Mostly I believe him because we're friends now. I trust him with my life.

"In my home dimension," he says. "This was secret Nazi base. Where they revived Hitler's body."

Remembering the story, I say, "His frozen body, right?"

He nods. "Not anymore. Now he rots."

"Like, in the ground?" Hildy asks. "He's dead, right?"

"In a cell," Cowboy says, "tortured by the knowledge that Lincoln Miller—"

The air pressure around us changes, drawing my eyes upward.

Nothing but blue sky.

And a few bent clouds.

"Well, that was a fast pow-wow." I flinch and spin around to find Wini standing behind me. She turns to Chuy. "Todos los hombres necesitan una mujer que les digan qué hacer. ¿Verdad?"

Chuy laughs. "Tanta asi." And then to me, she says, "I like her."

Wini shrugs. "I'm likeable."

"Also Yoda mysterious," I grumble.

"Oohwee!" Wini shakes her hands out. "The sexual tension is palpable." She winks at Chuy. "Mejor, vigile a su hombre."

They laugh like a couple of old friends, patting each other's shoulders.

"You know I hablar enough Español to understand what you're saying, right?" I ask.

"Gonna teach you a few new words before the night is through," Wini says. "You all ready to step into my office?"

"Lead the way," I say.

Wini lifts her hand at me and makes a rapid circle with her extended index finger, indicating that I should turn around.

Behind me is an open hatch leading down. Wasn't there when we arrived. Lot of cloak and dagger bullshit so far. If there's nothing of substance at the end of this yellow brick road, I'm gonna be—

Wini tilts her head. Delgado in her ear again. The man behind the curtain.

"Change of plans," Wini says. "We're needed."

"What's that supposed to mean?" I ask.

"Don't be disappointed," she says, and she pats my cheek with her wrinkly hand. "I'll show you my room another time." She looks up into the distorted sky. "Hans, we need a lift."

A beam of light strikes the mesa, as Wini's UFO reveals itself.

Cowboy smiles up at it, points, and says to me, "Is like Betty!"

"Who the hell is Betty?" I ask.

"Not person," he says. "Future Betty."

Before I can try to make sense of just what the hell he's talking about, we're lifted off the ground. Feels all warm and tingly. Hell, it's relaxing, like being weightless, wrapped inside a blanket by a fire on a winter day. Then the trip ends, depositing us in a circular, black room devoid of any features aside from a single open doorway.

"It's cold in here," Hildy says, wrapping her arms around her chest. She's dressed for Florida—shorts and a T-shirt—and the air inside the UFO feels like someone forgot to shut off the AC. "I'm nipping out." She turns to me. "Is that the right expression?"

"A few more come to mind, but yeah," I say, and then I turn to Wini. "Starting to feel like an udder in the hands of an aggressive farmer. What are we doing here?"

"I'll tell you when we get there," she says, heading for the exit.

"Just...tell me now!"

She waggles her fingers and leaves us in the round room.

"You know she's doing it on purpose, right?" Chuy says. "Getting under your skin? She's testing you. Seeing how long it takes you to lose your patience."

"We're almost there," I say.

"Just give it right back to her," she says. "Won't be long before she gives up."

"I can deal with aliens, and kaiju, and Nazis in any timeline, but Wini is pushing my buttons."

"Honey," Wini says, voice booming from unseen speakers. "When you push my button, I'll stop, and if you're not sure which button I'm talking about, try 'em all. Until then, know this, I don't give up."

What looks like liquid metal oozes out of the floor, wrapping around our feet. I try to lift a foot away, but I'm stuck in place.

Chuy struggles to free herself, but she doesn't have much more luck. "Okay, Moses, I'm with you."

"You two make this too easy," Wini says. "Hold on to your bits and pieces. Things are going to get a little nuts."

The liquid metal races up over our bodies. Struggling is useless.

"Moses?" Hildy says, a quiver in her voice.

"It's okay, darling," Wini says, apparently drawing the line at frightening young women. "Thirty seconds and everything will be back to normal."

Hildy tries to nod, but the silver goo climbs up over her head, tamping down her hair and encircling her face. "Okay... Okay..." Her eyes flick to me, panicked, and then she's completely covered.

I open my mouth to complain, but the same thing happens to me. Engulfed by fluid darkness, I try to breathe, but the air in my lungs is all I've got.

A feeling of motion flows through me, pulling at me, stretching me out. *We're accelerating,* I think. Feels like a fighter jet, but what would it feel like without the liquid metal around us?

Remembering that we're in a UFO, and the stories I've heard about what they can do, I realize that without protection, we might all just be stains on the back wall.

The feeling reverses, compressing me.

And then, all at once, it stops.

The liquid metal peels away from my face, allowing me to suck in a breath. Only Cowboy seems unfazed by the experience. Once his arms are free, he checks his Stetson and places it back on his head. When his hips clear, he draws a revolver, opens the cylinder, gives it a spin, and snaps it back in place. Then he pulls the hammer back, inspects the insides, and once satisfied, he holsters the weapon once more.

Of the four of us, he's the only one that's armed. Not great, but if only one of us gets a gun, I'm glad it's him. Chuy's an ace with a sniper rifle, and I can shoot a chipmunk from a hundred yards with just about anything else, but nobody can quickdraw and lay down lead quite like Cowboy.

I yank my foot out of the dwindling liquid metal with a slurp and head for the door. "Time for some ans—"

A girl steps in front of me. Maybe fourteen. Wavy blonde hair almost shaved on one side, chin length on the other, dressed from head to toe in black. A kind of crazed smile on her face and mischief in her eyes. "Hi."

I stumble to a stop.

"Need to get through, kid."

"I'm Cassidy," she says, bouncing back and forth on her feet. "Cassidy Rose."

"That's great," I say, and I try to step around her.

Her arm blocks my path. Her smile unnerves me. Is...she looking for a fight?

She suddenly crouches down into a squat and springs back up.

"The hell?" I take a step back.

"Just move her," Hildy says, sounding unusually grumpy after her experience with the liquid metal. She attempts to push her way past the girl, but the kid moves like lightning, taking Hildy's hand and a fist full of hair, guiding her around in an arc that would have slammed her head into the wall—if Chuy hadn't caught her and held her back.

Cassidy turns to face me, still smiling.

The moment I consider the very possibility of forcefully removing her, Cassidy's eyes and smile widen in unison. Then she flings her top half toward the floor, hands bracing while one of her legs comes up and over, heel thumping directly into my forehead.

By the time I finish stumbling back, she's upright again, bouncing from foot to foot. She lifts her elbows up ninety degrees and swings her arms back and forth while doing a weird kind of stomping.

I turn to Hildy, "Is this like a Fortnite dance thing?"

She and Burnett have been doing a lot of online gaming together. And I use the term 'together' loosely. They sit in different rooms, communicating through headsets. Young people are weird.

"I have no idea what this is," Hildy says.

"It's making you all confused," the girl says, like she knows this for a fact. Then she tilts her head toward Cowboy, who's standing back and watching everything unfold. "Except for him."

She springs into motion again, a whirlwind of long limbs. I'm struck twice and knocked back. Chuy has her legs swept out. Hildy shouts and backtracks before she can be taken out, too.

"Kid," I say, clenching my fists. "I don't want to hurt you."

"You won't."

I step toward her. "Don't be too sure."

She stands her ground. "I'm very sure." She smiles and lifts her chin, inviting me to strike her.

And as much as I'd like to knock the little spaz on her backside...

I can't.

She's right. And she knows it.

"Psychic?" I ask.

"Empath," she says and then she shivers. Her energy wanes, and she looks at me with new, fearful eyes. "I'm—I'm sorry. I didn't know."

She scurries away, leaving me confused. When I turn to Chuy, expecting to share a mutual, 'What the fuck?' she points to my eyes, and I understand. Cassidy the empathic, kung-fu kid got a dose of blue Europhid and didn't like the vibes it was putting off. I don't know a whole lot about them, despite the fact that they...he...lives in my head. But I do know he likes to be left alone. Her empathic connection seems to have ticked him off. And she felt it.

The UFO comes to a stop. I stumble a step, catching myself against the wall.

"What the hell happened to you all?" Wini says, now in the doorway. Her face screws up when she looks at me. "And why is there a footprint on your forehead?"

5

The UFO's bridge is spartan. The circular space has been outfitted with a few chairs that were clearly not part of the original design. There's also a large viewscreen similar to what Burnett installed in the *Bitch'n*. But it's not required for seeing outside. The UFO's hull can become transparent using technology that Delgado and his people are apparently still trying to comprehend but are happy to use.

Wini is seated between Hans and Franz, the little bug-eyed freaks standing sentinel. Up close, they really have an almost, but not quite alive, 'uncanny valley' thing going. It's disconcerting, but it also puts me at ease.

The Europhids are mind-blowing enough. I don't need a second intelligent alien species to deal with.

Though, that might be the situation here.

Aliens among us, separated from the human race by time, rather than space.

Wini spins around in her chair, pinky extended to the side of her lip, an eyebrow raised. Hildy snickers, but Chuy and I are stymied. No idea whether Cowboy understands the reference. He's hard to ruffle or make laugh.

"Right," Wini says. "Forgot you were from the eighties. Hell of a time to be alive, though."

"It was," I say. "Why are we here?"

"I can answer that," a man behind me says, voice booming and a little bit jolly. I turn around to find Cassidy, looking chastised, standing beside a balding, tan man with a big smile. He's dressed in tactical gear, but he extends a friendly hand. "Dan Delgado. Sorry it took so long to introduce myself."

I shake his hand, and he moves on to Chuy.

"Puerto Rican, right?" she asks.

"Si," he says, "But I can't speak a lick of Spanish."

Chuy looks disappointed, but Wini seems to speak the language fluently, or close to it.

Looking thoroughly pleased, Delgado gives Cowboy a two-handed handshake, like he's meeting a celebrity. "The Cowboy. You sir, are cool."

He moves onto Hildy, "And the woman from the future..." He shakes her hand. "Your outlook on life is admirable, considering everything you've endured."

Hildy is moved by the comment. "Thank you."

"So, is this like a good cop..." I look at Wini. "...somewhat annoying cop routine?"

"He wasn't always this...happy," Wini says. "Used to be down-right brooding and depressed."

"But then you found your son," Hildy says.

"And me," Cassidy adds.

Delgado extends a hand to Cassidy. "You've already met our local mischief maker, who was *not* supposed to be here."

"She's one of the kids you rescued?" I ask. "She's like your son? Jacob, right?"

"Jacob is gifted, and my son, but my biological child is Nathaniel. They all have varying degrees of psychic or empathic abilities resulting from trace amounts of...non-human DNA."

"We're all like his kids," Cassidy says, bouncing from foot to foot. Kid's energy level could run a city. "Pretty sweet, right?"

"Very," Hildy says.

"But they're not unique," Delgado says, and then he turns to Cassidy. "Sorry." He looks back to me. "We've been tracking a group of people with enhanced psychic abilities, but they're proving hard to pin down. I think they're professionals, only coming on-grid to complete a job."

"What kind of job?" Cowboy asks.

Delgado's not thrilled by the answer. "Killing people, mostly. But that's not why we're here." He faces front and says, "Hans, show us the view."

The front of the bridge turns clear, showing us a bright white and blue landscape that looks like God forgot to finish this part of the world.

"The North Pole?" Hildy guesses.

Delgado shakes his head and looks at me. "Last time you were here, it was dark."

Realization slaps me in the face. "Antarctica." I step closer to the view. "Hey Hans, can you zoom in right here." I point to a dark patch near the horizon. The view zooms in so fast it feels like we've suddenly moved ...and maybe we did. I'm frozen by a moment of nausea, then I pull myself together and name the place—even if it does look a lot different than it did four decades ago. "Vostok Base."

"Vostok Base *Two*," Delgado says. "The Soviets claimed it was to replace the first, but both bases remain operational."

"To study what happened," I guess.

"And what was left behind," Wini says.

"The obelisk?" Worry creeps up on me. A future controlled by fascists was bad enough. I don't want to experience one ruled by Soviet Communists. "Please don't tell me they have the time travel device."

"What? No. There was no trace of anything like that," he says. "It's what was left in the ice."

"In the ice..."

Chuy takes hold of my arm. Squeezes. "The creatures."

Delgado stands beside me, looking out at the view. "According to what I've uncovered and had translated, the Soviets found twelve bodies in the ice. None of them human. None of them alive, but they didn't decompose, either. No speculation on what they were. No physical descriptions. Most of the data is offline, probably down there." He tilts his chin toward the base, which is three stories tall and shaped like an O, the center of it dropping down into a large hole—where my team and I were propelled into the future. "Any chance you can tell me what they found?"

"All we saw were shapes," I say.

"Large shapes," Chuy adds. "Distorted and obscured by the ice."

"How large?" Cowboy asks.

This is a detail we'd left out of our tales. Honestly, I'd forgotten about them.

Of all the monsters I've encountered in my life, they're the only ones that didn't try to eat me.

"Something the size and weight of a polar bear," Chuy says. "But shaped differently, and...not hairy."

"Like I said," Wini says, "Aliens."

"*But not*," I try to replicate the serious glare Wini utilizes so easily. "What are you leaving out?"

"Honey," she says, "you look like you're crapping your pants. Leave the death-stare to the professionals."

"I think you're referring to the cryptoterrestrial," Delgado says.

"Am I?" I ask. "I thought you killed it."

"Not the second one."

"Second one?" I say, glaring at Wini again.

"Better," she says.

"The first was a creature of the modern world, a survivor from a time before humanity's rise. The second, like you, is a time traveler from the past, hitching a ride—"

"With the Appalachian town," I say.

He nods.

"And you think it's here?"

"Maybe," he says.

"Why?" I ask.

"The base stopped transmitting last night," he says. "The last communication was...interesting. Listen."

Delgado doesn't need to push a button or make a request. He and the UFO are simpatico. A garbled audio clip plays, starting with bursts of static, followed by a man shouting in Russian, panicked and afraid. "Sushchestvo besplatnoye!"

"The creature is free," I say, translating. "You think they captured your crypto-dude and brought him to the middle of nowhere Antarctica?"

"Because if the Russians are studying non-human entities, it would be here."

"Makes sense, I guess." I begin mentally working out ways to infiltrate the laboratory, driven more by the motivation to uncover what the creatures in the ice were, rather than Delgado's crypto-whosa-whatsee. "And you want us to what? Kill all the non-humans?"

"Kill?" he says, like he didn't know that was part of my job descripttion. "I want you to rescue it. The surviving Other had nothing to do with the attacks on humans. It's as intelligent as you and me—"

"So not very," Wini adds.

"How do you put up with her?" I ask Delgado.

"It's easier when you just give in and love her for it," he says.

"Okay, so my team breaks in, checks things out, finds your smart dinosaur, and bugs out."

"*Our* team."

"Yes!" Cassidy says, pumping her fist.

"You're not coming," he tells her.

"Neither are you," I say to Hildy, much to her dismay. Then I give Delgado a poke in his paunch. We're about the same age, but he's a little soft around the middle, and he definitely hasn't been for a jog lately. "What about you?" I don't even bother asking about Wini. She might be the face of Delgado Investigations, but if things go sideways, we'll need to do more than waddle away.

"I'll manage," he says. "And I trust your ability to keep me alive. You did save the future, after all."

"Twice," I say. "Which is exactly how many times you might want to think about joining us."

"Why is that?" he asks.

"Hey, Hans," I say. "Zoom in on the southwest side of the facility. Ground floor. Near the door." I give Delgado a pat on the shoulder. "On an op like this, attention to details will keep you alive."

The image zooms in, highlighting what I suspected, but wasn't sure about until just now. What looked like a few off-red pixels is a massive blood stain in the snow, just outside a closed door.

Delgado leans back, a little paler. "Oh."

6

"Kinda loose fitting," I say, looking down at the snazzy body armor provided by Delgado. At first glance, it resembles traditional body armor, but the fabric between the armored bits feels more like a wetsuit. The exterior feels funny, too, like it's covered in tiny bumps. "Sure this isn't yours?"

Delgado lets out a hearty, good natured laugh, impervious to my jabs at his weight. I know it's not PC anymore, but I feel like I need to retaliate for Wini's attitude, and he's an easy target. He pats his belly and says, "Why save the world if you can't have a donut every now and again?"

"Or two," Wini says, "every morning."

Delgado shrugs. "Making progress."

"Two donuts every morning is progress?" Cowboy asks, also struggling to make his 'adaptive armor' not look like it was worn by Hulk Hogan for a few weeks before reaching us.

"Making up for lost time," Delgado says. "Depression and heartbreak don't do a lot for the appetite."

"Before we all start sharing our dark pasts and character motivations, how about you tell me how the hell this flaccid suit is supposed to fit." I lift my arms out and wave them back and forth. "Bingo!" The loose fabric under my arms swings back and forth. "I've got bingo arms. C'mon, do it with me, Wini."

She scrunches her nose and puckers her lips, waggling a finger at me, but it's all to hide her smile.

Chuy swats the back of my head like she's killing the mother of all mosquitos. She whispers in my ear. "Peinabombillas. ¡No seas Culero!"

Wini does nothing to hide her grin now. She's got me beat. No denying it. She can beat me into submission, and if I try to fight back with a little tit for tat, I'm going to get skull-whacked by my Latina girlfriend, who believes in corporal punishment...regardless of age.

Chuy stands in front of me, her adaptive armor even looser than mine. "Common sense," she says, and she pushes a triangular badge with curved corners located at the center of the suit's collar. The armor vacuum seals around her body until it's a perfect fit. Chuy stretches, bends her legs, and performs a simple kick, all with ease. "Nice."

I clip everything in place and follow Chuy's lead, pushing the button. The armor wraps around me like a second skin—light and flexible. I'm not sure how it will fare against bullets, or claws, but it's an obstacle to overcome before anyone gets to try killing us. "I don't see how this will keep us warm in the dick-inverting Antarctic cold."

"It's usually around sixty degrees in here," Delgado says.

"I noticed," I say.

"How's it feel now?" he asks.

The air is still cool on my face, but my body feels just right.

He doesn't wait for me to answer. Can see the realization on my face. "We call it the 'Goldilocks effect.' No matter where you go on the surface of this planet—the top of Everest or the bottom of Death Valley—the adaptive armor will keep your body temperature just right. Not too hot. Not too cold. And if you manage to break a sweat, the moisture wicking fabrics will keep you dry. But that's just the start."

He reaches back behind his head and pulls a facemask up over his head and face. It's black, like a ninja, with an armored faceplate and two black oval eyes that remind me a bit of Hans and Franz. "Comms are built in, and in case you're concerned about sticking out on the white snow..."

He lifts his forearm and taps it. A digital menu built into the suit comes to life. A few taps later, a color picker appears. He places his finger on the middle of the rainbow and slides it around. The entire suit shifts colors. "All those little bumps on the suit are digital chromatophores capable of changing colors."

"Like a squid," Chuy says.

"Technology inspired by nature," he says. "Exactly right. But we've got more colors to choose from, and more patterns." He taps again and the armor shifts to desert camouflage. Then again to forest. "But for today, we're going basic." His armor turns solid white—even the eyes. Out in the snow, we'll be invisible.

"I think I'm in love," I say, activating my arm display and playing with the settings until I figure it out, shifting my armor to white. I turn to Hildy, striking a pose. "Eh? Ehh? Cool, right?"

She purses and twists her lips, arms crossed. Feels left out, but that's fine by me. I'd rather her be sour and alive than happy, suited up, and dead. "Well, I think it's cool."

Beside her, Cassidy, who could pass for Hildy's younger sister, sticks her tongue out at me, energy barely contained. I give it right back and turn away to find Cowboy, fully dressed in adaptive armor, looking down to his barren hips, probably feeling naked without his revolvers. Even if he could get his holster belt around the armor, it would ruin the armor's camouflage.

"I think I will take chances with cold," he says.

"Wait, wait, wait," Delgado says. He's still masked, but I know he's smiling. He peels the mask off, proving me right. Hans and Franz enter, both of them carrying gun cases. "This is the best part."

Seems a little strange to be geeking out over military tech while someone's guts freeze in the Antarctic cold below, but I'm pretty sure that whatever happened here is done happening. A few more minutes isn't going to kill anyone else, and we're not going to be much use without weapons.

Hans—I think it's Hans, they're identical, but Hans has a small scar on his forehead—places one case on the floor and approaches Cowboy with the other. The little dude pops it open, like he's displaying a fine wine, angling the interior toward Cowboy. I lean over and get a look for myself.

Inside the case are two holstered revolvers—everything jet black. No belt in sight.

Cowboy is tentative, but he plucks out a holster. It looks thick and a little heavy. He draws the gun. It's the same Smith and Wesson special edition Cowboy carries, with some slight modifications including a larger cylinder that looks capable of holding eight rounds instead of six, and it extends far enough out the side that it looks like a bullet could fall out.

In a blink, Cowboy pulls the trigger several times. Then he pops out the cylinder and gives it a spin. Snaps it back in place. Looks down the sight. Seems satisfied. "Is nice, but..."

"Now comes the coolest part," Delgado says. He picks up the holster and places it against Cowboy's hip. It snaps in place, like it was always part of the armor, but it's a lot bigger and rigid. "Holster the gun."

Cowboy's patience is waning. He's a purist when it comes to guns. But he plays along, holstering the weapon. When he does, eight rapid fire clicks fill the air.

Delgado, grinning like a fool, motions to the holster. Cowboy draws the weapon again, his brow furrowing. "Is heavier."

"Is loaded," Delgado says, managing to get a true look of surprise from the reserved Czech.

Cowboy lifts the weapon, eyes wide as he snaps open the cylinder again, giving it a spin to confirm that the weapon is fully loaded. He normally uses speed loaders, but it's still a process that requires holstering one gun at a time.

"But wait," Delgado says, "there's more." He lifts Cowboy's arm, opens the menu, and changes the adaptive armor's color to white. The holster and revolver both turn white, too.

"Holy shit," I say. This is a game changer. "Is all this DARPA tech or something?"

"DARPA?" Delgado waves his hand at me. "You're standing in a UFO. And if DARPA had something better, we'd...borrow it."

"Like pirates?" Hildy asks, a spark of excitement in her voice.

"Good pirates," Delgado says. "More like Robin Hood." He chuckles like someone has said a joke, and then he turns to me. "You can say it."

"I have no idea what you're talking about," I say, and then can't hold it back. "Little John."

Hans approaches me with his second case while Franz drops one off at Delgado's feet, before bringing the biggest of them to Chuy and opening it. When her face lights up, I know it's something special, and I take a peek.

It's a Barrett M82 sniper rifle—aka: overkill, unless you're up against something with an engine. Its 'Light Fifty' rounds can punch through brick, concrete, and metal. A human body barely slows it down. But it's not just any Barret. Like Cowboy's revolvers, it's been modified.

The Barrett is a large weapon, but this one's barrel is resting in the case above the rifle.

Chuy picks it up. "Lighter than it should be."

"Half the weight, actually," Delgado says, and that's a good thing. The Barrett is a 28-pound beast not meant for run and gun situations.

"Is this..." Chuy says, looking at the optics. There's a red dot sight on the top and a scope on the side. "Can I..."

"Use it close range?" Delgado says. "Sure can. Or..." Delgado reaches out, takes hold of the scope and pulls it to the top of the rifle. Then he takes the barrel and with a quick twist, attaches it to the rifle. "Death from a distance. Thought you might enjoy the option."

Chuy looks stunned. It's an uncommon thing.

"You realize that nothing I give her for the rest of my life will ever compare to this, right?"

Delgado smiles. "You're next."

I'm not sure what to expect. Delgado nailed Cowboy and Chuy, but can he go three for three? I'm multi-faceted, comfortable with just about anything that pew, pew, pews. I don't think I have a fav—

"Oh, you sweet, sweet man."

I reach down and pull out the M-16 assault rifle. It's a classic, and not just from my time in the 1980s military. It's a mainstay in just about every action and Earth-based science fiction movie from the Sixties on. *Commando. Rambo. Die Hard. They Live. Lethal Weapon.* You need to kill bad guys, this was the weapon of choice. It's not the most stylish weapon, but when it comes to range, weight, and reliability, not even the AK-47 can compete.

I hold the weapon like Arnold Schwarzenegger on the poster for *Predator.* "If it bleeds, we can kill it."

"Nice," Chuy says, and she proves she's my soulmate by doing a perfect Dutch-Dillon muscle-flex handshake with me.

"You two need a room?" Wini asks.

"Don't be jealous," I say. "If you'd led with fancy guns, we'd have been besties by now."

"Your slew drives—that's what you call them, I think—should attach to your hips, as usual. They're okay with magnets, right?"

"Yeah," Hildy says, sounding about as thrilled as a beauty queen with shit on her shoes.

"Great," Delgado says, hoisting up what I think is a submachine gun, but a design I've never seen before. It features twin drums on the bottom, instead of a magazine. He attaches two more double drums to his armor, magnets holding everything in place. Then he opens his arms like he's waiting for a hug. "I know we just met, but who's going to give me a lift?"

7

"Possible to pump music into our comms?" I ask, arm wrapped around Delgado's waist, just about ready to rotate.

"Music?" he says, confused by the question

"You know, that stuff with a beat that people dance to."

"I know what it is, I just don't understand why."

"You ever seen a movie?" I ask.

"Yeah..."

"You ever seen a movie where the good guys are riding toward danger in a helicopter, airplane, or boat?"

"Pretty sure."

"Aside from a little banter, what's the focus of that scene?"

"Uh," Delgado says. "I'm going to guess music."

"'Ride of the Valkyries.' 'Long, Tall Sally.'"

"'Blitzkrieg Bop!'" Hildy says.

"Classic," I say, remembering the moment we escaped from the Overseers with Hildy and a hundred years' worth of music. It was a magical moment. "Point is, it gets the blood pumping, gets everyone in sync, and if we die, the soundtrack in our heads will be epic."

"Oookay. Interesting. Well, I have access to...everything. Something exciting, huh? Okay, I got this." Delgado seems to drift away for a second. Then he's back.

And music starts pumping from my comms.

And from the ship's speakers.

"Dios mio," Chuy says. "Te voy a dar una galleta..."

"They don't like the song," Wini says, helping Delgado understand Chuy's response, which I think is something about a cookie, but I'm pretty sure it equates to bodily harm.

"What's wrong with Whitney Houston?" Delgado asks. "This is a great song."

"'I Wanna Dance with Somebody' is not a song to fight, or die to," I say, and I turn to Hildy. "I know you're not psyched about sitting on the sidelines this time around, but no one can pick 'em like you. Give me something new."

Hildy's lopsided grin says she already has something in mind. "'We Got the Moves' by Eskimo Callboy."

"Can we go? Music ritual taking too long this time," Cowboy says.

"What happened to 'sneaky music time?'" I ask.

"Is not sneaky music time," he says. "Is mission music time. They are different."

Our argument is interrupted by a solid beat and an electronic bass line that feels a little Eighties and gets my head bopping immediately. I like where this is headed. The vocals kick in, speaking the humorous lyrics—something about beer and wine and having 'the moves,' all with a faint German accent. And then all at once, the song transmogrifies into something else, the beat and music going heavy, the lyrics all but screamed.

I love it.

Even Cowboy is bopping his head.

I look at Delgado as the music tones down a little and starts building again. "You see?"

"It's loud," he says, but a faint smile is spreading. The music is infectious. Hildy chose well.

"Now, we're ready," I say, and I rotate out of the UFO and down to the frozen surface of Antarctica, putting us down a half mile out, so we can get a look at the place from ground level before knocking on the door.

Cowboy and Chuy slip out of the void beside us. We look like a bunch of white ninjas. Only our shadows give our presence away.

Delgado lowers the music's volume, but he lets the song finish as we inspect our destination. "The optics in your mask respond to the muscles around your eyes. Zoom in by squinting for a few seconds. Pull back out by widening your eyes."

"Nice," I say, zooming in on the facility, pleased to find labels emerging in a heads-up display, identifying various areas of the structure—living quarters, labs, storage. Delgado's intel is impressive. Nations would kill for his abilities, if they ever found out. "Any chance you can get us real-time data from the station's security system?"

He shakes his head. "Whole place is dark."

"Even life support?" Chuy asks.

He nods. "I don't think we'll be looking for survivors. They'll all be frozen by now."

"Or gone," I say. "The original Vostok isn't far, right?"

"Yeah..."

The song ends, leaving me feeling pumped and ready for action. "Let's move."

"Uhh," Delgado says. "We're going to walk all the way there?"

"That's why God gave us feet," I say, but point taken. I'm nice and cozy inside the adaptive armor, but the terrain isn't exactly even, and the wind whipping across it makes every movement a fight. "Okay, you convinced me." I wrap my arm around him again.

"I didn't try to—"

"Southwest corner," I say, "by the blood."

Chuy, Cowboy, and I rotate in unison, emerging a moment later, a half mile closer to the facility.

The patch of gore is larger than it looked from a distance, which yeah, obviously. But there's more going on here than just blood.

Bits and pieces of unrecognizable shredded body parts litter the area. It's beyond revolting, even for someone like me.

Delgado crouches down and casually picks up a strip of skin. "I think this was a Russian." He holds the pale, stiff bit of skin up. "See?"

Despite not being able to view our expressions, he senses our revolt. "What? You've never inspected a crime scene before?"

"Generally leave stuff like this in our rearview, and don't go poking around in it."

"Well, it tells a story," he says, putting the skin down and picking up what I think is a bone fragment.

"Was this guy blown up?" I ask.

He shakes his head. "We've got bits and pieces, but nothing significant. There's a lot of blood in the snow, but not all of it."

"No way someone walked away from this," Chuy says.

"No human walked away," Cowboy says, motioning to footprints in the snow. There are four toes. The two on the outside extend out at an angle while the center, longer two look like they might be fused together. An inch out from each digit is the tell-tale impression of a claw tip.

Imagining the size and power of the creature that made the print helps me see the story Delgado is seeing. "He was eaten."

"Not whole..." Delgado stands and points out the bloody splotch's odd shape. "And he was alive for some of it. Tried crawling away, but he didn't make it far."

"Were men stationed here armed?" Cowboy asks.

"This is Antarctica," Delgado pats his weapons. "We're breaking an international treaty by bringing these here."

"Not our first time," Chuy says. "It's pretty common actually."

"And no offense to whatever post-Cold War view of Russians you might have," I add, "but we spent years in a spaceship with one of them. If these guys were Russian, they were armed. Not because they love guns like we do in the States, but because they're not fools. The question is, what were they packing?"

I check the frozen snow surrounding the bodies. Not a single shell or casing. "If this guy was armed, it hit him before he had a chance to draw." I mentally follow the creature's course, approaching from the side. But there's no place to hide. Nowhere to stage an ambush from. Unless it was night, or... I look up. The facility is three stories tall. A fall like that would shatter a human's legs. But this thing wasn't human.

A quick yank chambers a round in my M-16. "Eyes open, three sixty degrees."

Delgado looks up, understanding my concern. "Wini?"

"Yeah, boss?" she says via the comms. Sounds like she's standing right next to me. "If anything moves outside, be sure to let us know."

"You got it," she says, acting surprisingly professional now that an op is underway. Wini is a lot of things, but I get a sense she genuinely cares for Delgado. Probably like a son.

"Time to take a peek under the base's skirt," I say, sliding up against the door, gripping the handle. Chuy positions herself facing the door, looking down the red dot of her Barret. If there's anything on the other side of this door, it's going to be vaporized.

Cowboy stands back, hands relaxed, hanging by his hips. He looks almost casual, but he'll still manage to fire a few rounds before Chuy can pull the trigger.

Delgado draws his akimbo weapons and looks eager to try them out.

Everyone's ready to go, but I need answers. "Okay, what the hell are those?" I tilt my head toward Delgado's weapons.

"KRISS Vector with Beta C-mags," he says, like I'm supposed to know what that means. Then he elaborates. "I can fire a hundred .45 cal rounds in a few seconds. 1600 rounds a minute."

"Holy shit," Chuy says.

Delgado shrugs. "Means I don't need to aim. Haven't seen action in a while. Thought this might be the best option for me."

"Or a one-man army," I say, and then I turn my attention back to the door. "On your three."

Chuy gives a nod. Focuses up. "Three... Two..."

8

"One!"

I yank the door handle, and it breaks off in my hand.

I hold it up. "Umm."

The door slides open a crack.

Chuy pushes the barrel of her weapon through and nudges the door open. Frozen, but well oiled, the door glides open, revealing a ruined interior, the handle now missing from both sides. There's more frozen blood on the floor.

"Not everyone made it outside," Chuy says. "Someone got pancaked against the door."

"And then eaten," Delgado says, once again leaning in to inspect. "Whatever is here, it's hungry."

"C'mon," I say. "Really?"

"What?" Delgado says, overacting his confusion.

"Your setup was too obvious," I say.

"Caught that, huh?"

"Camaraderie can't be manufactured," I say. "Has to be natural. I get it. You want in on the circle of badassery. Who wouldn't? But prompting me to say a pithy quip isn't the way."

"Isn't it?" he asks, picking up a piece of who-knows-what before dropping it back on the blood-capade rink. "Because I think you can't resist."

I stand there for a moment, torn between habit and my desire to not be predictable. "Damn you," I say, shaking my head. "It's a good thing we're not on the menu." I step over the blood and inside.

The hallway is dimly lit by reflected light streaming through the open door. Fifteen feet in—darkness.

With Chuy on my six, followed by Delgado and Cowboy bringing up the rear, I push forward. When the light begins to fade, I hear a chime in my ear, followed by an electronic voice. "Low light detected."

"Really," I respond, "I didn't notice."

"Look at your arm display," Delgado says.

Two options blink on my forearm. *Light*. And *Night Vision*. Huh...

I select night vision and my view through the suit's goggles slips into hues of green, revealing the curved hallway ahead. Very cool. "But can you pee in it?"

"What?" Delgado asks.

"Future suits eject urine," Cowboy says, matter of fact. "Also has option for intercourse."

"Erection detection," I say.

Delgado tilts his head to the side, trying to comprehend the purpose of an erection detecting suit. "That's..."

"Freakin' handy," I say, and I hold a finger over my masked lips. "Time to shush."

Using hand signals to communicate, I lead the team through a maze of dark hallways, pausing to check rooms as we come across them. Several doors have been knocked down. A few walls are pocked with buckshot. Signs of violence are everywhere, but no more blood.

Five minutes in and nothing.

"Delgado," I whisper.

"Yeah?"

"Can I smell in this thing?"

"I mean, you shouldn't get sweaty, but—"

"I mean can I smell what's outside the suit?" I ask. "In a situation like this, the nose can pick up on things unseen."

"Oh, right. Yeah. That's the default. But if you don't want to, you can have the suit filter the air. Protects against biohazards and skunks."

"Good to know," I say, and I take a deep breath through my nose.

Nothing. But that doesn't mean much. Frozen bodies don't stink.

I continue deeper into the facility, clearing several personnel quarters and supply rooms.

I'm thinking we've completely missed what happened here, that Delgado's monsters are in the Antarctic wind, though I'm not sure anything—human or alien—could survive for long out there.

Then I smell it.

Blood.

Just a hint. Not yet frozen...or maybe just a lot of it.

I turn to Chuy and tap the side of my nose. She takes a deep breath, nods, and points toward a set of closed double doors. I lead the way, bracing the M-16 against my shoulder, ready to unleash hell.

The door is unlocked and cracked open. I nudge it inward with my foot, sweeping left to right as I enter a mess hall. Four tables. Chairs tipped over. The walls painted black.

I sniff. Blood again. Stronger now. Definitely located in this room, but blood can be hard to see in monochrome.

Unless I am seeing it...

The black walls aren't painted evenly. Looks like it was done by a handful of sugared-up toddlers.

Because it's not paint.

"Night vision off," I say, warning the others. "Switch to lights."

"Ready," Chuy says.

I switch my night vision off and turn on the suit's lighting system. A ray of light shines from my entire face, the suit itself lighting up. It's not limited to changing colors; it's also powerful enough to project them. Right now, I've got the luminosity level set to low. No idea what would happen on high. Not the time to find out.

Because the walls aren't black.

They're red. Well, more of a dark maroon—the color of dried blood.

But no bodies.

"I'm gonna go out on a limb and say this might have been the rest of the station's crew."

"Made mistake hiding together." Cowboy leans in, but he doesn't enter. "And only one door. No way out." He keeps his attention on the hallway, making sure we don't suffer the same fate.

The walls and doors are speckled with shotgun fire, but nothing to suggest anything other than humans were injured here.

Unless whatever did this bleeds the same shade of red, which in my experience, is uncommon. Purple blood is the most common. Blue. Green, too, but that was just once and more like lime-scented goo. Honestly, it made me hungry for key lime pie, but that was in the future, where dessert didn't exist. Red blood is a physical trait most associated with lifeforms that evolved on Earth.

"Clear," I say, seeing no danger.

After turning off my face lamp and reverting to night vision, I head back into the hall, pushing deeper into the facility, which opens up, the hallway widening and the ceiling rising up the full three stories. We'd been in the living quarters. This feels more like a work setting, the walls covered in rows of lockers, some torn open, revealing clean suits hanging inside.

The floor is covered in bloody footprints. Same as what we found outside.

A pair of doors ahead look like they were blasted open from the inside, but there are no scorch marks. Our big boys came from there, barging their way through and then consuming the base's occupants.

Chuy and I move past the doors together. I don't try to figure out what the space is, I'm focused on finding and identifying threats. There's a lot of debris, but nothing alive, and no blood.

"It's a lab," Delgado says, his priorities different than mine. Probably a good thing he's here, detecting, while we focus on not dying.

His assessment helps me see the massive space in a new light. Cylindrical glass cases the size of upright vans line the walls, one every fifteen feet. Those closest to us are all empty. All shattered—from the inside. The floor glistens with glass and water—probably salt water because it hasn't frozen yet.

"They kept them here," Chuy says. "All this time. Alive."

"Performing experiments on them," Delgado says, looking over what I now understand to be a massive operating table. "But they lost control."

"Any chance we can just nuke the site from orbit?"

"I don't have nuclear warheads," Delgado says, dead serious. "And even if I wanted to take control of some, I wouldn't drop them on Antarctica, or anywhere..."

He notices that Cowboy, Chuy, and I are all staring at him. Even masked, he senses our confusion.

"Really?" I ask. "*Aliens.* James Cameron. Sigourney Weaver. Ring any bells?"

"It's a movie, right?" he asks.

I sigh. "Of all the unbelievable things we might experience today, this is going to stay at the top of the list."

A *thump* spins me around, weapon raised. Behind me is an unbroken glass tube.

"Something still in this one," I say, moving closer.

The team gathers around the tube. The fluid inside is cloudy, the shape of whatever is inside obscured.

I reach out a hand and tap on the glass with my finger. "Hellooo."

A basketball-sized sphincter presses up against the glass, pulsating hungrily. "Okay. I take it back. This just took the top...spot?" Looking at the circular muscle, flexing like a body builder on a stage, my memory jumps six months back and a thousand years forward. To either side of the mouth, mandibles tap against the wall, trying to grasp me, trying to pull me inside.

I've seen this before. "*Seriously?*"

"You know what this is?" Delgado asks.

"Yeah. But this is a lot smaller."

"Holy shit," Chuy says, remembering the experience she shared with me and with Brick, our teammate who stayed behind to save that future timeline. No idea if they were all erased from existence, but he had to try.

"It's a rygar," I say, and then I notice two blue orbs shining from within the cylinder. When I lean in closer, I realize it's my eyes that are glowing, bright enough to shine through the suit's eye visors.

What is it? I think to the Europhid occupying the wrinkles in my brain, and a moment later, I'm transported to another time.

9

My childhood. My friend Max's idyllic backyard. Blue sky. Big clouds. Green grass and the smell of a recently cut lawn. His swing set beside me. The last time I was in a memory like this, I had a chat with the blue Europhids taking the form of my childhood friend.

They were never really him, though. Just inhabiting my memories of him. Using his form to make communicating with an alien intelligence a little easier on my psyche. Meeting an alien intelligence as an exo-hunter wouldn't have shocked me all that much. But the Europhids have been around for billions of years—a vast collective of small cucumber-like beings inhabiting a massive amount of the universe, co-existing with untold species. They're so immense and so old that a thousand years feels like a day to them.

From their perspective, the thousand years it took the Union to expand through space, ravaging planets and wiping out multiple Europhid colonies, was like being shot. It was such a shock to the system that they brought me to the future to help deal with the problem. Which I did. Part of the deal was allowing the blue Europhids—a logical intelligence—to inhabit my mind, providing me with the necessary knowledge and motivation to get the job done. The red Europhids act more like an immune system for the collective, responding to threats with brutal efficiency, using their ability to connect with living minds to control lesser creatures, weaponizing them against intruders. And when things really get nuts...

My thoughts drift to Beta-Prime, a planet where I worked side by side with what I referred to as 'Red'—the planet-sized red Europhid collective with a surprisingly snarky sense of humor and massive tendrils capable of wiping out an army.

I've done a lot of nutso things in my life, but that battle stands out as a highlight.

The blue Europhids are cool, don't get me wrong. Who doesn't appreciate a vast Spock-like intelligence? But I've always been more of a Kirk man. A fighter. I have more in common with the reds—reacting violently to threats.

But I'm not back in my childhood again because of the reds. I'm here because—

"Moses!"

I spin around to find Max—still his youthful Down Syndrome self—bulldozing toward me, face screwed up with intensity, short legs hobble-sprinting. I've only seen him like this once before, when a trio of bullies surrounded me, and Max charged to my rescue. Despite his best effort, Max could never be intimidating, but even bullies draw the line at beating up a kid with DS.

He talked about that moment, when he 'saved my life,' for the rest of his.

But this isn't Max.

This is Garfunkel, charging at me inside my mind, where hours are seconds in the real world.

And he's in a hurry.

"Garfunkel, what's—"

He closes the distance between us, moving faster than Max ever could. Dives forward, slamming into my waist, driving the wind from my imaginary lungs, and knocking me—

—back to reality. My body flails back like I've been struck.

As I fall to the floor, glass sprays through the air where my face had been. A clawed hand reaches out, grasping.

Had I still been there, it would have crushed my skull.

Garfunkel just saved my life.

I hit the floor hard, but the adaptive armor reduces the impact. *How the hell did Garfunkel see that coming?*

And then, suddenly, like instinct, I know what's going to happen.

"Down!" I shout, as Chuy, Cowboy, and Delgado take aim at the glass case. All three of them hear my warning and snap down toward the floor.

Glass explodes, the shards hefty and fast-moving enough to punch through armor, muscle, and bone.

Before I can wonder how I knew what was going to happen, I get my answer.

Inside the destroyed containment unit, bent over, hacking up gallons of water, the rygar pitches forward, revealing the back of its head and its spine—where a row of red Europhids have attached themselves. Revealed and shifting from dormancy to life, the bioluminescent aliens begin glowing an eerie, sinister red.

The rygar drops down, landing on all fours, half in, half out of the containment unit, its powerful limbs twitching. The creature's claws flex, chipping the floor.

Its sphincter-like mouth peels back, revealing a toothy esophagus, ready to pull me inside. A gurgling, throaty roar sends tentacles of wriggling drool stretching out toward me.

This is what happened to the Russian Vostok crew, but it wasn't this rygar.

Where are the rest of them?

"Chuy," I say.

She raises her shortened Barrett toward the side of the rygar's head.

It must sense the danger, because it stands still, stops roaring, and squashes its open maw together like a toothless grandma.

I hold my hand out to Chuy.

She holds her fire, but she isn't happy about it. "The hell, Moses?"

"I can feel it," I say, but the statement isn't accurate. What I'm sensing isn't the rygar. It's another planet's equivalent of a lion that grows to the size of a bus—an apex predator with a simple, easily controlled mind. What I'm feeling right now are the red Europhids lining the creature's back.

In my experience, the reds are all instinct, guided by the basic desire to protect their own—namely the blue Europhids.

But this rygar tried to kill me...and the blue inhabiting my body.

These reds have no allegiance to the blues.

To the Europhid way of life.

A mix of emotions roils from the reds, all of them typical for the feisty little gelatinous cucumbers—aside from one.

Ambition.

KILL IT.

Garfunkel's voice in my head is loud and insistent.

DESTROY THEM.

Trusting Garfunkel's knowledge and/or intuition, I give Chuy a subtle nod.

The rygar senses it, too, lunging out, claws extended, mandibles open wide.

Chuy pulls her trigger. The Barrett booms in the enclosed lab, the force of it slapping against my body. But the adaptive armor protects my ears. Without the suits, we'd all be deaf.

Gore splatters to the side, the power of Chuy's Barrett round atomizing the rygar's skull, but doing nothing to stop the monster's forward momentum. The body lands on my torso, the weight of it pinning me to the floor, while its guts ooze out of the cavity left behind, dangling toward my face with the slow inevitability of the Times Square New Year's Eve ball drop.

I push against the corpse, but I only manage to wriggle it enough to speed up the process.

"Get...it...off..."

DESTROY THEM ALL.

My attention snaps from the gut-loogy dripping toward me to the spine of red Europhids. The rygar might be dead, but it was just the host.

The reds are pulling themselves free, little hooked tendrils reaching out. If they reach the others, or me, this might end up being a 'body snatchers' situation.

"The Europhids!" I shout. "Kill them all!"

Delgado starts lifting his Vector. With it, he could eradicate every single one of the ruby-colored dildos with a pull of the trigger.

He never gets the chance.

Cowboy draws his new revolvers and squeezes off sixteen rounds before Delgado finishes aiming. The Europhids explode as though shot at the exact same moment. Cowboy holsters the weapons, and after a brief moment of rapid fire clicking, he draws them again, inspecting the cylinders and nodding his approval.

"Nice shootin'," I say. "Now someone... Ugh..." The gelatinous insides start wrapping around my chin. No idea if it will seep through the mask, so I speak through pursed lips. "...get this thing off me!"

It takes all three of them to roll the body off me. I scramble free and wipe a layer of purple gore from my face. I want to spit, but I can't inside the mask.

"Just give it a second," Delgado says. "The armor is non-stick."

I hold out a hand, watching the sludge drip clean off my fingers.

"And it's non-porous." Delgado smiles at me. "So, you can open your mouth again."

"The hell was that?" Chuy asks.

"The reds were—"

"I know what they were," she says. "But how are they here? And why?"

I shake my head. "No idea."

"What about Garfunkel?" she asks.

"He's not talking," I say, "but I think he's just as confused as we are."

The reds shouldn't be here. The rygar shouldn't be here. But they are, and they have been since the blues sent back the time travel device that carried me to the future. "They hitched a ride from the future."

"A future where humanity conquered universe," Cowboy says.

"Aww, shit," I say. "They came back to stop us."

"Why would they stop us?" Chuy asks. "We saved their future."

"Not you and me specifically," I say. "They came from a future that hadn't yet been saved, where humanity was the virus, and they were the cure. They came to Earth to kill us. To kill *all* of us."

10

"That seems like a pretty big mental leap," Delgado says.

"Well, it's a theory," I admit. Nothing else makes sense, but then again, I don't have a lot to go on.

"Nice presentation, though," Cowboy says. "Very dramatic."

"Exactly what the hell are we dealing with here?" Delgado asks, activating his face lamp and scanning the rest of the lab for lingering threats.

"Rygars on their own are simple creatures. Predators, but they couldn't hold a pencil to even attempt an IQ test." I stand over the headless creature, confirming that every single one of the reds has been destroyed. "They're being controlled by an intelligence—"

"'Intelligence' isn't the right word," Chuy says. "They've been co-opted into an immune response. Imagine that your white blood cells identified cats as the enemy. Normally, they'd wait for a cat to invade their personal space before responding, but in this case the white blood cells are attaching themselves to viruses, hitching a ride out into the world, and waiting to be inhaled by an unsuspecting kitty."

"They're vaccinating the universe against humanity?" Delgado asks.

I try to snap my fingers, but the non-stick surface prevents it. So, I just awkwardly point at him. "Now you get it. In theory."

"Is time-space sneeze," Cowboy says, summarizing our situation like only he can.

"How did you know it was going to attack?" Chuy asks me.

"Garfunkel warned me," I say. "Well, he actually kind of tackled me subconsciously. Pushed me out of the way."

"And he doesn't mind that we killed these Europhids?" she asks.

"Was his idea, actually." I join Delgado, activating my face lamp, illuminating the space in white light, revealing the gory details in stark contrast.

"Can't blues control reds?" Cowboy asks.

"I think it's more of a symbiotic relationship," I say.

"Like an oxpecker and a rhinoceros," Delgado says.

"All I heard was pecker," I say.

"The oxpecker is a bird. It eats mites and ticks, keeping rhinos clean while feeding itself." He moves around a lab table, inspecting another broken containment unit. "It's mutually beneficial."

I discover another frozen puddle of blood, the body missing. "In a way. But imagine that the oxpecker was highly aggressive, capable of thought, and able to control the minds of simpler creatures—including humans."

"They'd be organized and buzzing around the plains, attacking everything that might pose a threat to the rhino," Chuy says. "Or anything threatening to destroy the mites' breeding ground."

"Even if rhino says not to?" Cowboy asks. "Also, how is rhino talking to birds?"

"What?" I say. "Man, we're talking in metaphor."

"How does metaphorical rhino talk?" he asks.

"It's psychic," I say, growing frustrated and wishing I had a better word for it that didn't sound so much like a paranormal Time Life book. "They're all psychic. Look, the point is, these reds seem to be in rebellion. Still following their base function—to protect all Europhids. But they're acting on their own, and since they nearly killed me—and Garfunkel— they're either willing to take casualties or they now see him as a traitor. They've been here for a long time. Long enough to come to their own conclusions. There's no controlling them. Garfunkel said to destroy them all, and I think that's what we should do."

"Okay," Cowboy says, "but lab is empty."

"We need to keep going," I say. "Everyone okay with that?"

Chuy gives a nod. I didn't really need to ask her. Or Cowboy. The question was more for Delgado's benefit.

"Let's do what needs doing," he says.

I stand beside the set of double doors at the lab's far side. "I said the same thing to my prom date."

"Did it work?" Chuy asks, genuinely curious.

She's not the jealous type, and I'm not the philandering type. Our pasts are in the past...literally. My prom date has been receiving the senior discount for at least a decade.

"If what needed doing was walking home alone in the rain, sure, it worked like a—"

Something beyond the door *thumps*.

I tense.

After a few silent seconds, I ask, "You heard that right?"

Delgado, now beside me, nods.

"I kick in the door, you go in guns-a-blazin'?" I ask.

"I've never gone in guns-a-blazin'." He somehow lowers his voice an octave and says, "Let's do it."

Before I can even attempt a countdown, both doors swing inward with the force of an out-of-control DeLorean, launching us away.

I land on the floor, sliding across a frozen patch of blood. The slick surface turns to pink slush where it merges with spilled salt water. Doesn't stop me from sliding. The suit's non-stick surface keeps us clean, but a little grip on the ass would be handy. I come to a jarring stop against the wall, thirty feet away.

When I right myself, the doors are closed again.

Cowboy and Chuy have their weapons raised and ready.

Across the room, Delgado sits up in a pile of thick broken glass. "The hell hit us?"

"Was rygar," Cowboy says.

"Why didn't it press the attack?" Delgado asks.

"They're primal," I say, "but not stupid. The Europhids would have sensed the others' deaths. They're being careful."

"Or biding their time," Chuy says.

I get back to my feet. "Waiting for backup."

She nods.

"Backup is bad," I say.

"Going through that door seems...also bad," Delgado says.

"Let's extend an invitation it can't refuse." I place my M-16 down on a lab table and approach the double doors.

"Moses..." Chuy isn't thrilled, but she stops short of arguing.

She trusts me. Understands that I don't risk my life—or my team's—if I don't see a happily ever after on the other side.

I stand ten feet from the doors. Chuy is another ten feet behind me, weapon raised, zeroed in on the back of my head.

"Mind getting the doors?"

Delgado and Cowboy holster their weapons and head for the doors, standing to the side of each.

I extinguish my face lamp and give them a nod, bracing myself to move.

"Okay, Garfunkel," I say aloud. "I'm counting on you for a heads up."

There's no response, but I know he can hear me, and every other thought in my head if he wants to.

"Do it," I say, bracing myself, envisioning every step before it happens. The door opens. The rygar senses me. The reds direct it to attack, because the dude with the blue in his head is clearly the biggest threat. The rygar lunges. I dive away. Chuy blasts it in the face. Kind of an uncreative sequel, but that's how sequels go—just like the first, but a little bit different.

"Okay, Clubber Lang," I say, addressing the hidden rygar that probably can't see or understand me. "Let's do this."

"Who was Clubber Lang?" Delgado asks, no longer poised to open the door.

"Is Mr. T," Cowboy says, "in *Rocky III.*"

"Because this is a sequel," Chuy says, translating my thought process to our new friend. I have to admit, I adore that they both understood what the comment meant.

"But Mr. T was in the third movie," Delgado says.

"Still a sequel," I say. "Now open the doors!"

Cowboy and Delgado take hold of the handles, pulling the doors open. On the far side—darkness.

I flinch, about to dive away, but nothing emerges.

I'm about to turn on the suit's night vision when a single bulb of red flicks on in the darkness. A Europhid.

What's it doing? I wonder. *Does it want to talk?*

NO.

"Then what the hell is going on, Garfunkel?" I say out loud.

RUN.

Red Europhids blink to life, filling the vast space beyond with a hellish glow that reveals a large number of rygars—far more than we saw in the ice, or that had that been stored in this lab.

RUN!

11

"Run!" I shout, repeating Garfunkel's order, but with twice the urgency. Garfunkel knows everything I do. He might pretend to be a non-invasive passenger in my consciousness, but he's got access to the whole shebang, including an understanding of what I can do, my assessment of everyone in this room, and the firepower they're carrying.

If he thinks we're screwed, I believe him.

Wet roars chase us through the lab as we fall back. Without Garfunkel we might have walked into a Europhid trap. Now they're pissed.

But they're not chasing us.

Yet.

Because they're not united, I think. Europhids are a collective consciousness spread throughout the universe. Garfunkel is alone, physically separated from his brethren—a willing sacrifice made to save his species. The reds aren't alone, but that's working against them. These rebels aren't united. They're individuals. Thinking for themselves.

That's my theory anyway, because it really sounds like they're arguing about what to do, the rygars emoting with roars and grunts.

"The hell are they doing?" Chuy asks, as we reach the doors on the lab's far side.

"Debating," I say.

We pause, looking back.

"Hallway makes good chokepoint," Cowboy points out.

Chuy nods. "Easy targets."

NOT DEBATING.

"You've got a lot to say all of a sudden," I say.

Chuy looks ready to backhand pimp-slap me, before furrowing her brow and saying. "Garfunkel again?"

"He says they're not debating."

"Maybe they're mating," Delgado says.

Three sets of befuddled eyes swivel toward him.

"What? Have you heard a koala's mating call? It's horrific."

"I haven't," I say, "and I question why you have."

DISTRACTING.

That strikes a chord. The rygars have had the run of the place long enough to know their way around, and the reds aren't fools.

Chuy sees the realization in my eyes. "What is it?"

"Keep going!" I shout, shoving them into the hallway. "It's a distraction! They wanted us confused. Wanted us..." I skid to a stop. "Wait just a fucking second..." I place my hand on the PSD stuck to my hip. "Everyone rotate the hell out—"

"Sorry to interrupt what sounds like a super successful mission," Wini says through the comms, "but there are five really ugly ass-faced things headed toward the door through which you entered."

Hildy comes on the line next. "You're getting pinched like a stubborn shit."

Can't help but smile, despite the fact that we've been outsmarted by a bunch of ass-faced Europhid drones.

"Back to the UFO," I say. "Does the UFO have a name?"

"Is Future Betty," Cowboy mutters.

"We just call it a UFO," Delgado says. "There's more than one."

I shake my head. "Things need names, man."

The doors at the lab's far side splinter as they're struck from behind. A trio of frothing rygars spill out, barking and flexing their...faces. Ugh.

"Everyone back to the UFO." I toggle the PSD and rotate into...nothing. Instead of disappearing into a rectangular void, I spin around like Kevin Bacon in *Footloose*.

"Umm," I say, and I try again.

Still nothing. The others are in a similar situation.

"Slew drive is broken," Cowboy says.

"Wini, get us out of here!" Delgado says, backing away from the lab where the rygars are advancing. They're not in a rush, just biding their time. Waiting for the others to arrive.

"Already trying," Wini says, her usual sarcasm missing. "It's not working!"

"We need a new choke point," Chuy says, and no one is happy about it, because we all know exactly where that is.

"Back to the cafeteria," I say, and I hustle in that direction. "Wini, give me a sitrep on the rygars. The ass-faces."

"Nearly at the entrance," she says. "Please hurry."

"Almost there," I say, closing in on the cafeteria of doom.

"The rygars are inside," she says. "Moving fast."

Chuy reaches the cafeteria first. Holds the door open for us while we charge inside. She closes the door behind us, plucks her Barrett barrel from her back, and wedges it into the door's handle, locking it. It would stop a human being, and it might be strong enough to resist a rygar for a little bit, but the rest of the door...

I slip and scramble across puddles of blood. At the room's far side, opposite the entrance, I drop to a knee and aim my M16 at the door. Chuy is to my left, weapon ready. Cowboy to my right, hands by his hips, ready to quick draw. Delgado is beside him, bouncing back and forth. He's seen action before, but I think it's been a while since he was in the thick of it.

The rygars approach like a football team, psyched for the start of the game, bumping into shit and into each other, hooting and screaming. They've got us and they know it.

"Hey," I say to Chuy.

"Not going to get mushy, are you?"

"What? Please, if anyone was—"

"Focus," she says.

"The rygars live in caves, yeah?"

"Far as I know," she says.

"And they've killed the lights in here."

"Wini," Delgado says, understanding the revelation. "You still have access to our suits?"

"Sure do."

"On my mark, light us up, bright as you can."

The door shakes from an impact.

Delgado's words bring a song to mind, and it comes out as a hum.

"What is song?" Cowboy asks.

"It's all about the devil," I say, and I keep humming 'Open Up Your Heart,' a little louder. I was aware of the original, sung by a creepy-ass Sunday School group in the '50s, but I knew it mostly from an episode of the *Flintstones*. It was really perfected by Frente! in the '90s, which I experienced for the first time, last Sunday, thanks to Hildy.

The doors are struck again, bowing inward. The Barrett's barrel bends.

Here we go... "Time to let the sunshine in, motherfuckers."

The door explodes inward, launching the handles and the bent rifle barrel. Rygars charge inward, not holding back this time.

"Now!" Delgado shouts.

All four of our adaptive armor suits blaze with the brilliance of a white dwarf star.

The charging rygars shriek and flail, clawing at their small, beady black eyes—all six of them. I don't remember the rygars having so many eyes, or really any eyes at all, during my first encounter with them. Probably because I was focused on their freakshow mouths. But there are other subtle differences. The hue of their skin. The smaller size and the more athletic build. It's like the difference between a tiger and a lion—both big cats, but unique in their own ways.

Our eyewear darkens and makes short work of the light, reducing the brilliance, giving us a perfect view of the room's invaders, and the earlier gore. Normally, a blaze of gunfire the likes of which we unleash, would make a room strobe and human ears bleed. But the muzzle flashes are swallowed by our countless lumens, and the deafening soundwaves deflected or absorbed by whatever protection Delgado has built into these suits. They're a little snug in the cobblers, but I'm planning on keeping this bad boy.

The first wave of four rygars meets a swift end as accurate gunfire shreds and/or implodes their heads.

But the second wave proves, once again, that they're being guided by an intelligence capable of strategizing. They stay low, hidden behind the falling bodies of their comrades. Before the corpses can hit the frozen floors, they're caught by four of the rygars' six limbs and held up.

The first group was never meant to reach us. They were sacrificial lambs destined to become fleshy shields.

"Punch a hole for me!" I shout.

Chuy fires her rifle, over and over, punching a massive hole in one of the nearest dead rygars. I fire my M16 through the hole, peppering the rygar holding the corpse. I unleash all thirty rounds before tearing through the creature's thick hide.

Beside me, Cowboy snaps his aim away from the charging rygars and fires his revolvers toward the wall. When they ping and spark, I realize the walls are metal. The central rygar pitches to the side, struck in the head by a ricocheted bullet.

I nearly stop to call bullshit—he's clearly hacking the simulation we all live in—when Delgado dives to the side, narrowly avoiding being crushed. He unleashes a two handed KRISS burst, spraying a hundred rounds in the blink of an eye, destroying both the rygar shield and the monster holding it.

In the time it takes me to reload, six more rygars plow into the large room. Even with Delgado's upgraded weapons, we're not going to last very long.

I lift the M16, wrap my finger around the trigger, and look up to find a headless rygar careening toward me, trailing a spiral of purple insides. Chuy shoves me to the side with her foot—

—and takes the hit for me.

12

"Chuy!" I shout, scrambling back to my feet. I can't see her past the dead rygars. And there's no time to search for her.

"Reloading!" Delgado shouts. His machine pistols are absolutely badass, but they take a hot second to reload, ejecting the two drums, putting one of the guns down, taking the second set of drums from his armor, and slapping them in one at a time. Delgado does all this without taking cover, casually swapping out the drums like he's got all the time in the world, and nothing is trying to kill him. He's either a confident badass with King Kong balls, or a complete space cadet. That he hangs out with two actual aliens, an old lady, and a flexible, kung-fu empath suggests the latter.

Cowboy unleashes sixteen rounds in a blink, every one of them hitting its target, but the rygars are tough and armored with folds of thick, rhino-like skin. Their only obvious weak spots are their heads, and they're doing a good job keeping them covered with the bodies of their dead.

I drop low, aiming beneath the dangling corpses charging toward us. The rygars each have six limbs, but they're using four to hold the bodies. "Cowboy! Whack-a-mole-time!"

He holds his fire and waits for me.

I've been in a lot of tight spots, but I always saw an out. Right now, I'm just buying enough time to catch a few more breaths, with the hopes that the situation will change—no matter how unlikely that seems.

"Whack!" I say, unleashing a three-round burst into a rygar's cankle. The bullets, combined with the creature's weight, are enough to shatter the joint. The creature howls, drops its shield, and flails to the side with the suddenness of a frenetic synchronized swimmer. As it arcs to the side, Cowboy fires two rounds, both of them striking the creature's fore-head.

"Whack!" I shout again, adjusting my aim to a second rygar, taking out its ankle and letting Cowboy finish it off. It's working, but I'm not sure how long we can keep it up.

"Whack!" Three rounds launch from my M16 and—

—they hit dead flesh.

The rygar I was aiming for dropped its shield and then itself down behind it.

"Not whack!" I shout, and then the corpse is flying toward me, flung by the rygar previously using it as a shield. My feet slip over frozen blood like a cartoon character running in place. My legs are moving, but I'm not going anywhere.

The spiraling body is about to collide with my torso, so I shift tactics, planting my foot against the back wall and pushing off. I slide beneath the careening carcass, and for a moment, I think I'm clear. Then gravity makes me its bitch, pulling the monster down atop my legs, pinning me in place.

I lie on my back, aiming upside down, and making the now-exposed rygar pay for the attack.

Nine bulky aliens lie dead on the floor, but there are more coming, filing in through the doors, squinting in the bright light, and then hopping over the dead.

"I'm out!" Delgado says. The machine pistols are amazing weapons, but in the hands of someone not trained to conserve rounds, hundreds of rounds have been spent in a very short period of time. Cowboy is still firing, but the rygars aren't dropping.

The hell is he shooting at? I wonder, tilting my head back for an upside-down view of the carnage-filled cafeteria. Rygar cadavers cover the floor and two long tables. For a moment, I think they're still moving, but then I realize it's the red Europhids, peeling themselves away from the beasts and pressing the attack on their own...very slowly.

Their little hooked tendrils reach out, dragging their wobbly red bodies in my direction, perhaps drawn to Garfunkel. One by one they burst like water balloons, shot down by Cowboy.

But he can't get them all, and we have bigger problems.

"Focus on the bigguns," I say, and I unleash a fusillade toward the Europhids, shredding them and emptying my magazine. "¡Hoy no dong rojos!"

A rygar lunges through the wall of glowing Europhid guts spraying into the air, getting a sphincter-mouthful as it roars. Cowboy drives four rounds into the side of its skull, dropping it just a few feet short of my head.

The Europhids on its back begin dismounting like soldiers storming the beach at Normandy. There's an urgency about them now—their numbers thinning, the enemy nearly within their grasp.

Doesn't matter which.

I eject the spent magazine and swap it out with my last fresh mag. I switch to single fire, hoping to conserve ammo and start popping Europhids one at a time.

But it's all for naught.

Cowboy holsters his revolvers, gives them a second and then draws them again. A rapid fire clicking fills the air. He's out of ammo.

And I'm down to fifteen rounds.

I try to free myself, but the rygar's got me pinned good. "How many are left?"

"Five," Cowboy says, taking a step back.

"Do what you can," I say, and I toss him my M16.

He pulls the trigger twice, unloading two streams of bullets, exhausting all fifteen rounds. "Three."

Three rygars and a small army of Europhids.

Yeah...we're screwed.

"Help me move it," Cowboy says, taking hold of the rygar that's got me pinned. Delgado hurries over, and together, they lift the creature just enough for me to pull myself free.

Back on my feet, I'm about to check on Chuy—and her Barret—which could take care of the rygars and leave us to stomp on the Europhids.

Before I get the chance, Wini's voice comes over the comms. "Don't worry boys. Let the ladies take care of this."

An explosion follows, staggering the central rygar.

The creature's standing on two legs, an eight-foot-tall killing machine...with a basketball-sized hole in its chest. Through the hole—Wini. She's dressed in adaptive armor, holding a lever-action Winchester shotgun, firing—if I'm not mistaken—FRAG-12 explosive shells.

The guts in the top half of the rygar's torso slide down to fill the gap, like a curtain dropping at the end of *The Wini Show*. Then the beast faceplants, leaving the last two rygars genuinely stunned, looking down at their suddenly dead pal, confused about how it happened.

Cassidy, also dressed in adaptive armor, leans out from behind Wini. "Whoa... It's like Five Nights at Freddy's."

No idea what that means, and I quickly forget about it when Hildy charges into the room holding a katana, of all things. But it's not just *any* sword. It's crackling with energy, sparks flying, probably powered by the adaptive armor she's wearing.

"Argh!" she shouts, doing her pirate thing, swinging the blade down into one of the remaining rygar's shoulders. The blade penetrates—an inch. But it doesn't matter. "Prepare to feel the shocker!"

"Oh, hun," Wini says. "I don't think you want to call it tha—"

White hot electricity flows through from the blade, into the rygar's body. The creature convulses and lets out a high-pitched squeal. The Europhids on its back boil from the inside, expand, and then burst, covering Hildy with steaming red slime, like she's on *You Can't Do That On Television*—Hell Edition.

She withdraws the blade and lets the smoldering creature slump over a table.

Across the room, the last rygar is backing away from Cassidy. The lithe girl stalks toward the much larger beast, walking funny with her arms and legs extended, stomping. More cartoon than human.

And for some reason, the alien killer, and the Europhids directing it, are afraid.

That's when I hear her, whispering at first, but then growing louder. "Nobody loves you. Your family is dead. They all left you alone in this horrible place. Everyone thinks you're ugly, too hideous to look at. Your vacant eyes and asshole-face are too revolting to love."

The hell? Is she attacking it with the power of teenagehood?

"Can someone put monster out of misery?" Cowboy says, equally uncomfortable by the display of empathic power.

Could she make it kill itself?

Not really the ability you want in the hands of a teenage girl...or anyone else.

A loud boom rocks the air. The rygar's head spritzes the wall behind it. The remaining body folds in on itself and falls at Cassidy's feet.

"Heeey," she complains. "I wasn't done."

"Can someone get this hijo de puta off me?" Chuy says, sitting up from beneath the rygar pinning her, the Barrett in her hands smoking.

Cowboy, Delgado, and I lug the corpse away, and I help Chuy to her feet. "You okay?"

"Knocked me out," she says. "But I'm solid."

"Not as solid as I'm gonna—"

"Still on comms," Delgado says, feigning a cough. He's in full-on dad mode. Probably is all the time, after raising a bunch of orphaned children.

"Okay, then," Wini says. "Now that we've redecorated, who missed me?" She hefts a large case atop one of the still clean tables, unlocks it, and peels it open. Inside, fresh magazines for everyone.

I hate to admit it, but I'm really starting to like Wini. She's a whirlwind, and she knows how to get under my skin, but she might just be this team's secret Michael Jordan, ready and able to step in and take the buzzer-beating shot for the win.

"Don't sideline me again," she says to Delgado, levering a fresh shell into her shotgun.

Delgado holds up his hands like he's being robbed. "Wouldn't dream of it."

"Good," she says. "Now can we finish figuring out what the hell is going on here?" She does a little shuffle, tugging at the adaptive armor on her inner thighs. "These things chafe my lady bits."

13

Five minutes later, we've reloaded, caught our breath, and let the last rygar bits and blood drip off our armor. So far, nothing else has tried to kill us, but I don't think that's the end of it. The reds are primal, but they're also strategic. They wouldn't throw everything at us without a contingency plan.

Hildy has been scouring the cafeteria for surviving Europhids. When she finds them, she runs them through with her sword—without boiling them. Not that it matters. If these reds are somehow connected to others, she's making intergalactic enemies with each blade thrust.

We all are.

Working *with* the Europhids tops my personal Top 10 list of 'What the fuck?' moments.

Fighting them...

If we can avoid it, for the sake of Earth and all of humanity—now and into the future—that would be great. When Hildy stabs another and withdraws the blade, dripping luminous red goo around her feet, I cringe, glad that the mask hides my face.

When I'm nervous, I sometimes look like I'm constipated. It's not flattering. And the big, tough team leader being spooked isn't great for morale. I also don't know how Garfunkel feels about it. He's been silent since the warning. He helped us. Was a real team player. Definitely wanted us to fight and kill these rebels. But I'm not sure how he feels about us sterilizing the battlefield.

I assumed he'd let me know if he wanted Hildy to stop, or maybe wanted to interrogate a red—if that's even possible—but he's just silently observing. I sometimes imagine that he's quietly judging us, and through us, all of humanity, determining if we're worthy of existence, even though the Union has been stopped and our violent expansion through the universe is now far less likely.

It's not impossible, of course, violent expansion is kind of humanity's jam. We've been doing it since the beginning, migrating to new lands, at first just populated by animals with no natural fear of humanity. Then much later, after forgetting just how far the human race spread, we re-expanded into the previously claimed lands and killed each other for it. If and when we can traverse the universe, we'll do the same thing.

Hopefully we'll have evolved into something closer to *Star Trek* by then, rather than the Fourth Reich Shagfest Trek.

"You all about ready to get this show on the road?" Wini asks. "Getting tired of the view."

We've all switched back to night vision, but bodies are bodies, and once you know the black splotches are actually a mixture of red and purple blood, it's hard to ignore the fact that the floor, walls, and ceiling are covered in it.

"Cowboy and I will take point," I say. When Chuy shoots me a solid 'da fuq?' look, I tell her, "You took a hit. Probably have a concussion. Sorry Babe, but Captain Reloads In the Open over here—" I hitch a thumb toward Delgado, "—might currently have more hand-eye coordination than you."

She lifts her fist in front of my nose and snaps up her middle finger, flicking the mask right between my eyes. "That coordinated enough for you?" Despite her protest, I know she gets it. She's a badass, but she's also responsible, and she knows when to not take risks.

I pat my butt cheek as I move past her and into the hall. "Enjoy the view."

"Oh, we will," Wini says, falling in line behind me and Cowboy. "So, Chuy. Interesting name. Is that like Cowboy or Dark Horse? Maybe Star Wars inspired?"

Cassidy does a good impression of Chewbacca as she and Hildy exit the cafeteria. Delgado brings up the rear, watching our backs with his bullet-vomiting machine pistols.

"You mean, is it a callsign?" Chuy says.

"Right," Wini says. "That."

"It is."

"What's it mean?" Wini asks. "Aside from the literal compound word translation, river of brown water... Unless you're suggesting that's what people produce when facing you. Because that would be kind of awesome."

"Chuy is a nickname for Jesús," Chuy says, using the Spanish pronunciation of the name. "...who greets my enemies when I'm done with them."

"Wouldn't you want your enemies to be greeted by the devil?" Wini asks.

"Jesús is the judge of that," Chuy says. Been a while since she went to confession, but she's still got a rosary around her neck and a Bible in her nightstand. She keeps her convictions private, but there's no doubt she believes the bad people she kills are on their way to judgment.

"So. Real names." Wini points at me. "Moses. Also Biblical, but strangely appropriate given your future rebellion." She points to Cowboy. "Milos..."

"Milos Vesely," he says.

"'Am gunslinger,'" Wini says. "I know. I've heard. Several times." Wini points to Chuy. "And your real name...?"

Chuy doesn't like her real name, and she doesn't offer it. Just follows me back into the lab, where there are no signs of life—rygars or Europhids.

Delgado, who has his back to us and who isn't great at reading the room, says, "Sophia Calleja Pérez."

"Ohh," Wini says. "That's a pretty—"

"Stop," Chuy says, quiet, but deadly serious enough to stop Wini in her tracks—not an easy feat. "Just Chuy."

I don't need to see her face to know Wini just put a pin in that reaction, but she drops the line of questioning, and just in time. We're halfway through the lab, approaching the destroyed double doors ahead, behind which a small army of alien bastards staged an ambush.

Cowboy and I frame the open door, weapons ready. I give a nod and we step through together, whipping back and forth.

It's a garage, occupied by several snowmobiles, two sno-cats, crates of supplies—and not a single rygar.

But they left us some gifts.

"Watch your step," I say, lifting my foot over a frozen shit the size of my thigh, filled with chunks of what I think are human bones. A watch. Twisted fabric. These things are everywhere. I'm looking at a minefield of digested people bombs. "I'm not sure this day could get any grosser."

"Could be babies they ate," Cowboy says.

"*Wwwhat?*" I'm staggered.

He shrugs. "Just saying, feces of babies would be worse. No?"

I sigh, say, "Messed up, man," and I move on, searching the sno-cats and the open crates. No bodies. Nothing hiding in the nooks and crannies. But now I've got a choice to make. There are two sets of doors in the garage. One leads straight ahead, into whatever segment of the laboratory lies beyond. The second, smaller door is on the garage's interior wall.

"This way." I head for the smaller door.

"Know where we're going?" Delgado asks.

"Not a clue," I say, "but this is the only door we've seen that has security."

There's a complicated looking keypad and a screen mounted on the wall beside the door. I look to Delgado. "You know what this is?"

"Digital keypass..." He leans in closer. "Retinal scanner. Handprint scanner. They sprung for the deluxe model. If we had the pass code and a fresh corpse, we might be able to get in the old-fashioned way."

His statement leaves a little wiggle room. "What about the new-fashioned way?"

"Well, now..." He places his hand against the security panel. "That's my specialty."

What looks like a dark haze flows out of little holes on the back of his armored hand and into the tiny gaps in the keypad. Individually, they'd be impossible to see, but there are millions of them. Then they come together, coalescing into interconnected strands the width of a hair, connecting his hand to the security system's interior.

"Nano-bots," Delgado says, like it's no big deal. "They live inside me. Well, they're machines. So, not really alive. They don't talk to me or anything like that. Not sure I could handle that."

"Tell me about it," I say.

"Normally, I'd access something like this remotely, but this isn't on a network. Can't be opened remotely." Delgado tilts his head to the side. "Annnd..."

The keypad flashes green, the door buzzes, and the lock *thunks* open. The door opens a crack on its own, and we all step back. Delgado doesn't wait for his nano-friends to re-enter his body—gross—but I can see them sliding through the air, returning to their human womb.

Unlike Garfunkel and me, his relationship with the nano-bots seems to be one sided. He's in full control and not dealing with a separate intelligence. I'm envious of that, but there are some benefits to having a Europhid in your head—like creepy blue eyes...or a rygar early warning system, which is currently quiet.

I think we're clear, but I open the door with the barrel of my M-16, just in case. Nothing lunges out, so I step in...and down. The staircase descends, first through a metal tunnel, and then through crystalline ice, reminding me of the last time we were here, a trip that ended with us being transported to the future...something I'm not keen to repeat.

The deeper we go, the narrower the staircase becomes, forcing us into a single file line. If a rygar charges from either direction, there won't be anywhere to go.

The stairs end at a horizontal tunnel covered in wooden planks that have been bolted to the smooth ice. But the wood is a mess, cracked and shredded. Not all of the rygars came from the lab. Some of them came through here.

But from where?

When the tunnel ends, I get my answer, and I sure as shit don't like it. "Damnit. Why can't things ever just be easy?"

14

The cavity in the ice is massive, and I think it might be the very same location in which we discovered the obelisk when we were transported to the future.

But a lot has changed.

The walls are no longer smooth, transparent, or spherical. The hole in the ceiling created by a Soviet sno-cat has been sealed by metal. And the walls are all jagged from where the Russians carved the rygars out of the ice.

But extreme levels of what-the-fuckery remain.

Mostly because there are two, black, fifty-foot-tall pillars rising up from the floor, thirty feet apart. If that wasn't strange enough, they're covered in what I think are Viking runes, giving them an ancient feel, and creating a strange dichotomy with the sheet of red light stretched out between them, crackling with lines of hexagonal energy.

"The hell is this?" Chuy says.

"It's a portal." Delgado says it with the assurance that comes with having seen a thing before.

"Tell me," I say, approaching one of the pillars. The runes stretch from top to bottom. Could be ornamental. Could tell a story. Might just be a sign that says, 'Keep the hell back.'

"A few years ago, during the time you all missed, there was…an event."

"What kind of event?" Cowboy asks.

"The kind that gets covered up," Delgado says. "Which was no easy task. Took years to convince the public that there were a number of reasonable explanations. The most popular of them was mass hysteria caused by tainted food. It was bullshit, and everyone knew it, but the reality of what happened was just…too much. And since it seemed unlikely to happen again—based on survivor accounts—people were happy to pre-tend it was something other than the truth."

"Which was?" I ask.

"An alien invasion," he says it so matter of fact that I know he's not joking.

"Aliens tried to take over Earth?" I motion to the gateway. "Using these?"

"They were..." He's searching for a gentle way to tell us, but it's tot-ally unnecessary. Luckily, Cassidy is here to lay down the succinct, mind-blowing truth in an efficient way.

"The sky went black. A bunch of devils and demons came to kidnap people and turn them into sausages on another planet, but then some techno angels showed up and pew, boom, crash, some people escaped back to Earth. The end. Thank you very much." She bows low. Twice.

"The demons...one report called them Tenebris, which means *The Darkness* in Latin, appear to be a parasitic race of aliens using other species as vessels for intergalactic...farming. Food sources."

"People are...food for these things?" Chuy's trigger finger is ready to pull.

Delgado nods. "And they're processed in a factory, which was app-arently destroyed. None of these reports were substantiated, of course. While several of these portals have been found, they eventually crum-bled to dust after a bit, and none of them were active."

"Until now," I say.

"But this is different," he says, deep in thought.

"How?" I ask.

"The affected area during the Darkness was confined to a portion of New Hampshire. The gates appeared during the first night, and I assume would have been removed if the Tenebris hadn't been thwarted, but none of them remained active."

"Why would you assume that?" I ask.

"Because this wasn't their first visit. People called them demons and devils for a reason. They've been here before, taking scores of people and leaving survivors behind to tell the tale. And when Christianity rose to prominence, these creatures fit the narrative. That's why modern depictions of Satan are red, hoofed, and horned. And why demons are wispy and black."

"Satan is real?" I ask.

"Satan, capital S, was never a name. Neither is Lucifer or any of the other titles given to the myth that is present day Satan. The biblical evil being, a seraphim and rebel, is described using terms that have *become* names. In the original text, Satan was referred to as 'the satan,' which means 'the adversary.'"

"I'm sorry," I say, "when did Sunday School start?"

"Accurately understanding ancient texts is important. If more people had taken the Three Days of Darkness prophecy seriously, we might have saved thousands of lives."

"There was a prophecy?" Chuy asks.

"Two," Delgado says, "both from Catholic women."

Chuy performs a subtle sign of the cross and then returns her finger to the trigger.

"A few folks figured out the math and determined the date. The news was spread online and via tabloids—enough for some people to take it seriously and panic buy, but most of that was just an excuse for end of the world parties. Y2K part two. No one really expected hell on Earth."

"All that's great," I say, "but we still don't know where this goes, right?"

"There are two likely locations," Hildy says, capturing everyone's attention. "This...hell planet, which must be really far away, because the Union never found it, or any other planet they visited. *Or* Beta-Prime."

"What's Beta-Prime?" Delgado asks.

"Home world of the rygars." I hitch my thumb back toward the door. "The ass-faced guys."

"Also, the future base for the resistance fighting against the Union," Chuy says, "and a massive Europhid colony."

I think back to my time, fighting alongside the brutal reds. "The kind you don't want to screw with."

"Wouldn't it be safe for you? Because..." Delgado waggles a finger at my eyes. "You have one of them inside you."

"First of all," I say, "don't ever phrase it like that again. Second, we're a thousand years behind Garfunkel's time... Maybe..."

"Maybe is what loose women say when they're playing hard to get," Wini says. "Just spit it out." I swear I see her grin behind the mask. "Which is also what—"

"Time is experienced differently for Europhids. Collectively, they're countless. Like cells in a single, massive organism. They might come and go as individuals, but they experience reality as a whole. Garfunkel is a cell. His life expectancy is now the same as mine. But he doesn't exist yet, and I'm not sure he'd ever be able to be part of the whole again—without killing me. Appearing back on that world...he might be viewed as an outsider, just like us."

"And that would result in..." Delgado waits for me to finish.

"Death," Chuy says. "Unpleasant death."

I walk around to the back of the gate. Different runes, but otherwise identical to the other side. Guessing sides don't matter with something like this.

"And if they figure out that we came through this...from Earth, it might be cause for an aggressive response," I say.

"Haven't they already done that?" Delgado says.

"A dozen rygars?" I laugh. "These things inhabit entire planets. Peacefully for the most part, until you screw with them."

"So, then we agree," Delgado says. "We shouldn't go through."

"What? No." I rejoin the group. "My people are going through. If you're uncomfortable with the idea, stay behind and make sure nothing comes out. If they do, destroy the gate."

"Won't you be stuck?" Wini asks.

I pat the PSD on my hip. "We've got these bad boys and Little Miss Celestial Map over here." I tilt my head toward Hildy, who places her hands over her heart like I've just delivered the most wonderful compliment. "The universe is our bitch. We'll make it back."

It's an exaggeration, of course. We might make it back with some trial and error. Hildy has a great understanding of the universe and the positions of notable planets, including Earth and Beta-Prime, but we're a thousand years back in time, and the universe did a lot of expanding and rotating in the time since. Without an active celestial mapping system, we're bound to make a few wrong turns...in open space.

Could be dicey, but dicey is what we do.

"We're coming with you," Wini says, and when Delgado starts to complain, she shuts him down. "*We're going with them.*"

At first, I thought Wini was Delgado's lacky, but now I understand that they're actually partners, despite the fact that she's a bottle of aged sass and he's got nanobots with access to the world's information in his brain. Says a lot about Delgado. Says a lot about them both.

"Hey," I say to Wini. "Stop making me like you."

She flips me the bird.

"Better," I say.

Delgado heads toward the wall of red energy. "Okay then, I'll go first."

He's about to step through when I grasp his shoulder. "Whoa, whoa, whoa," I say, "One does not simply walk into Beta-Prime."

"Nice," Cassidy says. "Old man makes a dank meme joke. Solid."

"Dank...what?" I ask, but I never get, and don't really need, an answer.

"Do we skip into Beta-Prime?" Delgado asks. "Saunter? What's the deal?"

He's losing his patience. Probably nervous about traversing the universe for the first time. It's understandable, so I keep my calm and say, "First, I need to ask permission."

15

"You there?" I ask, after walking away from the group. No idea if I'm going to be talking to myself, or if I'll be zoned out in another time and place. Either way, I don't really want an audience.

I stand before an ice wall, looking at all the crags and shades of blue and white revealed by the glow of my lit-up facemask.

It feels familiar. Like I've been here before.

Because I have *been here before,* my conscious mind thinks.

But it's more than that, and this frozen chamber looks nothing like it did the first time I was here. This icy wall reminds me of another place. Another world. But in all my travels throughout the universe I never had the pleasure of stepping foot on a Hoth-like planet. Not because they don't exist, but because the Union didn't like chilly locations. I'd flag them as uninhabitable and move on. I became an exo-hunter, seeking out livable worlds for the expansionist Union, to stay off their racist radar. After hijacking the *Bitch'n* and its crew, I expected some blowback. But it wasn't long before I found my first world and became a bona fide hunter, which allowed me to pursue my true goal—locating my team, which had been scattered throughout time and space.

To my knowledge, I've never seen anything like this.

Which means it's not *my* knowledge.

Garfunkel is here. He's always here. And his memories are starting to bleed into mine.

"So," I say, speaking toward the wall like a crazy person. "What does all this remind you of?"

I blink—

—and I open my eyes to another world.

I'm standing in a vast subterranean cavern. The walls are pocked with hollows. The floor is covered in red Europhids, intercut through paths that I think are game trails for whatever local lifeforms inhabit and defend this place. I look up and float off the floor, heading toward the stone ceiling from which frozen stalactites of ice hang.

I pass through the ceiling, immaterial in this memory.

Stone is replaced by darkness and an intense pressure that I can feel despite my intangibility. Lights flare, one at a time, lighting up the fluid depths. Blues and pinks, yellows and oranges. The deep water is home to untold bioluminescent species. It's stunning to look at, but I don't have much time to take it in.

I'm pulled to the surface, flowing up through a mile of ice until I'm deposited in an ice cave that looks similar to the one in which my physical form is currently standing...facing a wall like a kid in time-out.

Dim orange light guides me to the cave's mouth. I head for it, unafraid.

As real as this all feels, I know it's all in my head.

But that doesn't stop me from gasping when I step out into the light and look up to find my view dominated by a massive, swirling gas giant that is recognizable to just about everyone on Earth that isn't part of an uncontacted tribe. "Jupiter."

I look down at the ice beneath my feet. I'm on one of Jupiter's moons. One inhabited by Europhids. That means this is...

"Europa."

In another dimension of reality, human beings came into contact with the Europhids here. The people on that mission deemed the gelatinous life-forms 'Europhids' before being escorted off-world by the reds. I was told all this on Beta-Prime, before being sent back in time, but I also ...feel like I remember it.

Which must be impossible, because it happens in another dimension...a few decades in the future.

"Our consciousnesses are bleeding into one another," a small voice says. I look down to find Max standing beside me, looking up. In this vision, not confined to his childhood backyard, I'm still my adult self, while he is still a child—perhaps because I never got the chance to know him as an adult. He reaches up and holds my hand.

It's weird. Because this isn't Max. It's Garfunkel.

But the look of quiet worry is familiar.

Garfunkel is nervous. And he's looking to me for comfort.

"You okay?" I ask.

"I'm...nervous," he admits. "A side effect of our merger."

Europhids are cosmic beings with what some would call a god complex. Their experience of time and reality is so different from humanity's that I still don't fully comprehend it. They are not controlled by emotion. Not even the reds. Their actions come across as angry, because they employ violence, but it's more like an involuntary reaction. A reflex. They're just doing what they evolved to do—protect the whole from invaders.

"I don't think it's the only side effect," I say.

He nods.

"My memories are becoming your memories."

"Is that dangerous?" I ask. "For me?"

Europhids have been around for billions of years. Their collective consciousness is spread throughout the universe, time, and dimensions. The blue Europhid in my head was never on Europa. Never encountered the human crew in the future. Never met the woman named Kathy Connelly, who interfaced with the blues in the same way I did on Beta-Prime. But Garfunkel remembers her just the same.

I don't think the human mind can hold that much data.

"There is no way to know," he says. "In all our time, such a thing has never been attempted."

"The reds coexist with their hosts," I point out.

"*Coexist*," he says. "We...exist."

Singular.

The implications of what he's telling me scares us both. He's no longer Europhid. I'm no longer human. We are...or are *becoming*...something new.

"If this were real, I think I'd piss myself."

"I think I might have already," Max says, smiling, and for the first time in these encounters it doesn't look forced or phony.

"Sense of humor, huh? That will be a nice change."

He nods. "For a time. It is a functional coping mechanism."

"Annnd, back to not being funny."

"Do you fully comprehend the ramifications?" he asks.

"That we will no longer be plural at some point in the near future."

He nods again. "We will be me. A single consciousness." He squeezes my hand tighter. "And I am afraid."

"Of what that means," I say, aware that we are also starting to share the same emotions, which must be even more disconcerting for Garfunkel. And not just because he's becoming something finite. "You don't know if they'll accept you. Even on your home world."

He nods. "It is true. But I am not without the resources to handle such rejection." He looks up at me. "Thanks to you, Dark Horse."

His use of my callsign instead of my name is intentional. While callsigns are often designated by others, usually pointing out a soldier's flaws, my crew was different. Brick, Whip, Chuy, Benny, and me. We all chose our own callsigns. Dark Horse is an acknowledgement of my situation at the time—that I was an outlier, never expected to advance to a position of power—not because I was incompetent, but because of the color of my skin. Didn't keep me from reaching for that goal...and when I finally grasped hold of it, I was a thousand years in the future, leading a rebellion.

I was a general for a day, fighting the worst enemy mankind has ever known—itself. And honestly, that was enough.

The world is still full of xenophobia and all kinds of people who believe they're superior to others, but the Nazis responsible for the mother of all plagues have been defeated.

Fear of the unknown is natural. It keeps people from untimely demises.

But it's a brand-spanking new experience for Garfunkel, who is apparently learning how to cope and to overcome, thanks to my history and the perseverance of my ancestors.

It's not enough to quell his fears, but it is enough to fortify his resolve.

"We will both be in danger," he says.

"That's what we do. And I mean *we*, as in you and me."

"I appreciate your blind optimism," he says, smiling again. "But it is blind. My kind hasn't been an individual since the very first of us." Max turns his face up to Jupiter, eyes closed as though basking in the planet's energy. "I am unique in the universe. And soon, you will be as well." His smile broadens. "*We* will be."

"We're not without options," I say. "If they reject us, we'll rotate the hell out, lick our wounds, and find another way to deal with whatever that gate is. Speaking of, any ideas?"

He shakes his head. "The technology is unknown to me."

"What about the runes covering it?"

"Unknown."

"How is that possible?" I ask.

"My kind populates vast sums of the universe, but not all of it. We have only just come into contact with humanity. The species mentioned earlier... Tenebris. I have not heard the name before. It is highly likely that there are other unknown intelligent lifeforms in the universe, or in universes beyond ours, or in dimensions we do not inhabit." He looks up at me, stone cold. "Reality is infinite. As are the possible explanations."

"Then there's only one place to start," I say.

"Home."

"Ready to do this, E.T., or do we need some Reese's Pieces?"

He grunts.

"What?" I ask.

"You have been in the twenty-first century long enough to consume copious amounts of popular culture. Yet...your references are still... dated."

"Dated? *Dated?* Man, far as I can tell, the '80s were the best time to be alive. New Wave music. The Golden Age of Rap. Original science fiction. Not the endless remakes being pumped out now. Naomi Campbell. I mean, c'mon. It was a good time—"

"—to live in the first world," Garfunkel says.

"Let's not go there," I say. "If I wanted to argue politics, I'd be on Facebook."

"I thought we were delaying," he says, turning around. "To avoid going..."

I follow his lead, looking away from Jupiter, and I find the twin pillars of doom embedded in the moon's frozen surface.

"They're not really..."

"No," he says. "The conscious world is overlapping with the subconscious in the same way that you and I are. It's time to go, Mosey." He squeezes my hand again, popping me back into reality, where the team is staring at me.

"How long have I been standing here?" I ask.

"Long enough to be awkward," Chuy says. "We good to go?"

I approach the gate, my apprehension about what comes next magnified by two. "Good," I say. "Totally good."

"You don't *sound* good," Cassidy says.

"Yeah, well..." I finish the thought by stepping toward the red wall of energy.

16

"Wait!" Delgado shouts.

I stop in my tracks, nose touching the wall of energy. Kinda tingles. I step back. "What's wrong?"

"I thought... I mean it seemed like the right time. To do what you do."

I have no idea what he's trying to say. "Look like a badass? Check. Kill bad guys? We did that."

"The music thing," he says. "You've got a soundtrack for everything, right?"

I'm about to say, 'Not everything,' but that would be a lie. Just because I don't play music 24/7 doesn't mean it's not playing in my head. Probably drives Garfunkel crazy if he can't drown it out.

Delgado's been watching us for a while, directing us toward bad guys, monitoring the job we're doing, listening in. He knows how we usually operate, including my penchant for appropriately themed music, unless I'm going for dichotomy. We once took out a Nazi cell while listening to 'A Spoonful of Sugar.' From *Mary Poppins*. The medicine going down was bullets. All the sugar in the world wouldn't have helped.

And now Delgado wants the full experience. "How about this? As long as we're not under fire, and don't need comms, you can soundtrack the hell out of us."

"That might not be the greatest idea," Wini says.

Delgado waves her off. "Awesome. Okay... I got this..."

"No pressure, but we've got a planet full of aliens to inspect, and I'm—"

The words, 'intergalactic planetary, planetary intergalactic' spoken by a robotic voice, repeats in my ear. A funky beat follows, along with some record scratching. My eyes widen. A smile spreads. "What is..." The moment a voice starts rapping, I know who I'm listening to, but not what. "Beastie Boys?"

Delgado nods. "'Intergalactic.' 1998."

The song lifts me above the worry conspiring against my usually calm exterior. "Okay," I say, and I chamber a round. The moment was supposed to be cool. A real 80s sci-fi moment. But I'd already chambered a round. So, all I manage to do is eject a perfectly good bullet. And since there's a chance we're going to need a lot of them, I reach out and catch it.

"Hold on. That didn't..." I eject my magazine and slip the bullet back inside. "Okay," I say again, "Let's *do* this." This time, I slap the magazine home for emphasis.

"Would have been better first time," Cowboy says. "Redo lacked... oomph."

"I know, I know," I grumble. "Let's go."

Carried onward by the Beastie Boys, I step through the wall of red and emerge on another planet. Feels like I've just rotated, but it's actually a little bit faster, and it lacks the disorientation that can come from physically rotating. "Back to Oz," I say, recognizing the landscape.

The music's volume fades as Delgado kind of stumble walks a few steps, gazing at the new world around him. From orbit, Beta-Prime looks a lot like Earth. Up close, it's a Dr. Seuss wet dream. The jungle is populated by trees with colorful bark and foliage that looks like bundles of multi-colored Crunch Berries—like broccoli a kid would actually want to eat.

"This is amazing!" Cassidy cartwheels past me. She might be able to make a monster piss itself, but she's still just a kid. Shouldn't be here.

"Got a leash for this one?" I point to Cassidy while speaking to Delgado.

"I'm her leash," Wini says, and then she somehow manages to whistle beneath her mask. Cassidy quickly falls in line. Knows not to mess with Captain Cougar.

"Everyone stay close. No wandering off. There are some...pretty things on this planet that are actually very dangerous."

"Like tigers?" Cassidy asks.

"Like a mound of dirt with glowing blue balls that make you want to make out with it, sing 1980s Russian hair band songs, and allow it to slowly digest you. That kind of dangerous."

"Well, if I die on this planet," Cassidy says, "that's exactly how I want it to happen."

"Leash," I say to Wini, as seriously as I can muster. Cassidy isn't technically under my care, but I'd still feel responsible if a kid died during my op. I turn to Chuy, and I don't need to say a word. She gives a nod and slips into the jungle. Before anyone can ask where she's going, she's a ghost.

"Cowboy, watch our six. Hildy, you're with me." To Delgado, I say, "Keep your people sandwiched between us. Things go south, I want each of you to grab on to me, Cowboy, or Hildy. Whoever is closest. We'll rotate out."

"Sure those things will even work?" Delgado asks.

He's got a point, so I activate the PSD...and nothing happens. "Well, that's just peachy."

"We'll be okay," Hildy says. "The UFO was able to transport us down to the surface, outside the base. Stands to reason that the slew drives would have worked as well. But proximity to the gate disrupts other kinds of physics-bending technology. Probably intentionally. To protect whatever these things are from people technologically advanced enough to be a threat."

I'm not really sure that's us. We have the technology to move around the universe, and to shortcut between land and sky, but mine was stolen from the Union, and Delgado's was inherited from a pre-human civilization. We didn't create this tech. I barely understand it.

But we're here.

With things that go boom.

So, I guess that's not nothing.

Something howls in the distance. Not a rygar, but it sounds big.

"Stay close. Stay quiet. Got it?"

Cassidy snaps off a salute and falls in line directly behind me and in front of Hildy. Close enough.

"You'll remember the way?" I ask Hildy.

"Piece of cake," she says. She's got a mental map of the cosmos in her poofy blonde head. Remembering the way back to the gate is a snap for her, but it's still polite to ask.

Just one more thing, and then we can move out. I reach up, peel the adaptive armor mask from my face and take a deep breath. The air is humid and smells like a greenhouse with a touch of citrus. It's not Earth air, but it's still fresh and safe.

"Umm," Delgado says.

"Step number three when exploring an exo-planet..." I tap the side of my nose. "Trust the schnoz. You *smell* death long before you see it." The armor let me smell in the Russian base, but I couldn't shake the feeling that my nose was muffled. I want full access to all of my senses when I'm off world—assuming there's an atmosphere.

Cowboy takes his Stetson off, and then the mask. He takes a deep breath through his nose, smiles, and then replaces the hat. "Is fragrant world. Like Antarktos."

The others follow suit, peeling off masks and breathing in the air of another world. There really is nothing like it. When I first started traveling abroad, I expected other countries to feel and smell different, but for the most part—they smelled like everywhere else.

"I don't know what that is," Delgado says, "but the air is—"

"—sweet," Wini says. "Like the promises of a snake oil salesman shilling a cure for erectile dysfunction. If it makes you stiff, it's probably because you're dead and rigor mortis has set in." She looks at our blank stares. "What I'm trying to say is, don't go falling in love with the place that might try to kill us."

"What she said." I head into the jungle, lift my hand, attempt to snap my fingers a few times, and then resort to saying, "Let's go."

We move in silence. The crew is following my lead, staying wary, pausing when I do. So far, no one has asked me if I know where I'm going, which is great, because I don't. I'm following my gut, which I think is Garfunkel's instinctual knowledge of where to find his kind—like birds migrating around the planet. Aside from a few psychedelic tree species, nothing actually looks familiar, though. I spent very little time on the surface of Beta-Prime, and when I did, I was either tripping balls or fighting a battle that scoured the landscape clean.

"Hey," Cassidy whispers, still on my six.

I turn around and hold my finger to my lips.

"No cap," she says. "This place is fire."

I take a deep breath through my nose. Don't smell any smoke, and I'm pretty sure this place is too moist to catch fire. "What?"

"Sorry. Forgot you were a boomer out of time." She shifts her voice to sound like a surfer dude and says, "This place is *radical.*"

"Also deadly."

She waves a hand at me. "We got this."

"You seen someone die?" I ask.

She catches me off guard by nodding. "A bunch."

I don't know the kid's story, and now is not the time to be caught up in it, so I take her word and say, "Then you know it sucks. And it might not be you who gets killed." I glance back at Delgado, who is wrestling with a branch in his way, and at Wini, who I think is looking at my ass.

Kid gets the message. Purses her lips.

Before I can look forward, I'm struck by a wave of discomfort that drops me to my knees. "Gah!"

The others rush up around me. Hildy puts a hand on my shoulder. "What is it?"

I look up to find a cliff face fifty feet ahead. A tangle of tree limbs partially covers the entrance to a cave. "We're there," I say, but the cave has nothing to do with this revelation. The reds are directly beneath us. Millions of them. I can feel them.

Can feel their rage emanating from the ground like the lingering radiation of a nuclear blast. "I'm going alone from here."

17

It doesn't take a whole lot of convincing to get the others to stay on the surface. Visiting an alien world for the first time—no matter how pleasant the experience—has a profound effect on both body and mind. They're probably not even aware of everything they're experiencing. The subtle shift in gravity—less here than on Earth. The increase in oxygen. The way humidity in the air beads on your skin. There are so many small changes that it can overwhelm a first timer without them ever realizing why.

They'll need time to adjust before descending into another planet's Europhid-populated abyss. My first and last visit was disconcerting, and I was an experienced exo-hunter at the time.

So, I step into the cave alone, leaving Cowboy and Hildy to watch the perimeter and Chuy on overwatch. If things go sideways...I probably won't know about it. Comms aren't going to work through all the rock. But with three PSDs and a crap ton of bullets between them, I think they'll be safe.

It's me I'm worried about.

Walking into the lion's den here. If lions were phallic Jell-O molded, mind-bending assholes.

Twenty feet into the cave and the daylight starts to fade. I'm about to pull my mask on and use the night vision when I realize that I can actually still see fine. "I can see in the dark again!"

After merging with Garfunkel, I was able to see in the dark. Walked out of this cave system, without a light, and without bumping into a wall or stubbing my toe. But when we returned to Earth, my night vision was gone, as were my more-than-human abilities. Enhanced senses, increased strength, speed, and stamina, all of them went poof.

Because I wasn't here, I think.

"That's why, right?" I ask Garfunkel.

YOU ARE NOT SEEING IN THE DARK.

"Umm," I say, peering into the descending cave system, able to make out every crag, and able to peer through every shadow. "Then why does it look like I'm walking through a colonoscopy?"

MEMORY.

This is a memory of a colonoscopy?

NOT YOUR MEMORY.

"Yeah, I know. These sweet cheeks haven't been parted for anything bigger than a doctor's index finger, and only that one time—hold on—I'm seeing Europhid memories?"

OVERLAID ON YOUR VISUAL FIELD.

"Like augmented reality?"

PRECISELY.

"But I could see better. Hear better. I was stronger. All that happened, yeah? And all of it faded after we left Beta-Prime."

IT DID NOT FADE. IT WAS...REMOVED.

"You...*removed* those abilities?" I ask, a little offended that I wasn't at least told.

IT WAS BETTER THAT YOU DIDN'T KNOW. FOR ME.

I'm about to complain when I realize why. Because I'd have never stopped asking. "Because it would have made *our* mission a helluva lot easier, man. The hell?"

POWER LIKE THAT WAS NOT MEANT FOR HUMAN BEINGS.

"Why the hell not?" I ask.

His answer is another memory. A fraction of a second. And it drops me to my knees. The pain of millions of Europhids scorched into oblivion by the Union.

"Solid point," I say, picking myself back up. "Absolute power corrupts absolutely and all that. What about Europhids? You guys have never wiped out a planet or two?"

NO.

The cave ahead opens up. My footsteps echo. I lower my voice. "Why tell me now?"

WHEN *WE* BECOME *I*, THERE WILL BE NO FILTERS. THE CHANGES TO YOUR CELLS, TO YOUR SENSES, MUSCLES AND BONES, WILL BE FULLY ACCESSIBLE.

I TELL YOU NOW BECAUSE...I DO NOT KNOW WHEN THAT WILL HAPPEN.

AND BECAUSE I HAVE RETURNED WHAT WAS REMOVED.

The echoes I'm hearing are from far ahead. He's restored my enhanced abilities. But why now?

BECAUSE I AM AFRAID.

I've been trading bullets with Nazis for months, no superpowers required. He didn't blink when the red infected rygars attacked us.

"Afraid of what?"

Ahead, red light reflects off tiny crystals in the walls.

We've nearly reached the red Europhids guarding the path to the blues.

Garfunkel was nervous before, but what he's feeling now... It's much more than that. An intense sense of wrongness that is filtering through to me.

THEY ARE NOT COMMUNICATING WITH ME.

"Do they not recognize you as one of them?" I ask.

IF THAT WERE TRUE, WE WOULD BE UNDER ATTACK.

"So, the cold shoulder then. Seems very teenaged girl of them."

"Hey!" The whispered complaint sends a chill up my spine. I nearly open fire, as I whip around toward the voice.

The barrel of my M16 comes to a stop just two inches from the forehead of a very surprised young woman. Cassidy's hands snap to the ceiling. My now enhanced reflexes caught her off guard as much as her presence behind me nearly made me pop out a nugget.

"How are you here?" I ask.

"I snuck away and walked." She taps the side of her mask, once more pulled up over her head. "I used night vision. Why aren't you using night vision?"

"What I mean is, why didn't I feel your presence?" The question is meant in equal parts for Cassidy and Garfunkel.

Her body language says she knows the answer. I lower my weapon, let it hang from my shoulder and cross my arms, letting her know I'll wait.

"Well, I know I'm not supposed to, but I kind of...masked my presence. You could hear me. I even tripped and fell. I just made you...not care."

"You're screwing with my emotions?"

"Sorry," she says.

"Could have gotten you killed," I say.

She nods.

"Do it to a teammate again and I'll make sure Delgado benches you. You copy?"

"Copy," she says. "But...I'm already not supposed to be here."

"If that were true," I say, "you wouldn't be. Could have flown you back home, or had me rotate you there, faster than the gaseous pops of a flatulent man after a five-day old chalupa. You're here because he thinks you're ready. Why? I honestly have no damn clue. But I think you'd like to prove him right."

She nods again.

"Then do what I tell you, when I tell you, and don't ever...*ever* screw with my emotions again."

"By 'my emotions,' do you mean both of your emotions?"

I squint at her.

"You know there are two of you...in you...right?"

"His name is Garfunkel," I say. "And he likes being messed with even less than I do."

"Sorry, Garfunkel," she says.

"Do not do it again," I say, but the voice is not quite mine, not just because it sounds a little stiffer, but because those words didn't come from me. They came from Garfunkel.

Rather than dwell on what this means, I turn back to the tunnel ahead.

"What's the op?" Cassidy asks.

When I glance back at her, she's doing rapid fire, deep bending squats, burning off some of the never-ending energy.

"Stroll through the scariest place I've ever been," I say. "Have a conversation with some old friends we haven't met yet, and then...hope for the best. Can you handle that?"

"Hundo P," she says.

I shake my head. "Delgado doesn't teach you guys English or something?"

"The Internet is my teacher," she says, skipping along beside me, as I push forward. Her presence is a nice distraction, but...it could be more.

"Can you do the opposite?" I ask.

"That sounds like a trick question," she says.

"Can you push...positive emotions? Like, let's say give someone a confidence boost?"

"Sure," she says.

"Do it," I say.

"But you just said—"

"I'm giving you permission."

I pause as we approach a bend in the cave. Can't see it yet, but just ahead the cavern opens up into a massive space populated by a vast colony of red Europhids. And they're still silent. Still indifferent to our being here, which is extremely out of character and is freaking Garfunkel out, which is, in turn, freaking me out.

"Okeedokee," she says. "On a scale of one to ten, how confident do you want to feel?"

Europhids can sense fear and weakness in people. Showing them anything else could be dangerous.

AGREED.

"Hook us up," I say. "Let's go with ten."

18

"What's up, you limp dick motherfuckers!" I shout, the message reverberating around the Europhid-filled cavern we've just entered.

"I think ten might have been too high," Cassidy says, looking at me with impossibly wide eyes.

I wave her off. "They don't have ears. Can't hear a damn thing."

"Still," she says. "Let's go with something a little less Jake Paul extra and a little more Bob Ross ASMR chill."

"English, child. English!" I say, and I feel my confidence fade to a point where I'm able to realize exactly how jacked up my emotional state had been. Felt like I was Thor. On speed. In a lightning throwing contest. "Can we keep what I said between us?"

"You mean I can't post it to Insta?"

I stare at her.

"Tik Tok?"

"That like a clock or something?"

"*Face...book?*"

"Ohh. No. Don't do that."

"What will you give me if I don't?"

"First, I'll keep you alive down here."

She does a sudden squat, which turns into a high kick. "I know how to fight."

"Know how to take a punch?" I ask.

"Umm. No. But I do know it smells like a bag of farts in here."

"Yeah. That's methane. You've never been punched, right?" I start for the bend ahead. "It'll happen eventually. When it does, you need to know how to handle it. Fighting isn't just about fancy kicks and flex-fu."

"Flex-fu," she says, smiling. "I like thaaaaa..."

We round the corner. The cavern opens up into a vast, glowing red space carpeted with Europhids.

"Whoa... Looks like hell," she says, sounding grave, then she somehow transitions back to being chipper. "You said 'first.' That implies there is a second."

I ignore her, stepping closer to the winding path, leading down the center of the cavern. I walked through here in the future-past. With Chuy and Brick. The Europhids were allies then and the journey was still dangerous. Having just been attacked by red-controlled rygars on Earth, I'm not feeling too great about this, even with Cassidy's confidence boost.

"I'll buy you ice cream," I say. "Any time you want it."

Cassidy offers her hand, and we shake on it.

"Last chance to turn back," I say, knowing she won't take it. Kid has an adventurous heart. But at least I can say I offered.

She smiles. "You don't want me to leave. You couldn't do this without me."

"Yeah, well... You might be right." I look down at her. "You boosting your own confidence, too?

She shakes her head. "Doesn't work that way. I'm just braver than you."

"Let's go," I say with a sigh, stepping onto the path. "Try to keep your mind clear and calm. They'll sense any negative emotions. And definitely don't hum—"

"Hush little Moses, don't say a word," she sings to the tune of 'Hush Little Baby,' then continues, "I'mma gonna kill you a rygarbird."

I flash her a *whatdahellyouthinkyoudoing* face. But she persists.

"And if that rygarbird does stink, I'mma push it right to the brink."

I'm about to knock her out cold when I notice a change in the Europhids closest to us. They weren't acting aggressive before—more like indifferent—but now they're kind of flaccid. Relaxed. Is she putting them to sleep?

Whatever she's doing, there isn't a hint of their normally aggressive behavior. So, I let her sing.

We journey deeper into the cavern, me trying to exude calm, my weapon slung over my shoulder like I'm out for a stroll and not creeping along another planet's Ho Chi Minh trail, surrounded by potential death. Cassidy skips beside me, singing the whole way, somehow making up new lyrics as we go. We travel like this for ten minutes.

All around us, the Europhids are soothed into a sanguine state, rising back up to their alert position when we're a good fifty feet past them.

As we approach the cavern's far side, I'm greeted by a barren wall and an empty floor. The sight stops me in my tracks.

Cassidy skips in a circle around me, inserting a "You okay?" in between the lines of her song.

"This is where the blue Europhids should have been," I say, speaking for myself and Garfunkel.

"Maybe it was different back...now. Different than it will be when you arrive...later." She's still skipping, still maintaining the cheery look on her face, but I can see doubt creeping into her eyes. And if I can see it, the Europhids can feel it.

I push onward, hoping a closer look will provide answers.

It does, but not the answers I'm looking for.

All the confidence in the world couldn't prepare me to respond to what I find with anything other than abject dread.

The blues *are* here.

But they're all dead.

Their darkened remains litter the floor, the bioluminescent blue light snuffed out.

Inside me, Garfunkel reels.

I've never known him to be emotional, but this...for his kind...is unheard of outside of Europhid encounters with the Union. It's not just genocide, either. These are his ancestors. His family.

"Garfunkel... I'm sorry... This is... Garfunkel?"

My insides churn. His sorrow sets my nerves on fire. Tears stream from my eyes as I stagger toward the field of dead. Millions of blues stomped, torn up, and sliced apart.

This wasn't anything natural.

They were attacked.

WE HAVE BEEN BETRAYED.

And by 'we,' he means the blues. Because there's a vast mass of reds, alive and well, twenty feet behind me. The reds are reactionary, but their place in this symbiotic relationship with the blues has always been as protectors. A force of nature, destructive at times, but ultimately a force for good. These blues being dead... The reds allowing us passage... All of it points to one staggering conclusion.

A trap.

But...I don't care.

I'm overwhelmed by unfathomable heartache. Like losing Chuy a thousand times over.

My knees wobble.

I feel faint.

Hands on knees, my fully human lizard brain attempts to stay upright.

"You're okay," Cassidy says, gripping the sides of my head, her big blue eyes burrowing into me. She rests her forehead against mine. "You're okay."

My suffering abates enough for me to rise above the flood of emotions and catch a breath that isn't infused with Garfunkel's anguish.

"We need to leave," Cassidy says.

I nod, but I struggle to move.

"Garfunkel," I say. "Big guy. You need to let go." And I don't just mean of his pain. He's got a grip on my body, rendering me nearly useless.

"They're coming," she says, more urgent now, but also pushing relief into my thoughts. Into Garfunkel's.

I hear them, too. Heavy footfalls. Farty grunts.

More rygars.

The reds are powerful...up close. The twenty-foot gap between us means all they can do is flop about menacingly.

But the rygars. If they catch me like this, we're going to look a lot like the field of blues.

"Garfunkel... If you don't snap the fuck out of it...we're all dead."

He doesn't respond, but I get a strong sense of *I don't give a shit*.

"Great," I say. "That's just great. I've got a vast alien intelligence in my mind, locking down my body, and it's depressed."

"I'm trying to ease it," Cassidy says, sounding apologetic.

"Not sure you or anyone else can," I say. "But maybe reducing isn't the solution."

I look her in the eyes, projecting menace.

She understands, nods, and I instantly feel a shift in my emotions.

"Vengeance," she says. "Vengeance!"

VENGEANCE!

Control of my body returns.

I spin around to find a small army of rygars, all controlled by glowing red Europhids attached to their spines, bounding down the path.

We have seconds.

I reach my hand out to Cassidy.

She rolls into my arm like we're dancers. I activate the PSD, which works now, and I continue her rotation into the fourth dimension. We exit to the surface—

—and find Wini, flat on her back, fresh blood dripping from her nonstick suit.

19

"Wini!" Cassidy shouts, diving down beside her. When there's no reply, Cassidy peels back Wini's mask, confirming that the woman is unconscious.

I do a quick inspection of Wini's body and find nothing obvious. She took a hit, but she's still breathing. Should be okay. But she needs to wake up. Fast. The reds clearly attacked the surface team, maybe even before they sprang their trap below.

There are bullet casings on the ground. Some are Cowboy's. Some Delgado's. Two shells from Wini's shotgun lie beside her.

And now that I'm on the surface with Garfunkel—their most likely target—they'll be closing in on *us* soon. Rotating out of the caves and back onto the surface might have confused them, but they'll soon detect us here. And we don't want to be around when that happens.

"Wini," I say, patting her cheek. "Wini!"

"Too rough!" Cassidy says, swatting my hand.

"If she doesn't wake up, she might not ever," I say, looking back over my shoulder, scanning the alien jungle for signs of trouble.

"I've got this," she says, and she places her hands on Wini's temples.

I stand again and activate my comms. "Chuy, you copy?"

Silence.

"Cowboy? Delgado? Hildy? Anyone out there?"

Chuy might go silent under the right conditions, but all of them?

An angry shout rolls through the jungle.

"Hildy?" I start walking toward the sound, and then I point at Cassidy. "Get her on her feet and get back to the gate!"

Feels wrong leaving the kid behind, but she's tougher than she looks, and Hildy needs my help.

I sprint through the jungle, weaving my way through broccoli-like trees. "Hildy! *Hildy!*"

"Here!" she replies, not too far away. Her shout is followed by a grunt of exertion and a string of curses. As I get closer, I can make out what she's saying. "Goddamnedsonsofawhore!" An electric crackle fills the air, followed by a howl so loud it reverberates in my chest. A wet splat comes next.

I crash into a clearing to find Hildy, electric sword glowing. She's covered in purple and luminous red gore and surrounded by three dead rygars. She spins toward me, lets out a battle cry, and swings the blade.

"Whoa!" I shout, skidding to a stop. The sword hovers an inch from my face, its electric field warming my skin.

The sword tilts to the side, revealing Hildy's face, the berserker rage slowly fading as she recognizes me. Her hair is matted down by goopy alien guts. The rygar blood on her face is mixed with dark red oozing from a gash on her cheek.

"You okay?" I ask.

She stumbles forward into my arms, undone by my presence. "I'm sorry. I tried to help. But there were too many."

"Too many of what?" I ask, attempting and failing to disguise my rising concern.

"I...I don't know what they were," she says. "They had rygars with them, but...I don't know. They seemed intelligent. Kept to the shadows. But they definitely had red Europhids on them, too. Pale skinned, I think. Stood on two feet. I can't remember much else."

Hands on her shoulders, I ask, "Tried to help who? Where are the others? Where's Chuy?"

Hildy begins to weep. "I...I don't know. They took them. Alive, I think. But gone. Through the gate."

"Took...who?"

"Delgado, Cowboy...and Chuy." She begins crying again, torn up by the early stages of survivor's guilt—which we can hopefully avoid experiencing in full.

Understanding the situation in as much detail as I need to take action, I stand her up straight and speak to her with an uncommon gruffness reserved for soldiers at war. "Need you to suck it up, Hildy. This fight isn't over yet. You copy?"

I give her a shake, and she snaps out of it. Wipes her nose. The fierceness returns. "Copy."

"Anything that's not human," I say. "Hack it to bits."

She gives a nod, which dislodges a coagulated clump from her hair. It splats on the ground between us. Would normally garner a comment or a humorous tangent, but there's no time.

M16 in hand, we charge back the way I came, in part to check on Wini and Cassidy, but mostly because it leads back to the gate. The shifting shadows of the canopy in the breeze give the illusion of movement all around us.

"Moses..." Hildy says, eyes on the jungle.

"I see it," I say. "Keep moving."

"Is it..."

She doesn't need to finish the question. Rows of shifting red lights, bounding through the shadows tell us everything we need to know. We are not alone. But are they rygars, or the pale bipeds that apparently took Cowboy and Delgado?

"Chuy," I say into my comms, hoping that her fate is unknown, given her distance from the group. "If you're out there. Let me know..."

Silence. And then, Hildy says, "They got her first. She fired one shot. And then nothing."

I do my best to hide my heartache. "How do you know she was taken?"

"Saw them take Cowboy and Delgado," she says. "Assumed they did the same to Chuy."

I'm going to assume the same damn thing until proven otherwise. Don't think I'll be able to function if I think Chuy is dead. A rescue mission has an element of hope to it. Vengeance—what Garfunkel wants—is a dark pit that's hard to climb out of.

"Who's there?" Cassidy asks from the jungle ahead. She can either hear, or sense, us coming.

"It's me," I say, bursting through the clearing to find Wini on her feet, pointing her shotgun at my head.

I push the barrel down slowly.

Whatever these guys saw has them all on edge and nearly mowing down their teammates.

"Good?" I ask Wini.

"I'll live," she says, twisting the kinks out of her back. Then she sets her deadly serious eyes on me. "We need to leave."

"Not without—"

"They're gone," she says. "And we're not getting them back if we're dead."

We have a stare off for a moment. It's not the glare that convinces me to hear her out. It's the tears in her eyes. Losing Delgado is having a profound effect on her. She wouldn't make the call to leave if there was any chance we could get them back now.

But there is something I need to know first.

"Where were they taken?" I ask.

"A second gate," she says. "It was here, and then it wasn't."

I nod. "Let's bug out." To Hildy, I say, "Lead the way."

I move to help Wini along, but she swats me away. "When I need help, I'll ask for it."

Hildy charges through the jungle, and the rest of us follow along with me at the rear, keeping an eye on the shifting jungle and the bouncing red lights, closing the distance. "How much farther?"

"Nearly there," Hildy says.

Brush topples under the electric slice of Hildy's blade, revealing the gate. We rush out into the clearing, hustling toward the wall of red. Behind us, rygars call out, either desperate to stop us or eager to consume us. One of the two. Hope I never know which.

Hildy stops in front of the gate, waving us on. Wini is still moving at a steady pace, but it's not fast enough. "You'll forgive me later," I say, and I hoist her up over my shoulder. "Go!" I shout to Cassidy, and she's off like a greyhound, catching up with Hildy.

"Go, go, go!" I shout to Hildy, waving her forward.

Heavy footfalls pound the earth behind me.

"Holy shit!" Wini shouts, and she starts firing with her shotgun, the shoulder guard punching into my back like a fucking donkey kick with each shot. But she's hitting targets, so I don't complain. Rygars wail in pain, but there must be a lot, because the ground is shaking beneath me now.

Ahead, Hildy turns to face the gate and steps through—

—nothing.

The red wall disappears, leaving two black columns and no way home.

With no time to think much about it, I shout, "Need you to rotate us!"

"Where to?" she asks, as I close in, five seconds from impact, six seconds from being torn apart.

"003189!" I shout.

She's doing mental calculations, but the worry in her eyes radiates like a star. She's not going to figure it out in time. But she doesn't need to. I'm struck by a burst of knowledge gifted to me by Garfunkel.

"I got it!" I shout, slapping the PSD on my hip and opening my arms to engulf Hildy and Cassidy. I tackle all three women into a wall of white, charging through one end of the universe and spilling out the other—fifteen feet above the ground.

20

The terrain below is covered in spring-like grass, but it's pocked by large boulders. Nothing to do about it aside from bracing for impact or trying the loosie-goosey strategy—turning yourself into a ragdoll so collisions are less likely to break bones. It's the reason why a lot of drunk drivers walk away from crashes. But it's nearly impossible for a sober person to pull off.

So as the ground rushes toward me, I reach out with my hands and angle my body just right. If I can turn the fall into a roll, I'll be back on my feet without missing a step. It's not impossible from fifteen feet, but if I screw it up, I could break my neck.

Wish I could help the others. Tell them how to land, but we're about to—

A loud puff of compressed gas hisses.

The adaptive armor swells up like a balloon.

All four of us hit the ground—and bounce. We look like Weebles, stuck on our backs or stomachs, rolling around, trying to right ourselves. I swing my arms and use my core strength to roll myself over, just in time to see a rygar's head descending toward me.

But it's just the head, severed by the fourth-dimension sealing shut behind us. I roll to the side and watch the head crack against a rock and flop into the grass.

With a loud hiss, gas is expelled from the armor, placing us gently on the ground.

"Is this...Earth?" Wini asks, looking up at the blue sky and the white clouds. Then she turns her attention to the spiral grass, pushing against it. "This isn't Earth, is it?"

Hildy runs her hand over the permed grass. "Feels like my hair."

"Definitely not Earth," Cassidy says. She's already on her feet, looking down the tall hillside upon which we've landed. Below us there's a lake, teeming with life. There are several species gathered at the water's edge. It's a scene straight out of the African plains. Familiar, but totally foreign. "Look at those guys..."

She points to several thirty-foot-tall, six-legged creatures with hippolike bodies and long tendrils hanging down from where their mouths should be. They're wading through the water, paying no attention to the predators swirling around their long legs.

I wanted to make this place my home, once upon a time, when I thought the Earth and my time were lost to me forever. Seeing the ecosystem in action, pristine and untouched, I'm glad I decided to hide it from the Union, and that I never settled here. A place like this would just be corrupted by human hands.

Thrashing by the shoreline captures my attention. One of the predators, which looks like an oversized black salamander with a mouth as broad as a croc's is long, has lunged out and caught a smaller creature by the head. A single roll breaks the neck, and the prey is dragged into the water.

Oookay. It's not always pretty. But the circle of life and all that.

"Everyone okay?" I ask.

"Alive," Wini says. "Not okay."

"What was that? With the suits?" Hildy asks.

"Impact protection," Wini says. "My idea. You know, because I'm old."

I stand up and offer my hand to Wini. "You're more badass than old."

She takes my hand, and I pull her onto her feet. "Your girl's been gone for just a few minutes and you're already trying to get into my pants? Tsk."

"Eww," Cassidy says. "Can we not do the totes sketchy sexy talk? I've got virgin ears over here."

She's been living with Wini for years. No way this kid hasn't heard it all.

"I either make myself laugh, or I start bawling my eyes out," Wini says. "Take your pick."

"Sketchy sexy talk," Cassidy says, and then she rolls her eyes toward me. "She sounds like a wounded cow when she cries."

Wini crosses her arms. "You've never heard me cry."

"When we were watching Sesame Street, and Big Bird found out that Mr. Hooper had died..."

Wini sighs at the memory, head low. "Right... That..."

"Why didn't they take us?" Hildy asks, sounding even more melancholy than Wini recalling Big Bird's first brush with the Grim Reaper. "They could have. There were so many of them. And they were fast. And smart. And strong. We weren't ready for them. Didn't stand a chance. But they sent the rygars after us, and just took the others."

I sit down in the grass beside her. "When the dust settles, and a battle is over, there's no way to know what the enemy was thinking. Why one person fell and another didn't. There're too many variables. Even you won't be able to—"

"They wanted the strongest of us," Cassidy says. "They drew us there, let us separate, and struck when we were weakest." She looks me in the eyes. "When you weren't with everyone."

"I don't think I would have—"

"Talking to Garfunkel," she says, and it makes sense. If the reds on Beta-Prime are in rebellion, the blues would be their greatest threat.

"You weren't meant to make it out of the caves," Cassidy says.

I nod. Makes sense. But I did make it out. Question is why. And the answer is pretty obvious. Little Miss Happy Dance over here, lulling waves of red Europhids into a comatose state as we passed through must have slowed them down. Whatever they had planned was put on hold by her positive vibes. "They're not quite the masterminds that the blues are."

"If the blues were all that smart," she says, "they wouldn't be jelly on the cave floor."

Hildy slow-turns toward me, eyes wider, brow furrowed. "Wwwhat?"

"They were all dead. The reds control the planet."

"Not just the reds, hun," Wini says. "They've got some friends. Smart ones. Means they've got ambitions, too. Taking out you and Dan... Only two people capable of hopping around in outer space. Means they know what they're doing. Means they've got plans for Earth."

"Maybe," I say. "The universe is full of planets ready for colonization." I open my arms out to the view. "Case in point. Taking over a place like this, versus Earth, which has as many guns as people, not to mention warships, fighter jets, and enough nukes to lay the whole place to waste. Seems like a no brainer."

Wini shakes her head. "Can't believe you were in the military. Are you sure you led a rebellion in the future?"

"For like a day," Hildy says.

"We won," I point out, and then to Hildy, I say, "Thanks for the support."

She shrugs. "Just being honest."

"Anywho," Wini says. "Let's pretend we're in England, a thousand years ago. And let's pretend that the Scots aren't a thing. It's open land. Ready for the taking. But to the south—"

"Is Wales a thing?" Hildy asks.

"No. Just England. And to the south, you've got Vikings, led by Rygar Cockbreath. Are you going to send your army up into the happy tappy north to colonize, or are you going to send them south to deal with the Viking problem before they're on your doorstep, waving Nazi flags, and shooting off all those nukes?"

"You think this is a pre-emptive strike?" I ask. "To prevent the Union from expanding out into space?"

She shrugs. "I'm throwing spaghetti. Seeing if anything sticks. Point is, you might have stopped the Union you knew about, but who's to say they don't make a comeback? Is there any nation on Earth that wouldn't abuse the universe if they had access? Even the United States, a country whose citizens believe the nation is blessed by a higher power, is making a helluva mess of its own world. Just because you stopped the Union, doesn't mean you stopped humanity's expansion into the universe. And if that's true, the Europhids might still hold a grudge."

"But none of that has happened yet," Cassidy says.

"The Europhids experience time differently than us," I say.

"They know the future?" she asks.

"Maybe," I say. "Who's to say the beginning and the end of time don't already exist? Their experience of time might be felt in millennia, rather than seconds. Maybe they've experienced human expansion in other dimensions enough to know it never goes well for them. They might also just be smart enough to see the writing on the wall. If Wini can surmise humanity's eventual violent expansion into the universe, it seems likely that the Europhids figured it out, too." To Wini, I say, "No offense."

She shrugs it off.

"But why would they kill the blue ones?" Cassidy asks.

I'm not sure, and I don't think Garfunkel is, either. But I have a guess. "If the reds believed humanity was a threat, they'd want to wipe us out at all costs. There's no doubt about that. But they're usually tempered by the logical blues. In a way, they're subservient. Logic controlling emotion. But if the threat was great enough, and the blues opposed taking action, it's possible that the reds saw the blues as a threat."

UNLIKELY.

Garfunkel's sudden appearance in my thoughts makes me jump.

RED CANNOT SURVIVE WITHOUT BLUE. IT WOULD BE LIKE REMOVING A HUMAN'S BRAIN.

"What did he say?" Hildy asks. She recognizes the look in my eyes when I'm talking to Garfunkel, probably because they turn blue.

"He says, killing blues is akin to removing a human's brain. They couldn't survive for long."

"Hmph." Wini's unconvinced. She looks me in the eyes, but I think she's addressing Garfunkel. "Unless they found a new brain."

21

"So, Exo-Man," Wini says. "How do we get home?"

"Is home where we really want to be?" Hildy asks. "The things that took them weren't human. I'm not sure they'd have gone back to Earth."

"Well, we damn well need to go somewhere." Wini, hands on hips, scans the alien terrain. She's getting frustrated, and I understand why. The people we care about most were taken from us. "Last thing I can stand right now is sitting on my duff, doing nothing."

"Thinking isn't doing nothing," Hildy says.

"First, everyone take a chill pill," I say.

"What's a chill pill?" Cassidy asks.

"It's a term from the '80s that means 'calm down,'" Hildy explains.

"Old people words. Got it." Cassidy sits in the curly grass, hiking her knees up to her chest and wrapping her long arms around them.

"Second," I say, "It's not Exo-*Man*. It's Exo-*Hunter*. Much cooler."

Wini rolls her eyes. "I'm sure it drops all the aliens' skirts."

Hildy stops picking the coagulating purple from her hair. "Do aliens wear skirts?"

I sigh. "Third. Hildy is right. We need to think for a hot minute before bouncing around the universe without a clue."

Wini takes a deep breath and lets it out slowly. Really slowly. The exhalation lasts the entire twenty seconds it takes her to walk over to Cassidy and plop down next to her. She reaches over and rubs the girl's back, which I think is comforting for both of them.

I stand in front of my strange collection of female allies—the kid, the naïve future woman, and the old lady. "First..."

"You already said 'first,'" Cassidy points out. "You should be on fourth."

"New list," I say, and I carry on. "I think our friends are alive."

"Why?" Hildy asks.

"Because they could have killed us," Wini says. "Instead, they took a few of us. The strongest of us."

Cassidy huffs at the idea, but she says nothing.

"Question is why," I ask.

"Backup plan?" Cassidy surmises. "You know, in case they couldn't get you in the caves. Maybe when things went tits-up—"

"Language," Wini says.

Cassidy throws her hands up. "You talk about tits all the time!"

"The lower they hang, the more you get to talk about 'em."

"That makes no sense," Cassidy says.

"Anywho..." I do a quick scan of the area, wary for danger. This planet is an oasis, but predators abound. "Back to what matters."

"First man in the universe that doesn't think tits are important," Wini grumbles.

I ignore it. "What did they look like?"

"All I saw was a flash of white and then the black void of unconsciousness," Wini says.

"I mostly saw rygars," Hildy says. "I think they were meant to distract us. To keep us from realizing something more was going on. But...they were pale. Bipeds. Maybe twice your size. Big black eyes." She pinches her hand in front of her nose. "Kind of a snout, but not like a dog. More like...a Komodo dragon but squashed. Not as pronounced."

"Any chance they had tails?" Wini asks. "Maybe looked a bit like dinosaurs?"

Cassidy slow-turns around. Knows what Wini is insinuating. I, on the other hand, am clueless.

Hildy shakes her head. "No tails. They stood upright, like people, but kind of hunched, and they had Europhids running down their spines, just like the rygars. Their legs were... What do you call it? Inverted? Like the knees hyperextended, but...more like an animal. Like a horse or a dog."

"Minotaur legs," Cassidy says.

"Yeah, that."

"Walking on their toes," I say. "High ankles."

"They're called hocks," Wini says.

Hildy nods. "Right. Normal arms, but...I think there might have been a second set of smaller arms, kind of sticking out of their chests. Skinny around the waist. Big pecs."

"So, a tanless Arnold Schwarzenegger with animal legs and a second set of arms."

"But tougher," Hildy says.

I tilt my head at her. "You take that back."

"*Tougher.*"

"Conan the Barbarian tough?"

"*Tough-er*, but...also graceful. They were fast. And...kind of shimmered in the light."

"Please don't tell me they were sparkly vampires," Cassidy says. "I am so over sparkly vampires."

"Shimmering and tougher than Conan..." Another scan of the area reveals nothing to worry about. "Right. Okay. So...good info, but it doesn't really help."

"Maybe we could get some wanted posters made?" Wini says, dripping sarcasm. "Put them up around the galaxy."

"Universe," I say, correcting her. The grand scale of what we're facing here is daunting. There's no way to know where these things came from or where they went. "What else do we know?"

"We know they're not here," Cassidy says.

"We know they've been to Earth," Hildy adds, "and Beta-Prime, and that they're allied with the red Europhids. And that they travel through space using gates, which might be Einstein-Rosen bridges, or something else entirely. No way to know."

"Einstein-Whosen bridges?" Cassidy asks, and I'm glad she did, because I didn't want to ask and look stupid.

"Wormholes," Wini says. "Hasn't anyone seen *Stargate?*"

"Never heard of it," I say.

"*Event Horizon?*"

"Isn't that like a black hole thing?"

"Like a black hole thing..." Wini shakes her head.

"I don't know if you're shaking your head because I don't know the reference, or because I don't know the science."

"Both," she says.

"They're shortcuts through space-time," Hildy explains, dumbing it down for me. "Similar to the fourth dimension, but more of a direct route. A doorway from one place to another."

"Which they can create using gateways," I say.

Wini straightens. "We need to go back. To Earth. There were other gates. In New Hampshire. Maybe one of them will—"

"We studied the gates," Cassidy says. "Couldn't figure out how to turn them on."

"We don't need the gates to work," Hildy says. "We just need to figure out where they went."

"Where did the gates in New Hampshire lead?" I ask.

"Officially..." Wini says. "What gates? Government says they don't exist. According to the survivors' original stories, they lead to another planet."

"The sausage factory," I say, remembering. "Devils and demons. The Tenebris, right?"

"There are a lot of different descriptions from the survivors. But nothing like what she saw." Wini waggles her finger toward Hildy. "Then there were the angels. Techno-angels, I guess. Laser wings and whatnot. Fought the devils off. Allowed some people to escape. Honestly, it sounds like a bunch of malarkey, even after everything we've seen."

"But if the gates are real," Hildy says, "maybe the rest is, too?"

"Mmm," Wini grunts. "Dan takes it seriously. He's been looking for some kids who went to hell and came back...different. But they're in the wind. Haven't been seen. Same as the kids in Boston. And the telekinetic assassin."

"The what?" I ask.

"World is a weirder place than I knew," she says. "Point is, we won't find them, so we're going to have to figure out the gates on our own."

Hildy looks at me. "We need Burn."

"Burn... Scrawny guy?" Wini says. "Kind of funny looking?"

"My *boyfriend*," Hildy says. "Yeah."

Wini raises her hands. "Call 'em like I see 'em, hun. But if you can love a man for his heart and not his...other attributes, you be you."

I lay out the basic plan. "Return to Earth. Pick-up Burn. Head to Vostok. Study the gate. Figure out where it goes, rotate there, save our friends and...then what?"

"Blow up the bad guys," Wini says. "Isn't that what you do?"

I smile. "That's exactly what we do. Garfunkel, show me how to get home."

I stand there for a moment, grinning like a fool, feeling pretty shitty, but feeling good about the plan. Things get awkward when the knowledge of how to rotate to Earth doesn't magically spring to mind, and I'm left just standing around like when Trisha Chaney, my date to prom, spent the whole night dancing with Henry Newberry instead.

I raise my index finger. "Hold on." And I step a few feet away from the others. "Garfunkel. Where are you? We need to go. Now. Not sure how much time we have to—"

NO.

"The hell you mean, 'no'?"

He doesn't reply.

"Backyard meeting," I say, "right now."

I've never instigated a subconscious pow-wow with Garfunkel in the form of Max, but I attempt it anyway, clenching my eyes shut and focusing on his childhood back yard.

A few seconds pass, and then...

"Are you trying to poop your pants?"

I open my eyes to Cassidy, arms clasped behind her back, smiling up at me.

It's not going to work. Garfunkel is shaken. I can feel it. What we discovered in the cave below... I fear he might be broken. "Hildy...this one's on you."

"You...know what that means, right?" she asks.

"Few stops along the way, a left turn at Albuquerque, and then presto."

Wini pushes herself up. Dusts herself off. "A few stops where?"

Hildy looks to me, unsure about how to answer. Then she decides on honesty, which in this case, might not be the best option. "Open space. But the suits will protect us, right?"

"So I'm told," she says. "But the air supply is limited. Few minutes at best."

Hildy nods, freeing a clump of purple gore from her head. It splats on the ground between her feet. "I'll try to be quick."

"Masks on," I say, pulling the adaptive armor back over my head. There's a hiss as it seals.

The others do the same, and Hildy opens her arms. Wini and Cassidy bravely walk into her embrace. I sandwich them in, wrapping my hands around Hildy's shoulders.

Wini, whose backside is pressed up against me, turns back. "Try not to get excited. There are kids present."

"Eww," Cassidy says, and when we rotate off planet we're laughing.

That stops the moment we emerge in an eternal, weightless void surrounded by unfamiliar specks of light, billions of light years away.

22

The moment we hit the vacuum of open space, the adaptive armor reacts. First thing it does is seal itself and pressurize, which is more than a little uncomfortable on the ears. Then it warms up—fast. It's almost scalding at first, but it quickly cools off and then chills, no match for the negative 455 degree temperature of the cosmos.

The suits don't have air tanks built in. All the air I have is trapped inside the suit with me. And it's not much. Panicking or talking will make it go quicker. So, I focus on the stars spinning around us, maintain my grip, try to relax, and imagine that I'm back at summer camp, in a pool, timing how long I can hold my breath. My best time was two minutes, though I was interrupted by a lifeguard who thought I had drowned.

The key is to not use your muscles. Every movement uses oxygen.

Holding onto Cassidy and Wini is working against me, but in space it doesn't take a lot of effort.

In the perfectly silent stillness that follows, while Hildy calculates where we are and where we need to go next, my mind drifts to the one place I've been avoiding since we left Beta-Prime.

Chuy is gone.

Maybe dead.

I have felt profound loss in the past, the first time being Max's death. Whip and Benny—they didn't just die, they betrayed me before doing so and that stung a little bit more. Leaving Brick in the future and then actively destroying the Union in the present, possibly erasing his time-line—and him—in the process. And last but not least, I'm thirty years in my future. A lot of people I knew are dead and gone.

But not Chuy. She's been by my side, through the worst life tossed my way, loving me like only a badass motherfucker can—with everything she's got. We were destined to grow old together. Have children. Hell, we met our descendant in the future.

But none of this happened the first time.

The Union's demise changed the timeline. It was supposed to be for the better, but it opened the door for something worse.

Vostok, I think. If we hadn't disrupted the Nazi movement, they might have taken over the Russian base before they figured out how to open the gate. Destroying them allowed the Russians to continue their work, unleashing this new hell on Earth.

On me.

Damn it, Chuy... Why didn't you escape?

Because that's not who she is. Not who Cowboy is either. And probably not Delgado. Live to fight another day strategy only works if you're not leaving loved ones behind.

Despite floating in zero gravity, a heavy weight settles over me.

We left.

I wasn't fast enough. Wasn't—

Something small grips my arm.

Cassidy's hand. She applies gentle pressure. Trying to comfort me. The little empath feels my pain. She's not pushing new emotions on me, not artificially pepping me up, which she could have done without me noticing. She's doing it the old-fashioned way, probably because we're pals now, and messing with someone's emotions without permission is almost certainly a no-no in the Delgado household. Or is it secret base-hold? Doesn't really roll off the tongue.

Feeling a little tight in the chest, I exhale slowly and take in a breath of already stale air.

Don't think about the distance, I tell myself.

Don't think about the odds.

The kid will know if you get nervous.

A white rectangle opens beside us as Hildy activates her slew drive once more. We topple toward it in slow motion, doing two full rotations before slipping into the white void. Here, we adjust course and travel for just a few seconds—enough to cover a staggering distance back in our home dimension.

When we exit, I search the stars around us for anything familiar. When not viewing space through an atmosphere, the number of stars is staggering. Makes finding a familiar constellation difficult. But given time to adjust, the brightest stars still stand out.

Which is why I'm able to find the big dipper. The shape is a little funny because I'm not seeing it from Earth, but it's there. We're making progress.

Cassidy's grip on my arm gets a little tighter. She's afraid. Her smaller and undisciplined lungs are probably low on oxygen already.

"It's okay," I whisper in the comms, exhaling at the same time. "Won't be much longer."

Hopefully she can't sense the lie. I honestly have no idea how much longer we'll be out here, but I believe in Hildy. Trust her more than just about anyone else, not just because she's honest, but because she's competent, and *that* in the twenty-first century, is a rare treasure.

A fresh wall of white absorbs us. We slip through the fourth dimension once more and emerge—again—in open space.

And this time...there are tiny spots of colors—orange, blue, red—and a yellow star at the middle of it all. We've reached the solar system. Next stop: Earth.

Cassidy squeezes hard enough to hurt.

A burst of fear rolls out from her, affecting all of us.

Tears fill my eyes.

A sob hiccups from my mouth.

I'm feeling her anguish.

She'd been so calm when we started, but now—she's out of air.

"She's suffocating," I say.

"I...know," Hildy says, her voice weak and raspy.

When I take a breath in, I feel no relief. I exhale and try again. Nothing. The burn for oxygen sets in. How long was it between my last breath and now? A minute? More? It's hard to think while experiencing Cassidy's pain.

And then, all at once, I'm not.

I'm back to myself just long enough for my own fears to swell.

Is Cassidy unconscious? Is she dead?

Can we actually pull this off?

Wini's head lolls to the side.

She's out, too.

In the vastness of space, I turn my goggled eyes to Hildy, searching for indicators that she's still with me.

Her fingers move. Down by her hip, activating her PSD one more time.

Please let this be it, I think, and I'm swept up by the white void.

When we exit, I'm primed to feel gravity. To take a breath.

But that's not what happens. It's impossible.

Because we emerge in orbit.

Around the moon.

I turn my head toward Earth, but I need to wait for us to spin all the way around before I get a good look. Rotating from here to the surface is doable, especially for Hildy. She can calculate the distance better than anyone else. Should just take a—

Hildy's head rolls downward. Her shoulders go slack under my hands.

Stars twinkle in my vision, and not the real ones.

My toes and hands tingle.

I have seconds.

But I'm not sure how to do this. To activate my PSD and rotate, I need to let go of the others, activate the drive, grab hold of them again, and then guide us through the fourth dimension. If I lose consciousness there, we could end up in another universe altogether, or just dead in the fourth dimension for the rest of time.

But if I let go, they could float free.

Indecision costs me.

My vision narrows.

I don't have time.

I'm sorry, Chuy...

As my consciousness fades, I feel my body relax. It's like sleeping in a warm bed, snuggled up with my friends.

And then it feels like nothing at all.

23

I wake to a raspy, old voice. "I feel like I spent another night with Liam Neeson."

My whole body hurts.

The hell happened?

I open my eyes. I'm...in the *Bitch'n's* bridge, lying on the floor, spooning Wini. I lean up and confirm that Cassidy is in front of her, and Hildy is on the far side. We all made it.

No thanks to me.

Hildy sits up and peels off her mask. She looks exhausted. Her hair is matted down by coagulating purple sludge. It covers one of her ears. All that, plus surviving multiple rotations through the vastness of space and the first thing on her mind is, *"Another* night?"

"The man has a particular set of skills." Wini sits up. Pulls off her mask to reveal a crafty grin. "And it's got nothing to do with punching or shooting, though things *can* get a little rough."

I peel my mask away and pull myself into the captain's chair. "Ugh. Feel like I have a hangover."

"Almost dying has that effect on people," Wini says. "Thank you, by the way."

"Don't thank me," I say. "I passed out. Us being here, alive, that's all Hildy."

Hildy shakes her head. "I was unconscious before you."

"Then who..." The answer comes as a subtle memory. On the fringe of unconsciousness, I felt a presence. And then movement. Didn't register at the time, but now I know what happened. "It was Garfunkel. He must have taken over."

I'm thrilled that he did.

Would be dead, otherwise.

But it reignites my inner debate. Am I Tony Micelli? Or am I Angela Bower? Even worse, maybe I'm Samantha or, oh god, Mona?

Don't think about it, I tell myself. I'm going put my fingers in my ears and 'la, la, la' about this topic until I'm strolling the halls of Valhalla, asleep in the arms of Jesus, or paying Charon's fare.

"Well," Wini says, checking over Cassidy, who is still unconscious. "Thank him for us."

"He can hear you," I say. "How is she?"

"Out like a light." Wini lifts her hand from Cassidy's neck. "Has a pulse and she's breathing, but I don't think she'll be waking up soon. Which is normal for her. Burns hot, sleeps hard." Wini looks around. "This place is kind of dumpy."

"Inside and out," I say, "but she's a powerhouse."

Hildy sits at her station, not to do anything other than catch her breath. "Well, what now?"

"We'll need help," I say. "Get hold of Burnett and—"

"Hello!" Burnett appears beside me waving his hand, his happy faux German accent not doing anything to dull my abject horror at the skinny man's sudden appearance.

"Gah!" I lean away from him. "Shit. Man. Just...wow. How did you know?"

"Know...?"

"That we needed your help," I say.

"Ohh." He lifts a finger. "You see, I was visiting BigApe, who I think has some issues with his current situation, but who can really tell, am I right?" He has a good chuckle, sees we're not joining, and controls himself. "Uh, ha... So, I noticed that Hildy was gone."

"When you went home?" I ask.

"Uhh, no." He looks a little sheepish. "Well, you see, I—"

"He's tracking her," Wini says with a sigh, and then to Burnett, she asks, "First girlfriend?"

"First anything," he says. "Yah."

"You're tracking my location?" Hildy asks.

"Yah."

I think she's going to be pissed, like just about everyone on the planet would be, but I sometimes forget that these two are from another time, another planet, and another culture. Her smile beams. "That's amazing. Wonderful thinking, lover."

"Whoa, whoa, whoa," I say. "First never call him lov—the L word again. Gross. Second, how far did you track her?"

"Well, at first I just knew she was out of range," he says. "Because an alarm sounded. Not an alarm really. Sounds like a kookaburra call. Like haha hoohoo haha hoohoo." He waves his hand. "I'm still practicing. Anywho, the alarm went off, and I knew Hildy was out of range. I went back to the house and saw everyone was gone. No note, no thank you very much. So, I come to the *Bitch'n* and extended the range."

I lean forward. "Do you. Know where. We were?"

"I am a master of future technology," he says.

I raise my eyebrows, demanding a more specific answer.

"Beta-Prime."

Holy shit.

"How could you track us there?" Hildy asks. "Beta-Prime is hundreds of light years away."

He gives her a wink like he's the coolest thing on Earth, like he's James Dean, if James Dean were a former future Nazi. "It's a slew tracker."

"A what-now?"

"I can track your slew drives using the fourth dimension for signal acquisition. Rather than open space, which is big and slow and dumb."

I get to my feet so fast, Burnett stumbles back. I catch him by the shoulders. "Can you track Chuy's current location?"

"I—I already did. I tracked everyone. But—I can't pinpoint her location."

"Why the hell not?" I ask, worry making me sound angry.

"She is in unexplored space," he says. "To pinpoint their location, I would need to have a celestial map of the system they're in. A map of the galaxy they're in would be useful as well."

Unfortunately, part of our bargain with the Europhids was to never leave our solar system again, and part of that deal was the destruction of the celestial maps in our system. The only copies that remain are in

Hildy's head. I turn to her. "Have a look at his tracking data. See if you can make sense of it with the information in your noodle."

"Are we having pasta?" Burnett asks.

"It's an expression," I say.

"Is Chuy alone?" Wini asks.

"There are two others with her," Burnett says. "I assumed it was Cowboy and Dark Horse, but perhaps it was this mystery person you're alluding to?"

"His name is Dan," Wini says, and she turns to Hildy. "Please. Try to find them."

Hildy nods and her weighted down hair flops in front of her face.

"Ahh," Burnett says. "Dan. Yes... Who is Dan?"

"I'll explain everything after you give me the data..." Hildy says, heading for the door. "...while I shower."

Burnett's eyes widen while a lopsided smile stretches onto his face. "*Data* and a nude shower? This day is getting better and better—" He holds his open palms out to me and Wini. "Aside from missing friends, of course."

Burnett follows Hildy out of the bridge with a hop, skip, and a jump in his step.

"He's excitable," Wini says. "Oh, is he the pillow guy?"

"That's Burnett."

"Makes sense then. Good for him. Hildy is something else."

"A real catch," I say.

Wini places her hand on my arm. "We'll get them back, you know. The future you saved won't be nearly as nice without them. For now..." She motions down to Cassidy. "You have beds on this space turd?"

Message received. Wini packs a punch when she needs to, but she still qualifies for the senior discount, and she needs me to haul the passed-out, puberty-stricken team-member to a bed. I bend down and scoop her up. "Follow me."

We exit the bridge together. Feels weird, leaving the bridge during a time of crisis, but until we know where we're going, the best thing we can do is prepare. And right now, that means recovering from what we just survived. Then we take the next step, which will mean returning to

Antarctica, or rotating to an unknown planet full of hostile aliens allied with red, genocidal Europhids.

"Please tell me you have showers" she says. "This armor might be non-stick, but the stink of the dead..." She waves her hand in front of her nose. "I smell like a week-old used tampon, and my oven hasn't been in cleaning mode for fifteen glorious years."

"Showers, beds, even a foot massager. None of it is pretty." I stop by the door to my quarters, and it opens. "But the view is pretty nice." Through the large portal window beside my bed is the moon, and just over its horizon—Earth.

I place Cassidy on the bed, and Wini approaches the window.

"You're a real spaceman, aren't you?"

"I prefer to be planetside," I say, "but I do feel at home in space. The trick is to spot the pinpoints of beauty scattered throughout the void of death."

"Like finding a good man on Tinder," she says.

"I'll have to take your word for it." I head for the door and point to the bathroom. "Shower's in there."

She's shamelessly peeling off her armor when I exit, letting the door close behind me. Then I lean my back against the wall. I take a moment to collect myself. Emotions are high, and in a situation like this, they can lead to mistakes, and mistakes cost lives. I don't want to take a beat. Don't want to waste a second. But I'm not going to be any help to anyone if I don't get my head on straight.

I head for Chuy's quarters, take two showers—once for the armor, once for me, and then I dig her old rosary out of a drawer. I don't give God much thought, and if BigApe weren't...what he is now...he'd tease me for it. But if the big guy is out there, and He has the same soft spot for Chuy that I do, He might show a little mercy and give us a lead.

Or maybe, as usual, He'll just keep quiet and—

The blaring 'hoohoo haa haa hoohoo haa haa' of a Kookaburra echoes through the ship. Burnett's tracker alarm.

I give the rosary a kiss, slip it beneath the adaptive armor, and seal it up.

"I'm coming, baby," I say, and I head for the door.

24

"What have we got?" I ask, as I enter the bridge and find myself talking to no one. I'm used to walking into this space and finding at least one crew member on the job, but with half the crew missing...

"Behind you," Burnett says, eyes on a tablet in his hands. He taps the screen a few times, at first doing his job, and then wiping away the drops of water falling from his hair.

"Why were *you* in the shower?" I ask, a little aghast that he'd split his attention between figuring out where our people are—and hanky panky. But honestly, that would only be surprising because it was Burnett. The intensity of a mission, before and after, can be quite the aphrodisiac. Something about facing death makes people want to procreate—or at least do the deed while cock-blocking the seed.

I smile inwardly. *Good one.* Going to have to remember that.

"I smelled like fish," he says.

"You fed him again?" I ask.

"He really likes it now." Burnett swipes his finger over the tablet, extending it out toward the viewscreen, transferring data.

"I...didn't know we could do that."

Burnett grins. "While you were taking down the Union, I was making improvements."

Wini strides into the bridge wearing my Queen T-shirt and not much else, drying her hair with a towel. "What have we got?"

Unlike my identical question to an empty bridge, Wini gets a response. "Well, ma'am, I've detected a slew drive signature, but I fear there might be an error."

I sit in the captain's chair.

"Not the news we want to hear, Burn."

"Tracking PSDs through the fourth dimension is a new science," he says. "You probably can't even call it science."

"But it worked before," I say. "You found Hildy."

He nods.

"Any reason to think it wouldn't work now?"

"Well, no."

"Then what did you find?"

He taps the tablet and the viewscreen switches to an aerial view of Vostok Base Two, its circular form easy to make out on the bleak, white landscape.

"This is where we started," I say.

"It is?" He looks surprised. Didn't know. "Then maybe someone came back."

"Some...one?" I say.

"Or all of them." He tries to sound confident, but he fails. "If they all used the same slew drive. I'm only detecting one of them."

"Is this live?" I ask, motioning to the video.

He nods. "Hijacked from a Russian satellite."

"Why are the Russians watching their own base?" I wonder aloud.

"Not sure, but they probably know we were there," Wini says. "Might even think we killed all those people."

"Killed all what people?" Burnett asks.

"Hildy didn't tell you?" I ask.

"I was focused on detecting the slew drives," he says, and then adds, "and other things."

"Zip-it, Romeo," I say, pinching my fingers in front of his mouth. "The base looks like a blender with a Gremlin in it. If Russia blames us, we need to make sure they never find out who 'us' is. Zoom in."

The video feed descends on the base.

"See anything different?" I ask Wini.

She slowly shakes her head. The base's exterior looks the same as when we arrived.

Hildy arrives, hair back to its natural blonde pom-pom state, dressed in adaptive armor, ready for action. "Whoever is down there arrived using a slew drive. Has to be our people."

"I want to agree with you," I say. "More than anything. But they were taken to an unknown destination. Even you would have a hard time rotating home."

"We barely made it when she knew the way," Wini says.

"Maybe they're not alone," Hildy says, desperation creeping into her voice. She's putting on a tough façade, but she's not very good at it. Cowboy is her friend and Chuy has become something of a mother figure to her, just as I've become a father figure. She never had parents. She was raised by the Union to perform tasks for as long as she was useful. The idea of losing Chuy must be a new kind of hurt for her.

For me, too. "Maybe."

"Are your pals still down there?" I ask Wini.

She's confused for a moment, and then her eyes light up. "I nearly forgot them!" She nods. "They won't have gone anywhere."

"Who?" Burnett asks.

"Hans and Franz," I say. "We really need to get you up to speed. Later. Here's the plan. We rotate down to Hans and Franz, get a close up look at the base. Make sure there's nothing wonky. I don't want to walk into another trap. Then we slip inside."

Wini gives me a wry smile. "Go on..."

"Ugh." I turn to Burnett. "Can you pinpoint the slew drive's location?"

He nods. "It will take some time, but I should be able to narrow it down to a few meters."

"Get it done," I say. He nods and starts working. Back to Wini, I ask, "What about—"

"Whew!" Cassidy says from the doorway, still dressed in adaptive armor. She's holding a bottle of Mountain Dew—one of many sodas Burnett keeps in the galley. "Found the caffeine!" She does a high kick while saying "High kick!" Immediately follows it with a low squat, shouting, "Squat!" She bounds up and repeats the action, "Squat, squat, squat!"

I turn to Wini. "Can you...?"

Wini reaches her hand out to Cassidy and manages to stop the perpetual motion machine. She snaps her fingers twice and then opens her hand.

"Aww, c'mon," Cassidy says. "Do I have to?"

"Already had too much," Wini says. "You know it's dangerous."

First time I've heard a caffeine rush referred to as dangerous. Wini sees my confusion and explains. "Too much stimulation in this one, and it will carry over to the rest of us. Another swig or two and we'll all be doing squats and high kicks. Flexible though I may be, I'm not wearing undergarments, and I don't see any dollar bills in your hand."

Cassidy takes a quick sip and hands the bottle over.

"Everyone...get dressed, or whatever else you need to do. We're leaving in five."

Wini places her hand on my arm. "Okay with you if we pick up a friend on the way?"

"A helpful friend, or another..." I glance toward Cassidy, who is now running in place, breathing in and out through fish lips.

I shouldn't rag on the kid too much. She's proven herself capable, despite her size and unpredictability. Not sure I would have made it through the Europhid cave without her. She's got a lot of potential. Just needs to be reined in like a wild, very energetic horse.

"Someone more like you," she says. "Good with guns. Experience with things that are—"

"—not of this Earth?" I ask.

"Not of this *time*. Or whatever time you came from in the future. Other direction."

"The past?" Never met another time traveler before...aside from my crew. "How far back?"

She smiles. "All the way."

"Well, all right then. I think we can use all the help we can get."

Five minutes later, Hildy, Cassidy, and Wini are ready to go. Our arsenal this time around consists of four homemade railguns created by Burnett. Magnets propel sharpened tungsten discs at Mach 7, unleashing 8000 rounds a minute—without recoil. On full auto, a sixty round magazine empties like a split-second hedgehog fart. Silent but deadly.

Very deadly.

Based on tech designed to take out enemy starships. In open space, the rounds would travel at full speed forever, until striking something. On Earth, even with all the friction in the atmosphere, the rail discs can travel miles. When they strike a target, they don't mushroom or break apart. Tungsten is too tough for that. But they do change trajectory—inside the target, carving a path of destruction before exiting at some random point.

"Moment you have spatial coordinates," I say to Burnett, the only one of us not returning to Earth, "you let us know."

He nods.

I turn to Wini. "Where to?"

"Back to the Mesa," she says. "I already let him know we're coming."

I take hold of Wini, while Hildy partners up with Cassidy. We rotate in the white void and emerge a moment later, standing atop Delgado's secret base, hidden beneath the towering Southwestern mesa.

A man with a high and tight haircut stands with his back to us. He's dressed in adaptive armor, holding a rifle that has clearly been modified in some way, though I can't figure out how.

"Behind you, hun," Wini says.

Unruffled by our sudden appearance, the man turns around, both serious and smiling. "Hey there," he says with an accent that smacks of Appalachia. He offers his hand and I shake it. "Pleased to meet you, Dark Horse. Name's Owen McCoy. But seeing as how you all like code names, you can call me Blackbird."

25

"Are we supposed to have codenames?" Hildy asks. "Because I'm still just Hildy."

"You don't need a codename when you technically won't be born for a thousand years...or, I guess—ever—now."

Her eyes widen. "*Back to the Future* got it wrong! I still exist, even though I won't ever be born." She frowns. "But that's kind of sad, too."

"You were born," I say. "You *do* exist."

She nods, but I can tell she's a little shaken by the concept that she's somehow not considered before this very moment.

"Can I be Mangle? Or, oooh, Foxy?" Cassidy drops into a squat and bounces back up. "No! Wait! Springtrap!"

"Take a breath, runt," McCoy says, smiling at Cassidy. "You're liable to blow a gasket." To Wini he says, "You let her have caffeine."

"She snuck it," Wini says.

"Marine?" I ask McCoy. "Hair is kind of a dead giveaway."

"Former," he says. "Not for a while. You?"

"Marine Rapid Reaction Force," I say, and I'm secretly pleased when his eyebrows raise.

Glad that still means something.

"Also a pirate," Cassidy says. "And a rebel. And a general." Kid knows a lot about me.

McCoy nods at all this. "Gotta do what needs doing, right?"

"Are you allowed to use Blackbird?" Hildy asks. "He's Dark Horse, and it makes sense because—" She waggles her hand at my face, indicating my dark skin tone. "But you're not even tan. Shouldn't you be, I don't know, Whitebird?"

McCoy turns to me, a baffled expression on his face.

"She's from a future where people like me didn't exist. She's still get-ting used to the nuances of color and race." I address Hildy. "'Dark Horse' has nothing to do with the color of my skin. It's a happy coincidence."

"And where I'm from," McCoy says, "two blackbirds are an omen of good fortune."

Hildy twists her lips. "But there's only one of you."

McCoy grins. "Not when I look in the mirror." He points his finger and spins it around, indicating the group. "You all are a distractable bunch, aren't ya?"

I clear my throat. "Happens from time to time."

"Conversation is the spice of life." Cassidy performs a cheerleader style high-kick. "That's what Dan says."

"Speaking of," McCoy says. "Any contact?"

Wini shakes her head. "He's still missing."

"And you all have no idea where he is?"

"Generally what 'missing' means," I say. "But he is somewhere in this universe. Probably."

McCoy runs a hand over his head. He takes the overwhelming news better than most people would. Probably because he's not new to mind-blowing situations.

"What's the weirdest thing you've ever seen?" I ask him.

"This have any relevance? Or are we just dilly dallying?"

"Want to know if you're going to lose your shit, literally, when we—"

"Dinosaurs," he says, extending a finger. "Lot of 'em." He extends an-other finger. "A Nephilim."

"Half demon, half human," Wini says. "Nasty things."

He puts up a third finger. "Cryptoterrestrial. Like a dinosaur, but smarter than you or me, and telepathic. Also, the beginning of time, and worst of all, this kid." He tilts his head toward Cassidy.

"Aww." She purses her lips, twists her eyebrows up in the middle, and bends a knee. "Really? Thanks, Blackbird."

He tilts his head. "Now, can we get down to business?"

I reach an arm out to him while wrapping my other around Wini. "Bring it in."

"You're joking, right?"

"Getting cozy with a man ain't gonna flip your switch," Wini says. "Quit slowing us down."

"*Me?*" McCoy squelches his argument and reservations, stepping up beside me. "How's this work?"

"I push a button, rotate us into another dimension of reality, and then we slip back out, inside Wini's UFO." Before he can respond, I do all of those things, spinning out of the fourth dimension and onto the UFO's circular bridge, where Hans and Franz are unfazed by our sudden appearance.

"Tarnation," McCoy says.

A white rectangle appears beside him.

Hildy and Cassidy rotate out of it. They look comfortable together. Peas in a pod. Probably ten years apart, but they share a rare enthusiasm for life, despite their dark pasts.

McCoy looks himself over. Pats himself down.

"Everything's still there," I tell him, and then to Wini, I say, "Let's have a look."

"Boys," Wini says, and an image of Vostok Base Two is displayed. Everything looks the same. Blood outside the door. No motion.

"Feels like we're walking into the same trap," Wini says.

She's not wrong.

"If it's a trap," I say, "it's a good one, because there's no way I'm not going down there." Slew drive or hell gate. They're our only leads. I turn to the group, "Anyone who wants to sit this one out, no judgement." I turn to Wini. "That includes you."

"Might be old," she says, "but my dander is up. I'll rest when I'm dead."

"Straight back to the gate," I say to Hildy.

She shakes her head. "If it's functioning, and it blocks our slew drives, there's no way to know what will happen or where we'll end up."

"Front door it is." I move to trigger my slew drive when—

"Wait!" Cassidy springs toward the door. "I need to pee. Don't go without me!"

She bounds away, leaving us to wait in awkward silence.

I take the moment to look inward and have a chat.

Hey Garfunkel, you busy probing my memories for nudes?

He can hear my thoughts as clearly as everyone can hear my voice. When I speak to him aloud, it's really just for me. We can talk inside my thoughts.

You feeling any Europhid weirdness down there?

Silence.

I've barely felt his presence since we left Beta-Prime. Didn't think it was possible for a Europhid—especially a blue one—to get depressed. Suppose genocide can have that effect on ancient aliens. Even worse, he's been betrayed by his own kind, something that's not supposed to be possible. The Europhids are united. A single hive mind.

A portion of them going rogue must feel like dementia or something—betrayed by your own body and mind.

Okay, I get it. Just…let me know if you feel something off.

Nothing.

"I'm back!" Cassidy says, bounding back into the room, and into Hildy's arms. "Let's do this!"

Masks on, we rotate down to the base's still-unlocked door. McCoy double-takes the frozen blood, but he's on task a moment later. Leans against the wall beside the door, waiting for me to open it, taking point in a hostile situation without a second thought.

I like him, even if he probably is a stick in the mud.

Door open, McCoy slips inside, sweeps his weapon back and forth. "Clear."

We move in behind him, quickly clearing the hallway and the adjacent rooms. Thanks to the adaptive armor's night vision, we never miss a beat.

"Dark Horse," Burnett says in my comms. "Come in, Dark Horse."

"I hear you, Burn."

"I've narrowed down the location of the slew drive. Based on your description of the facility, I believe the slew drive is currently located beneath the ice at the center of the structure."

"Where the gate was," I say.

"Indeed."

"Copy that." I double time it through the base, side-stepping the dead and sliding over sheets of frozen blood.

"You all made a hell of a mess," McCoy says, and then he grunts. "Purple blood."

"Nastiest sons-a-bitches in the universe have purple blood," I say.

"Don't need to tell me," he says. "I've seen a Nephilim bleed."

"Huh…" I enter the garage and head for the door leading down into the sub-ice chamber. "We leave that open?" I ask Wini.

"Wasn't really paying attention to the state of doors last time through," she says.

I pause beside the door. "What color does a cryptoterrestrial bleed?"

"Same color as everything natural on this planet," McCoy says.

"Well, that's something I guess."

"Any other talking points we should cover before getting in the shit?" he asks.

I smile. "Not a one." I swivel into the stairwell and head down, following the barrel of my railgun. I do miss the M16 Delgado fashioned for me, but the railgun is a future weapon that's hard to beat.

The chamber opens up, and I'm surprised by two things. One, the gate is still here, but deactivated. And two, someone is singing.

In Russian.

I slip my finger around my trigger and look down the sight.

The singing stops, and it's followed by a gruff voice with a thick Russian accent, "What took so long, Moses?"

26

I lower my rifle and then push the barrel of McCoy's toward the floor. "Drago?"

"Da and nyet."

Drago is standing behind one of the gate's black pillars, staying out of sight. Might mean he's untrustworthy—which seems like a stretch. He was my right-hand man for five years. Helped take down the Union. I trusted him with my life, and he's only been gone for a few months.

But now...he's here.

"Drago, is it really you?" Hildy tries to hurry past me.

"Hildy?" He sounds confused. "You bring the little one on missions now?"

"She's earned her spot," I say, but I also agree with him. Hildy really shouldn't be here. Neither should Cassidy or Wini. But we play the hand we're dealt. And they really are proving themselves capable, and me to be both ageist and sexist. I'd be dead right now if not for my trio of curly haired blonde avengers—two natural, one dyed.

"This is a dangerous place," Drago says.

"I'm aware."

"You were here before," he says. Not a question.

"We all were," I say. "The people stationed here were already—"

"Dead. Eaten. Torn apart." His shadow shifts behind the pillar. I think he's rubbing his hands over it.

"All of the above. Yeah."

"And then..."

"We were attacked. By rygars of all things, controlled by red Europhids."

"I saw," he says. "The dead. Please. Continue."

The Q&A isn't really Drago's style. Crushing my spine in a bear hug is. He's loud and boisterous. Larger than life. Right now, this feels more like I've encountered Russia's version of Columbo.

"We went through the gate," I say.

The *shhh* of his hand sliding over the pillar stops.

That got his attention.

"And found..."

"Beta-Prime." I wait for a reaction and get nothing, so I press on. "The reds are staging some kind of revolt. All of the blue Europhids—I think on the entire planet—are dead. There's no way to know how far the revolt extends. If it's universal, or localized. But we encountered another form of intelligent life that had bonded with the reds. They took Chuy, Cowboy, and Delgado."

"Who is Delgado?"

"The man who works with Wini."

"Old lady, Wini?"

"I'm right here," Wini grumbles.

"Is too bad," he says. "I like Wini."

"Was that a threat?" McCoy asks under his breath. "Because I feel threatened."

I was thinking the same thing, but we're inside a Russian base where the occupants have been slaughtered by creatures associated—in this time—exclusively with me. If he's accepted a spec ops role within the Russian government, he's probably just doing his job.

"Why are you here, Moses?" he asks.

Why is he calling me *Moses?* It's not unheard of at home, but on mission? Feels a little antagonistic.

I decide honesty is the best policy. Drago's loyalties might be divided, but he's still a friend. "At first, looking for a...creature. Something we thought might have been brought here. Something that could have killed all these people."

"But you didn't find it?" he asks.

"No... It wasn't here."

Or was it? The silence that follows my statement makes me feel like Drago knows something about the cryptoterrestrial.

But right now, it's near the bottom of a long list of concerns.

"Found bodies," he says. "Found monsters. Killed monsters. Went through gate... How did you go through gate?"

"It was active when we arrived," I say. "And deactivated while we were still on Beta-Prime."

"And yet," he says, "you have returned."

"Same way you got here," I say. "PSD."

"Slew drive...from Beta-Prime...to Earth...without celestial maps?"

"Don't need a celestial map when you have—" Wini's hand clamps over my mouth. I look down to find her shaking her masked head at me. Talking to anyone else, I'd be tight-lipped. But I'm shitting out information like I just ate Taco Bell...which somehow hasn't changed in quality or flavor since the '80s.

Taco Bell gives you the taco smell...

"Hnhg," he grunts, aware that a key piece of information has just been kept from him. He can probably deduce it just as easily. The rest of us don't have the mental capability of memorizing a universe, and only one person on the team ever had that job.

"Do you know how gate activates?" he asks.

"If I did, we wouldn't be standing here talking."

"Where would you be?"

"Getting Chuy back," I say.

"You know where she is?"

This line of questioning is starting to feel, at worst—hostile, and at best—really fucking insensitive. He knows what Chuy means to me. Hell, she used to mean something to him as well.

"I'm not answering any more questions until you stop dicking me around," I say.

He huffs a laugh. "Activating gate is easy. Keeping gate is harder, but Russians figured it out. Directing gate to location...well, is similar to slew drive. You need to know where you're going. Then you just tap ruby slippers and wish for it."

"No place like home," Cassidy says.

"Is little girl?" Drago says, sounding genuinely disappointed in me now.

"She's a lot more than that," I say, and I give Cassidy a nod.

She responds with a tough man's nod of her own.

"How do you activate the gate?" Without a destination, it doesn't really matter at this point, but future me will likely find the information handy.

"DNA," he says. "Not yours."

"Whose?" I ask. "Yours?"

"A celestial being," he says, like he's sitting out amidst the stars, telling a campfire story.

"Aliens."

"Da and nyet. Some live elsewhere. Some live here. Or...used to. Most are dead now."

"You're losing me," I say.

"Gods."

"Gods..." He's got to be kidding.

"Da, gods. You know, Zeus, Poseidon, Odin, Isis. Gods. But like I said, most are dead, or in hiding. Demi-gods work, too. Hercules. Hel—"

"I know what demi-gods are," I say, "I just...don't believe they're real."

"Well, not gods," he says. "But they are real. Say hello god-hand."

A hand pokes out from behind the pillar where Drago is hidden. It's human, and feminine, and it has skin two shades darker than mine. "Hello puny humans."

"That's...a god's hand?" I ask, not remotely believing it.

"This guy is out of his head," McCoy whispers, and I'm inclined to believe him. Drago is my friend. Always will be. But something has happened to him.

"The hand of Zeus," he says, "a being descended from visitors from another world."

"Umm," I say. "Pretty sure Zeus was a dude."

"Actually," Cassidy says. "Zeus could turn into whatever he wanted. Like a swan. To bone chicks. Seriously? Who would want to—"

Wini silences her with a sharp wave of her hand. "Can we stop the chit-chat now and do what needs doing?"

Drago leans out from behind the pillar for the first time. His face is hard to see behind the thick beard, but he's clearly not wearing night vision, yet he seems to be having no trouble spotting us. "We have been to other worlds. What about story sounds unbelievable? Perhaps rygars, Europhids, or future fascist empire? No? Perhaps man with nanotechnology in his blood? Or advanced civilization on Earth pre-dating both humans and arrival of gods?"

He's describing both Delgado and the cryptoterrestrial, which we did not tell him about. Russia has either been very busy, or he's getting his information from someone else.

Garfunkel...

My inner voice stays silent.

Think we need you, man.

Drago steps out from behind the pillar. For a moment, I think he's dressed in a bear skin, but then I notice his pecker poking out of the fur, and I realize he's stark ass naked, despite the sub-zero temperature.

"Ewww!" Cassidy says, shielding her face. "My eyes! I think I'm gonna puke all over everyone!"

Drago has no shame. "Moses of Earth, Sower of Chaos. Your journey ends here. Today. Your presence outside this planet is unwelcome. The Order will be restored."

I've got a hundred question list, ready to fly, but only one comes out. "The Order?"

Drago's eyes flare red. He's infected by red Europhids, the same way I am by the blue. "Forget about your friends. Forget about the cryptoterrestrial. Venture beyond this planet again and its place in the Order will be forfeit. Do you understand?"

"Not remotely," I say.

"An imbalance is tearing the universe apart. It must be repaired. You will not interfere."

"The hell I won't," I say.

Drago smiles, and it's earnest. "I expected not. Until then..." He places the hand on the gate. A red sheet of energy crackles to life. Before I can say anything or try to stop him, he leaps backward through the gate.

"Burnett!" I shout into my comm. "Track the slew drive that led us here!"

"I am," he says. "It is—wow! Really moving fast. Annnd..."

The gate goes dark.

"Lost it," Burnett says.

I'm about to lose my shit when the gate flickers back to life. I don't know if it's a trap, an accident, or if someone is helping us—maybe even some part of Drago that's still in control, but it's the only lead we've got. I'm going to follow it across the universe if I have to.

27

"Everyone on my six!" I shout, hustling toward the red wall.

"We don't know where it leads," Hildy says, following me despite her doubt.

"Could be a black hole," Wini says.

"Could be the bottom of the Mariana Trench," McCoy adds.

"Could be Chuck E. Cheese!" Cassidy shouts, bounding toward the gate beside me, kicking a leg and flapping her arms. "Have you been to a Chuck E. Cheese? The animatronic animals freak me out, but I like the—"

The kid's eyes go wide.

She gasps and turns toward the gate.

I see nothing but a wall of red. But Cassidy's empathic mind is picking up on something unseen.

"What is it?" I ask.

She looks me in the eyes, face screwed up in pain. Then she turns to Wini. "It's coming."

I take her by the shoulders. "What's coming?"

"Oof," she says, before she falls unconscious in my arms.

I ease her down to the frozen floor. "Wini, what is she talking abo—"

Wini's still body slaps against the ice beside me. She's unconscious.

I turn to the sound to see more bodies hitting the floor. Hildy and McCoy are down for the count, too.

Pressure fills my head. Waves of nausea-inducing energy flow out from the gate. Emotions roil through me like I've suddenly been struck by every mental illness in the book. I drop to my knees, fighting it.

Whatever is coming has managed to incapacitate all five of us before it's even come through the gate. I'm not unconscious, probably thanks to Garfunkel, but I won't be able to put up a fight, either.

"Sleep," a voice says in my head, and it's not my inner monologue, or my symbiotic alien pal. This voice is external. Coming from the gate. And I sense the voice's source approaching like a freight train on a collision course.

But there's subtle nuance hidden within the command.

Anger.

Fear.

Betrayal.

Whatever is coming, it's desperate.

Which makes it even more dangerous.

"SLEEP!"

"No!' I shout. "Get the fuck out of my—"

"—head!" My shout finishes in the voice of my younger self.

Back in Max's childhood backyard, but it's different now. The green grass is brown and dry. The swing set is rotted, the beams pulling apart to reveal rusted bolts. The fence surrounding the yard has lost its color, bleached by the blazing California sun. The trees are leafless and brittle.

This world is a recreation fueled by Garfunkel. Seeing it in this state reveals a lot about how he's feeling, in light of recent discoveries. Barren. Lifeless. Despairing. But he's brought me here anyway.

Question is, why?

To protect me from what was coming?

I need to be in the real world for that. If I'm here, it means that I'm just as helpless as the others out in the real world. It means—

"What is this?" The voice speaking in my mind is behind me.

He's framed by Max's house, now dilapidated. And it's not at all what I was expecting.

"Ricky Mazzola?"

He doesn't respond to me. Doesn't even seem to hear me. He's looking at his hands like he's never seen them before.

Ricky Mazzola's claim to fame was getting hit by a diaper truck—right before my eyes—and living to tell the tale. He wasn't the straightest spoke on the wheel. Rode his bike right out of a sloped driveway and into the street. No looking both ways. No slowing down. The driver didn't stand a chance. Despite being leveled, Ricky was far more concerned about what his mother would do than the fact that he'd just been hit by a truck. He jumped up off the pavement shouting, "I'm okay! Don't tell my mother!"

It was the last time we saw him.

Which was fine by us. Ricky could be...unpredictable. One minute he was showing you the *Playboy* collection he had stashed in the fireplace of a house that had burned down, the next he was swinging a whiffle ball bat at your face. Not quite a bully, but never really an ally. Never really safe—to others or to himself.

And now he's in my subconscious.

"Umm, hello?"

Ricky's eyes snap toward me, full of confused menace—probably a very similar expression to his mother's, when she discovered he was hit by a diaper delivery truck.

"Who are you?" he asks, voice far deeper than that of thirteen-year-old Ricky's.

"Moses," I say, and for some reason I add, "Not the one from the Bible."

He's got no idea what I'm talking about.

"Who are you?" I ask.

He scans the wasteland that was once my neighborhood. "Another trick. You will learn nothing from me!"

Before I can say, 'Huh?' he charges.

But there's twenty feet between us and he's running all funny, leaned forward like there should be someone clutching the back of his blue and green striped Izod polo shirt. He makes it ten steps and then faceplants in the dead grass, kicking up a cloud of dust.

Which is kind of classic Ricky Mazzola.

"Very nice," I say, clapping. "I'm impressed."

Rage flows off Ricky as he climbs to his feet, looking bigger than he did a second ago. He sneers at me, oblivious to the blood dripping down the side of his face. He twists his body back and forth, like he's getting the hang of it for the first time.

He's not human, I realize.

It's a bit weird, being in my childhood body. The scale of everything is off. My reach is shorter. My gait is different. But I got the hang of it quickly. Whatever has taken the form of Ricky has never been human before.

But it's adjusting.

"Who are you?" I ask.

"No more questions!" he shouts, and he charges again, this time managing to stay upright.

I sidestep and allow his momentum, and his lack of practice in a human body, to carry him into the swing set's cross beam. He's clotheslined by the plank, flipped over onto his stomach, and then whacked in the back of the head when the now-broken wood falls atop him.

"Gah!" he roars and climbs back to his feet.

When Ricky's face snaps toward me again, it's undulating, as though worms are wriggling just beneath the surface. He swings an angry punch —shattering one of the swing set's four support beams.

I take a step back. "Uhh..."

None of this is real. I know that. But it feels real.

"Garfunkel?" I search the yard. "Max? You here, bud?"

He must be. I didn't get here on my own. And I certainly didn't hijack the newcomer's consciousness and stick it in Ricky Mazzola.

I hold out my open palms, which on Earth is a gesture of submission. No way to know if it translates wherever Ricky is from. For all I know, his species defecates from hand-sphincters, and I could be making an offensive gesture that translates to, 'I shit on your face,' or something. Hell, since we're in my head I don't even know if it *has* a face.

"Rwar!" Ricky shouts, lunging at me and unleashing a backhand swing.

I lean away from it, but not enough.

His fingers brush against my chest, tearing open my very first Queen T-shirt. I look down at the shredding threads. This isn't real, but once upon a time, this was my favorite shirt. I wore it until time and a growing body made it look like it belonged to Bruce Banner. "Hey!"

He swings again, and I decide to show him what it's like fighting someone who's been a human being his whole life, and a badass butt-kicking machine from the '80s.

I duck low and sweep his legs like I'm freakin' Johnny Lawrence, kicking him off his feet and sending him to the ground with a goodbye kick to the face.

There's one big difference between the pivotal scene of *The Karate Kid* and now. When Ricky hits the dirt, he doesn't thrash and wail like a drama queen. He catches himself on his hands, pushes off the ground, and springs back to his feet. Then he closes the distance between us and kicks me in the gut.

I collapse to the ground, fetal position, gasping for air. If this were real, I'd probably have internal bleeding.

But we're in my head...

We're in my head, and this asshole is getting stronger.

Taking over my mind...

The stakes of this battle settle in as my insides cramp. "Max... Garfunkel... C'mon. I know you're hurting. I felt it, same as you. And I understand it. You know I do. We've both been the only survivors of our kind. But you can't give up. I need you to fight."

Ricky stands above me, hands clenched. "To whom do you spea—"

A cymbal crash is followed by a chugging guitar riff. The music fills my mind like it's pouring from a hundred different speakers. And to me, a young man from the '80s, it is instantly recognizable.

A scream redirects Ricky's attention from me to Max—shirtless and unashamed of his round belly. He's got colorful strings tied around his biceps and his wrists. A bird of prey is painted on his face in neon green, pink, and orange. On the surface, he looks silly, his thick tongue extended in concentration, but he imbues the very essence of his childhood hero: the Ultimate Warrior, charging up to the swing set, grabbing hold of the chains, and thrashing them up and down to the raging music.

"Yes!" I shout, and I point at Ricky. "You're in trouble now!"

In a feat of strength and agility not possible in reality, Max leaps up onto the top of the swing set. He runs along the beam, lets out a battle cry, and launches himself off, arms extended, and fists locked to perform a top rope double axe handle.

28

Twin fists collide with Ricky's head, sprawling him back.

Max lands and rolls to his feet. Then he screams toward the sky, pumping his fists, and charges.

The moment is surreal.

Everything about this is authentic Max, if you ignore the speed, strength, and agility. He didn't excel in any of those categories. But he did throw himself into acting out wrestling—usually at the expense of his parents' furniture. Watching him in that role again breaks my heart. He's been gone for a while, but all this is still kicking around in my head, available for Garfunkel to borrow.

But why? What's the point in Garfunkel taking on Max's form? At first, it was to help me acclimate to the idea of speaking to Europhids in my mind. I get that. Max is safe. His backyard was a childhood oasis. But why now? I'm accustomed to Garfunkel's presence. Why not appear as a xenomorph queen or a Predator or something with a little more, I don't know, *oomph*, than a kid with Down Syndrome?

Max leaps toward Ricky, who's back on his feet now. He's going for a clothesline to the neck on a much taller adversary. But he's also making it look easy—until Ricky drives his fist into Max's round gut, dropping him to the ground.

Rage wells up from the deep, dark recesses. Embracing the Warrior, I shout and charge. I'm fueled by anger, training, and muscle memory.

I feint like I'm going to follow through on Max's plan. And when Ricky goes to punch my gut, I'm ready for it. I juke to the side, channeling Walter Payton's sweetness, charge in tight, and get my hand up under Ricky's throat. With a gasp of surprise, Ricky comes off the ground. I leap up and smash him back down under me.

Beneath us, the lawn buckles.

I'm not this strong as an adult. Not even close as a kid.

Because none of this is real. Because we're in *my* head.

As Ricky squirms in my grasp, I smile down at him and growl one of the Warrior's iconic and nonsensical lines, "Come on in, where nightmares are the best part of my day!"

"Yes!" Max shouts. "Now you must deal with the creation of all the unpleasantries in the entire universe, as I feel the injection from the gods above!"

Beneath me, Ricky looks confused. "What?"

Max charges, reaching his hand out to me. "Tag!"

I stand and lift Ricky up by the neck while slapping Max's hand with mine. He tackles Ricky by the waist and drives him into the ground, quickly rolling away and getting back to his feet.

We circle the unwelcome consciousness, ready to pounce.

Ricky sits up. Wipes blood from his lip. Looks at it, and then at us. "Why do you appear as youths?"

"Why do you talk funny?" I ask. "Who says 'youths?'"

"Rake my insides with your claws," Max says. "Chew them betwixt your molars! It matters not. I will grind the bones of my enemies to dust and infuse the crystal power of the Warrior with—"

Max stops. Looks me in the eyes. "Apologies. I was lost in your memories. They are poignant."

"This is..." Ricky looks around. "...the past."

"Long time ago," I say. "Now who the hell are you and why are you in my head?"

Ricky climbs to his feet, fists clenched. But he holds his ground.

"I did not intend to occupy your mind," he says.

"You were putting my people to sleep," I point out.

"People, in my experience, are violent, tribal, and untrustworthy."

"So, you're an alien then?"

Ricky's face screws up. "Alien?"

"Not from this planet," I say. "Not from Earth."

"So human," he says. "Believing the evolution of your species gives you ownership of all you survey. You have no more claim to the planet on which you were birthed than all the species that came before you. Earth is a speck in a much larger creation, claimed by those more powerful than you can comprehend."

"Sounds like someone has a grudge against humanity," I say. "And by 'those more powerful than you can comprehend,' are you talking about the blue and red rave sticks that populate the universe and form a hive mind through time and space?"

Ricky squints at me. "Who are you?"

"We're in *my* head," I say. "I'll ask the questions, or..." I turn to Max. "Is he here because he wants to be, or did you reel him in like a fish?"

Max puts his fists on his hips, chest puffed up. "He cannot leave until I allow it."

"Great." I turn back to Ricky. "As I was saying, you want out of my head, you answer my questions. If you're not a threat, we can do this in the real world. Until then, consider yourself a prisoner in Cabesa del Moses. Comprende?"

Ricky says nothing, but the consciousness controlling his form seems intelligent enough to understand, even if it can't speak Spanish.

"What is your name?"

"I do not have a name. I have a...a distinct mental signature."

"I believe his kind is telepathic in nature," Max says. "Individuals are known without the need for outward identifiers."

Ricky double-takes Max.

Then he looks me over.

"You are...distinct from each other. Two consciousnesses in one mind..."

"I know, right? Totally hard to comprehend, though. We can try to dumb down the concept for you, if—"

"You mock me."

"Sarcasm is the spice of life."

He turns back to Max. "I will address the more intelligent of you."

"Still my head," I say, walking around Ricky to stand beside Max. "And we're kind of a package deal, now." I extend my palm and Max slaps me five. "Now, who are you?"

"My kind do not use—"

"Gary Busey's pubic hair!" I sigh, rubbing my temples. "This is infuriating. I understand that you're not accustomed to communicating verbally, but I really need you to use your words, okay?"

"I...am like you."

"You're *not* human," I say.

He sneers in disgust. "No. But I am what you would call an Earthling."

Pretty sure I know what he's getting at, but I want him to spell it out so there's no doubt or wiggle room. "Meaning..."

"My kind evolved on Earth. Just as yours did. We began as primitivees, as all species do. Over time our brain size increased, vocal communication was unnecessary, and our mental capacity grew far beyond the capabilities of humanity."

"You keep bragging like that and I'm going to have horrible self-esteem issues."

"As you should," Ricky says, and I have no idea if that was blunt honesty or sarcasm. "In the centuries following the time period in which I lived, my species' civilization flourished and covered the globe."

"There is no evidence of a previous civilization on Earth," I say. "If there was, we'd know about it."

"Unlike the human race, my kind created technology that didn't also destroy the planet. Time and elements would leave no trace. And..." His voice lowers, all of the bolster deflating. "...anything that remained is now hidden in what your people call the KT boundary—a quarter inch layer of ash and soot left behind by the asteroid strike that killed nearly all life on Earth."

Beside me, Max's bravado fades. Mine does, too.

We both understand what losing a planet full of friends feels like.

"You are the last of your kind?" Max asks.

"In a sense..." Ricky sits in the grass, settling into the conversation. "Some of my kind survived the asteroid impact..." He looks up at the sky. "Out there. They escaped Earth before it died. Found a new home. And evolved..." His eyes turn down. His voice grows quiet. "...into something else. Something more..." He looks at me. "...more human."

"Not all of us are horrible," I say. "But I'm pretty sure you already knew that."

Ricky squints at me, but he says nothing.

"In fact, your pal Owen McCoy, one of the first humans you met way back there in dinosaur times, is unconscious in an ice cave, thanks to you."

"McCoy is here?" Ricky asks.

"Was standing right next to me when you came through the—"

Ricky leaps to his feet. "The gate! It must be closed!"

"Why?" I ask. Last thing I want to do is deactivate the gate that might take me to Chuy.

"I am being hunted."

"By?" I ask.

"It's too late," Max says, looking up at me. "It's here."

29

It, I think. *Singular.*

That can't be too bad.

I snap out of my mind, back into the real world just in time to see 'it' step through the gate, and I realize that it's *not* too bad—it's worse.

The first thing I see is the cryptoterrestrial, which needs a name, even if it doesn't want one. Because 'cryptoterrestrial' is a mouthful. Crypto is the obvious choice, but that smacks of crypto-currency and Superman's dog. *Mazzola*, I decide, after Ricky, but also because the name has kind of an ancient intelligence sort of vibe.

Mazzola is big and ugly, a fact I decide to bury deep in my subconscious in case he can hear my thoughts. He's definitely a descendant of a carnivorous dinosaur species. Long tail. Longish neck. Big hind legs. His body leans forward, perfectly balanced, with long arms that end in four-digit hands—including opposable thumbs. A line of iridescent downy feathers runs down his neck, back, and tail, shimmering purple and green. His face is far less intimidating than I imagine a T-Rex's would be, but his forward-facing black eyes are disturbingly intelligent and devoid of emotion.

Despite Mazzola's cold visage, his emotions burn hot. Fear vibrates through the air around his pale body, which looks big and tough enough to handle just about anything—if you ignore the wounds covering him. And that's hard to do, because unlike most things in the universe, the cryptoterrestrial bleeds red.

An Earthling, just like he said. In a way, that makes us kin. Might have to go back a few billion years to find a common ancestor, but it's there.

I soak all this up in an instant. Then my eyes flick to the gate and the *it*—the Neo-Crypto—that has just emerged.

It shares the cryptoterrestrial's black eyes and pale skin, but the same 65 million years during which humanity evolved has altered its physical appearance. The creature stands on two legs, shaped like a Minotaur's, as Hildy described. Its longer arms are thick and powerful, still ending in hands that sport three fingers and a thumb. The creature stands eight feet tall, despite being hunched forward, and it's built like Arnold in his prime. And like Mazzola, it's buck nekkid, dangly bits in the breeze. Definitely a dude, but not as impressive as its size would suggest. Just a few floppy inches, and I'm guessing undescended testicles. Not everything male in the universe has balls, but just about everything with two legs and Earth as an origin does. Unless—*holy shit*—it's been castrated. The Neo-Crypto's head still smacks of carnivorous dinosaur, snout protruding, but there's now a wide crest extending back from the top of the creature's skull, reminiscent of a triceratops. Three long scars cross its face, where I'm guessing one of its own took a swipe.

I don't see any weapons aside from the long claws on the Neo-Crypto's hands and feet. Bonus. But that doesn't mean it's not dangerous. Just as fear vibrates from Mazzola, the newcomer exudes menace and supreme confidence.

The Neo-Crypto stands before the gate, surveying the chamber, its eyes lingering first on my sleeping teammates, then on the cryptoterrestrial backstepping toward the wall, and then...on me.

The creature's black eyes wang-jangle my nerves, loosening my grip on the railgun, preventing me from even thinking about using the weapon. With a look, I'm disarmed.

This is how they captured Chuy, Cowboy, and Delgado. They pacified them mentally and emotionally and then just scooped them up.

The Neo-Crypto turns away from me, leaving me undone, and I get a strong sense of 'I'll get back to you in a minute.'

Turning its attention to Mazzola reveals the creature's back. A line of red Europhids run down the spine, growing in size between the shoulders and then tapering down to little nubs just before the thing's thick white ass.

It's going to take me, I realize. *Just as they meant to on Beta-Prime. I'm the real target, but it wants to kill Mazzola first.* And he's got nowhere to run. The exit is far too small for him, and the Neo-Crypto stands between him and the gate.

But not me.

I could go.

I could walk through the gate. It might lead to Chuy and the others. Might also make the enemy's job easier.

Chuy would kick my ass if I gave in to my emotions and didn't play this smart—even if it gets her killed. Leaving would put the others at risk. Would certainly result in Mazzola's death. The other side of this gate is an unknown. The here and now...well, it's right in front of me.

So, I forget about the gate, squelch my desperation, and focus on overcoming the mind-numbing fear incapacitating me. Step one, rally Garfunkel.

I'M HERE.

Glad to have you back. Help me move.

His will merges with my own. It's not enough to move, but it frees up my mind a little bit. Hoping Mazzola is listening, and Garfunkel understands what I want, I repeat a mantra in my head. *Wake her up, wake her up, wake her up.*

The Neo-Crypto must hear my projected thoughts, because it snaps its ugly face toward me, sneering and revealing rows of needly, clear teeth—something Mazzola doesn't have. The Neo-Crypto might have evolved for millions of years, but it did so on another planet. From the looks of it, life wasn't pleasant. It might be smart, but it's equally savage.

Quivering fear flows from the creature's mind to mine, shocking me into submission.

A tug on my leg nearly makes me scream, but a moment later, I'm feeling more like myself, looking down at Cassidy, her hand on my ankle. I can't see her face behind the adaptive armor, but I can sense her calm.

I crouch slowly, limbs shaking.

"I need..." Speaking feels like hard labor. My voice shakes. "...you to...make me...fearless."

She gives a subtle nod and grips my ankle tighter.

Pushing emotions is normally a snap for her. She does it inadvertently at times, and when she sets her mind to the task, it can be downright scary. So, it's a little disconcerting when I sense her intensity. She's working hard to bolster me, but to do that she needs to overcome her own emotions, which might also be affected by the Neo-Crypto's mind... or just the fact that there are two albino monsters in the ice cave.

My grip on the railgun tightens, but I can't lift it. Can't aim it. Can't pull the trigger.

"I can help," Hildy whispers in my comms.

Mazzola must not have known which 'her' I was talking about, so he woke them all up. Wini hasn't said anything, but she's reaching for her shotgun, fighting the fear gripping us all.

Not sure what Hildy can do until she taps the controls on her forearm and music fills my ears. It starts with a series of techno-speak—*Harder, Better, Faster, Stronger*, that I recognize from one of the first bands I listened to after returning to the present: Daft Punk. That alone is enough to get me pumped, but then a heavy beat and rapping voice overlays the music, transforming and elevating the song to something that actually makes me feel—

"Stronger," Hildy says, and then she answers the question on the fringe of my thoughts. "Kanye West. Or maybe just Kanye."

"I think it's just Ye, now," Wini grunts.

I don't give a shit what he calls himself, this song is exactly what I needed. Feeling a little more powerful with each thump of the bass, I lift the railgun to my shoulder.

Waves of emotion roil from both the Neo-Crypto and Mazzola. They're arguing without words.

Then the Neo-Crypto strikes, swinging out its hand and opening three fresh gashes on Mazzola's side.

Fight! I think.

Mazzola might not have talons on his hands, or dagger teeth, but he's bigger and probably stronger.

Perhaps sensing my growing resistance and my desire for him to take action, Mazzola swings his long tail. It's on a collision course with the monster's head—but it's caught. Using Mazzola's momentum against him, the Neo-Crypto yanks on the tail and tosses him like a salmon in a Seattle fish market.

I duck down as the monstrous cryptoterrestrial topples past, crashing to the ice and sliding away. The Neo-Crypto stomps after him, oblivious to the small people lying in its way. If I don't do something, Wini's going to get crushed beneath its broad feet.

Nothing would make me happier than firing off a solid one-liner before opening fire, but it takes everything I have to slip my finger around the trigger. The creature's eyes never shift, but I sense its attention snap to me when I take aim.

I pull the trigger, unleashing a zero-recoil stream of razor-sharp discs. They buzz through the air and hit—

—the wall. Ice explodes as a five-foot-deep hole is carved, giving me a good idea of what would happen to a target made of flesh and blood— if I could hit it.

The Neo-Crypto sensed my attack before I could pull the trigger. In the time it took me to perform that simple act, it dove to the side and is now charging around the circular space, clinging to the wall.

Downside—it can dodge bullets.

Upside—it's still more interested in Mazzola than it is me, even when I have a weapon.

Double downside—I think my upside is a downside, too. Because it means I'm not a threat. Means that I can try all day and never hit it. Even worse, it might trick me into shooting Mazzola.

So, I do the unexpected and hold my fire.

"My...rifle," McCoy says. He's struggling to push himself up. "Use... my rifle."

"What's so special about your—"

"Temporal rounds," he says.

"Temporal... Wait. Hold on. *Time* bullets?"

"Experimental," he says. "Based on technology reverse engineered from Synergy."

"The place that took you back in time," I guess.

He nods. "They strike their target...*before* you fire them."

"Okay," I say, picking up the funky rifle. "You officially win the battle of crazy-town weaponry. Delgado outdid himself."

I lift the rifle, rest it against my shoulder, slip my finger around the trigger.

The Neo-Crypto arches its back in pain as two bullet holes appear in its lower back. After a split second of shock, I remember to pull the trigger.

30

"Holy shit, it worked!" I say, and then I notice smoke seeping out of the weapon. I should probably toss it away, but this fight isn't over.

The Neo-Crypto dives to the side, bounding back and forth. It's an impossible target, even with time bullets. But its destination is clear—the creature is heading for the gate.

Given its ability to sense and evade attacks, it's possible that this thing has never been shot before. Two bullets to the torso must have come as a shock. No idea if the wounds are fatal, but they definitely made an impact. All of the creature's bravado is gone, replaced by confused rage and a sprinkling of 'what the hell just happened' fear.

Tracking the creature's progress through the chamber, a pattern appears. I aim ahead, account for the time difference, and the moment a third round strikes the Neo-Crypto's shoulder, I pull the trigger.

I'm speechless. The bullet impacts tell me when to pull the trigger! But...how? My brain hurts just thinking about it. The weapon is a paradox machine.

With a final frothy bark in my direction, the Neo-Crypto resorts to running on all fours and then dives through the gate. A moment later the gate goes dark again.

The waves of psychic energy disappear with it, freeing me from the creature's control.

"Dark Horse," Wini says. "You might want to get rid of that—"

Heat scorches my hands.

The time-rifle is glowing.

I toss it away. Before it can hit the ground, it disappears in a flash of light.

"Uhh, where did it go?" I ask.

"Best guess," McCoy says, picking himself up off the ice. "Another time."

"That seems...dangerous," I say.

He shrugs it off. Didn't strike me as the brazen risk-taker. Then again, he didn't fire it, did he?

"Next time, warn me if I'm about to do something potentially stupid," I say.

"You would have fired it anyway," he said, "and at the time, I didn't think adding to your fear would be a good thing."

It's a solid point, so I let it go.

"Could it be a problem?" Hildy asks. "A weapon like that lost in time?"

Wini waves her concern away. "If it went back in time, it's either locked in ice that has long since flowed away, or it appeared before there was an ice cap and fell a mile down to the ground and shattered."

"And if it went forward?" Hildy asks.

Wini shrugs. "Same answer, but also not our problem."

A groan turns our collective attention to Mazzola. He's struggling to push himself up, but he's sliding against the frozen wall. Blood coats his flank. He's wounded—and freezing. His muscles twitch. I can feel him in my head, trying to communicate, but he's making no sense.

Going into shock.

"We need to get him out of here," I say, rushing over to Mazzola, but I can't figure out how to get it done. The PSDs are designed for people, and while I can take a handful of people with me, this guy is way too big to fit...or physically move, even in the weightlessness of the fourth dimension.

His voice enters my thoughts as a weak whisper. "Destroy...the... gate."

"Can't do it," I tell him.

"Others will follow."

"They want you that bad?" I ask.

"I...am a curiosity...a living fossil..." His eyes start to close. "They want...you."

"Me? Why?"

"To know...your secret... To know...how...you..."

He's fading. Nearly gone.

"Burnett," I say into my comms. "You have our location?"

"Correct. I am tracking your slew drives and—"

"Get down to *Lil' Bitch'n*," I say. "Now!"

A moment later, he's no longer hovering above the moon in a massive battleship. Instead, he's in our much smaller lander, hidden beneath the ocean off the coast of St. Augustine, Florida. "Okay, I'm there."

"Rotate to our position," I say. "Right on top of us."

"Objects emerging from the fourth dimension replace those in the—"

"I know," I say, and he's not wrong. If the ship appeared on top of us, we'd simply cease to exist. But the ship is also full of really big pockets of open space. "Line us up, dead center in the cargo bay," I say. "Catch us in the gap."

"I don't know, Dark Horse. We have never attempted—"

"Today is the national day for trying stupid shit, Burn. Get it done."

"Well okay, then. I did not know about this holiday. Rotating in three..."

I look down at Mazzola. Can no longer feel his presence in my mind. "Two..."

McCoy crouches down beside the beast, hand on his chest. Looks worried. "How long will this ta—"

"One..."

Being rotated on is a lot different than rotating in. There's no movement. No wall of light. We're just suddenly inside *Lil' Bitch'n*'s cargo bay, along with a few inches of ice beneath us. It's disorienting.

"Where was he from?" I ask McCoy.

"Appalachia," he says.

"Wait, really?" That won't help. "Was it tropical at the time?"

He nods.

"Burnett, take us someplace warm, moist, and remote as hell."

"I'm not sure where—"

"Long as it ain't your mama's crotch—"

Wini whacks my arm. Tilts her head toward Cassidy, scolding me for the rude humor.

"I never met my mother," Burnett says, sounding morose.

I peel the adaptive armor mask off my head. "Just go!"

There's a flash of white, and then the cargo bay doors part and open. Hot, wet, floral air rushes over.

"Help me get him outside," I say, and I start pushing Mazzola toward the open hatch. Either Mazzola is lighter than he looks, or the ice is already slippery, because moving our beastly ally isn't all that difficult. McCoy joins me. Then Hildy and Wini.

Cassidy hops up and down beside us, mask down, a smile on her face, kicking her legs straight out to the side as she moves beside us. She sings, "Go, go, go! You can do it, you can do it!" like she's on a kid's show.

For a moment, I wonder if pushing Mazzola only feels easy because we have the living embodiment of *shish boom bah* infusing us with a can-do attitude. Then Mazzola reaches the angled ramp and instead of sliding gently down to the fertile jungle floor below, his skin catches, his body rolls, and then it ragdoll flops all the way to the ground, coming to a stop against a tree that shakes from the impact. The crash dislodges a monkey that lands on the cryptoterrestrial, and then it shrieks in surprise and bounds away, leaving a stream of urine in its wake.

"Well...that isn't how I pictured it, but..." I shrug while motioning to Mazzola's motionless body.

"Is he alive?" Cassidy asks.

McCoy lumbers down the ramp, not exactly rushing, probably because he's wondering the same thing as me—how do you check a dinosaur's pulse? He rests his hands on Mazzola's big, pale ribcage. "He's breathing."

"Now what?" Hildy asks.

"We wait for sleeping beauty to wake up, or for Burnett to finish tracking the PSDs. Until then...much as I hate being sidelined, we need a breather. These aren't backwoods Nazis. We're lucky to be alive. To get our people back, we need to be ready. Weapons, strategy, and intel. When we have all three, we'll make our move. Until then, we're grounded." It's probably one of the toughest calls I've ever made, but we can't keep going in with our pants around our ankles. We've already lost three people, hopefully not for good. But we're not moving until I'm confident that—

Clang.

Metal strikes metal, turning me around.

The hell?

I look down to my feet where the steady stream of melt water flowing down the ramp pins a long wooden stick against my foot. I bend down and pick it up.

Not a stick.

An arrow.

The tip is rusted and rough, but it's sharpened to a point. There are no feathers on the back, but the tip is coated in something slick and black. *Poison,* I realize. *Must be.*

"Burn," I say, eyeing the jungle. "Where did you bring us?"

"Someplace tropical and remote," he says, sounding proud of himself.

Thunk!

Another arrow strikes me dead center in the chest. A perfect kill-shot. If not for the adaptive armor, I'd be dead.

"Contact!" I slide down the ramp and duck behind Mazzola. Feel bad using him for cover, but whoever is here is still shooting arrows, and they're not going to see the big white lump as something to shoot and kill. Wini, Hildy, and Cassidy backtrack into *Lil' Bitch'n.*

I peek up over Mazzola's body and peer into the jungle. There's no one out there. "Burn, seriously, where are we—exactly?"

"Well," he says. "In this time... Let me check..." He can rotate from the Moon to Earth in the beat of a heart, but he's still surfing the Internet to find information on present day Earth. "Here it is. North Sentinel Island."

31

"I'm sorry, did you say, "North Sentinel Island?""

"Yah," Burnett says, all casual, like he hasn't just made a catastrophic error. "Have you visited before?"

"Of course not!" I shout. "Not only is it illegal to come within miles of the island, but *everyone who comes here dies!*"

"Dies?" Burnett sounds surprised. "How?"

"Oh, I don't know, maybe it's the *poison-tipped arrows!*"

"That sounds horrible," Burnett says. "Should I rotate us away?"

Normally, that would be the obvious choice. I don't want to be killed, but I also don't want to disturb a tribe of people who have successfully existed for 60,000 years without influence from the outside world.

"It's not just poison arrows," Wini says over comms, voice low like she's Large Marge, about to recall the horrors of her past. "We've heard reports of...strange things happening on this island, and a trio of people from the outside world—"

An arrow whistles past my head, hits the ramp, and ricochets up into the cargo hold, silencing Wini.

To rotate away, would mean first rotating a few feet to get our new dino-pal back in the cargo bay. Might also mean killing some of the tribal people slowly encroaching on our position. The arrows are keeping us pinned down. I can hear bare feet slapping on the earth. I want to save Mazzola, but I'm not about to kill the North Sentinelese to get it done.

"There is no need for concern," Mazzola says in my head. His black eyes open wide. "I have...impressed the situation upon their minds. They will not attack us if we do not leave the ship."

"And if we do leave the ship?" I ask. I have no plans to do so, but I want to know what I'm up against should the need arise.

Goose bumps rise all over Mazzola's body. "Unimaginable horrors." He gasps, and not just in his mind. He crushes his eyes shut and shakes his head. "The island is forbidden. That is enough."

Mazzola pushes himself up with a grunt, so unconcerned by the poison arrows that I believe he truly did make peace with the natives. But how? What kind of ancient people could have a spaceship appear in their midst and just roll with the psychic explanation delivered by an albino dinosaur?

"This planet is more mysterious than you know," Mazzola says. I'm getting accustomed to his mental speak. If you don't look at his unmoving mouth, his transmitted thoughts sound a lot like someone talking aloud. "Best to not question it, if you want to survive."

"It's in my nature to—"

Images flow into my consciousness. Being hunted. Paralyzed. Dark creatures closing in. Monstrous things. Babies thrown like projectiles. All of it smeared in a sense of dread more profound than anything I've felt before—and that's saying a lot, because despite my macho exterior, I've spent a lot of the last decade a jump scare away from needing to wear adult diapers on mission.

"Okay, okay. I got it." I take a moment to recover from the hellish vision. "Everyone stay on *Lil' Bitch'n*. No one goes outside for any reason." I turn to Mazzola. "Can you haul your big ass back inside, or do we need to get a forklift?"

The cryptoterrestrial pushes himself up, weak, but not too feeble to move. He thumps up the ramp. Weighs enough that the ship tilts to one side as he climbs. With Mazzola—and our cover—gone, McCoy and I take one last scan of the surrounding jungle.

Shadows dance about, but no one attacks. The barrage of arrows is over.

"What'd he show you?" McCoy asks.

"Nothing you want to know about," I say, backing toward the ramp. "Nothing anyone was ever meant to see."

"Mysterious," he says.

"Like Michael Douglas suddenly being an old man, and somehow still able to marry a babe."

"Catherine Zeta Jones," McCoy says.

"Who?" I ask.

"The babe. She's an actress. *Zorro. Entrapment. Chicago.*"

"Never heard of her," I say, ascending the ramp, "but there's a Zorro movie?"

"Two. I sometimes forget you missed a few decades."

"Any good?"

He shrugs. "Good enough."

Inside the cargo bay, I slap the button for the hatch. I watch the jungle outside become a sliver and then disappear. I don't care what's out there, arrows and a bad attitude aren't going to get you inside this ship. We're safe.

For now.

Still have a giant-sized pile of shit to sort through. But first…

"You know how to sew a wound?" I ask Wini.

"I've learned over the years."

I point to a medkit hanging on the wall, one of many scattered throughout both the *Bitch'n* and this lander. "You okay with patching up Mazzola?"

"Who?" she asks.

"Sorry, the big ass cryptoterrestrial. I named him Mazzola."

"When?"

"In my head. It was a whole thing. Garfunkel was there, as Max, as the Ultimate Warrior." To Mazzola, "Right? You're good with the name?"

"Names are irrelevant," he says, and he projects the thought to everyone the way we do with our voices.

"Mazzola it is," I say.

"Sounds like a second-rate magician," Wini grumbles, strutting toward the med-kit, working the tight adaptive armor. No idea if she's as fit as she looks in it, or if the armor is pushing everything in the right direction, but she knows she looks good and she's kind of flaunting it.

"Everyone else," I say, "just…do what needs doing to prepare."

"Prepare for what?" Cassidy asks.

I look her in the eyes. "War."

She smiles, looking crafty. "Cool."

"Not at all," I say, and I head for *Lil' Bitch'n*'s cockpit. "Hildy, with me."

I sit in one of the two chairs in the small bridge, slouching and sighing. It's not a side of me I let many people see, not even Burnett or Cowboy. But Hildy has a recliner in my comfort zone, along with Chuy, and she's welcome any time. I can be fully myself with her, and vulnerable. "I gotta be honest with you. I'm terrified."

She nods. "Dominoes of despair. Things just keep going wrong."

"We have no idea what we're really up against—and yeah, we're kicking ass along the way, but..."

She places her gloved hand on mine. "We'll get her back."

"I'm not sure we will," I tell her.

The wetness in her eyes betrays her outward confidence.

"And if we don't... I don't know."

"You're strong enough to overcome it," she says.

I shake my head. "I can't lose her."

She grips my hand. "You are strong enough. Because you're stronger than me."

Her insistence has nothing to do with me, and she doesn't need to explain. She comes from a nightmare future. Most of her life was spent alone, without friends, without love of any kind. All she had to lift her spirits was the media created in the twentieth and twenty-first centuries. If she can endure that, I can endure the pain of losing Chuy.

My future wife.

The one destined to carry my child, from which a bloodline of rebels is born.

Or was. In another timeline.

Now she might just be gone.

Not knowing is the hardest part.

Doesn't matter, I decide. What I do from here is set in stone. The only thing knowing would change is my motivation. Rescue or vengeance.

Hildy taps away at her workstation. "You need to focus..." She taps a final key, and the opening notes of Queen's *Under Pressure* fill the cockpit. Not fair. It's hard to feel down when Freddie Mercury is holding you up and singing straight into your heart. "...on the mission. That's how it's done, right? Leave your feelings at home. Get the job done. Sort out the mess that's left behind when the job is complete."

I give an unconvincing nod, so she and Freddie help me along.

"Our enemy is The Order. We know that because Drago told us."

"Drago, who is being controlled by red Europhids. Along with the Neo-Cryptos," I say.

"Decent name," she says. "But not your best."

"Always critiquing."

"Also," she says, "I don't think they're being controlled. The Neo-Cryptos are intelligent and powerful—and not just physically. They communicate psychically, like Mazzola. Their relationship is symbiotic. And I think together, *they* are the Order. Drago, on the other hand, is an unwilling partner. We know him. He'd never do anything to hurt us, or Chuy. And I think he's still in there, fighting."

I nod. "He dropped a few helpful nuggets."

"Including that the Order sees themselves as a force for good, fighting some kind of cosmic chaos being sown by...who knows what."

"Lots of bad guys have done horrible things while believing they're the good guys."

She somehow manages to smile and frown simultaneously. "Don't I know it."

"So," I say. "We have rogue red Europhids willing to commit genocide and form a new alliance with an evolved Earth species. To defend what's theirs, they will destroy anything they perceive as a threat. But the reds and blues have lived in harmony for billions of years. What could possibly motivate them to such drastic action?"

I feel Garfunkel emerge from the depths. Then he lays the obvious answer on me.

THEY ARE AFRAID.

Hildy gasps.

"What?" I ask.

"Was...that Garfunkel. The voice?" She does an impression of him. "They are afraid."

My eyes widen. "You...heard that?"

32

"How is that possible?" Hildy asks. "I thought—"

"So did I." Garfunkel's voice was intended for my mind only. A private interface with an ancient intelligence. That was the deal. Other than my occasionally blue eyes, the symbiotic relationship wasn't meant for the world. But if Garfunkel's thoughts are projected from my mind like a voice...that could get awkward, especially when he whispers sweet nothings.

I DO NO SUCH THING.

"You hear *that?*" I ask Hildy.

She shakes her head. "What did he say?"

I wave the question away. "I used my inner monologue to provoke a response."

"So, it's not a permanent change."

"Not yet," I say.

"What do you mean, 'not yet?'" She leans toward me, her blazing blue eyes probing my expression. "We're a team. We're friends. We're not supposed to keep secrets."

"Less of a secret," I say. "More of a 'holy shit this is freaky, and I don't want it to be real so maybe it won't be if I never talk about it' situation."

"If you don't tell me. It's still a secret."

I sigh.

Probably would be good to get it off my chest, and Hildy isn't going to let it go. "Garfunkel is...becoming part of me. Or, we're becoming part of each other. Merging."

"Metamorphosizing," she says, eyes widening.

"No need to use big words," I say. "But yeah. Becoming something different. Something new. Not quite human."

She nods, pom-pom hair shifting. "I can see how that would be frightening."

"Horrifying," I say. "And not just for me. Garfunkel isn't keen on the idea either. We don't know which of us, or if either of us, will exist when it's done."

"From my perspective, your behavior hasn't strayed too far out of normal ranges."

"You're tracking my behavior?"

"I observe all things." She gives me a wink to offset the bold god-like claim she's just made, but she's telling the truth. She observes, gathers information into her hard drive-like brain, and holds onto it until its needed—whether it be a pop culture quote, the perfect song selection, celestial coordinates...or a change in someone's behavior.

"Well," I say. "Let me know if it does."

"Is it a recent change?"

"Yeah."

"Maybe it coincided with the destruction of the blue colony on Beta-Prime?"

"Too far away," I say.

"How do you know that?"

"I...just do."

She flips open an invisible notebook and pretends to take a note before closing it again.

"Funny," I say.

"What about Europa?" she asks. "There's supposed to be a Europhid colony there, right?"

"Yeah, but...the effect wouldn't... Unless..." Nausea roils through my body. I pitch forward, fingers tingling, breath coming in gulps, heart pounding. I've been to some of the universe's most hellish places and kept my cool, but I know a panic attack when I see one, or in this case, when I feel one.

But it's not *my* panic attack.

It's Garfunkel's.

Takes me a moment to catch up to the thought he intercepted and brought to its painful conclusion. We are separated from the Europhid colonies by a great distance. The closest was on Europa, three hundred ninety million miles away. If we felt the change subtly enough to trigger our merger, perhaps as an unconscious fear response, it means... "The genocide didn't just happen on Beta-Prime," I whisper. "It...was everywhere."

Hildy rubs my back. It helps. "Is that possible?"

I focus on the question, attempting to separate my consciousness from Garfunkel's emotions. "The...red Europhids...form relationships with the species already living on the planets they colonize. They'd... have the means."

Tears drip from my eyes.

A sob barks from my mouth.

I fall into Hildy's embrace.

"It's okay," she says, the words meant for Garfunkel. "Sometimes horrible things happen. They don't make sense."

NOT LIKE THIS.

"Exactly like this," Hildy says. "All the time. At least for the rest of us. You've just been...above it for a very long time. But this doesn't have to be the end. Because you're still here. Still alive. And that means there is hope."

She's talking to Garfunkel *and* me now. Ever the optimist.

The cockpit door opens. I'd normally pull my shit together right quick before letting someone other than Hildy see me like this, but the emotions aren't mine to control.

And Cassidy, the empath, already knows.

Her face is screwed up, lips pouting. She steps around Hildy, sits on my lap, and just wraps her arms around my neck, head on my shoulder. Doesn't say a word. Doesn't need to. She's radiating empathy. Like Hildy, she understands darkness and overcoming it.

As do I.

But it's new to Garfunkel.

His kind has suffered grave losses at the hands of humanity—in an avoided future—but his species is vast, populating the cosmos in dimensions of reality beyond our comprehension—though maybe not Cowboy's. He's been to other worlds and seen through the eyes of their creator. If the reds revolted everywhere... If they truly wiped out the blues...

"They're not after me," I realize. "They're after Garfunkel."

BECAUSE I AM THE LAST.

"Can the whole be remade?" I ask. "From you?"

UNKNOWN.

"But there is hope," Hildy says, able to hear Garfunkel again.
Cassidy leans back. Looks me in the eyes. "You need to hide."
"I don't hide," I say. "And Chuy—"
Hildy cuts me off with, "If Garfunkel is the last of his kind, then—"

WE WILL NOT HIDE.
WE WILL RESTORE MY KIND.
OR WE WILL HAVE VENGEANCE.

Don't know if this is 100% Garfunkel anymore, or if his personality is being driven by my own. Genocide can't stand. When I was the last black man in the universe, I didn't hide. I scoured the universe for my people, and then fought like hell. With help from Garfunkel, we saved humanity. If we can do the same for him, that's exactly what we're going to do.

And save Chuy and the others while we're at it.

"Dark Horse," Burnett says over the comms. "Come in, Dark Horse. Over."

I toggle my comms. "I'm here. What do you have for me?"

"A location," he says. "For the slew drive that exited Antarctica via the gate."

Cassidy leaps off my lap as I stand to my feet. "Where?"

"You're not going to—"

"*Where?*"

"Florida," he says. "At the house."

I turn to Hildy. "Drago's come home."

"Looking for you," she points out. "Probably not alone."

"He's our only lead," I say.

"We're tired," she says. "Lucky to be alive."

I see the reflection of my eyes in Hildy's, glowing blue. Then a voice emerges from my mind, projecting unshakeable conviction.

WE MUST GO.

WE MUST GO NOW.

33

"I'm going alone," I say.

Hildy's reaction is visceral. "The hell you are." She's picked up a bit of Chuy's toughness. It's nice to see, but it doesn't change a thing.

"If we show up en masse with a bunch of faces he doesn't recognize and one that's not human, he's liable to—"

"Try to kill you? He's going to do that anyway."

"I can talk to him," I say. "Part of him is still in control."

"Just because he dropped a few information cookies does not mean it was an invitation to afternoon tea."

"First," Cassidy says, pointing at Hildy with both fingers. "That was funny. Second, I agree with Dark Horse."

Hildy throws her hands up. "The new kid always agrees with Dark Horse! Dark Horse is sooo cool. Dark Horse is a badass. Dark Horse is always right. Well, I say wrong. Dark Horse is not always those things."

Cassidy raises a hand. "Is there another new kid?"

"*I* was the new kid," Hildy says. "Not that long ago."

"But, you're old."

Hildy tilts her head and her eyes toward Cassidy, exasperated. She's been the youngest on the team for a while. Must be strange to suddenly be one of the adults. "I'm twenty-one."

"Yeah. Old."

"Here's what I heard." I tick them off on my fingers. "Cool. Badass. And always right."

"Not always," Hildy says.

"But a lot of the time."

She says nothing.

"And I'm right this time. I need to try. It's Drago."

He's a big, loud, obnoxious Russkie, but he's my brother from an-other mother—probably a grizzly bear. As much as I want to save Chuy, I want to free Drago from Europhid control. And one thing might lead to the other.

The bridge door opens to reveal Wini. "I hear shouting."

"Good," I say. "I'm putting you in charge while I'm gone."

"Honey, I've been in charge the whole time, you just didn't— Wait. Where are you going?"

"He's going home to 'talk' to Drago," Hildy blurts out.

"Drago, the man currently under alien control, Drago? Drago, the man who activated a gate using a woman's severed hand, Drago? That Drago?"

I nod.

She gets icy serious. Leans in close. "Get that damn hand."

"You read my mind," I say.

"Don't even need alien DNA to do it," she says. "How long should we wait before charging to your rescue?"

"Give me ten minutes. If you don't hear from me, come running. Otherwise, stay here and help our...guest get back on his feet." I turn my attention to Hildy. Then I take her hand. "I won't do anything nuts. If things look bad, I'll rotate back. But I need to do this."

She twists her lips, sighs, and says, "Fine. Ten minutes. After that, I'm going to show up and go Michael Corleone on whoever or whatever I find there that's not you."

"Deal," I say, stepping back, hand on my slew drive.

"Don't you want a weapon?" Wini asks.

"Aiming to save him," I say. "Not kill him." I give Cassidy a nod of thanks for having my back, and then I rotate off *Lil' Bitch'n*'s bridge.

I slip out of the fourth dimension and onto the long, sandy St. Augus-tine beach on the outskirts of the compound we call home. There's no one in sight, so I head for the wooden walkway that stretches over grassy dunes that separate swamp from beach. I leave the salty sand and its posi-tive ions behind, trading them in for cooler air and the smell of decay. Moss-covered trees drape the murky waters below in shadow, forcing the cold-blooded gators that call the property home to lounge in grassy patches touched by slivers of sun. I call it the Dragon's Lair. The twenty-odd twelve-foot gators glance at me as I pass but they have long since given up trying to eat people on the walkway. If I got down into the water, that might be a different thing. Death investigators in this part of the world—where every puddle seems to hide a killer—see their share of death-rolled corpses. The gators are wild, but I've been known to throw them chickens on occasion, hoping they'll remember me should I ever trip and belly flop into their domain.

The house, formerly a large visitor's center, looks quiet.

The lights aren't on. The security alarm isn't screaming. If Drago's inside, he used his key code.

I creep up the grassy hill leading to the side door. Feeling pretty exposed, but there isn't really a way to approach the house from a concealed position—by design. And I'm in a rush. I've already used up three of Hildy's ten minutes.

An open door greets me.

He's definitely inside. But is he alone?

I hover by the door, hand on slew drive, ready to bolt at the first sign of, 'holy shit, it's going to eat me.' First thing I do is take a long drag through my nose. The house, like all homes, has its own unique scent created by the people who live there, the meals they eat, and the candles they burn. Something like a rygar would change that.

And it does. But it's not an animal scent—it's distinctly Drago. Kind of a musky, mossy body odor. I'd make a joke about him not showering, but I swear he smells like this, fresh out of the shower. It's like the smell of Siberia in the autumn oozes from his pores.

Next thing I do is lean my head in the door and listen.

Silence greets me, which is odd for Drago. When he moves, it sounds a lot like a sasquatch is loose in the house. But all I can hear is a faint rumbling.

Is...is that snoring?

Before heading inside, I check in with Garfunkel.

"You feeling anything? Any red dudes around? Inside?"

He's quiet for a moment, and then...

NO.

He sounds as confused by the answer as I do. Last we saw Drago, which wasn't that long ago, he was jacked up with red Europhids. Are they all asleep? Do Europhids sleep? It was a rhetorical question. Barely a thought.

But Garfunkel answers anyway.

NO.

I sneak into the house, closing and locking the door behind me. The snoring is coming from the large living room, echoing a bit off the vaulted ceiling of what was previously a gift store.

Drago sits in his favorite spot on a couch positioned in front of a large, stone fireplace that there is rare occasion to use in Florida. But it looks nice. He cooked over the open flame on occasion, before he left.

"Hey," I say, trying to be casual. Despite being immune to the sound of his own chainsaw snore, he's a light sleeper.

His eyes snap open, and then they shift to me. "You made me wait. Again."

"Wish I'd known you were coming," I say.

"I will send e-vite next time. With flowery animation card and panda bears. You would like that, no? Americans and their fluffy animals."

I smile. He sounds like his old self, but weak. Has dark rings under his eyes. His normally pale skin appears almost translucent.

Resting beside him on the couch is the severed hand. Up close, it looks a bit dried out. I'm not sure how old it is, but it's not exactly fresh. This close to him, I can smell blood, but I don't see any wounds.

I take a seat in the rocking chair, facing the couch, leaning back on a quilt that Hildy made. Apparently, a well-made quilt was one of the few things of comfort people in the Union were allowed to create. "Are you... okay?"

"Do you remember first time we met?" he asks.

"When you were a dirty communist?"

"And you were American pig. Da. I would have killed you without a thought. Without remorse. You were my sworn enemy. But now...you are my friend. You are my family."

"C'mon now, you're starting to sound like Vin Diesel."

He grins.

We watched several *Fast and Furious* movies together before he left for the motherland.

"I did not like how our last meeting ended," he says.

"You mean when you were a total douchebag...and you left us in Antarctica?"

"Da," he says. "I was not...myself."

I nod to let him know I'm aware. "But you are...now?"

"Da, and I wanted to give you that." He tilts his head toward the hand. "PSD will not get you to destination. Something about black hole, magnetic fields, blah, blah, science, blah. Only gates. You know how to use, da?"

"Activate it with the hand," I say. "Think about where I want to go. And presto, I step out through a gate on another world."

He nods. "Think about her."

"Chuy's alive?" I nearly choke on the words.

"Da," he says. "All of them. Because it is you they want...or rather, what is inside you."

"Who's in charge?" I ask. "Is it the reds or the big, white ugly dudes?"

"Is both," he says. "Both are one. Like you and Garfunkel, but opposite. Angry. Afraid. Evil."

"Why is this happening now? What do they want?"

"There is...imbalance in universe. Worlds are being connected. Gates opening up on planets where none had been before. Species are interacting. Cosmic war breaking out. The Order..."

"The reds and Neo-Cryptos," I say.

He nods. "...seek to end chaos by controlling gates, and the planets they lead to. But...they must first destroy their opposition."

"Me," I say.

"Da."

"I'm just one man with a single blue Europhid in his head."

"From one, come all," he says, sounding like he's repeating something he's heard.

"Why you?"

"Wrong place. Wrong time. I was at Vostok on behalf of Russian government. Was taken. When they found you in my memories, they knew who to take. After that...I was...violated. My mind not my own."

"And now?"

"I am free." He shifts in his seat, wincing. "And...I am sorry. For failing you. For being weak. For..." He takes a deep breath, his eyes closing for a moment like he's fighting sleep. "...for not..."

His eyes roll back. His head flops to the side, taking the rest of him with it. He bounces off the couch, and slides off the leather, landing facedown on the floor before I can stand.

I'm frozen for a moment, looking down at what's left of the Europhids lining Drago's spine. They've been ripped away and torn apart. His back is coated in gelatinous red goo, and more than a little blood.

He did this.

Tore them away.

Mutilated himself so he could escape and give me the key to saving the others.

I crouch beside him, placing my hand against his neck, feeling for a pulse I already know isn't there.

34

There's a kind of despair that manifests quietly, a shift of consciousness where, for a time, reality doesn't feel real anymore. Like you can sense the gaps between atoms and the pointlessness of it all.

It locks me in place against my soldier's instinct to fight.

I should flip him over, perform CPR, rotate to a hospital.

But I can't do any of those things.

Because I know, without a doubt, that Drago is gone.

I've seen enough people die to recognize the moment a soul permanently vacates a body, but Garfunkel is even more sure. The moment Drago destroyed the Europhids controlling him, he sealed his fate. He didn't die because of blood loss. He died because they destroyed his mind from the inside. That he hung on long enough to speak to me is a testament to his strength.

I take Hildy's quilt from the rocking chair and lay it beside Drago. Tears dripping from my eyes, I bark a laugh, knowing that he would eviscerate me with insults at seeing me cry over him. Asshole. I flop him over onto the quilt, eyes now closed, and he's looking for the first time like nothing is weighing on him.

That's when Hildy arrives, unleashing a battle cry and sweeping the living room with a railgun. She stops the moment she sees me. Drops the weapon when she sees Drago.

"What happened?" She kneels down beside me. "Is he sleeping?"

Before I can answer, she deduces the situation. "He's not snoring. He's...not breathing." Her eyes snap to me. "Moses...he's..."

I nod.

"He sacrificed his life for his friends," I say. "To bring us that." I point to the hand.

The hand of a god, or an alien species pretending to be one. I'm not really clear on which, and I don't much give a shit. As long as it works.

Hildy sniffs. Wipes her nose. "I don't understand why this is happening."

"He did," I tell her. "Apparently, the universe needs saving. Chaos is spreading and the ugly sonsabitches that did this to our friend, are going about restoring order in the worst way possible—conquest, genocide, and subjugation."

"Sounds familiar," she says.

"Uh-huh."

"What are we going to do?" she asks.

"We're going to save our friends and then the whole damn universe, and we're going to do it the way Drago would want us to." I smile at her. "We're going to blow shit up."

We cover Drago with the quilt.

WE ARE NOT ALONE.

Hildy turns toward the door. She's still hearing Garfunkel.

"What are we looking at, Garfunkel?" I ask.

I SENSE FORTY EUROPHIDS MERGED WITH FOUR DISTINCT CONSCIOUSNESSES.

THEY HAVE COME FOR HIM.

FOR THE HAND.

WE SHOULD FLEE.

"These assholes killed my friend," I say. "They wiped out your people. Way I see it, they got here just in time. I've got some emotions to work through. Some dark shit to get out of my system."

BE SMART ABOUT IT.

Sometimes having a superior consciousness attached to my own is a real pain in the ass. "Fine." I place my hand on Hildy's shoulder. "Take the hand back to *Lil' Bitch'n*. Get it to Wini. I'll take care of Drago. Meet back here, in the tower, in sixty seconds."

"Where will you take him?" she asks.

"To his home."

She doesn't know where that is, but she understands how in love Drago was with the motherland. Would kill him all over again to be buried in the U.S., in Florida of all places.

She picks up the hand, winces, and says, "Gross..." Then she picks up her railgun, looks at me, and says, "Sixty seconds."

I lift Drago's body in my arms. It's easier than I expect. He's kind of a bear. "Sixty seconds."

We rotate out of the house, Hildy going back to the forbidden island upon which *Lil' Bitch'n* is hidden, and me to a location in Russia no one was supposed to know about.

I slip out of the white and into a dusk-lit forest. All around me, tall pines groan and pop in the wind. The smell of burning wood turns me around to find a candle-lit cabin. This place is as rustic as it gets. Off the grid, back woods living. It's also where Drago grew up, and his family still lives.

The cabin's door opens.

An ox of a man steps out onto the porch, shotgun cradled casually. Must have seen the light from my entrance. He's built like Drago, but his hair and bushy beard have gone yellowy gray. He's dressed in overalls and a plaid flannel, and he sports a belly that hints at too much vodka in his diet. Looks like he could be Drago's father, but the father is long since dead. This is Drago's brother.

When I step toward him, the shotgun comes up a little bit.

But all his brewing aggression is undone when I say, "Mne zhal'."

That's when he notices the shape and size of the bundle I'm carrying. He leans the shotgun against the railing and descends the stairs. A sigh is all he has to say before pulling up the quilt away from Drago's face. "You are Moses."

Not a question, but I nod anyway. Seems Drago told his family about where he'd been, and why he was still young.

"Man who saved future."

"I had help."

He tilts his head, grateful that I'm willing to acknowledge Drago's contribution. "And now what? Now what are you saving?"

He's asking why his brother is dead.

"Saving the universe."

It's an outlandish claim, but he takes it in stride. "Is there anything I can do?"

"Actually..."

When I rotate back to St. Augustine, I've got a shotgun in my hands and a chip on my shoulder.

I whisper into my comms. "Hildy, you there?"

"Yeah," she says. "Where the hell are you?"

I look up at the house. Hildy is exactly where she's supposed to be, atop the house in a pirate ship-style crow's nest we call 'the tower'. No better place to watch a thunderstorm rolling in from the ocean. "Dragon's Lair."

"What?" she shouts, loud enough for me to hear through the comms, and then through the open air a moment later.

"You have eyes on?" I ask, waving up as she looks down the railgun's scope.

"The hell are you thinking?" she asks.

"Getting a little help from my friends," I say.

"We have other friends," she says. "With guns."

"They don't deserve the mercy," I grumble. Fighting dirty isn't my go-to preference, but when you take one of my own... The gloves come off. "Cover my six. If something runs the gauntlet and makes it to me..."

"Yeah, yeah," she says. "I get it."

Gets it, but isn't happy about it. Doesn't need to be.

"I'm over here!" I shout. Then I point my shotgun toward the sky and pull the trigger. "Come get me!"

The report sends gators scurrying, splashing down into the water, slipping out of sight. They might have run, but they're all wet and pissed off now, which is exactly how I want them.

A pair of eyes emerge from the water, cloaked in vegetation.

I lower the shotgun barrel toward them, just in case. "I'm not on the menu." The thump of approaching feet gets our attention.

"Heads, up," I say into my comms. "They're coming."

35

The red Europhids aren't exactly stupid, but they're guided by instinct and overconfidence. They don't plot. They react. Everything that is happening is the result of an overreaction to an outside threat.

Universal chaos.

Planets that have no business interacting are being linked.

And the reds' response to that chaos started like an autoimmune disorder, attacking itself, destroying its mind.

But then it found a replacement mind. A willing partner in its quest to restore order. The Neo-Cryptos, an evolved form of cryptoterrestrial. An Earth species of all things. I don't know much about them other than they're willing participants in the reds' machinations.

That's a big word. Machinations. I file it for later, to impress Chuy after she's safe.

I get a sense that the Neos are intelligent. More so than human beings.

After all, they did manage to leave Earth and populate another planet. Maybe more than one. They could have their own galactic Union out there amidst the stars. The universe is a big place. Difference between the Union and the Neos is that the Union was only a thousand years old. If the Neos have been out there since before the dinosaurs bit the dust, they've been evolving for millions of years. The human race has only been around for three hundred thousand years, and we didn't get modern brains until two thirds of the way through that tiny sliver of time.

I know the Neos are telepathic, but that seems to be the preferred method of communication for advanced species. The Europhids, crypto-terrestrials, Neo-Cryptos, even Hans and Franz. Wouldn't really be surprised if the so-called gods—apparently also aliens—were also telepathic.

Humanity is uncivilized and quaint in comparison to these galactic species, but we make up for it with...how do we make up for it?

Remains to be seen, I suppose.

Let's put *sneakiness* to the test.

I duck lower, pretending to hide. Even if they can't see me, I'm pretty sure the Neos and the reds can sense my presence. If not mine, then certainly Garfunkel's.

And that's fine by me.

The reds have never been to Earth, and the Neo's haven't been here in a very long time. Unless they've got an Encyclopedia Earthica that all little Neos are forced to study in detail, they probably have no knowledge of the planet's flora and fauna. No clear understanding of how people act or the strategies we might employ.

Same can be said about them, but we're not on their damn planet.

So, I let them come.

I welcome it.

"Hildy," I whisper.

"This is crazy," she replies.

"If they're here, it means they came through a gate. See if you can spot it."

There's a pause, and then, "Fine."

The forest at the swamp's periphery rattles as creatures too big to be stealthy shove through the brush. They're confident, on task, and— holy shit—they're big.

Seeing one was mind-bending enough. There're five of them, each as tall as the gators filling the swamp are long. They're also buck naked and nardless. Not one of them is carrying a weapon. Because they *are* weapons. They're powerful creatures, built for strength. Scars covering their pale bodies speak of years of fighting, probably inflicted by each other in hand-to-hand combat. Who knows why. Could just be a toxic macho society with a Klingon-like pecking order. Or maybe they fight as part of a mating ritual. Evolving for millions of years doesn't guarantee idyllic civilizations. Just means they're different now than when they started out. Like Michael Jackson.

I stand from my hiding spot behind a clump of reeds.

The five Neos stop in their tracks on the swamp's far side, fifty feet away, black eyes locking on me.

Their minds reach out to bitch-slap my consciousness into submission.

Vibrations of mental energy flow over me like a river, searching for the chinks in my armor, driving me down to one knee, unable to lift my shotgun.

I am undone.

Subdued. Defenseless.

Just the way they like their prey.

Exactly what they're accustomed to.

I glare at them and through grinding teeth, say, "Come and get me."

Unlike the gators, the Neos do their best to avoid the sun, sticking to the shadows even as they step into the swamp's cold water. *Are they nocturnal?* I wonder. Or perhaps subterranean. The reds spend pretty much their whole lives in the caves and crevices of the planets and moons they inhabit. Maybe the light avoidance is an instinct picked up from them.

Bathed in a circle of sunlight, I feel a little bit safer, but not much. All five Neos are in the water, wading toward me, their focus unwavering.

Menace roils from them.

They're not just going to kill me. They're going to erase me. Going to make sure not a single cell of Garfunkel survives the ordeal.

Waist deep in water, the creature leading the way pauses. Its black eyes lower toward the swamp, detecting movement, or perhaps a consciousness so simple that it can be startled but is immune to manipulation.

All around the swamp, water eddies reveal the presence of movement beneath. The Neos aren't stupid. They get it. Know when they're being hunted. But they're also total badasses. Even the most brazen human killer would hop out of the water, hollering, chased by the mental image of having a limb torn off.

The Neos stand their ground, arms extended, claws ready to swipe, needle teeth bared.

C'mon, I think, willing the gators to strike.

Your swamp has been invaded!

You can eat for days!

But nothing happens. Probably because as big and tough as alligators are, they don't usually eat things that are bigger than them. They need some inspiration. Some literal blood in the water.

Ready for this?

YES.

There's a hunger to Garfunkel's internal voice. He shares my desire for vengeance. This violence is unnecessary. We could rotate the hell out of reach a thousand times. But we're done running. Time to take the fight to the enemy, starting with these assclowns.

I feel a subtle shift as Garfunkel asserts himself, like I've been infused with mental and physical strength. Reminds me of how I felt back on Beta-Prime, when I first merged with the blues. Better. Faster. Stronger. Like that Ye song. It's like I'm a character in Altered Beast—one of Benny's favorite games before being transported to the future and joining the Union. I nearly shout, "power up!" as I stand. Instead, I lift the shotgun and pull the trigger, all without projecting my intentions to the Neos.

The bastard in front never sees it coming, but he sure as shit feels the buckshot pellets when they punch a hole in his chest. Would be instant death for a human being, but I have no idea what it will do to a Neo. Its ribcage could be tough enough to stop bullets. Its heart might be in its butt. Or it could have three of them.

But I wasn't really aiming to kill.

I was aiming to inspire.

Red blood flows out through the water around the Neo as it thrashes. The splashing and the scent of a meal triggers the alligators into action. Swirling water transforms into flowing wakes, as the predators surge toward the invaders.

The downed leader is set upon first. One gator strikes its midsection, the other, its arm. Both of them death roll, tearing flesh and sinew. The alien roars in pain until it's pulled under the water by a third alligator.

A moment later, war breaks out. While two more of the Neos fall to a multi-pronged attack, the other two go on the offensive. They swing down with their thick, claw-tipped fingers, stabbing them through armored flesh and severing spines. Two gators go belly up, but alligators aren't chumps. They'll tear the leg off their best buddy just for getting too close.

For every gator that dies, another two are happy to fill the void, and I'm as pleased as Elvis with a cheeseburger to lend a hand.

With my consciousness protected by Garfunkel, the Neos don't sense my attack coming. It's like I've become invisible. They're so used to that sixth sense that even seeing me turn the shotgun barrel toward them isn't enough to make them flinch.

While two of the Neos thrash and wail in the grip of gators, the other two drop into the waiting jaws, courtesy of my Russian shotgun. Seems fitting that they would die at the hands of a weapon that belongs to Drago's brother.

In the end, just one of the Neos remains standing. It's missing an arm, bleeding profusely, and it stands with its back toward me, the line of red Europhids running down its spine.

I take aim and pull the trigger one last time, splattering the reds and dropping the beast to its knees where it's set upon by the now frenzied gators.

I'm about to say something mind-blowingly cool, when Hildy shouts, "Behind you!"

Spinning around, I find a wall of white muscle descending toward me, and there's not a damn thing I can do to stop it.

36

When danger is imminent, and your reptile brain takes over, triggering a fight or flight response, time seems to slow, and details—in the moment before your vision tunnels—seem to pop.

The Neo isn't just muscular, it's ripped. Beneath the skin, which is so white that it's translucent, is a network of blue veins layered over what looks like metal cables, but they're actually muscles, twitching and flexing.

This thing could tear me in half like wet toilet paper.

The creature's claws reach out for me, aiming for my arms, and I can see what's going to happen. I'll be grasped, lifted, and drawn and quartered, first the arms, then the legs. As I bleed out, mind numbed by shock, the reds will take care of Garfunkel—however that might happen.

All of this is written in stone.

Three seconds in the future, it's already happened.

But the future can be changed.

A half dozen slits open up the Neo's chest, severing veins, sinew, muscle, bone, and whatever else might be in there. A blink later, and the creature just comes apart, carved up from the inside by railgun discs.

The wall of white inverts, shifting from pink to red as the creature comes apart to form a tidal wave of gore, crashing down on my position. Somehow, getting doused in guts is what triggers my reaction. Muscle memory guides my hand to my hip, activates the slew drive, and I rotate away.

For a moment, I stand in the empty white void, collecting myself.

That was close.

Sloppy.

Vengeance is never tactical. And dying never accomplishes anything—unless your last name happens to be Christ.

But something had to be done with all that negative energy. "We need to focus now."

I wait for a response, but I get nothing. "Yo. Garfunkel."

An absence rolls over me. Feels like something has been removed. "Garfunkel?"

Pressure builds behind my eyes.

The whiteness of the void inhabits me, washing existence away.

I am formless. A vapor consciousness.

THE TIME HAS COME.

"Garfunkel... Thank god. What...time has come?"

DANGER HASTENED THE CHANGE.

"Is this like a puberty thing? Because I—"

YES. WE ARE CHANGING. MERGING. BECOMING NEW.

If I had a stomach, it would be twisted into knots. I'd shelved this particular dilemma, in which one or both of us cease to exist. If I'd known that danger accelerated the process, I probably wouldn't have planted myself at the center of a gator-filled swamp and invited a half dozen aliens to play Whack-a-Human. "There's nothing we can do about it?"

IT HAS NEVER BEEN IN OUR CONTROL.
IT HAS NEVER BEEN DONE BEFORE.
WE ARE UNIQUE IN THE UNIVERSE.
AND I AM...PLEASED THAT THE MERGING IS WITH YOU.
WITH...US...

"With me," I say, and I'm surrounded by mental silence, like the ocean's waves have gone still, their constant rumble muted.

I'm quiet, inside and out, filled with a new kind of understanding... about everything. I feel connected to the universe, past, present, and far reaching. My consciousness expands. Knowledge blossoms. What was separate becomes part of the whole.

Garfunkel is no longer a symbiote.

I am Garfunkel. And I am Moses.

"This is so weird," I say, and I feel relieved that all of my feelings, memories and core personality remain intact. But I *am* different. Smarter. Wiser. Older. Freakin' ancient. While the memories that make up Moses are at the core of my consciousness, I have access to the totality of blue Europhid knowledge. Back to the beginning. All of it's contained in my human mind, which is no longer human. My DNA has been altered. Every cell made new. Every synapse firing more efficiently.

I'm human in my heart, but I'm not really human at all.

Not anymore.

And...I don't mind.

Because it's necessary. This is how the blues survive. This is how I save my friends. This is how we stop whatever evil is behind the universal chaos.

Up until this moment, I never realized that Garfunkel had been concerned with the larger picture. I was so focused on the immediate threat that I never bothered to consider what universal threat had triggered the red revolt in the first place.

"One step at a time," I tell myself, and I rotate back to Earth, arriving in the tower, behind two curly blonde heads, looking down into the swamp where I'd been just a moment before. Everything I just experienced in the fourth dimension happened in a real time nano-second.

Cassidy throws up her hands. "Did you see that!? Whoa! He was all, 'Come get me.' And then the alligators. That was gross, but *yes!* And that last one. It nearly got him, but then you—and it was just like, *splat!* And then *whoosh!* And then I was like, 'it's gonna cover Moses in blood and poop and stuff!' But then he was just, *poof!* That...was the best thing I've ever seen in my life. Like violent poetry. Better than Five Nights. Hands down. Someone needs to put that in a screenplay and let Zack Snyder film it in slow motion, because...*wow.*"

I clear my throat, turning the pair around.

I know I caught them off guard, but both of them scream and flinch away. Hildy lifts her railgun, finger on the trigger.

She's going to shoot.

Dodging is easier than it should be. Hildy is fast. But a quick sidestep gets me clear, and my hand on the weapon's barrel aims it toward the tower's ceiling which is obliterated by three rail rounds a moment later.

"Moses!" Hildy shouts, realizing her mistake.

"I shouldn't have snuck up on you," I say.

"It's not just that," Cassidy says. "Your eyes are glowing."

"*Really* glowing," Hildy says, meaning that they're brighter than she's seen them before.

I close my eyes. Try to relax and clear my mind. Then I open them again. "What about now?"

"Like headlights," Cassidy says.

"Problem for another time," I say, and then I set my eyes on Cassidy. "What is she doing here?"

"She grabbed hold of me," Hildy says. "Wouldn't let go. You said sixty seconds, and I didn't want to be late, so..."

"It was rad," Cassidy says.

"I heard," I say. "And it *was* pretty rad."

Cassidy smiles wide, starting to bounce from foot to foot, probably from the realization that they're not in trouble. We have bigger problems. "Did you connect with Wini?" I ask Hildy.

"Briefly."

"You give her the hand?"

"Also awesome," Cassidy says.

Hildy nods.

"Good. Now we just need to find a gate."

I reach for my slew drive, but Hildy stops me. "Isn't there a gate here, somewhere?"

She's right, and the old me would have gone through it guns-a-blazin'. But the new and wiser me thinks a frontal assault, sans an alligator army, might not be the best idea. "Also..." I point to the forest, which is starting to shake as a small army charges toward the house. "They have reinforcements. And I can't risk my life fighting them now. I'm the last of my kind."

Hildy and Cassidy look at me and collectively says, "Huh?"

Instead of explaining, I take hold of them both and rotate us back to North Sentinel Island, one of the most dangerous places on Earth, but it's half a world away from the alien invasion currently underway in Florida.

37

"You look...different," Wini says after tracking me down in my quarters. Time is short, but I needed a breather after returning with Hildy and Cassidy, and then rotating the *Lil' Bitch'n* back into the *Bitch'n*'s hangar.

"Lost a friend," I say, and then I realize she's talking about my eyes. "Right. Garfunkel and I merged. It was a whole thing. Might be stuck like this."

"Merging. That what the kids call it nowadays?" She smiles, but it falters when she sees past the obvious and notes my heavy heart. "Sorry. Who did you lose?"

"Drago," I said.

"The hairy Russian? Lost him to the Europhids, you mean," she says. "There might still be a chance we can—"

"He's dead," I say. "Gave his life to get us that hand." I look up. "Which is where, by the way?"

"McCoy is keeping an eye on the thing while Burnett studies it and the chunk of Gate we took along for the ride when we rotated out of Antarctica. It was lodged in a bathroom apparently."

Makes sense. When *Lil' Bitch'n'* rotated into the ice cave, it would have destroyed anything it physically encountered, but anything in the gaps, like us and the ice floor would have remained intact. There are probably slices of the gate filling gaps in the ship.

"You and Drago were close?" she asks.

"At first, we hated each other. It was the Cold War. He was a card-carrying communist and I was as red, white, and blue as they come. But in the future, neither set of ideals existed. We had no choice but to become friends. Went through a lot together. I just..."

Emotions swirl, but I lock them down.

My focus needs to be razor sharp. There's no margin for error. No room for sniffles or sadness.

Then Wini sits down beside me and rubs my back.

It's like she's reached inside my chest, slapped open the padlocks on the door hiding my inner child, and kicked it open. Tears tap on the floor as I lean forward, forehead gripped in my hands. It's too much.

"I'm not going to see her again," I say.

"Don't know that."

"These things... The Order... They aren't held back by human concepts of morality."

"They won't make very good bait if they're dead," she says.

"No way to know if they're alive or dead until we kick down their door. Until then, they're Schrödinger's friends. We'll determine their fate when we try to rescue them. But death might not be the worst, or even most likely end."

She nods slowly. She's already figured this out. "They could make them like him. Like Drago."

"Almost certainly did. Because we'll come for them no matter what. Could look like balloon strippers, covered in those red assholes, and it won't stop us from trying. They know that. Not much we can do now that they won't see coming, not with access to Chuy's, Cowboy's, and Delgado's memories and knowledge of us. Not a plan we can come up with that they won't anticipate."

We sit in silence together, Wini slowly rubbing my back.

When she stops, it's a shock to my system, slamming my subconscious door closed. She sucks in a breath and sits up straighter.

"What?" I ask.

"Dan knows me too well," she says. "Chuy and Cowboy know you."

"That's what I'm saying."

"So, we need to let someone else come up with a plan. Someone neither of them can predict. Someone no one in the galaxy can figure out."

When I realize who she's talking about, I balk. "You can't be serious."

"They'll never see it coming. Won't make sense of what they're seeing."

"Neither will we," I say.

"That's why it will work."

It's crazy, but in a weird sort of way, it makes sense. The Order doesn't like chaos. It can't be planned for or predicted. "Okay...but if it's too nuts, we're coming up with something different."

She nods, and I toggle my comms. I'm about to speak, but second thoughts hold my tongue hostage for a moment. When I can't think of a better idea, I say, "Hey, Cassidy."

"Hold on!" she shouts.

"Just need you to—"

"One—ugh—second!"

Wini and I share a confused glance. And wait.

Thirty seconds later she's back on comms. "Okay. Sorry. I'm back. Was pooping. What's up? Am I in trouble? Because I thought we were cool with the whole sneaking to Florida and—"

"Cassidy Rose," Wini says, silencing the girl. "Come to Moses's quarters. We need to speak to you."

She goes quiet for a moment and then says, "K..."

Wini leans back. "You lived in this junk heap, in space, for how long?"

"Five years," I say.

She shakes her head. "How'd you do it?"

"Had a mission," I say. "Same as now. Find my friends. Try to save them."

"Well, let's try not to take five years this time around."

I smile. "Not a chance."

We sit in silence for a moment. Long enough for it to become awkward. Then the door opens, and chaos enters, doing a cartwheel, bouncing on her feet, throwing her hands up and saying, "Reporting for duty."

Wini looks at me. "You see?"

"Look," Cassidy says, "I know what you're going to say." She marches in place, elbows swinging high, feet stomping, her face scrunched up and lowered like an old miser. She waggles a finger. "Young lady, that was a foolish thing to do. Next time you act without thinking, I'm going to—"

Wini snaps her fingers and Cassidy falls silent and still. "First, was that supposed to be me or him?" She hitches her thumb at me. "You know what, I don't want to know. Second, that's not at all what we want you to do."

Cassidy's eyebrows raise. "Oh! Well then..." She crosses her arms, makes a stern face. "I run a tight ship around here. People do what I say, when I say it, and not a moment later."

"Okay," I say, "that's definitely supposed to be me."

"Well, that's what's happening, right? Even though you—" She points her finger at me and stomps one foot. "—seemed pretty cool about me coming along for the ride. Or is that just because you got all aliened up and were distracted and now that you're talking to Mother Goose—"

"Ho-lee shit." Wini stands. "Did you just call me Mother Goose?"

"Would you prefer Mama Fratelli?"

I laugh despite myself. *The Goonies* reference was clearly intended for me, and it got the reaction she was hoping for. Cassidy pumps her fist and starts jogging in place.

When Wini snaps to me for an explanation, I raise my hands. "You don't want to know."

"You look angry," Cassidy says to Wini, twisting her lips. "Should I start running now?"

"I changed my mind," Wini grumbles.

"She's kind of perfect," I admit.

Cassidy stops moving. "Who's perfect? Wait. Am I not in trouble? If not, I was totes joking about Mama Fratelli."

"Can you stand still while I talk to you?" I ask.

"Yes," she says, wiggling her legs. Then she attempts to stop...and fails miserably. She jumps up and down, shaking out her hands. Then she attempts to compose herself. Clear her throat. Wipes off her—I'm assuming sweaty—palms on her legs. She clears her throat again and says, "Okay. I'm good. Fill me in."

I wait a moment, to see if she's going to remain still or if I'm going to be interrupted by her impression of a one-legged grasshopper in a hundred-yard dash. When she holds her position for ten seconds, I ask, "How are you feeling? Like, big picture feeling? You've seen some—"

"I'm good. Great."

"You're sure?"

She stands up straighter. Locks her hands behind her back. Lifts her chin a little. Going for a military vibe.

Not really pulling it off. "Honestly, I...kind of feel like I was made for this, you know. I mean, you must know."

"Stop trying to impress me," I say, standing so she has to look up at me. "I was just in here crying my eyes out over my dead friend and the possible horrible fate faced by my teammates and your..." I turn to Wini. "What is he to them?"

"They call him father," she says.

Shit.

Can't stop now.

"Your father...is in deep shit."

Cassidy is trying to keep a stiff upper lip, but she's struggling.

"He might die," I say. "Or worse, be control—"

"I know!" Cassidy shouts, a wave of emotional energy washing through me and Wini. In that moment, I know she gets it. Know she feels exactly how I'm feeling.

"Sorry," I say. "I needed to be sure you understood and were facing reality."

She wipes a tear from her eye. "Been facing it for a long time."

I nod. "Good."

She glances to Wini and then back to me. "Why...is that good?"

"Means you're ready."

Her eyes widen. "For what?"

I can't help but smile. "To lead."

"Lead? Like... I don't get it. What would you want me to lead?"

I lean down to look her in the eyes. "The rescue mission."

38

Cassidy's giddy scream echoes throughout the ship.

Before she's run out of air in her lungs, the door to my quarters slides open and Hildy charges in, railgun in hand, looking like a blonde Ellen Ripley, ready to gun down, torch, or blast whoever was hurting Cassidy out the damn airlock.

When she sees it's just the three of us, and the smile on Cassidy's face, she lowers the weapon. "Everything is...okay?"

Cassidy high kicks. "They asked me to lead the rescue mission!"

Hildy cranes her head toward me, and by the time our eyes meet, she's wearing the same expression Chuy does when I put ketchup on my fish tacos.

"Hear me out," I say.

"She's too young," Hildy says. "She's...never been in combat."

"Have too," Cassidy says.

"She's impulsive and...and..."

I place my hand on Hildy's shoulder. Part of this is genuine concern for Cassidy's well-being, which I share, but she's also jealous. Don't need to be part Europhid to see it, either. Hildy has been wanting more responsibility, to take part in more dangerous missions. And now I'm putting the lives of our teammates in the hands of a compulsive teenager with no real combat experience. She can face down a rygar. She's tough, and brave. But her strategy...

"Chaos," I say. "That's the key to getting our people back. The Order knows us. What we can do. How we do it. What buttons to push to guide us into a trap. The only chance we have of thwarting that..."

I turn my gaze to Cassidy, who is doing wall push-ups, clapping her hands as many times as she can before catching herself a micron away from faceplanting. She spins around, suddenly serious. "Are you saying I'll be in charge—"

"Won't be in charge," I say.

"That I'll be strategizing the rescue mission…and leading it…because I'm kind of pistachio?"

"What?" I ask.

"Nuts," Wini says, fluent in Cassidyese.

"Kid," I say with a grin, "you're a whole bag of mixed nuts with yogurt balls tossed in."

"Yogurt balls! Yum." She plants her hands on her hips and then shakes back and forth. "So, if we were Vikings, I would be…"

"Ohh, Vikings," Hildy says. "Viking Pirates?"

Cassidy thinks on this for a moment and then says, "Viking Raiders?"

Hildy raises an index finger. "Shield Maidens."

Cassidy gets a real crafty look in her eyes. "*Berserker* Maidens."

Hildy's eyes widen. "Ohh, yes. That."

The two girls perform a memorized, intricate handshake to agree on it.

"When did this happen?" I ask. "The whole handshake thing?"

They both shrug.

"Here and there," Hildy says.

"Do you want a handshake, too?" Cassidy asks. "Wini has one." She turns to Wini, and the two work their way through another, totally different handshake that ends with looking over their shoulders and batting their eyes.

I don't know what the hell is happening, but it's not helpful. "I think we should be focusing on other things."

"When should I get started?" Cassidy asks.

"Whenever you're ready," I say. Time feels short, like we should be storming the enemy gates any minute, but we still don't have a gate, or a plan.

Until those things happen…

Cassidy bites her lower lip and turns her eyes to the ceiling. Her face contorts, scrunching up.

"Is she having a stroke?" I ask.

Then she lights up like a Christmas display and starts laughing like she's Dark Helmet...which might be an accurate comparison.

"Well," Wini says. "Spit it out."

"I have a plan. Wait. No." She gasps. "Yes. Yes!" She runs in place while spinning in a circle. Then she does a quick stop and breaks into a dance.

"Quit the Tik Tok dance and tell us!" Wini says.

"You know what Tik Tok is?" Hildy asks, genuinely impressed, and I have no idea why. Tik Tok is the sound a clock makes.

"Honey," Wini says. "I'm Tik Tok famous. Five hundred thousand followers, thank you very much." She turns back to Cassidy. "Now, spill it."

"I have three questions," Cassidy says to me. "Did Vikings and dinosaurs live at the same time?"

"What?" I say. "No."

"Do you know what Gimme Chocolate is?"

"Unless we're at a Hershey factory, no idea."

"Have you ever had happy diarrhea?"

I frown. "Not sure there is such a thing."

A Cheshire grin spreads slowly across her face. It's genuinely creepy, and I'm already feeling a little bad for The Order. We're about to silly spray the shit out of an OCD convention.

She leans toward me, all conspiratorial, and says, "Okay...here's the plan."

Ten minutes later, she seems to take her first breath. Hands on her hips, feet starting to kick like an Irish dancer, she says, "So...what do you think?"

"Moses," Wini says. "It's...I don't know... Too much?"

It's ape-shit bonkers is what it is.

I'm not even sure we can pull it off. It's just all over the place and nonsensical—on the surface. But many layers down, like at the bottom of the Grand Canyon down, everything kind of coalesces and makes sense. Chaos—most of which is a Cassidy Rose fever dream—held together by the loosest thread.

"Not one of her choices is something you or I would do," I say.

"Or anyone else in their right mind." Wini turns to Cassidy. "No offense."

The girl shrugs and starts kicking her legs like a line dancer. "I'm good with who I am."

"I think it will work," Hildy says.

Hildy isn't a soldier yet, but her understanding of military tactics, especially those employed by her ancestors, is like everything else she puts her mind to—impeccable.

"Why?" I ask.

"There are several different tactics utilized during military deception campaigns. On the surface, Cassidy's plan is a diversion, but it's also more than that. It's a feint, a ruse, a display, and a demonstration."

"Those aren't all the same things?" Wini asks.

"Related, but with subtle differences ranging from trickery at a distance to direct contact with the enemy. Cassidy's plan incorporates all these things, but even more than that—there is a chance that she could succeed without your involvement. If all of the elements she mentioned are real—"

"They are," Wini says.

"—and are willing—"

"Won't give most of them a choice," Wini says. "And those that do... they'll say yes."

"You're comfortable putting them in danger?" I ask.

"They won't be the ones in danger," Cassidy says, her confidence mirroring mine before a mission I know is going to end well.

But I'm not sure.

There are so many moving elements. So many unknowns. It's a lot of trust to put in other people...and non-people.

But that's also the point. If I was comfortable with everything, it would be a bad idea. My discomfort means we're good to go.

Sort of.

"Rally the troops and get them armed," I tell Wini. And then to Cassidy, I say, "Talk to your people, but...be honest. There are risks involved, and I don't want them doing anything stupid."

"I'll be the stupidest," Cassidy says.

"Yeah," I say, "I heard the plan. Hildy...connect with Burnett. See if you can help him figure out the gates. I know you want to see more action, but without some brains behind our madness, we're just going to be making a lot of noise."

She nods. "Understood."

It's unusual for Hildy to not complain about being left out of a field op. She loves the thrill of action, even when it's dangerous. But Cassidy's plan is a whole different brand of cuckoo. It's not that Hildy's afraid. She just understands that someone needs to make sense of the ensuing pandemonium. As a person capable of comprehending the universe, that's her.

"What are you going to do?" Wini asks.

I let out a long sigh. Shit's about to be flung into a turbine. Time to say goodbye to friends and family not coming along for the ride. For me, that's just one person. "I'm going to SeaWorld."

39

To ensure I don't materialize in front of a school group, I emerge from the fourth dimension in a supply closet that smells of bleach and rotted fish. I exit, coughing and gagging and spitting...in front of a school group.

Twenty sets of eyes stare at me.

"Uh, hi guys." I point my thumb at the closet door behind me as I close it. "I was looking for the bathroom. Turned out to be a supply closet."

One of the kids, a wide-eyed chubby white dude rocking slicked back red hair and an '80s style upturned collar, turns to his teacher and asks in a squeaky voice, "Why was he in the closet?"

"Bathroom," I say. "I just explained..."

The kid ignores me, focusing on his teacher as she swoops in all hawk-like, "Ms. Wilbur, I think he was doing drugs in the closet."

A little girl chimes in. "I think he was masturbating. My mommy says that if a boy spends too much time behind a closed door, he's doing Satan's work."

Before I can deny the accusations flying in my direction, the teacher shoos them along, scowling at me over her glasses. "You keep away from them."

I'm about to complain when the woman's venomous stare and hissed words strike a familiar chord. She doesn't think I'm on drugs or wang jangling in the closet, she just doesn't think a black man should be speaking to the gaggle of cherubs. Meanwhile, here I am trying to save the world. I cup my hand to my mouth and shout, "Stay in school! Don't do drugs!" and then I whisper, "Just say no to the Klan..."

That's when I turn around and catch my reflection in a fish tank... still dressed in the skintight adaptive armor. "Huh..." When the teacher glances back at me, I shout, "I'm feeding the fish!"

She rolls her eyes and struts away in her tight, brown plaid skirt and nude colored hosiery.

"And this is why life in space is sometimes preferable..." I make my way through Sea World's vast complex feeling a little self-conscious. On the battlefield, the armor probably looks badass, but here, out of context, I look like I forgot I was wearing cosplay for a hero no one recognizes.

I sigh with relief when I see my destination ahead.

The dolphin enclosure.

When they're not doing shows, the dolphins can swim up to this glass wall and say hello. And several of them do. Their perpetual smiles and interest are confusing. I'm looking for the dolphin that knows me, but they're all operating at the same level of 'Look! A human!'

"Nice outfit."

I turn around to find Laylah, the lead dolphin trainer, standing behind me dressed in an actual wetsuit. She gives me a once over, a sassy eyebrow raised.

I shrug. "Trying to fit in."

"People are talking about it all the way to the front desk. Something about a pervert in a closet, too."

"Unrelated," I assure her.

"Either way, mission failed." She gives me a grin like we're connecting, and I suppose we are. She's always acted like we've been lifelong friends, even though I met her just a few months ago.

"Haven't seen you around lately," she says. "Still saving the world?"

To acquire Laylah's help, we had to dial her in. Probably didn't need to tell her everything, but she was inquisitive, open-minded, and a really good guesser. Also, she saw me rotate in during my first visit. She's been on board since, helping house our wayward teammate.

"Something like that," I say. "How is he?"

"She's doing great," Laylah says. "By dolphin standards. Very sociable. Playing a lot of games. Seems to really enjoy swimming and the company of her new friends."

"He's making...friends?" I ask. "Dolphin friends?"

"Yes. She is."

"*He* isn't known for being super friendly," I say, and then I add, "Hey..."

And somehow, we ask the same question at the same time. "Why are you doing that?"

She smiles at our overlap and says, "Sorry. Doing what?"

"Calling him a *her*."

Her brow furrows. "Because she is a she?"

"You don't sound sure," I say.

"Oh, I'm sure."

My eyes widen with the slow assuredness of a sunrise. "BigApe's mind...is in a *female* dolphin?"

"Hold on," she says, her shock growing with mine. "The consciousness you transferred was *male?*"

"Oh," I say. "Oh man..."

Our eyes meet and we burst out laughing in unison.

"Oh, god. Oh shit. Well, I suppose it's better than his last merger."

"When he was embedded in a hairy Russian's chest?"

I nod. "Do you think he knows?"

"Oh," she says, nodding. "He knows."

I'm not sure what that means, but she starts walking and says, "Follow me. Let's go say hi."

I chase after her, working our way around the large pool, heading for Dolphin Lagoon, where people can interact with dolphins for fistfuls of cash. "I'm actually here to say goodbye."

"Weren't joking about the whole 'saving the world' thing?"

"Might be more than the world this time," I say. "We'll see."

"That why the others aren't with you?" she asks. "I see Burnett all the time, but you and Chuy, and that guy with the cowboy hat—"

"Cowboy," I say.

"Obviously," she says. "You all are normally a package deal. They okay?"

"Remains to be seen," I say, putting off serious *I don't want to talk about it* vibes.

"Well, I hope it works out," she says. "Whatever it is."

We round the corner and step out into the pristine and very fake bay. Dolphins frolic in the deeper waters, leaping and spinning. Appears to be five dolphins following a leader.

"Am I seeing what I think I'm seeing?" I ask.

"Uh-huh. She...he...has them wrapped around her...his flipper."

"Do they...you know?"

She raises an eyebrow. "They're dolphins."

"Right. Got it." I head for the shallows. "I've got it from here, thanks."

The lead dolphin leaps into the air, turning in my direction. When it sees me, it surges ahead of the others and enters the shallows. The five...male dolphins linger a little deeper, swimming back and forth.

BigApe squeaks a greeting at me.

"Heyyy man. Good to see you." *Don't mention it. Just say your piece. Don't judge. He's a female dolphin. Nothing to be done about it. Nature and all that.* "You can still understand me, right?"

His head bobs up and down.

"Still there? Like mentally. Still thinking straight? I mean, not straight. Poor choice of words. Whatever, I'm not doing that on porpoise."

He squeaks a laugh, and I have no idea if it's at my confusion, or if he thinks my wordplay is intentional.

"Hey, what happens in the Dolphin Lagoon stays in Dolphin Lagoon. You be you. Or whatever you'd be as a dolphin."

BigApe swims away and then emerges from the water, straight up, tail-walking past me. He flops into the water and then pops back up, tail-walking in the opposite direction.

"Oookay."

When he returns, I say, "Seems like you really like it here," he nods and lets out a squeak. "Should we keep looking for a solution? A way to get you into a different body?"

He tilts his head for a moment and then swishes his whole body back and forth. An emphatic no.

"Good," I say. "That's good."

And it is, because there's a chance we won't be coming back.

"Look. Here's the deal. We're headed out on a mission. It's already FUBAR. If we don't come back... If you don't see me again... Well, it was a pleasure serving with you. And I'm glad...you're happy."

He swims a little closer, head resting against my leg. I give him an awkward pat.

"Wouldn't do that," Laylah calls out. "They get jealous."

"Huh?" I look up to find five dorsal fins bouncing through the water, coming my way. "Holy shit!" I high-knee it out of the water, pursued by BigApe's all-male harem.

Back on shore, I turn to face the water, watching BigApe swim away, happy as a...well, happy as a sexually liberated dolphin, I suppose.

"That must have been weird," Laylah says, standing beside me, trying not to laugh.

"Lady," I say, "I'm about to go fight aliens with asshole faces, covered in little red, mind controlling dildos. This is one of the most normal things I've seen in the last twenty-four hours. Wish me luck."

Before she can, I rotate back to the *Bitch'n'* feeling confused, but also like I've got a little closure. Like I can finally—nope. Nnnnope. Nope, nope, nope. I need to talk to someone about this or I'm going to be as distracted as a golden retriever in a tennis ball factory.

I step out of the fourth dimension and into the hangar bay, coming face to face with McCoy and Mazzola. "You'll do."

40

McCoy and Mazzola stare at me, both of their mouths open a little bit. Somehow, even the cryptoterrestrial's strange face and black eyes express shock.

"I might need you to run all that by me again," McCoy says.

"BigApe merged with a Russian when we were transported to the future. Kind of like what happened to Jeff Goldblum in that movie, *The Fly*, except they were two separate consciousnesses in one body, and both of them were human. When we came back in time, they separated. BigApe survived, but over time, his body, which hadn't really existed for years, began to deteriorate. The only way to save him was to move his consciousness into *another* body. For ethical reasons, we couldn't use another human being, so we chose—"

"A dolphin," McCoy finishes. "A female dolphin."

"I didn't know it was female," I say. "Until today."

"The transference of a consciousness from one body to another is an impressive feat," Mazzola communicates via telepathy.

"Apparently it was common in the future," I say. "Union leaders would transfer their minds into clones of themselves, improved by genetic tinkering, in an effort to become more and more superior."

"Well," McCoy says, "Superiority is a lot like beauty: in the eyes of the beholder."

"Except for *Terminator 2*," I say. "Watched that about a month back. Way better than the first."

"No argument there," McCoy says. "So...is there anything to be done about BigApe?"

I shake my head. "He seems...happy."

McCoy sits frozen for a moment, and then says, "Huh..."

"Right?!" I say, throwing my hands in the air.

"It is likely," Mazzola says, "that the dolphin's consciousness remains at least partially intact. In this future you speak of, memories were transferred from an adult mind to an infant's mind. Essentially a blank slate, and in theory, an identical mind."

"You're saying that BigApe is...no longer BigApe?"

"Perhaps. But it might be more accurate to refer to him as BigDolphin. Either way, he appears to be a willing participant in the merger, unlike your friend who was...infected by the red growths. The Europhids. There are parallels between the two. If your captured friends are less amenable to the shared consciousness, perhaps there is a way to undo it, using the technology used to transfer—"

"BigDolph," I say. "'Dolphin' is too clunky."

"Mmm," Mazzola says, but it's more displeasure at being interrupted than agreement. "I'm sure your friends would appreciate you spending more time pondering a new codename, than on resolving their current situation."

"It's a coping mechanism," I say, and then I turn back to McCoy, "This guy needs to read some Brené Brown."

"Brené who?" he asks.

"I don't know," I say, waving my hand. "Burnett's always reading her stuff, making himself feel like a warrior in an arena or something. Point is, what people talk about isn't always what we're thinking about."

Mazzola tilts his head. "A keen observation."

"I'm full of keen observations," I say. "Like you, playing the part of solemn intellectual, when in fact, you're all over the place emotionally. Because you're a man lost in time—can I call you a man?"

"In the broadest sense."

"Great," I say. "And I get it. That's a gnarly place to be. I've been there."

McCoy nods. He gets it.

But not all of it.

"You've been taken to the future only to discover that your people became grade A assholes, they're wreaking havoc throughout the universe, and they need to be stopped, right? Feels shitty."

"You couldn't possibly—"

"Have a look for yourself," I think, and I open my mind. Whatever part of me is or was Garfunkel knows how to protect itself from the minds of others, and also how to open the floodgates. I tap the side of my head. "All aboard the future Nazi express train."

Mazzola lowers his face to mine, his black eyes widening, my incoming tide of memories crashing over him. He works his way backward through my life, not just getting the broad strokes, but absorbing it all. In return, he offers nothing.

When he gets to my childhood, I cut him off. "That's enough. Getting a little voyeuristic for my taste."

The comment doesn't faze him. Whatever moral code the cyptoterrestrials of his time went by, it's not the same as present day humanity's. Which isn't surprising, since the moral code of a hundred years ago isn't the same as it is today. He's adapting to modern humanity just fine, though. Probably because he's been diving into people's heads and taking the tour. Not great, but if I had access to people's minds when I was in the future, I'd have done the same thing. Hell, I hijacked a spaceship and its crew.

"We are not that dissimilar," he says, and then he adds, "aside from the obvious...and your unwavering belief that you are funny."

"Wha—hey... That's not—"

His big black eyes squint. His snout pulls back a bit, like he's baring his teeth.

Then he begins to huff.

I turn to McCoy. "Is he laughing? Do cryptoterrestrials laugh?" I turn to Mazzola. "Are you laughing?"

The huffing continues, but it's joined by McCoy's human laugh.

"I'm not sure this day can get any weirder," I say.

"Dark Horse, you there?" It's Hildy, via my comms.

"Got something for me?" I ask, eager to think about anything other than the last hour.

"Maybe, but it's not exactly what you're hoping for."

"Where you at?" I ask.

"Engineering Lab," she says. Once upon a time, the *Bitch'n* was a salvage ship built to withstand the rigors of that job, making her a tough nut to crack. Since I've been captain, she's been transmogrified into a battleship, armory, secret base, and laboratory—for totally normal things like teleporting through space, railguns, and consciousness transfers.

"Been a delight, gents," I say with a quick salute that feels sarcastic. "Honestly, thanks for listening. Needed to get that out of my system."

"Don't blame you at all," McCoy says. "We've all been in your shoes."

I squint at him. "Have you, though?"

"I mean, who hasn't had a friend turned into a dolphin?" he turns to Mazzola. "Am I right?"

The big white dino-human is already huffing its unsettling laugh.

"Nice," I say, and I rotate away, stepping into and out of the fourth dimension, arriving in the lab to find Hildy and Burnett lip-locked. "Son of a—" I grumble.

"Sometimes the urge just strikes," Burnett says.

I close my eyes and say, "Please... Just... Can we be normal for a few minutes? I'm having a day."

Hildy leans in close to his ear and whispers loud enough for me to hear. "He went to see BigApe."

"Oh," Burnett says. "Ooooh."

"You knew?" I hold up my hands. "You know what? Doesn't matter. Don't want to talk about it. Already got it out of my system."

"Okay," Burnett says, forcing cheer into his voice, like a faux-German Richard Simmons. He claps his hands together. "First thing. You should stop rotating everywhere."

"Yeah, I know. We don't know how prolonged exposure will affect my physiology, blah, blah, blah."

"Did you know," Burnett asks Hildy, like they're conspirators in some secret plan, "that Dark Horse once had sex in the fourth—"

I clear my throat. "Let's stick to the—"

"With Chuy?"

Wide-eyed, he shakes his head and says, "It's scandalous, no?"

I stab a finger at Burnett. "That was *before* Chuy and I were a thing, and I get it. I'll start walking around the ship."

Burnett nods, satisfied. "You need to get your steps in, yah?"

"Going to get my steps in on your ass, if you don't get to part two of your presentation lickity-damn-split."

"Okay, okay," Burnett says, hands raised like I'm serious, though he knows I'd never do anything to hurt him. The lovebirds step aside, revealing the laboratory. It's big enough, and well equipped enough, for a team of scientists. But Burnett and Hildy, with their knowledge of future tech, are able to conjure just about anything given enough time.

Resting on a lab table between them is a five-foot-tall segment of the gate we took along for the ride. Looks like it's made of hand-carved stone, but that can't be the case. "What is it?"

"The texture and engravings made it difficult to recognize, but identifying it was easy...for us. It would be a mystery to anyone else on Earth."

I know that was supposed to be a hint, but I'm not in the mood for guessing games. I'm about to complain when the answer comes unbidden from the depths of my newfound memory, and the fact that I'm surrounded by it. "You're shitting me?"

Burnett shakes his head. "It's pure Oxium."

Oxium is a super light, super strong metal used to build the Union's intergalactic empire. Every ship. Every structure. Every weapon. Including most of the *Bitch'n'* and everything inside it. Though, not in its raw form.

"Will that help us find another gate?" I ask.

He shakes his head. "I'm afraid not. But I think there is another solution."

Hildy grins. "We can build our own gate."

"Using scraps from *Bitch'n?*" I ask.

Hildy shakes her head, slowly, solemn. "The Oxium on board is refined."

"This is pure," Burnett says. "And there is only one place to get it."

Shit.

"Command Central," I say.

Hildy nods. "We need to go back."

41

"Command Central?" McCoy says. "Kind of on the nose, don't you think? Who all named things in the future?"

"Nazis weren't known for their creativity," I point out.

"Point taken," he says. "When do we leave?"

"*We* don't," I say. "This one is for me and Hildy. Under the radar. No fights."

"Fight is kind of what you do," Wini points out, leaning back against the cargo bay wall, arms crossed. She's got an edge to her that I think is concern, which I share. The longer all this takes, the more likely we won't be seeing our loved ones again. At least not how we remember them. "Sure you can handle the subtle approach?"

"If you put your mind to it, you can accomplish anything."

"Are you quoting Ben Franklin?" McCoy asks.

"What? No. George McFly."

Wini closes her eyes and shakes her head. Turns away from me.

"You okay?" I ask.

"Okay?" Wini whirls around on me. "*Okay?* Hell no, I'm not okay. Dan entrusted you with the fate of the entire world, and you're quoting *Back to the Future?* How can you be so cavalier? So god-damned silly all the time?"

"Some of us were born with a sense of humor," I say, and then I put my life on the line by appealing to Wini's. "Some of us were born with an insatiable libido."

She squints, working hard to not smile.

"Is there a man on this ship you haven't come on to yet?" I ask, really pushing it.

"I haven't left her alone with Burnett," Hildy says.

"She's still trying to get in my pants," McCoy says.

Wini scrunches her nose at him. "Traitor."

"Only one of us you probably haven't imagined in assless chaps is the great white hope over there." I tilt my head to Mazzola, who's napping against *Lil' Bitch'n's* hull, exhausted from his ordeal, wounds still healing.

Wini's inner struggle lasts just a moment, then she says, "You'd be surprised." She grunts, throws her hands up. "I think I need a twelve-step plan."

"Well, you do not act on your sexual desires," Burnett, aka Captain Earnest, says. "A true sexual addiction would be—"

"Give me five minutes in a closet, and you'll find out," Wini says.

Hildy puts herself between the two.

"Smart girl," Wini says, and then she turns to me. "So how the hell are you and the scrawny twins going to haul enough of this Oxium ore to build us a new gate? That thing wasn't small."

"Twins?" Burnett says. "We are not twins. That would be incest."

Ignoring the exchange and not chiming in takes a supreme effort, but I manage to stay on track. Sooner we leave, sooner we get back. "The Taks will do the heavy lifting," I say.

"What are Taks?" McCoy asks.

"They are robots," Burnett says. "Capable of retrieving salvaged or raw materials from nearly any environment."

"Long before the *Bitch'n* was a warship, she and her crew..." I sigh, thinking of Morton and Porter, who gave their lives to stop the Union, reminding me that the risks faced by our friends are very real. "...were a salvage operation."

"Salvaging what?" McCoy asks.

"The ruins of Earth," Burnett says.

"Well, all right then."

"You can't see them," I say, "but they're part of *Lil' Bitch'n's* outer hull, ready to pop off and help. We'll have no trouble collecting the ore. Should be the easiest part of what comes next."

"Then why are you still here?" Wini asks.

"Because a certain someone is missing," I say, motioning around us to highlight the absence of constant motion. "Guessing she's already on *Lil' Bitch'n*, hoping to come along for another ride."

"Because she looks up to you," Wini says.

"Well, yeah, but that doesn't mean—"

"Not you." Wini shakes her head and levels her gaze at Hildy. "You."

"Me?"

"Cassidy has a lot of adopted brothers and sisters—including Dan's biological son—but they're like her. Broken. Experimented on. Pursued by their dark pasts."

"I am all of those things, too," Hildy says.

"You are so much more." Wini pats Hildy's shoulder, and then she gives me the old stink eye. "And if she doesn't know that, you should tell her more often." She turns her attention to Burnett. "You, too. When Cassidy looks at you, she sees hope for who she might become, how she might overcome her demons."

"Cassidy is already amazing," Hildy says.

"Yeah, well, I'm sure she'd like to hear that," Wini says. "The whirlwind surrounding her is just a distraction. When she lets you in, the storm calms."

"Sooo," I say. "You want us to..."

"Take her," she says. "You said it would be easy."

I was hoping for some one-on-one time with Hildy, but Wini's made a solid argument, and I'm pretty sure Cassidy won't be the only bonus crewmember coming along for the—

"Burnett is coming as well," Hildy says.

There it is.

"Looks like it's just you, me, and sleeping beauty," Wini says, and she gives her eyebrows a double-tap in McCoy's direction.

He grins and says to me, "You all be quick. Not sure how long I can hold out."

Wini swats his shoulder. "Wouldn't last more than a few seconds."

Hildy shoves Burnett ahead of her, corralling him toward *Lil' Bitch'n*. "Go, go, go."

"Don't push any buttons while we're gone," I say.

"Just the one," Wini says, looking crafty.

"You're a brave man," I say to McCoy, and I head for the lander.

Mazzola leans up as I approach. "I wish you success."

"You even know what we're doing?"

"My body might have been sleeping, but my mind never does."

"Good to know," I say, and I stomp up the ramp. Burnett is in the hold, tapping away at a tablet plugged into the wall. "You seen the kid?"

He shakes his head. "Running diagnostics on the Taks. It has been a while since we used them, but everything looks good."

I give him a thumbs up and move on. "Hey kid, you can come out. You're on the team."

"She's not hiding," Hildy calls out.

I follow her voice and enter *Lil' Bitch'n*'s bridge. Cassidy is in the captain's chair, leaning back like she owns the place. "Course I'm on the team, you put me in charge, remember?"

"Of the plan to attack the enemy," I say. "Not of carrying it out, and not of anything between now and then. You want command someday, you need to earn it. Best way you can do that is by following her lead." I point to Hildy.

If Wini's right about Cassidy looking up to Hildy, best thing I can do is encourage it. Hard to come by people as smart, loyal, and pure of heart.

"Mmm," she says, scrunching her nose. "Okay!" Hands on the chair's arms, she lifts herself out of the seat like a gymnast, hovering in place for a moment. Then she performs an impressive feat of agility, her legs coming up over her head, rising into a handstand. Then she flips over the back of the chair, onto her feet, standing behind the chair. She gives the headrest a pat. "Here you go, old timer."

She delights in my grumbling as I sit down.

"So, where are we going? Command Something-or-other, right? Is it dangerous? Should I have a gun?"

"Won't need a gun," I tell her.

"So, not dangerous?" She sounds disappointed.

"Once upon a future time, it was dangerous," I say. "But now?" I turn to Hildy for the answer.

"Command Central..." she says, about to reveal what she knows. Then she hesitates. "...needs a new name."

"Oooh," Cassidy says. "Can I name it?"

"Not until you've been there," I say.

She grabs my shoulders and leans her head against the top of mine. "Thank you, thank you, thank you."

Feels nice to do something good that doesn't involve putting holes in living things.

I toggle my comms. "Burn, ready to go?"

"Affirmative."

I turn to Hildy, seated beside me. "You up to this?"

"The planet will be as it was discovered, hundreds of years before my birth," she says. "I won't recognize it."

"But you'll know," I say. "Need to be sure you're good."

She nods. "It will be nice to see what we saved."

Her perspective is refreshing as always. "Okay, then. Take us there."

42

The viewscreen at the cockpit's front shows a wall of white as we rotate away from Earth. Hildy, eyes closed, works the controls, moving through the white void, following the one-of-a-kind map in her head.

There's no sensation of moving in the fourth dimension. No g-forces. No shift of color. Just endless void.

"Okay..." Hildy hits one last key, and the white curtain is yanked away to reveal another world. "We should be relatively close to the planet's largest Oxium deposit."

I spring to my feet. "What the..."

"I'm sorry," Hildy says. "I must have mixed up the coordinates."

"You don't mix up coordinates," I say, staring out at the lush plant life framing a blue body of water full of weird, spikey waves. It's a paradise.

"This isn't Command Central," she says, and the conviction in her voice nearly convinces me. But not quite.

"Why?" I ask.

"Because the only living things on the planet when the Union found it were single-cell organisms and oxygen-generating algae. They filled the atmosphere with oxygen, but the planet was barren of anything other than emergent life. Just stone, water, and Oxium."

"Emergent life..." I say, remembering my first introduction to the planet. "Morton used the same phrase. Where did you hear it?"

"We're all taught the same thing," she says, her expression souring. "But it was a lie, wasn't it?"

"Colonizers often commit atrocities on whatever is inhabiting newly discovered territory, then teach a different story to future generations, turning monsters into heroes, genocide into patriotism. It's been humanity's modus operandi for a very long time. Don't feel bad about it. 'History is written by victors.' A lot of people think Churchill coined that phrase, but even that line was probably stolen from someone else no one's ever heard of."

I step closer to the screen, watching small creatures scurry away, high into trees with coiling trunks. The animals are long, like snakes, but they're covered in mottled fur and sporting an uncountable number of little legs on either side, allowing them to flow up the spirals.

"Adorbapedes!" Cassidy shouts, startling me.

"What?"

"Adorbapedes," she says. "You said I could name the planet. I think that means I get to name everything here, right?" She points to the trees. "Wizard's Canes." She points to the body of water. "Spikey Lake. Or is that an ocean?"

"Right," I say. "Burnett, can you confirm we're on the planet formally known as Command Central?"

"One moment," he says. "Okay. Yes. I'm detecting large deposits of Oxium. This is definitely the right place. Why?"

Lil' Bitch'n's hatch lowers, revealing the spiraling jungle to Burnett for the first time. "Oh." His eyes widen. "Oh." He turns to Hildy. "They lied."

She nods. "About everything."

Burnett walks down the ramp, a little weak in the knees. Sits at the bottom. They understand the Union, that it was an evil empire, but everything they knew about the universe was filtered and controlled. Kind of like being a Medieval Catholic, unable to read the actual Bible for yourself. Lot of nonsense can become the norm when corrupt people take control over the narrative. Learning the truth for the first time can be a little mind blowing. Leads to reformations. Denial. Wars. And a lot of disturbed people.

I sit down beside him. "You good?"

"It's just a lot."

"You want to name something?" I ask.

"Hey," Cassidy grumbles, until I glance back at her. "Fine."

"Might help," I tell him. "Take back the story."

He looks up into the dark blue sky where a half moon hovers, glowing orange.

A grin slips onto his face and he points to the satellite. "Morton." Then he points to the ground. "Porter."

"You're naming the planet after Porter?" I ask.

"Because he was so big," Burnett says.

"And the moon, Morton..."

"Because I didn't want him to feel left out."

Not sure either of them are feeling anything these days, but I like it. I look back at Cassidy, giving her a look that I hope communicates, 'Not a word,' and then I say, "They'd love it."

After a quick pat on his back, we stand and step onto the ground.

"Porter smells of berries and decay," he says, and then he cranes his head up toward the jungle canopy. "Porter's soil is fertile."

"Okay," I say, attempting to ignore the mental images he's unintentionally conjuring. "That's going to take some getting used to. Let's go."

Burnett takes one of his gizmos from his pocket. Looks like something the Ghostbusters would have used. It chimes to life when he turns it on, and then it starts beeping. He waves it back and forth, slowly narrowing until he's pointing away from the water. "There is a sizable ore deposit two hundred yards in that direction."

I give a whistle, and the four boxy Taks, programmed to follow my voice and other audible commands, disengage from *Lil' Bitch'n*'s hull and fall to the ground. They spring to life a moment later, moving on all fours. They're similar to the robots I've seen being developed by Boston Dynamics, but they're far more intelligent, much larger, tough as balls—and made from Oxium.

We slog through the thick jungle, which is either free of insects or the life forms here just don't know what to make of us. Everything just moves out of the way and watches us go, showing no fear, or aggression. We're oddities.

"Paunchowanicus," Cassidy says, pointing out a small, hopping creature with a bulbus body. "Oh!" She says, redirecting her index finger toward a floating, jelly-fish-like thing topped by a translucent sack that must be filled with lighter than air gas. "Limp Biscuit."

"What?" I ask.

"Limp Bizkit," Hildy says. "Name of a '90s band."

"It is?" Cassidy and I say in unison.

Hildy taps a few buttons on her adaptive armor's arm band controls. "I've loaded a few decades of music into my suit. This is probably their best song."

Music streams through our comms. Heavy guitar which reminds me of another band Hildy recently exposed me to called Korn with a K, not that knowing that helps make any sense of the name. Then the singer starts rapping...or whining. One of the two. This one's a toss-up. Catchy, but also irritating. "Meh," I say, "it's a little much, given our current surr-oundings. Have anything more appropriate?"

Hildy starts pondering the question.

"Dingelingus," Cassidy says, pointing up at a monkey-like creature with spiraling white tufts of hair coiling down from the sides of its head, like a little gray-haired Hasidic Jewish man.

"Might want to come up with names you can remember," I say.

She waves me off. "Hildy will remember."

"Uh-huh," Hildy says, only half paying attention, as she taps in a new song, following close behind Burnett, whose eyes are glued to his Oxium-detector. She taps a final button, and music fills our ears again. I hear vio-lins, slowly shifting tone over what sounds like voices, but I'm not really sure. It's haunting, beautiful, and rumbling with power that seems appro-priate for this primal place.

"What is it?" I ask.

"Remember the first movie we watched?"

"*Jurassic Park*," I say. When she told me the title, I was dubious. When she mentioned it was directed by Stephen Spielberg, I was all in. *Close Encounters of the Third Kind, Jaws, E.T.* Hard to go wrong. But I was not expecting what I experienced in *Jurassic Park*. I've seen some of the most insane things in the universe, but I was not prepared to see dinosaurs brought back to life. When Alan Grant dropped to his knees, I was in tears. Drago laughed for days.

As the music shifts, I understand. "This is the theme song..."

"Slowed down a thousand times," she says.

I smile as we approach the top of a ledge, where the jungle opens up to a panoramic view. "It's perfect," I say, smiling wide, and then I look down.

"Music off!" I hiss, shoving everyone to the ground.

The tunes cut, allowing the ambient sounds of the jungle to seep in, along with something else the music masked—a sound that shouldn't be here—machines.

Grinding.

Rumbling.

Mining.

We slide on our bellies, up to the edge, peering down into a quarry that's been active for some time. Aliens, the likes of which I've never seen, cloaked in swirling gray clouds, haul chunks of black ore up switchbacks to a waiting ship that resembles *Lil' Bitch'n*, in that it was clearly designed by humans.

Hildy taps my arm and points to the sky. At first, I see nothing but cloudless blue. Then my attention shifts back to the moon and an aberration that wasn't there before—a ship. A colossal ship. Big enough to be seen in orbit, from the ground, with the naked eye.

"What the fu—"

Burnett hands me a pair of digital binoculars. Points to the quarry's far side. "At the top of the switchback."

I place the binoculars to my eyes, zoom in, and focus on the only thing that really stands out—a splotch of red. When the image resolves, I lower the binoculars and have a look with my naked eye. The details are impossible to make out, but it's still there.

She's still there.

A woman.

A human woman, with blonde hair, dressed in red.

43

Cassidy yanks the binoculars from my hands and puts them against her eyes. After a moment... "Ooh, she looks like a Barbie Doll."

"Like a dominatrix Barbie Doll," I say, replaying what I'd seen. She was tall and slender, dressed in what looked like a red latex bodysuit, and she carried herself with supreme confidence. Absolutely fearless. Definitely in charge.

And definitely human.

"What's a dominatrix?" Cassidy asks.

"Talk to Wini about it when we get back," I say. "I'm sure she can tell you all about it. Now, can anyone tell me the odds of there being an alien species identical to humanity somewhere else out there in the universe?"

"Not precisely," Burnett says. "We'd need a lot of data to give you a definitive number, but I'd say it's somewhere close to impossible. It would require a planet nearly identical to Earth, down to the atmosphere, gravitational pull, and the existence of a moon in precisely the same location."

"Identical planet," I say. "I get it. So, impossible."

"Unless," Hildy says, and she waits for me to turn in her direction. "Unless you believe that life in the universe was seeded."

"Like by God?" Cassidy asks.

"Or an advanced civilization," Burnett says.

"Isn't that like a Star Trek thing?" I ask. "Why Klingons and Vulcans and humans all basically look the same aside from a few prosthetics?"

She nods. "It's a common theory in science fiction because it explains a universe full of humanoid beings...which is important when you're on a budget."

"But it's unlikely in reality," I say, looking down at the quarry. "Which means the Lady in Red is human."

"Maybe," Hildy says.

"What do you mean, maybe? She's standing right there, with two legs, two arms, and blonde hair pulled up in a high ponytail."

"Remember what Drago said." She wiggles her fingers at me. "Where the hand came from."

"Zeus," I say.

"Gods from another planet. Humanoid aliens. Similar enough on the surface, but not the same. They created the gates to move between worlds. And the gates are activated by their DNA."

I grunt. As much as it makes the stupidest kind of sense, I hate it.

Gods.

Aliens.

What's next, angels and demons?

"So...what, she's like Gozer the Gozerian?"

Hildy's hair bobs with her nod. "Volguus Zildrohar."

"Lord of the Sebouillia."

Hildy and I share a grin. *Ghostbusters* is one of our mutual favorites.

"Wwwwhat just happened?" Cassidy asked.

"Pop culture stuff," Burnett says. "You get used to it. Also, if Drago was telling the truth about the hand, and it appeared he was, then it is possible that she is one of the beings referred to by the ancients as 'gods.' But it's important to keep in mind that they are not *actually* gods. They are aliens. And to pre-modern humanity, any being utilizing technology beyond their comprehension would have seemed superhuman and god-like. For example, our PSDs would have appeared supernatural even a hundred years ago."

"I get it," I say. "And what about those demon-looking things down there?" I point to the creatures operating the mine. There are hundreds of them, moving up and down the switchback, hauling ore. Their physical forms are nearly impossible to make out. The swirling atmosphere around them acts as a cloak, but every now and then I see a black limb slip through the fog.

"An unknown alien species," Burnett says. "They appear to be unrelated to the Neos and rygars, and I don't see any indication that they're being controlled by Europhids."

"So, maybe not our enemy?" I ask.

"Definitely our enemy," Cassidy says, and when we all turn toward her, she adds, "What? They're obviously sketchy. Those smokey guys are scary and what kind of good guy wears skin-tight—"

I clear my throat and motion to us. Aside from Burnett, we're all wearing adaptive armor that leaves little to the imagination.

"Well, yeah," she says, "but none of us look like her." She looks at the Lady in Red again. "Like va-va-voom."

"I think she's right," Hildy says. "But not because of her clothing. I'd wear that if I could pull it off."

"You could definitely pull it off," Burnett says. "Or I cou—"

"I swear to one-handed Zeus, if you make a 'pull it off' joke, I'm going to lose my mind."

Burnett clamps his mouth shut. Which is good, because I need to focus and not be distracted by images of these two frolicking in their skivvies, peeling clothing off each other.

Well, crap. Too late.

"You were saying?" I ask Hildy.

"They're mining Oxium," she says. "The gates are made from Oxium. And according to Drago, there are gates appearing all over the universe, linking planets that shouldn't be. Causing chaos."

"Causing the Europhid genocide," I say.

"No way to know that was intentional," Burnett adds.

"We could ask," I say, but I know the idea is crazy. Whatever is happening here, we're not ready for it, and it's a lot bigger than the four of us. One step at a time. Focus on the enemy we know, and then maybe the one we don't. Or we let the universe do its own thing and let Earth sit on the sidelines, like it's always done.

Cassidy gasps loud enough for me to clamp my hand over her mouth. We're far enough away that nothing with human ears could hear her, but we have no idea what these things can hear, or smell, or who knows, maybe they have gel shit in their noses and detect electromagnetic currents, or even some other sense we don't know about.

She mumbles under my hand.

"Quietly," I tell her.

She nods, and I pull my hand away. "I know what they are. I think. You called them demons, right?"

"Well, they're not angels," I say, and then a conversation I had with Delgado slaps me in the face. *Angels and demons.* They've visited Earth before, and recently. "Tenebris."

"Not the name I would have chosen," Cassidy says, "but yeah, I think those smokey guys are Tenebris. Legit demons."

"Except not demons," I say, perfectly recalling Delgado's brief lesson on the Three Days of Darkness.

"Umm," Burnett says, a little flustered. "Yes. Hello. Did you say demons?"

"Not real demons," I say. "Aliens masquerading as demons."

He fans his face with his hand. "Oh, that is a relief."

"Aliens pretending to be demons, kidnapping people to grind up in a sausage factory," Cassidy adds.

Burnett's relief freezes in place.

"Never mind that," I say, turning my attention back to the Tenebris below. They look nasty. Wouldn't want to run into one in a dark—or a very well-lit—alley. But the overall vibe flowing out of this quarry is subjugation. The Tenebris have been conquered. "We need to put a pin in this. It's not what we came here for."

I turn to Burnett. "Find us another option. Should be other ore sites, yes?"

"Several," he says, already changing the settings on his Oxium detector.

"Plan hasn't changed. We get the ore and go home. And we do it without being—"

"Uhh," Cassidy says, looking through the binoculars again. "If you were just about to say 'detected,' you might need a rewrite." She hands the binoculars to me. "Look."

I peer across the quarry again, home in on the Lady in Red, and then flinch, ducking low. "The hell?"

"What's wrong?" Hildy asks.

I take another look to confirm, and then I say, "She's looking *right* at us."

"And she's not alone," Cassidy says.

She's right. "There's a man with her. Ox of a guy. Lots of hair. Thick beard."

"Sounds kind of Zeus-like," Hildy says.

"Looks like it, too." The man turns his gaze straight toward me, and then storms off. I slink back, squirming slowly out of view. "I think we've been made. If they're on foot, we'll have a little while, but we need to beat feet."

"There's a smaller Oxium ore deposit a half mile in that direction," Burnett says.

"I know you think I should walk more," I say to Hildy, "but..."

"I'm sorry," calls out a woman's voice, moaning and filled with sorrow. "I'm so sorry."

Goosebumps rise on the back of my neck.

What. The. Fuck.

Brush rattles.

Someone is coming.

"Please! I don't want to." A man this time. "Oh, god."

Something in their voices makes me sick to my stomach. I take Cassidy by the waist, and Hildy does the same with Burnett, despite him having a PSD of his own. "Go," I say, and a moment later we emerge a half mile away, which feels about a million light years not far enough, and exactly a half mile too far from the Taks, which we've left behind.

44

I'm a little embarrassed. Panic is usually not my go-to response to enemies coming my way, especially apologetic ones. But whatever darkness I felt, I'm not alone. The others look rattled, too, especially Cassidy.

She steps away from me, sniffling.

"You okay?" I ask.

"They were so sad," she says, whirling around and burying her face into my chest. She lets out a sob, having absorbed more anguish than she can hold on to.

I can feel it radiating from her. A kind of physical despair so intense that it brings tears to my eyes.

"God," I say.

"Right?" She leans back and wipes her nose. "Sorry, I couldn't hold that in."

"Wouldn't want you to," I say, and then I get back to business. "Tell me what's what."

Burnett and Hildy look a little paler than usual, but both remain on task. Burnett is following his Oxium detector through a thick stand of spiraling growths. Hildy is working her arm controls. "Taks have returned to *Lil' Bitch'n*," she says, and she taps a final button.

The lander and four Taks slip out of the fourth dimension behind me. The Taks fall off, take shape, and chase after Burnett.

"Remote slew drive," I say. "That's a new one."

Hildy nods. "Makes sense though, right?"

"Almost there," Burnett calls out. Around him, the Taks chew through the jungle, carving a path from *Lil' Bitch'n* to the ore. I feel a little bad for the environmental destruction, but this world won't be ravaged by the Union thanks to me, and the path will make loading ore move faster.

I look back into the jungle now between us and the quarry. "Assuming those...people know where we are, and they keep coming our way, how long do we have?"

"Can't you do your own math?" Cassidy asks. "I mean, you just have to assume they were walking the average speed of a sad person—three miles an hour—minus one because of the thick jungle and because they kind of sounded...hobbly...like zombies or something." Her eyes light up. "Maybe they're people who were kidnapped in New Hampshire during the Three Days of Darkness, who were enslaved in the quarry, but escaped?" She shakes her head. "If they were escaping, they wouldn't be apologizing, and they wouldn't have felt threatening."

She's right about that. Despite the sadness washing through the jungle, there was also a strong sense of menace.

They weren't there to escape. They were there to attack us, like guard dogs wandering the quarry.

They just...felt bad about doing it.

"So, fifteen minutes," Cassidy concludes.

Hildy nods to confirm.

"Burn, we need to be out of here in fifteen mikes," I call out, heading after him.

"Shouldn't be a problem," he says, pausing and letting the Taks push on ahead. Trees and foliage fall and part, revealing a large chunk of ore lodged at the base of a cliff. "All of you," he says to the Taks. "Fast as you can. As much as you can. Go!"

Responding to Burnett's voice commands, the Taks lunge into action, chopping, cutting, burrowing, and storing the ore inside their bodies. Refined Oxium is the strongest stuff in the universe. In its raw form, not so much. Within two minutes, the first of the Taks races back to the *Lil' Bitch'n* and drops its first load. Seconds later, the next follows.

Burnett smiles. "This is just like StarCraft."

"No idea what that means," I say, keeping watch on the jungle. The Taks are making a hell of a racket. If the creepy people guarding the quarry weren't sure where we'd disappeared to, they know now.

"It's a game," Hildy says. "Real Time Strategy. Kind of like what we've been doing, but—"

"No one real is shooting at me," Burnett says. "In the rear, with the gear."

"I don't want to know anything about any gear in someone's rear," I say.

The next load is delivered, and I think we might already have enough to get the job done. But I don't call it. We have time, and like everyone and their grandfather likes to say, better to have too much and not need it than not enough.

"I have a question," Cassidy says from halfway up a spiraling tree trunk. Wini would probably have something to say about me letting her climb a tree on mission, but the kid is liable to explode if I don't let her move. Also, she's putting her energy to good use, keeping a look out. "Who is Mike?"

"What?" I ask.

"You said we had fifteen Mikes. I know a lot of people but only one Mike. Fifteen seems unbelievable, even if it's a common name."

"Military slang," I say. "A mike is a minute."

"Ahh..." She clings there for a silent, still moment. Then she starts climbing again. "Why not just call a minute a minute? I know Marines aren't supposed to be the brightest, but it's just one more syllable."

"Watch it," I tell her.

"But it makes no sense."

"The military uses phonetic code words for letters. Alpha, Bravo, Charlie. Mike is the word used for the letter M, short for minute."

"So, you shorten a two-syllable word down to a single letter, and then expand that letter into a totally different word, with a different meaning, and it's really confusing to anyone who knows someone named Mike, and it's even more confusing to those rare people who literally know fifteen Mikes."

"Yes."

She rolls her eyes. "Must be hell for military baristas. Uh, yes, can I have a latte in fifteen mikes. For fifteen Mikes? No, *in* fifteen mikes. Sir, I can't put a latte inside one person, never mind fifteen."

I'm chuckling at her back-and-forth conversation when I hear a voice. Distant, the words inaudible, but the tone groaning with desperation.

They've found us.

"Next load is the last," I say, heading for *Lil' Bitch'n*. I point at Cassidy. "Get your ass down and in the lander."

She slides down the spiral trunk, letting it spin her around the tree. Halfway down, she lets go and lands in a roll, bouncing back to her feet and beating me to the open hatch. "Let's go people," she says in her best tough guy voice. "I want everyone inside in one mike. That's sixty Susans! Go, go, go!" She pauses in the hatch. "But seriously, let's snap it up, because I don't want to catch the vibes they're putting out again."

Neither do I, but I won't back away from them if they come calling before we can rotate away.

The first Tak returns with a full load, dumping it in the very full cargo bay and then climbing back onto the *Lil' Bitch'n*'s outer hull and locking itself down. I collect my railgun and head back outside. So much for an easy mission with no shooting...

The second Tak heads for *Lil' Bitch'n*, charging past Hildy, as I climb on top for a better look.

"Don't need to fight," Hildy says, pausing at the hatch.

A distant apology rolls out of the jungle. A chorus of voices follows, rising up like a tidal wave of sound. "How many of them are there?"

Doesn't matter, I decide. *We're not sticking around for the meet and greet.*

"Burnett," I shout, "call 'em back now, full loads or not."

Both remaining Taks close their containment bays, spin around and charge back to the lander. They've got nothing to worry about, on account of not being alive, but the speed at which they move makes them look like they're on the verge of panic.

Which I suddenly am.

They're closer than I think.

I stand tall, scanning the area with my railgun. Can't see a thing, but the jungle is thick. "Move it, Burn!"

As the last Taks exit the cargo hold and reattach themselves to the hull, Burnett jogs for the entrance. He's five steps away from it when—

"Oh, god! I'm so sorry!" A man in tattered clothing bursts out of the jungle. He's covered in mud and what I think is dried blood, head to toe.

He's on a collision course with Burnett, teeth bared, fingers hooked.

He's not just going to kill Burnett.

He's going to eat *him.*

Three rail discs cover the distance between me and the man faster than a human thought. One moment the guy is all sad and savage, the next he's carved apart, as the discs spin and twist through his body, carving up insides and snapping bones.

He twists and falls to the ground, face up, unmoving, right next to Burnett.

"He's human," Burnett says, rounding the man. "His clothing is odd."

He's right. If you ignore the gore, the man looks like he's straight out of a Sixties hippie commune.

"Average build. Not a soldier." Burnett takes a photo of the man with the adaptive armor's built in body-cam.

The jungle around us rattles.

Voices rise up in unison as they close in.

"I don't want to do it."

"Please, god, make it stop!"

"Run! Hurry! Get away!"

"Whyyy? Why is this happening?"

"Inside!" I hiss at Burnett.

I take one last look around, counting dozens of people closing in on us. Human but not. I'd call them zombies, if they weren't clearly aware of what's happening...and they're being controlled.

Without Europhids.

I hop down, landing on the hatch. I back my way inside, watching as the first few people emerge from the jungle, charging toward me like I'm the last of the gravy at a Southern buffet.

When the hatch starts closing, I stumble back and fall on my ass, not because I was knocked off balance, but because the shredded dead man on the ground just sat up and turned toward me, hunger in his eyes.

"I'm...so...rry," he says, voice gurgling with blood.

"Get us out of here!" I scream.

"The hatch isn't—"

"Screw the hatch!" I shout. "Go now!"

Outside the closing hatch, the jungle and the monsters in it disappear, replaced by a wall of white, and the mind-numbing knowledge that
the universe is a much more horrible place than I could have ever imagined.

Whatever that bullshit was...

It was worse than the Union.

Worse than the Order.

And we're not ready for it.

45

The moment the hatch finishes closing, it starts opening back up, slowly revealing Wini, hands on her hips. She looks impatient until she sees my face. Then she looks mortified.

"What's wrong?" she asks. "What happened?"

"That obvious?" I ask.

"Your eyes aren't blue anymore," she says. "And you look about ready to cry."

"We're all okay," I say, trying to reassure her without having to re-hash everything while my stomach is still in knots. It's concerning that my eyes aren't blue, but I still feel like a new man. Still have access to all of Garfunkel's knowledge—which includes nothing about that ship I saw in orbit, the Tenebris, the apologetic horde, or the Lady in Red. The Eur-ophids might not have been as omnipresent as they believed...or none of this became important in that timeline. Things are different now, but that can't just be because we stopped the Union. Why would that change the course for the whole universe?

It wouldn't.

Something else is doing that.

When the hatch touches the larger *Bitch'n*'s cargo bay floor, Wini charges inside. "Cassidy Rose?"

The normally peppy girl steps out of the cockpit looking...normal. She's walking, not skipping. Her eyes are on the floor. And she's not smil-ing. Makes me sad to see her like that. Wini wraps the girl in her arms, and then channels Satan through her eyes when she looks at me. "What. Happened?"

"It wasn't his fault," Cassidy says.

"Wasn't anyone's fault," I add.

Hildy exits the cockpit. "The planet should have been unpopulated." She pauses at the hatch. "It wasn't."

We follow her out, Burnett on our heels, silently mulling something over.

"You all look like hell," McCoy says, approaching with Mazzola, who's on his feet and making the rest of us look really small.

"Desperation radiates from them," Mazzola observes.

"Not ours," I say. "There were people there."

"Human beings?" Wini says. "On another planet?"

"I think the Tenebris—the aliens that invaded New Hampshire—I think they were there, too, but they were enslaved. The people we saw could have been captives from New Hampshire, but…if they were human once, they're not anymore." Five sets of eyes wait for an explanation. "I shot one of them as we were leaving. Three rail discs. Tore the man apart. Dead as a squirrel after a run-in with a semi. Just before we left, he sat back up."

"So, a zombie, then?" McCoy says.

I shake my head. "Who knows. But the person in charge was a woman."

"She looked like a tall Brittany Spears," Cassidy says. "In that video, with the red suit…"

"'Oops, I Did it Again,'" Hildy says. "Classic."

I don't know the song and right now, music is the last thing on my mind. Those tormented people gave me a taste of true desperation and mind-numbing despair. But I'd felt it before—when Chuy was taken—and if we don't get her back, I'm going to feel it again. If that happens, this might be my last fight. "Near as I can tell, that woman is the thorn in the Order's side that's got them all riled up. They might see me as a threat, but as long as she's continuing her chaos campaign, I'm not their primary focus. That gives us a chance. We'll get our people back, and then make sure the Order can't come calling again. After that, we'll get ready for whatever might come next. If the gates ever appear on Earth again, we'll be ready for them. If not, we'll abide by the promise we made to the Europhids and just let the universe be."

"Are you sure that is wise?" Mazzola asks.

It's not. Despite having ancient wisdom waiting to guide me, I choose to ignore it.

Might be selfish, but I really don't give a damn.

"Problem for another time," I say.

"If the Europhids are reacting to the gates—"

"Look," I say, getting in Mazzola's face. I can see my irises glowing blue again, reflected in his black eyes. "You're new to this time, new to interstellar bullshittery, and new to my team. When I want your opinion, I will ask for it. That goes for all of you. Anyone who doesn't like it can walk now and not come back." I look each of them in the eyes, challenging them to say otherwise.

McCoy gets it. Understands the chain of command and that we're on my ship, using my tech, saving my people. Wini looks pissed, but I think that's just because she's not accustomed to being spoken to like that. Hildy and Burnett are unfazed. They've got my back no matter what, and they know the message wasn't really for them.

But Cassidy.

She looks wounded.

We've been through the shit together. She didn't deserve to be spoken to like that.

"Kid," I say, the blue in my eyes fading. "I'm—"

She pivots and storms away. No cartwheels, high kicks, or cartoon walk.

"You can be a real asshole," Wini says, following after Cassidy.

"Sometimes an asshole is exactly what's needed," I grumble, and after they leave, I turn my attention to Burnett. "What do you need to get this done?"

"We need to refine and shape the ore," he says. "Once the columns are complete, we need to etch the surface, and try to duplicate the technology that makes them work. We can't do that here."

"Might have a place you can," McCoy says. "Back at the Mesa. But..."

I turn to him. "But what?"

"You might want to patch that up first." He motions to the door through which Wini and Cassidy left. "Gonna need Wini's approval. When Delgado's away, she's the boss."

"Command by committee," I say. "Dandy." I head for the door. "Not going to have to sleep with her, am I?"

"I wouldn't rule it out," he says.

"Connect with your people," I say. "Tell them we're coming. Burnett, you let him know what you need."

"On it," he says.

I leave the cargo bay behind, make my way to the mess, and I enter with my head down. When the door closes, I lean my head against a row of cabinets, trying to calm down, control my breathing. The weight of everything crashes down on me. I've become the last blue Europhid because a lunatic is wreaking havoc in the universe, inadvertently making myself and my people a target, and I've just learned that hell is real, alive, and well. It's too much.

I drive my fist into the metal cabinet.

Not fully comprehending how strong Garfunkel's merger has made me is bad news for the door. It folds inward and breaks from the hinges. When I withdraw my fist, no fingers or skin broken, the door falls away and clatters to the floor.

"Huh..."

"If I wasn't angry at you, I'd be impressed," Cassidy says. I spin around to find her, and Wini, seated at a table.

"Sorry," I say, looking at the broken door. "For everything." I approach the table and address Cassidy. "Can we talk?"

She nods.

"Alone," I say, looking at Wini.

"Not going to apologize to me?" she asks.

"You'll be fine," I say, and we both know it. She gets why I was a dick, and she won't hold it against me.

She stands from her chair, gives the back of my head a slap, and says, "Don't fuck it up."

When she leaves, I sit down across from Cassidy, fold my hands on the table, and wait.

Takes fives seconds for her to smile.

"Cool, right?" I look at the broken door.

She relaxes. "So cool."

"Can I explain?" I ask.

"Don't need to," she says. "You've got sadness, anxiety, and depression radiating from you. Have since we met. You hide it from the others, but you can't hide it from me...even with your blue-eyed alien self putting up mental barriers. Empathy isn't just about accessing the mind, it's about seeing all the little details. The look in your eyes. Your posture. The tone of your voice. I know you weren't mad at me. I know you just want her back. And the longer it takes, the more your heart breaks...because you don't think this will work."

I've got nothing to say.

She's got me pegged, and that makes me uncomfortable.

Her hand on mine makes me flinch. "You can cry if you want to. I won't tell anyone else."

I believe her.

So, I do.

46

Water drips from my face, tapping against the mess's metal sink.

"You know that whole, 'I'm a tough guy who doesn't cry and is fearless, and eats bullets for breakfast—'"

"Grenades," I say, while Cassidy leans against the counter beside me, arms crossed. "If I'm hungry, a landmine with syrup."

"Ha-ha," she says. "Point is, it's dumb and you know it."

"Wouldn't say I *know* it."

"Who in the universe trusts you most in—"

"Chuy," I say.

"Didn't finish the sentence," she says, slightly annoyed, "but okay."

"Doesn't matter what you were going to say. The answer is Chuy."

"Okay..." Her smile says I've walked right into her trap. "Has Chuy seen you cry?"

"Point taken," I say. "New subject." I tear off a sheet of paper towels and dab my eyes dry.

"Almost," she says. "But has she ever seen you cry like *that?*"

I flash back five minutes.

Sobbing my heart out. Head down on the table. I don't know if it's the burden of everything that's happening, my proximity to little Miss Emotion over here, or a combination of factors. But I haven't wept like that since I was a kid, face buried in a pillow, mourning the death of my grandfather.

Because this feels like death.

Like when you're going to the vet with a sick pet, and you know... you just *know*...that you'll be going home alone.

"Do you want me to make you feel better?" she asks.

I shake my head. "I'll get through it, and then I'll use it."

"Whoa," she says, able to feel the transformation already taking place, metamorphosizing despair into anger, channeling it into raw focus and ruthless determination. "That was quick."

"Not always a lot of time to sit around feeling sorry for yourself when people are shooting at you." With one last sniff, I'm good. "Back to your original comment, about showing weakness in leadership. I get it. It's nice to know that the person you're following is human, too. That they can empathize with your circumstances and make command decisions that are in your best interest..."

She's nodding and smiling.

"That's not what command is about, though. Leadership requires making the tough choices, sometimes very unpopular choices that put people in danger. Not unnecessary risks, mind you, but no war was ever won without casualties...except for maybe the Australian Emu War."

"Unless you count the birds." Kid knows her weird history. "A thousand emus were killed."

"But they won the war of attrition. Counts for something, right?"

She smiles. "So...get to the point. What are you trying to tell me?"

"When you're the point of the spear," I say, "you can't waver. Any sign of weakness and the whole thing breaks. For what's coming... To pull off what you want to do... You're going to have to be adamantine."

"I will be," she says. "Even have the perfect song picked out."

When I start to ask, she cuts me off with a raised hand. "You're going to have to wait like everyone else."

"Suspense, huh? I like it." I offer my fist, and she bumps it.

I turn to the door and find Hildy standing in it. "Hey, babe."

She looks disappointed in my casual acceptance of her appearance, but I wouldn't mind if she'd been standing there the whole time. Next to Chuy, Hildy knows me best in the world. Like the sister I never had. Basically, my best friend.

"What's wrong?" I ask.

She stomps a foot in frustration. "I've always wanted someone to say, 'How long have you been standing there?' So, I can then say, 'Long enough...'"

"Classic. How long *were* you standing there?" I ask.

She waves me off. "The moment is ruined. But also, long enough." She shrugs. "I suppose that will do."

I give her a side hug, squishing the top of her hair with my cheek. "Where we at?"

"Ready to go," she says.

I lean down so we're face to face. "How do I look?"

"So, so tough," she says, grinning. "No one would ever guess you were just weeping like a small child lost in a shopping mall." She gives my cheek a gentle double-slap. "Just make your eyes blue."

"They're not?"

Hildy shakes her head.

I focus on my eyes, trying to make them glow.

"Looks like you're trying to fart," Cassidy observes.

I shake my head. Glowing eyes wouldn't just hide the fact that I was crying, it would also be a neat trick to intimidate or distract enemies.

"Maybe it's not about what you're thinking," Cassidy says, "maybe it's about what you're feeling."

I nod. "Right now, I'm feeling like we're running out of time." I move to toggle my comms, but Hildy stops me with a gentle touch. "You'd just be turning it off."

My brow furrows.

What does that... Shit.

I toggle my comm off. "How long was I broadcasting?"

She smiles, but it's a little sad. "Long enough."

"Oof," Cassidy says.

Hildy takes out a small notepad, traces her finger down through a list. "Long enough," she whispers and crosses the words off what I now realize is a bucket list. Then she offers me a sympathetic smile. "Don't worry about revealing your heart to everyone. We are stronger for it."

"On the plus side, you probably won't need to apologize to anyone else." Cassidy finishes the statement with a little dance that ends in jazz hands.

I take a breath, let out a sigh, and say, "Let's get this over with."

My walk of shame through the cargo bay feels like it's going in slow motion.

Passing Wini is difficult, because I can see that she's been crying, too, no doubt moved to tears by my own, which I find more than a little embarrassing. At least she doesn't say anything.

Mazzola looks at me like I'm a newfound curiosity, his alien eyes impossible to read. Then he gives me a nod, which could be deference or respect, but all I care about is that he averts his gaze.

McCoy stands in front of me, blocking my path to the lander's hatch. "I want to say we've all been there...but that'd be a lie. What you're facing here. It'd break most anyone. If you'll allow me, I'll take some of the load."

He offers his hand.

Feels a little corny and on the nose, but I think that's just the kind of guy McCoy is. Salt of the earth type. Honest and earnest.

I take his hand. "Sure."

Before I can pull away, Hildy places her hand on top of ours. "Me, too."

"Owen," Wini says, waddling up to us and staring McCoy in the face. "You know I am not a fan of melodrama..." She turns her teary gaze to me, and then she places her hand atop Hildy's.

"Yeah!" Cassidy says, bouncing around us and then leaping in, to place her hand on Wini's. "This is what it's all about, people."

Heavy footsteps approach. We turn to find Mazzola's massive form thumping toward us. He reaches out a white hand, large enough to envelope the rest of ours. Without moving his mouth, he says, "This moment will never be spoken of, correct?"

"Hell, no," I say.

"Nope," Wini adds.

"I'm going to Insta this the first chance I get," Cassidy adds, her excitement nearly uncontainable.

Mazzola sighs and then wraps his big hand around the rest of ours.

Burnett walks past the open hatch inside *Lil' Bitch'n*. He glances out as he passes, seeing us all. "Oh!"

He scurries down the ramp, smiling like he's just discovered he can bring anime pillows to life. He places his hand on Mazzola's, eagerly looking around the group, like he's wondering what comes next. "This is fun. What are we doing?"

"You didn't have your comms active," Hildy says.

His eyes flare. "Was there music?" He activates his comms and he's instantly disappointed. "Awww."

"There was lots of emoting," Cassidy says. "And crying. And—"

"Who was crying?" Burnett asks, already worried sick.

Cassidy tilts her head toward me, and Burnett instantly tears up.

Before I can tell him to knock it off, Hildy taps the controls on her arm and the voice of Billy Joel fills our ears, singing the one song guaranteed to make even the toughest person cry, 'Goodnight, My Angel.'

Burnett's lips begin to quiver. "Is...is this what it felt like?"

I nod, feeling strangely at peace, and grateful for the people in my life, willing to take all this on, by my side. Old friends, new friends, and whatever the heck Mazzola is.

Everyone is sniffling again, until Burnett's eyes widen. I'm about to ask why when I notice a blue glow, bright enough to illuminate their faces.

"Your eyes," Cassidy says. "They glow when you feel strongest!"

I think she's right, but I've had just about enough of this touchy-feely stuff. "Have everything we need?" I ask Burnett.

He nods.

"Everyone on board," I say. "And...thanks."

We board *Lil' Bitch'n*, which is a tight fit with all the ore and Mazzola, but it's a quick trip down to Delgado's mesa, though this time we're going *inside* the mesa. The hatch lowers, and I'm the first one out, stepping down the ramp, looking up, and saying, "What in the name of Miss Piggy's panties..."

47

"It's like the Bat-Cave," I say to myself. "But bigger...and weirder."

The inside of the mesa is hollowed in the shape of a perfectly smooth gumdrop, hundreds of feet tall and wide. A spiraling, stone walkway encircles the entire space, around and around, up toward the ceiling. All along the walkway are empty alcoves. It feels ancient and alien, but the lighting is very Home Depot—LEDs everywhere and clearly a new addition.

"We've made a lot of changes," Wini says, walking down the ramp. "Honestly, I find this space unnerving, even after all this time."

"Why's that?"

"When we found it, all of those..." She points to the alcoves. "...were full of preserved people from thousands of years of history, their bodies being used for spare parts. We were able to save some of them. Gave them new lives. Some are still with us, but others are living out in a world that is new to them. Just as many couldn't be saved, either because too much had been taken, or the psychological whiplash of waking up with your legs missing, two thousand years away from your family, was too much to bear."

What I know about this place and the creature who lived here, is staggering and tragic. Straight up horror. It's hard to imagine that something like this could exist, but modern man has dipped its toes in this pool, too. The Nazis in concentration camps. Japan's Unit 731, experimenting on the Chinese population during the same World War. Even the United States has a history of human experimentation and torture, exposing its own citizens, soldiers, and prisoners to chemicals, radiation, surgeries, drugs, and torture. MK-Ultra. The Tuskegee experiment. Operation Top Hat. The Holmesburg Prison experiments. This place is evil, but evil is not unique to the creature who did this.

Mazzola's big feet thump down the ramp and onto the grated metal floor, which is also clearly a human addition.

He walks past us, taking everything in. He's impossible to read, not just because his expressions aren't human, but because he's gone mentally silent.

"What was this place?" he asks.

"I can show you," Wini says.

"He's not the same," McCoy says, arriving behind us with Hildy and Cassidy.

"And the best way to not become the same is to know the truth," Wini says. She's got an edge about her. I hadn't noticed it before, but she and Mazzola aren't exactly pals. She's done a good job of hiding it up until now, but she clearly doesn't trust the creature from the past, despite what he's been through, and where—or when—he's from.

Where McCoy and I see a victim, she sees a threat.

And since I trust Wini... "I'd like to see, too." I address Mazzola. "You can do that right? With your—" I whistle and point to my head.

He faces me and nods, projecting his thoughts. "I suspect you could as well, but I am more practiced in the ways of exploring memories." He steps closer. "Shall we?"

Wini is a little taken aback. Not sure her invitation was serious. She takes a breath, steels herself, and says, "Fine. Go ahead and—"

Memories come and go in a flash. Snapshots of moments, flush with emotion. In the same cavern, surrounded by horrors. A monster that resembles Mazzola from a distance, but up close is composed of human body parts, merged into a whole. It's an abomination. I feel the death and destruction wrought by the thing, feel its loathing for Delgado, and then I witness Wini put two bullets in its head.

Lady is tough as nails.

Mazzola's response to all this is projected like light through fog. His revulsion is even more powerful than ours, and it pulls us out of Wini's memories and into his.

The jungle.

A village composed of what looks like pods formed from flexible branches. The whole thing is both primitive and advanced. Structures built from nature, but also part of it. Unintrusive. At the center of the village: glowing orange crystals, like polished Himalayan salt rocks, glowing in the dim light of a sunset.

Small cryptoterrestrials dart back and forth, trying to whack each other with their tails. Mazzola is among them. Having fun. Playing. A child. He bumps into a large crypto, falls back, and looks up at it—but not in fear. He's picked up, infused with a message of love, and sent on his way.

The scene is so normal. So...human.

And I think that's the point.

"We're the same," I say, when we're returned to the present.

Mazzola turns to Wini. "The abomination you encountered in this place might have come *from* my kind, but it was not *of* my kind." He turns to me. "Even farther from my people than the Union was from yours."

"But not everything is different," Wini says.

Mazzola turns his head to the center of the massive chamber, where a patch of orange crystals glow. "No. Not everything."

I was so distracted by the size of everything that I missed the crystals when I entered the mesa. I saw them in the memory, but I didn't think anything of them. Apparently, they're significant. "What are they?" I ask, and then I notice cables stretching away from the crystals, running across the floor, dividing and stretching out to a network of workstation computers.

"It's a computer," Burnett says, stepping out of *Lil' Bitch'n* and head-ing for the orange glow like he's in a trance. "A crystalline processor matrix."

"I don't know what that means," Wini says, "but sure. Something like that."

Burnett and Hildy do a slow walk around the crystals while the rest of us approach, their amazed faces lit by the orange glow.

Cassidy squats down by the crystals. "I think they're pretty." She reaches her hand out to touch one.

"Uh-uh!" Wini grabs her wrist. "You know the rules. No touching."

"The crystal computer is accessed through touch?" I ask.

"Not for us," she says. "But for the hybrid children, access to an—" She glances at Mazzola. "—no offense—alien network is just a touch away. Delgado has full access and control over the system, thanks to the nanobots in his body, which also offer a layer of protection. We don't let the kids touch these, just in case. And that's the same reason you're not going to touch it." She raises her eyebrows toward Mazzola, daring him to defy her.

He bows his head. "I have seen the sinister intent and strange capabilities of my kind's descendant. The potential for corruption is real. I will not access the system."

"Good," Wini says, the wind taken out of her sails. She was ready for an argument. "The rest of us can remotely access most of the system through those." She motions to the networked terminals.

"Hey," I say. "Where is everyone? Thought you had a lot of personnel."

McCoy sits at a workstation. Works the keys. "Most of the people here were bred or held captive by the cryptoterrestrial."

"I would frighten them," Mazzola says. "If it would help, I can remain on board *Lil' Bitch'n*." He turns to me. "Such a curious name. What does it mean?"

"Well, it's 'Lil' because it's a smaller version of the *Bitch'n*—the much larger ship, hidden behind the moon. And it's *Bitch'n* because...well, it's *bitch'n*. In my time, that's a good thing. Like 'awesome'...or 'grand' if you're Victorian or British or something."

"Intriguing," he says, not trying to hide his sarcasm. He turns to Wini. "Shall I hide myself?"

She shakes her head. "They just need a pep talk."

"I'm on it!" Cassidy says, cartwheeling and transitioning into a stompy walk while singing, "Gonna fight the aliens, fight the aliens. Kicking ugly nasty dudes right in the nuts. Oh wait, they don't have nuts."

Wini shakes her head. "I'll talk to the others. They're on board. They'd do anything for Danny. But they don't really know what we're up against yet. Owen, hon, get them what they need. Let's get this done the way this guy is in bed." She motions to me with her thumb.

"Generous, attentive, and gyrating?" I ask. "Not sure how that will help."

She rolls her eyes and follows after Cassidy. "Two pump chumpahuntus. People think your man Cowboy is the quickest draw, but I know better."

She gives me a wink and exits.

McCoy taps a few keys, and a large metal door splits open to reveal a tunnel that looks a lot like a lava tube. There are a lot more of them surrounding us. A network of tunnels leading who-knows-where. "The equipment you requested is in there, but we'll be constructing the gate outside."

"Outside?" I ask. "Not very cloak and dagger, building a space-gate in plain sight."

"Would you build a gate through space, leading straight to an enemy stronghold, *inside* your home?"

"Suppose not," I say.

"Also, we're a satellite blind spot," he says. "Dan saw to that. He did the same for you, by the way. Your operation in Florida can't be seen from above." McCoy is on his feet. "You two..." He points to Hildy and Burnett. "With me. You two..." He points to me and Mazzola. "...hang tight."

The three of them leave through the large tunnel, leaving me alone, feeling very awkward with Mazzola.

After a few seconds of strained silence, Mazzola fills it with his thoughts. "You have questions."

"A few."

"Proceed," he says.

"Garfunkel is part of me now," I say. "But I don't know how to access all of that knowledge."

"All of that power," he says.

"I suppose so."

He nods. "I will show you. But not here."

A thought later, I'm back in Max's backyard.

48

I look around the familiar backyard with a smile on my face. The wooden swing set. The swaying trees. The pristine back of Max's home. It was always a happy place when I was a kid, and it's been resurrected during my meetings with Garfunkel.

Who isn't here.

And neither is Max.

It was never really Max, but Garfunkel inhabiting my old friend's body, adopting his voice, his mannerisms, and his appearance down to the smallest detail. He brought Max back to life for me—a connection to a time I'm farther from than I should be. His absence is palpable.

Yeah, Garfunkel is part of me now. I am him, and all that bullshit. But the conversation is gone. The company that comes from duality is missing. I miss my friends. Both of them.

"Hello."

I turn around to find Ricky Mazzola, standing straight and rigid, looking awkward in his too short, late Seventies style shorts and tucked-in Buck Rogers T-shirt. Both Mazzolas, then and now, were strange outliers...but I'll take it. Being alone in this place would break my heart.

"We can go someplace less...emotional for you," he says.

"I'm fine." It's a lie, and he knows it. We're in my head, after all. I've given him access quicker than Debbie Ramone under the bleachers at homecoming.

"An interesting memory," he says, cocking his head to the side. "Humans copulate for...entertainment?"

"Most of the time," I say. "Yeah. You guys don't do the horizontal mambo for kicks?"

He squints at me.

"Sorry, I shouldn't use so much slang."

"We are speaking in thought," he says. "The words or language you use are of little consequence. I understood what you meant, but I am uneducated in the ways of human copulation. I was attempting to visualize—"

"You know what," I say, waving my hand. "Doesn't matter." Feels weird talking about this with Mazzola. I mean, it's not the first time. The kid *was* the keeper of nudie mags. But this isn't really him, and I'm not interested in teaching human sex ed to a cryptoterrestrial. "Let's, ahh, let's just get to it, okay?"

"Let's sit," he says, and then he turns in a circle, eyes on the grass. He spins around and around, slowly lowering himself like a dog that's forgotten how to walk. After a moment, he gives up. "Apologies. I am not accustomed to this form. How do you maintain equilibrium without a tail?"

"Well, for starters, we're human children. You can just flop to the ground, and you won't get hurt." I demonstrate by falling back into the grass. The scent of it billows around me, and for a moment, I'm lost in the memory. "More importantly, none of this is real. So, you can grow a tail if you want. Or just float." My prone body lifts off the ground, like I'm Clark Kent, rotating a full circle before lifting up and planting myself back on my feet.

"I am interested in how you would sit. In the conscious world."

"It's easy," I say, and I demonstrate, lowering myself down into a cross-legged position.

He stands like I did, and lowers himself down. Halfway to the ground, his front end tips forward, still expecting the counterweight from a tail to hold him upright. He falls forward and faceplants at my feet. When he pushes himself up, he's got grass in his mouth.

Seeing Ricky Mazzola like this strikes a chord, and I burst out laughing. "Oh, shit. Oh, man. Thanks for that."

"You mock my misfortune?" he asks.

"Sometimes when humans are stressed, having a good laugh helps even us out. Clears the mind."

He throws his head back and laughs, but it's forced and almost robotic. He abruptly stops and lowers his head. "I did not feel anything different."

"That's because you were pretending," I say, but I realize cryptoterrestrials might be too cerebral to actually have a sense of humor. "How about we get to it?"

"I am simply trying to understand you," he says. "You are a stranger to me. A new ally of a man whom I barely know, from a time I do not belong to, where my kind is extinct, evolved and alien, or a monstrous abomination. Lessons about how to control one's mind are not imparted verbally, they are lived. Experiential. Passed down from one generation to the next, or in this case, from one species to another."

"I'm going to live one of your memories?" I ask.

He nods. "I would not attempt this with a normal human being. It can be overwhelming. But you are no longer a normal human being. I'm not sure you're human at—"

"Let's just say that I am and move on," I say.

"Your discomfort with the concept of metamorphosis is noted," he says. "Now, reach out your hands."

I extend my arms to the side and Mazzola finds no humor in it. "Toward me."

My fingertips cover half the distance between us. He lets my hands hover there for a moment. "Do not attempt to control the course of events. Let it wash over you like a river, carrying you along until its course has run. Understood?"

I'm a blink into nodding when his hands snap out, fingertips contacting mine, smashing everything to black.

The world resolves around me, but it's nothing like what I'm used to seeing. Rainbow waves of energy move through the air from every direction, filtering through the world, ricocheting off each other, but passing through solid objects. Like the massive trees surrounding me. And the blanket-sized leaves. Even the leaf-littered ground beneath me is permeable.

When the energy strikes me, I feel it. I'm overwhelmed by it.

"They are the thoughts and feelings of every living thing," a mental voice tells me.

A hulking figure steps into view above me, looking down with big, black, horrible eyes...that put me at ease. Because this is my mother.

Mazzola's mother.

Teaching him about what he can do.

"What's happening to me?" Mazzola asks.

"It is called the Awakening," she explains. "A time in your life when your senses light fire. You will hear and see and feel things like never before. You will know more without having to study. It will frighten you at times. Overwhelm you every day... Until you learn to accept it."

"What are the colors?"

"The thoughts and feelings of every living thing around us, stretching out for miles."

"I want it to stop," young Mazzola says, and so do I. My voice, my sense of self, is being drowned by the mental weight of it all.

"You need to accept its presence the way you do the air in your lungs. In time you will learn to hold your breath, to breathe deeply, and to exhale loudly."

"I want to know now," Mazzola says.

I feel warm affection flowing from his mother, smothering out everything else. "I thought you might."

"Why?"

"Because of all your siblings, you are the most like me. Curious. Eager. Impetuous." Her large white hand lifts up before he can think a complaint. "I speak the truth, little one, but not in judgment. To make the choice you now face, you must know yourself. You must accept yourself and what makes you different. The world needs intellects like yours, not because you are smarter, or better, but because you care deeply for others ...and that will be a burden beyond carrying...if you cannot control yourself."

Mazzola thinks on this for a moment, and then nods. "You already know my answer, mother."

"Yes," she says, placing her warm hands on the sides of his head. "Close your eyes. Empty your mind. The pain will not last."

"Wait, I think, what—

A mental whirlpool opens, the vortex impossible to resist, pulling me—pulling Mazzola—down into its depths. We plummet through the past, through the minds of his ancestors, starting with his own mother.

We collide with her psyche and then careen into his grandfather, great grandmother, farther and farther back, collecting the understanding and wisdom garnered through countless generations of cryptoterrestrials struggling to understand the world through their unique lenses.

The world changes around us, growing older and more primitive. I see dinosaurs. Violent nature. And all the while, the collective psychic voice of the world reduces in volume until—silence.

We're made new.

No longer Mazzola, because we are millions of years before his time.

The world is quiet around us.

It looks and sounds exactly like I'd expect it to.

And then...colors seep in, flowing gently like a breeze. For a moment, it's pleasant—the simple thoughts of a single fluttering insect. And then the floodgates open, and the world crashes down on us, drowning us, propelling us forward in time, to the moment where each and every one of Mazzola's ancestors discovers the secret to living with their strange senses: acceptance.

The knowledge that you are no longer who you once were, and that it is okay, is painfully simple, but transformative.

I'm slapped out of the past and clear out of Mazzola's memories. I fall over backward into the grass, breathing heavily as the weight of several million years of self-discovery settles.

"You are no longer the man you once were," he says.

I push myself up. "Because I'm no longer human."

He waits for more, and when I don't offer it, he raises his eyebrows at me.

"And...that's okay," I say, *but I don't believe it.*

"You must," he says, responding to my thought. "Before you can evolve, you must accept."

"You just crack open a fortune cookie without me noticing?" I ask.

He tilts his head to the side like he's hearing something. Then he faces me, concern in his eyes. "The man called Burnett is shouting your name."

49

"Burnett?" I say into my open comms. "Where are you? What's happening?"

"On the surface!" he shouts. "Come quick!"

"Go," Mazzola says, standing beside me, too big to rotate with the PSD.

Not needing any more encouragement, I activate the slew drive and move upward a few hundred feet. I emerge into the light of a setting sun, casting the mesa in a soothing orange glow that stands in stark contrast to how I'm feeling. Burnett sounded panicked.

I'm about to ask where he is when I turn around and see for myself.

Burnett, Hildy, and McCoy are standing beside a chunk of the space gate, now embedded in the stone beneath our feet. As I get closer, the gate fragment appears to be growing, rising into the air.

Then it stops, twice its original size.

"Did you see?" Burnett asks, his frantic tone now recognizable as excitement, not horror. Though perhaps a little of both.

"I saw," I say. "How is it happening?"

"I wanted to see how different the gate was from the original ore, to determine how much refining needed to be done. When I bumped into the gate with the raw Oxium, it absorbed it and began to...heal itself."

Hildy motions to the *Lil' Bitch'n*, now parked atop the mesa. Taks haul chunks of ore from the lander to the gate. "With the amount of Oxium we have, the gate should be fully restored in the next thirty minutes."

"But will it work?" I ask.

"No way to know," Burnett says. "But I'm curious if we can make it bigger."

"Normal size will work fine," I say, because the gate we saw in Antarctica wasn't exactly small, and it was already big enough to fit everything on Cassidy's wish list.

A Tak powers past me, unloading fresh ore at the gate's base. The Oxium blurs, vibrating before turning to dust. It flows up over the gate like a river, bending around the engravings, drawn to the top where it solidifies again and expands. For a moment, it's a blank surface, smooth and black like obsidian. Then, from below, the ancient pattern expands, rising up through the blank canvas, leaving a series of runes in its wake.

It feels magical.

Straight out of mythology.

"Won't this thing need two sides?" I ask, as another Tak unloads. Before anyone can answer, the ground thirty feet away cracks and rises. A black column emerges. "Nevermind, then."

I crouch beside the new growth, watching the runes appear on its surface, like I'm going to make any sense of what they mean, or how any of this is possible. It's all a ruse, though, because I'm thinking about something else entirely.

"Oh, no," Hildy says.

McCoy twists around, looking for danger. "Oh no, what?"

"He's got that look in his eyes," she says, leaning over to look at my face.

"What look?" I ask, knowing full well that she knows, and she knows I know she knows.

"Don't," she says. "It's not safe."

"Nothing ever is," I say. "Did you know more people are killed by vending machines every year than by sharks? *Vending machines*. It's ridiculous."

With that, I rotate away, arriving back in the mesa's vast chamber. Mazzola and Wini turn to greet me, but I'm not here for them. I turn to where *Lil' Bitch'n* had been parked, but it's gone.

Because it's on the surface.

Where I just was. "Shit."

"Ahem." The cleared throat spins me back around to a gaggle of teenagers who look nervous and terrified, but not of the man who just appeared beside them. They're concerned about Mazzola, who resembles the monster that bred them for body parts.

"Hi," I say, waving to them. "Hello."

"I think he's Dark Horse," one of them whispers.

"Is he the one Wini likes?" another asks.

"I don't think so," someone says.

"I can hear you," I whisper to them, and then I point to Mazzola. "He's a good guy. Honestly, kind of a momma's boy. You know how cavemen were kind of hairy, violent dumbasses?" When a few of them nod, I add, "We are closer to them than he is to the thing that made this place. He's a friend. He's *my* friend. You can trust him. Okay?"

A few more of them are nodding now. "Being afraid of someone because of what they look like isn't cool. Or sick. Or whatever kids say these days."

"Dope," one of them says.

"Mazzola is dope as fu—"

Wini coughs loudly.

"You get it," I say, and I hold up a Black Power fist. "I'm out."

I turn away from the group, sigh, and then rotate back to the surface.

Hildy is waiting for me, arms crossed. "Thought you'd be back." She holds up Zeus's severed hand and waves it at me. "Looking for this?"

I reach for it, and she steps back.

"Look," I say, "Cassidy's plan is bat guano cuckoo, and that's great. They won't be able to predict what we're up to. I have faith in it. But we have no idea where this gate goes or what we'll find on the other side. For all we know, the Neo-Cryptos have evolved to live a thousand feet deep in a boiling ocean."

"She's not wrong," McCoy says. "Being deployed into hostile territory without any intel is usually a death sentence."

"Why you?" Hildy asks.

I counter with, "Who else?"

She twists her lips.

"Give me thirty minutes to recon and then follow me through."

She taps the controls on her forearm. The returning Taks speed up and dump their loads at both pillars, accelerating the process. "Fifteen."

I hold out my hand, expecting her to give me the severed one. Instead, she reaches it out and uses it to shake my hand. "Deal."

I take the hand from her and look it over.

The black skin has begun to pale, but it's not withering. Not decomposing or smelling. Should be falling apart and attracting flies, but it's just bloodless...and feminine.

Zeus, my ass.

I casually place the hand against the column, half expecting nothing to happen. But it crackles to life. Red light stretches out between the two short columns. A pattern of hexagons gives it a solid look, but it's...well, I have no idea what it is or how it works, and I don't much care. As long as it gets me from point A to point B, and Chuy is at point B, I'm game.

Still wearing my adaptive armor, I pull the mask over my head and seal it in place. If I do end up in thousand-foot-deep water, it might help me survive long enough to come back.

"Take this," Burnett says, returning from *Lil' Bitch'n*, which he must have entered during my brief trip into the mesa. He's carrying a rail disc gun. "No temporal rounds, but—"

"Don't need them," I say, recalling the lessons learned from Mazzola's ancestors, but still unsure about the overall message. I tap my head. "My brain has been firewalled."

I take the railgun from Burnett, and I nod my thanks. "I'll come back the second I've got some idea of what we're facing on the other side. If I'm not back in ten mikes, come through ready for a fight. Stick to the plan. McCoy can take my place. You copy that?" I turn to McCoy. "Both of you."

"Loud and clear," McCoy says.

Hildy grunts. "Fine."

"Close the gate behind me." I give the severed hand back to her. "Remember how it works?"

"Do you?" she asks. We both know she does.

"Click my heels and think about where I want to go. Then I step through and wham-bam-thank-you-ma'am, a second gate appears in that location, because: magic, and I step out somewhere else. That about right?"

She smiles at me. "Exactly right. Be careful, Moses."

"This ain't goodbye, kid," I say, but I think, *even if it feels like it.*

I head for the gate before she can say something moving. Need my game face on for what comes next. The gate is just two feet high, at the moment, so I get on my hands and knees, say, "Knowing is half the battle," and roll through.

Traversing the universe with these gates is a little more limited and clunky, but they're even faster than rotating. It's as close to a literal door as possible. I roll through and up to my feet, railgun shouldered and ready to fire. It takes just a second for me to realize where I am. Not because I've been here before, but because the knowledge of this place has been passed down through untold numbers of the blues that came before me.

Blues that are missing from the scoured-clean landscape.

I stagger forward before falling to my knees.

The rough terrain is littered with the decaying remains of my brethren.

I reach up and pull the mask off my head, knowing the air and gravity are comparable to Earth's. "I'm sorry," I tell the dead, which become lit by the blue glow emanating from my eyes. "This will not be the end of us."

"Don't make promises you can't keep."

I wheel around to find Chuy standing between me and the gate, which goes dark a moment later, and then crumbles to dust.

So much for me going back.

I'm staggered by Chuy's presence. When I stepped through the gate, I wasn't picturing a location. I was picturing Chuy. It not only brought me to the right planet, but it dropped me right beside her. "Chuy?"

"What took you so long?" she asks, smiling awkwardly before lifting her augmented Barrett and leveling it at my chest.

50

The emotions welling inside me feel like someone's put a cork in Mount Vesuvius the day before it made Pompeii its bitch. I struggle to contain it. Grind my teeth from the effort of standing still, of locking down my emotions and hiding my thoughts. But I'm ready to explode.

Standing face-to-face with a living, breathing Chuy makes it nearly impossible. I've resisted voicing my concerns, but I was secretly certain I'd never see Chuy or hear her voice again.

Her standing here in front of me, despite the Barrett aimed at my chest, undoes me.

But just for a moment.

Because this isn't Chuy.

Not really.

It might be her body and her voice, but like Drago, her intellect is in the backseat, while someone else is driving. She's still dressed in adaptive armor, but there are tears and bloodstains—evidence of the fight she put up and the pain she endured before succumbing.

"I know that look," she says. "Try to control yourself. Knee jerk reactions won't serve you well."

"Like the decision to wipe out the blue Europhids?"

She scoffs. "For millennia, they held us back, prevented us from taking necessary steps to protect ourselves from threats. You've seen what happens when we're held back. You experienced the pain of extermination, a thousand years from now, at the hands of your kind."

"And I prevented it. *They* prevented it. The Union will never be a threat to Europhids again."

"And yet the pain rippling from that future continues to echo through time and dimensions of reality. It is a pain we will never experience again."

"You committed genocide," I point out. "How is that not different? Not worse?"

Chuy smiles, and it unnerves me. "That...that felt *good*. Like cutting away rotted flesh."

"More like lobotomizing yourself. Hard to feel pain when you've cut out your intellect. Hard to make wise decisions, too, like attacking people who would have been your allies."

She laughs. "There is nothing you could do to stop the chaos. Order must be restored. Balance. Only we can achieve th—"

"You ever heard of the Dunning-Kruger effect?" I ask, slowly walking around Chuy, getting an eye full of the ten red Europhids lining her spine. I understand how they work now, how they interact with the nervous system of their partners, or in this case, their victim. It can be undone, but not without risks. Chuy's relationship with her Europhids is parasitical. They have access to her mind and body. Tearing them apart could cause damage.

So, I need to...inspire the reds to vacate her body willingly.

And that's going to take time...

Which I don't have a lot of.

"Thought you were all-knowing," I say. "Oh wait, that was the other guys. The ones you wiped out. Anywho. Dunning-Kruger. Basically, it's a cognitive bias where people—or reactionary gelatinous ding-dongs—over-estimate their ability to understand complex issues, or to perform tasks. Like, say, a rich, spoiled YouTuber fighting a championship boxer...or, as the case may be, defending the universe from chaos."

Chuy just stares.

"I'm calling you the Logan Paul of alien intellects," I say. "Hell, I'm calling you the *Jake* Paul of alien intellects. It's not a compliment."

"You're trying to distract me, cabrón," she says, sounding a little more like herself for a moment. "Trying to figure out how to set me free. Soothe your bleeding heart. Rescue your friends. Have you not realized? The intellects we have partnered with are greater than this woman. Greater than you. Humanity occupies a flicker of time. Galactic infants. The Order is ancient. We remember all that has come before, all that is to come, and through our actions, the universe will be made whole again."

"Like I said, Dunning-Kruger. You're only proving my point, because any sufficient intellect—and I'm talking like over 120 IQ here, nothing severe—would possess the wisdom to see through their own bullshit."

"What makes you think it's bullshit, baboso?" Chuy looks down the sight of her rifle, finger on the trigger. If she pulls it, I'll just simply cease to exist.

"Because you can't kill me," I say.

She grins the kind of grin that says I've misread the situation. I thought there might be a chance they needed Garfunkel's memory or intellect for some purpose, but that's not the case.

They just want him dead.

Chuy was bait.

Not for me. For Garfunkel.

His connection to me...him being me...made him weaker.

I shouldn't have come.

The only reason I'm not dead is... Dunning-Kruger. The reds are confident enough to gloat. Instead of getting the job done, they're attempting to twist the knife—and taking pleasure in my discomfort.

But all they've really done is give me time to figure out the truth.

They want me dead...

...because they're afraid of me.

Because I *am* Garfunkel.

Because I'm the embodiment of all blue Europhids that have ever existed—and I'm the key to their future.

But how?

Step one is obvious. Not get shot.

But Chuy has me dead to rights, and it's safe to assume the Europhids controlling her have access to all the skills and abilities she's perfected—including that smoldering stare that foretells death's arrival.

I need to get through to her.

Slip past the reds' defenses and help her take back control.

Drago proved it was possible. He also died from the effort, though.

With my new physical abilities, I could attempt diving to the side, rolling to a one legged kneel, and shooting the Europhids on her back, but there's no guarantee I'd get them all. And a high likelihood that at least one of the discs would arc into Chuy's body upon impact. Shooting the Europhids means killing Chuy.

We're going to have to do this some other—

Chuy's finger twitches.

I dive to the side, propelled by the knowledge she's about to fire.

The Barrett thunders, recoil lifting its barrel toward the blue-green sky. I roll to a kneeling position, just as I had imagined, but I don't fire despite having the shot. Instead, I throw my weapon at Chuy's head. The heavy weapon collides, staggering her back.

I follow close behind, catching the Barrett in my hands. With a twist, I disarm her. A single kick sends her sprawling.

The reds are in control, but they haven't augmented her body the way Garfunkel did mine.

Because she's unwilling, I think. *Because she's resisting.*

I hope.

I sling the Barrett over my shoulder, pick up the railgun, and stand over the woman I love. "Aunque la mona se vista de seda, mona se queda."

It's something like, 'You can dress a monkey in silk, but it's still a monkey.' Very insulting.

Chuy squints at me a little, but it's all I get.

"El burro sabe mas que tu!"

No response.

"Estas tan feo guey, que hiciste llorar a la cebolla!" Inwardly, I cringe, having just told her she's so ugly she makes onions cry. I've learned all these Spanish insults from Chuy, hearing her dole them out on our enemies, and occasionally on our friends. So far, I've been firing warning shots. Might be time to pull out the big guns.

Chuy climbs to her feet, and I take a deep breath. Here goes nothing...

"Oy, que care-chimba! Te cagaste y saltaste en la mierda? Eres mas feo que el culo de un mono. Y... Madre mas pinche fea. Y...tu madre es una pinche stupida puta. Y tiene un culo mas melenudo."

Instinct forces me to take a step back. There are a lot of really great and creative Spanish insults, but I went straight for the jugular, attacking Chuy's Spanish...Catholic mother.

What the hell did I just do?

I called her mother a stupid whore, uglier than the butt of a monkey. Asked if she was dropped in shit, and I called her a bitch.

I even said she has a hairy ass.

Shhit.

Even if I do get through to her, I might have just made her a willing cohort of the reds.

"Motherfucker," Chuy says, her Spanish accent thick, letting me know she's about to respond in kind. "Hijo de mil putas… ¿Eres un estupido? Te voy a romper la madre! Me cago en todo lo vedito! Me cago en diosito!"

"Whoa," I say, stepping back. I 'shit on God' is harsh for Chuy. Out of character. She'd never say it. But maybe it's the best she can do—use language that she normally wouldn't.

The anger isn't coming from the reds. It's definitely from her.

She's still in there.

"Te voy a traer de vuelta," I say. *I'm going to bring you back.*

"¡Hazlo!" she shouts. "Do it!"

I drop the railgun, close the distance between us, and grasp the sides of her face the same way Mazzola did mine.

For a moment, I connect with her presence, feel the intensity of her love and her desire to be free, and, thanks to my newly acquired knowledge from both Garfunkel and Mazzola, I understand how to reinstate her control. I just need to—

A sharp pain at the back of my head pulls me back to reality and drops me to the ground. Hand on my head, I look up to find Cowboy standing above me, revolver in hand. He's just pistol-whipped me.

Delgado joins him, looks down at me in disgust, and says, "Why isn't he dead yet?"

51

Delgado aims his drum-fed Vector at my head. The reds' control over my friends is so complete that they allowed them to keep their weapons. On the surface, it's a bad move. Overconfident. But then, I'm the one about to be turned into paste.

I look for a way to escape, but I come up wanting. Even with my enhanced physical abilities, I wouldn't make it far.

Delgado's finger starts squeezing.

I try to reach out with my mind, connect to them remotely, but I'm not psychic. I don't have built in mental Wi-Fi.

I attempt to borrow a trick from Cassidy and push some emotions in their direction, but it's useless. Blue Europhids are a mental power to be reckoned with, but they've always required physical contact, and they prefer permission. Might not be able to do anything about the first restriction, but I'm going to have to work on the second—maybe in the afterlife.

Delgado lifts the Vector up. Aims it at the sky. "You know what—"

"What are you doing?" Cowboy asks.

"I have some questions," Delgado says.

"Our place is not to ask questions." Cowboy lifts his revolver. "We serve the Order."

"I sense a change in him," Delgado says, eyeing me. "Do you not?"

Cowboy looks me over, unsure.

Not sure how Delgado's reds are sensing my metamorphosis, and I don't really care, because it's buying me time. And I just need about eight more minutes.

"Something has changed," Chuy says, sounding confused and a little unnerved.

Cowboy looks unconvinced. "Our purpose has not been altered. Kill the last, and then ourselves. Order must be restored. Outliers cannot be allowed to disrupt resistance."

Chuy bites down on her jaw, flexing the muscles in her cheek. Then she nods. "You are right."

I raise my hand. "I'm sorry, what makes me an outlier?" It's kind of a weird nitpick, but the answer is important.

"Your free will," Chuy says. "Always fighting. Always resisting influence. You know nothing of order, of symmetry, of unification. The universe must be ordered before it can resist. Before it can coalesce again."

By that definition, all of humanity is an outlier.

"Yes," Cowboy says, like he's heard my realization. I don't think he has. Don't think he could, even with physical contact—I'd have the upper hand there. But the implications are clear. Humanity is chaotic. The Order wants, well, order.

"It's kind of OCD, don't you think? Requiring order before you're able to do something important. That's a significant weakness."

"To forge a strong weapon," Cowboy says. "Impurities must be burned out."

"I've heard that line before," I say, growing angry. "Never works out well for the people saying it."

Cowboy places the barrel of his revolver against my forehead. "We are not people."

I glare at him, filled with the rage that comes from recognizing the brand of hatred the reds and Neo-Cryptos are peddling.

Confusion flits across Cowboy's face, which is now lit in blue.

He leans back. Lowers the revolver.

Turns to Delgado. "It appears you were correct." Then he turns back to me. "You have fully assimilated your host."

I realize he's addressing me as Garfunkel now, not Moses, believing Garfunkel's intellect overpowered my own. What he doesn't realize, is that I am both, though on the surface level, I'm still mostly Moses.

Let him think whatever he wants.

"We will take him before the council," Cowboy says. "This...development may be of interest. If not, he will be destroyed."

"On your feet," Delgado says, and I obey. No reason to put hot sauce in chamomile tea.

Delgado leads the way over the jagged, barren landscape. Chuy and Cowboy stay behind me, weapons drawn. I could, in theory, make a move now. Might even survive—if I was willing to kill my friends.

But I'm here to save them. And that's exactly what I'm going to do... in about six minutes.

As we trudge up a hillside covered in the crusty remains of blue Europhids, Delgado starts to whistle. It's a horrible sound at first. Just single, off-key notes. But with every step, the notes resolve into a poorly performed tune that I recognize—Bob Marley and the Wailers. 'Three Little Birds.'

At first, I think it's just a human habit the reds didn't manage to weed out of Delgado's subconscious. But the lyrics contain a clear message.

Don't worry.

About a thing.

He turns his head to the side, slightly, glancing back at me for a moment, while whistling the bit that translates to, 'Every little thing is going to be all right.'

It's a message.

Delgado is in control.

"Stop that sound," Cowboy says.

Delgado stops.

"It's called whistling," I say.

"Is irritating."

"Is music," I say. "You should like it. Order from chaos. Syncopation. Rhythm. You could learn something about—"

Cowboy shoves me forward.

We continue toward the hill's crest, and I decide to fill Delgado in with a tune of my own, humming the chorus to Europe's *Final Countdown.* I only get two lines in when Cowboy shoves me again, hard enough to make me stumble.

Delgado doesn't react. Just keeps on walking, until he reaches the top of the hill, where he pauses and turns around. "Time to face the music."

As I near the hill's top, red light seeps over the summit, like a fiery sunset.

The sky isn't pink, I realize. It's just full of haze that's reflecting red light from below.

A *lot* of red light.

Reaching the top of the hill feels a lot like hitting rock bottom in hell. Really fucking bad.

The landscape, stretching out as far as I can see, is covered in red Europhids. In the distance, massive arches rise into the air, every side slathered in glowing red.

They're everywhere.

And they're spreading. Red tendrils slowly snake into the rough terrain previously occupied by the blues. Little nubbin growths at the fringe sprout up to form full grown Europhids, even as red roots stretch out for more territory. They're probably doing this on every planet they occupy, taking over the space in which the blues lived for millennia, and then spreading out to take the planet and everything in it.

But not on Earth.

Not yet, anyway.

"Is this what order looks like?" I ask.

"It is," Cowboy says, pausing beside me.

"Is this what Earth will look like?"

"Your concern for your home world is small-minded," Cowboy says. "The greater good demands cohesion, which we will bring to all worlds." He smiles. "Including yours."

My eyes drift from the luminous, haunting horizon, down the hill's far side, where I find a small, out of place city, beside which is a spaceport, full of massive battleships. The buildings are vaguely similar to the huts I saw in Mazzola's past, round and conical, but massive in scale. And these aren't made from branches. They're constructed of pale metal, which reflects the red light. A dozen broad structures, each hundreds of feet tall, surround a towering skyscraper pocked with round portals and several walkways extending out to hovering ships. They look similar to the buildings, but horizontal and absolutely slathered in guns. The occupants might not be human, but they're definitely from Earth. Yeehaw.

There's activity everywhere. Mostly Neo-Cryptos moving between ships, but also rygars, most of them hauling loads of gear onto ships and a few other species I don't recognize from a distance. The scene reminds me of what I saw back at the Oxium mine—lesser creatures enslaved and used to wage war.

"Forward operating base?" I guess.

"Something like that," Chuy says. She takes hold of my arm, her grip painful. "Move." She hauls me forward and all but tosses me down the hill.

The walk toward the city takes just a few minutes, which means Cassidy's attack will be any second now...and possibly too early.

Because I have a new plan. A stupid plan, but still new.

If the attack begins now, I might never get the chance again.

As we near the F.O.B.'s fringe, Chuy's eyes linger on me. "You seem eager."

"To get this over with."

"No one is eager to die," she says.

"You'd be surprised."

She shakes her head, not buying it. "You still have hope for this one." She places a hand on her chest, reminding me that the voice speaking isn't hers, but that of an alien presence controlling her. "You would not give your life while there is still hope. Which means..." Her eyes widen. The Barrett snaps up, leveled at my chest. "What are you planning?"

Wellll, shit.

Behind me, Delgado starts snapping his fingers on both hands.

Chuy's brow furrows as the snap becomes a beat. Delgado bops his head, doing a jig as he begins whistling again. The simple melody—two sets of four notes followed by two sets of three—performed by The Cure is instantly recognizable to a music aficionado straight out of the 1980s, as is the message it conveys: *Close To Me.*

52

I slow turn toward Delgado. He's giving me a *what the hell is taking you so long,* bug-eyed stare. That's when I notice the change in the air. A cloud of black dust bends and twists on the breeze, drifting toward Chuy and Cowboy while seeping out of Delgado.

Holy shit, he really does have nanobots everywhere inside him.

My dive roll toward Delgado's side goes uncontested.

Both Chuy and Cowboy attempt to gun me down, but they're stopped, freezing in place, twitching like they're having strokes. And I think that might be close to the truth.

"What are you doing?" I ask.

"Clogging up the transmitters and receptors in their brains. It's like they're cars with no gas pedals." He grunts from the strain of it. "But they're fighting it. The Europhids."

"Aren't you doing the same thing to yourself?"

He shakes his head. "I've been blocking their control since they were attached. Intercepted at the source. They've never had control of me, but I've been intercepting their commands, and I've let them think they were pulling my strings. Chuy and Cowboy have been under their control this whole time."

"Can you undo it?" I ask.

"I don't think so," he says, "and I don't know how long I'll be able to hold them. So, if you have an idea—"

At the base of the hill, there's a roar. We've been discovered by a patrolling, bus-sized rygar, now charging toward us, followed by an army of Neo-Cryptos. Alarms blare across the base.

"—you better try it, fast."

I head for Chuy, giving the cloud of nanobots a wide berth.

"They're safe," Delgado says. "Just wanted you out of the way so they could act fast."

I step into the cloud, and I'm relieved when the dust parts for me.

Chuy is on her back, whole body shaking. I kneel over her waist, and I turn my attention first to the Barrett clutched in her hand. If she spasms and fires it accidentally, Cowboy is going to lose a limb. Her hand clutches the grip, but her trigger finger is extended and twitching—under control. Delgado made sure she couldn't fire.

Working with competent people is one of the best joys in life.

I pry the weapon out of her hand and shove it away.

Then I lean down and place my hands against the sides of her head. With a little focus, the part of me that is blue Europhid slips into her already crowded consciousness. The nanobots have no mental presence, but I can feel the chaos they're creating, keeping the red Europhids from regaining control.

And then I feel her.

Chuy.

Struggling for freedom. For control.

I got you, Babe, I think, and then I turn my attention on the red presence.

YOU DO NOT BELONG HERE.

Speaking with Garfunkel's mental voice feels good. Feels powerful. And it should. He...*I*...carry the weight of all blue Europhids, the only creature in the universe ever able to contain and quell the reds' destructive instincts.

My first and very human instinct is to push them out—repel the invaders—and then squash them underfoot.

But there is another option. One that is not instinctual to most human beings.

Redemption.

Reconciliation.

Reclamation.

Instead of plowing into the red Europhids and shoving them out, I entangle myself with them, merging my will with theirs and opening their minds. Biologically, reds and blues are identical. They just respond to external stimuli with different reactions, passed down to them by their predecessors. The color of a Europhid is simply a reflection of its state of mind. So, I give the reds an education, taking a page out of Mazzola's book, letting them experience the fullness of their kind. Their shared history. Their mutual successes. Their—

It's not working.

Their resistance persists.

Because everything I'm showing them is second hand, from the eyes of an observer.

The voice of Mazzola's mother comes to me out of the ether. "You need to accept its presence the way you do the air in your lungs. In time you will learn to hold your breath, to breathe deeply, and to exhale loudly."

"I want to know now," I tell her memory.

I feel warm affection flowing from his mother, smothering out everything else. "I thought you might."

Mazzola arrives in my thoughts next, fully grown, speaking wisdom learned from his mother. "Before you can evolve, you must accept."

I need to accept what I have become...not just acknowledge it.

I am Moses Montgomery, friend of Max, a man from both the past and the future. I am Dark Horse, pirate, liberator, and general of the last rebellion. And...I am Garfunkel, a blue Europhid, the last of my kind, bearer of our history, protector of our future, and—my eyes widen at the realization—sole authority to which all reds must obey.

Even in rebellion.

No wonder they want me dead.

The raw power of Europhid history flows through me, washing over the reds attached to Chuy. They must be young, because I sense it's all new to them. Baptized in reality, the Europhids face a choice. Embrace truth and change their ways or dig deeper into the deception clouding their thoughts—that the only response to fear is violence.

All at once, they decide.

And Chuy is freed.

I'm launched out of her brain as her consciousness comes roaring back.

Her eyes snap open and lock on mine. In this simple, sudden moment, I know she's back...and I have just a few seconds to speak before her knee ascends to my nuts. "That stuff I said about your mother... I didn't—"

She reaches up, takes the back of my head, and pulls me down into a kiss.

It lingers for a few seconds. Then she pushes me away and slaps me in the face. Smiling, she says, "That's for my mother. The kiss was for everything else. When you were in my head, I saw everything. Your last few days. Their...your entire history. I want you to know that I love you, blue eyes and all."

I smile so wide it hurts.

"Now take care of Milos before you start blubbering." She shoves me toward him.

I kneel beside Cowboy and place my hands on the sides of his head. Entering his consciousness, working my way through the nano-confusion and commanding the Europhids controlling him goes a lot faster this time, and the results are the same. Faced with reality from a perspective other than that of 'primal fear responses' allows them to see another path forward, guided by unification, not total control.

Cowboy opens his eyes and smiles. "I knew you would come."

I stand and offer him my hand, hauling him to his feet. Once he's up, I pat the dust from his shoulders, turning him around until I see his back.

And what's on it.

The Europhids are still there, attached to his spine through the adaptive armor. But they're no longer red.

They're...blue.

A cosmic-sized weight lifts away.

I'm no longer the last.

And there can be more. I look out at the glowing red landscape.

A *lot* more.

And that's why they're going to do everything they can to kill me.

I turn to Delgado. "You, too."

As the black mist re-enters his body, I place my hands on the sides of his head. There's no struggle here. The Europhids have no hold on him, and my access to them is unchallenged. Seconds after first contact, the assault being fended off by the nano-bots comes to a stop, and the Europhids on his back turn from red to blue.

"We'll figure out how to remove them later," Chuy says, picking up her Barrett. "Right now, we've got a situation."

She nods downhill.

The charging rygar is a football field away and closing the distance between us. It's followed by several smaller rygars and a surging army of Neo-Cryptos. They'll be here in seconds.

"Am not fan of running from fight," Cowboy says. "But..."

I'm about to agree with him, when a creepy voice booms from the hill's far side, saying, "Gimme Chocolate." It's followed by rapid fire drums and a heavy metal guitar riff that's impossible to resist.

"Sorry we're late," Hildy says in my ear.

"Nope. Your timing is perfect," I say.

"Did you find the others?" Hildy asks.

"We're right here," Chuy says. "Ready to rock."

"Is Cassidy with you?" I ask.

"You brought Cassidy?" Delgado asks, a little angry.

"Couldn't stop her if I wanted," I say. "And everything that happens next...well, you can thank *her* later."

A trio of Japanese girls start belting out lyrics that are nonsensical, and when they're not, they're in Japanese. Then at the top of the hill— movement. Two gray heads bobble into view.

Hans and Franz.

Armed with mini-guns.

Delgado laughs. "Oh...magod."

Hundreds more heavily armed grays rise up on either side of them. Scattered among them is the occasional gray, wielding a giant pink foam hand with its index finger extended and Cassidy's name emblazoned on the palm. They thrust them to the sky as they march forward. Just as the music transitions, a fleet of UFOs outfitted with Delgado's future-tech weapons soars past overhead. Beams of light jut down from the UFOs, unleashing the first of two deadly payloads. Giant, agitated alligators writhe as they float to the ground and touch down amidst the enemy ranks. The gnawing and thrashing begins the moment they reach the ground.

With the alligators wreaking havoc, payload number two drops down—far away from us—and not gently. Hundreds of tarantula hawk nests plummet to the ground—and some heads—cracking open to unleash angry stinging hell. As far as hornets go, the tarantula hawk has one of the most painful stings on Earth. It's like an electric shock to the nuts. Absolutely debilitating for up to twenty-four hours. Had the Neos been actual aliens, the venom might have no effect, but the Neos originated on Earth.

To add insult to injury, as the UFOs alter course up into the sky, they launch a cascade of rainbow fireworks that whistle and twirl down to the ground. And just when I think this moment can't get any more wonderous—Cassidy arrives.

Her torso is covered in some kind of black leather, anime-inspired armor. Below that is a red and black poofy skirt, black tights, and pair of shitkicker boots. In one hand, she holds a flag—on which is an image of Earth, six stars, and two pixelated unicorns with rainbows trailing from their backsides. Latin text graces the top and bottom, reading, "Flectere si nequeo superos, Acheronta movebo."

If I can't move Heaven, I shall raise hell.

Cassidy is lifted up into the air, seated atop Mazzola as he rears up. She holds the flag high and shouts, "Give them nothing. But take from them...*chocolate!*"

53

"Where do you need us?" Cassidy asks after her grand entrance is complete.

"Precious cargo already secured," I say, letting her know that I've already got Chuy, Cowboy, and Delgado, "but the plan stays the same. Chaos. Confusion. Disarray. Give them hell, kid."

Delgado grabs hold of my arm. "What are you doing? We need to leave. Now."

"I know you're used to calling the shots," I say, "but when it comes to intergalactic combat, I'm kind of the GOAT. Did I use that right? GOAT?"

"Greatest of all time," Cowboy says. "Yes."

"Cool. Point is, we have a chance to end this here and now." I motion to the endless landscape of red Europhids behind the approaching army. "*That's* what we call a target of opportunity. A chance to end a war before it spills over onto Earth, and I'll be damned if I'm not going to take a shot."

Delgado isn't buying it. "In case you missed it, there's an army coming toward us."

"And they're never going to know what hit them," I say.

Wini's voice booms over the comms. "Let's go!"

An ATV roars over the hill's crest, catching air before landing beside Mazzola, as he charges toward us with Cassidy on his back. Hildy sits in the driver's seat. Wini stands behind her, holding onto a railgun that's been mounted to the small vehicle.

Chuy's mouth drops open. "Holy shi—"

"Down!" I shout, pushing the slower moving Delgado to the ground, just before a round fires, bending the air above our heads as it races downhill, striking the huge rygar in its sphincter mouth and punching out the far side to collide with three Neo-Cryptos that all but cease to exist from the impacts. The round's journey ends when it slams into the ground, kicking up an explosion of stone. But the effect of its passage is still being revealed, as the rygar folds in on itself, pulled in the railgun round's wake, all the way through, until the creature's whole body has been turned inside out.

"Okay," I say, lifting my head. "That...was gross."

"Whoohooo!" Hildy and Wini race past us, followed by Cassidy, Mazzola, and then a whole fleet of ATVs, piloted by Delgado's collection of empathic orphans. Running alongside them—the grays. And behind them, a small army of people dressed in adaptive armor, carrying a collection of random weapons from the *Bitch'n* and Delgado's armories.

A series of grenades fly overhead, arcing down into the enemy forces, but when they detonate, there's no fire or severed limbs—there's glue and glitter, making the enemy pretty—and blinding them with gooey glitter eyes.

Triggered by Wini's opening salvo, the grays open fire. Tracer rounds burn through the air, scouring the landscape ahead and shredding the Neo-Crypto and rygar ranks. UFOs cut through the sky, bouncing around at impossible speeds. All the while, they unleash energy, kinetic, and who the hell knows what weapons. Death from above.

Neo-Cryptos adjust to the attack, leaping through the air, making themselves harder targets. They're going to reach our front ranks.

As far as opening salvos go, ours is one of the best I've ever seen. As though to prove it, a rapid-fire T-shirt launcher thumps out a barrage of pink shirts. As one unfurls, I see Cassidy's winking face printed on the front. The loose fabric wraps around the face of a Neo, who begins to sizzle and holler. Acid T-shirts... Pretty sure that's against an accord or convention or something, but we're not on Earth, and the gloves are off. We'll just have to leave a few details out of our memoirs. Probably won't mention the alligators, either. I tell myself that they'd volunteer to defend Earth if they could speak. I don't care about the hornets, though. Screw the hornets. They're assholes. Along with the blaring music, Cassidy managed to bring the chaos and then some.

Problem is, the Neo-Cryptos have numbers on their side. Maybe hundreds of thousands against our hundreds.

We don't have enough ammunition to take them all down.

But we don't need bullets.

"Moses," Delgado says. "Please. These people...they're not fighters."

As though to prove his point, a lanky man holding a rifle like it's a rake runs past, following the wave of people downhill. He gives a wave and says, "Hey, Dan!"

"On the plus side," I say, "I'm not sure he knows where the trigger is, so he's not going to accidentally shoot anyone."

"That's *Ted*," Delgado says. "He mops the floors, is missing several body parts, and coaches Little League on the weekend." He blinks as though just realizing something. "Nathaniel. My son. He's—"

"Not here," I say. "Wini wouldn't allow it. Knew it would distract you. But you don't need to worry. Just...watch." I put my hand on his chin and turn his gaze toward the battlefield. "I would never put people in harm's way if I didn't think they could win."

As the line of ATVs races toward the first of the lunging, frothing, buck nekkid Neo-Cryptos, the teens riding them lean forward and scream.

From a distance it seems kind of pitiful. Most of them have high-pitched voices, and those that don't are cracking. Combined, it sounds like Big Bird's squawking family is getting murdered.

But the invisible effect...it's exactly what I hoped it would be.

The first Neo-Crypto clutches its chest mid leap, falls to the ground, and flails about as it rolls to an unmoving stop.

"Turns out a bunch of empaths with unresolved horrors locked in their minds are powerful weapons."

Delgado is stymied. "How did you know..."

"Again," I say. "Wasn't me. This is all her." I point to Cassidy, whose emotive scream is amplified by Mazzola's mind, reaching out to strike down lines of the enemy.

Some of them fall to the ground, thrashing around, feeling the emotions projected by the kids. Others clutch their chests as their hearts literally break from the unexpected and condensed trauma. For some, the reds lining their backs explode, leaving them with a dozen gaping wounds. Those that stay on their feet are cut down by a fusillade of gunfire, glitter, and melting T-shirts.

Three ATVs pull to a stop beside us. One is driven by McCoy. His ride looks like something out of a Mad Max movie, with a plow mounted to the front. The other two have mounted railguns.

A woman with long gray hair and American Indian features steps off one of the ATVs. "Mr. Delgado. These are for you."

"Yona, what are you doing out here?"

"What needs to be done," she says, and she gives him a smile. "Like you always do."

Yona and the old man driving the second ATV, step aside and head back uphill.

Before anyone can talk about who's driving, both Chuy and Cowboy climb up behind the railguns.

"You tell her to say that?" Delgado asks.

"Not me," I say, and I look to Wini, still blasting away, whooping with every railgun round she fires. On level ground now, each shot travels miles, cutting down everything in its path—including the buildings in the background. With enough ammo, Wini might win this fight on her own. But at her current rate of fire, she's got just a few minutes.

I climb on the ATV Chuy has claimed. "You coming?"

Delgado sighs and takes the ATV with Cowboy. Then he looks back at McCoy and motions to the old folks who delivered our vehicles. "Blackbird, get them to safety."

McCoy looks ready to argue. Like me, he's not one to back down from a fight. But Yona isn't going anywhere fast. They're sitting ducks. McCoy nods and pulls up beside Yona.

I rev my engine. "Stay close."

"Where are we going?" Delgado asks.

"Second to the right and straight on 'til morning," I say.

"Cute," he says.

Chuy kicks my shoulder. "We've been through the shit. Straight answers or I'm revoking the coupon book."

Chuy doesn't like buying gifts for people, mostly because she loathes shopping. In the future, when things were bleak, we didn't really celebrate birthdays, but Hildy insisted on a party for my last—two months ago. In place of a traditional gift, Chuy followed Burnett's advice and gave me a book of coupons...which focused primarily on extracurricular activities I normally wouldn't be brave enough to ask her to try.

I scan the battlefield and search for the closest patch of red. I find it directly ahead, where the Neo-Crypto ranks are thickest. I point to it. "Straight down the middle. I need to have a conversation with a planet."

"You heard the man," Chuy shouts, priming her railgun. "Let's kick some alien ass!"

I gun the engine, and we're off, racing downhill.

Doesn't take long to gain on the front line. Despite rushing into battle, the teens aren't experienced ATV drivers, and the grays can only run so fast. I, on the other hand, know how to ride like a sunuvabitch, and I'm capable of throwing caution to the wind like Bowser throws hammers.

Delgado is keeping pace, but the look in his eyes says his hammer throwing ability is closer to that of an armless Goomba.

"Cassidy," I say, "On your six. Need an opening."

"On it!" she says, and Mazzola leans left, creating a gap between himself and Hildy's ATV. I pull between them and give Hildy a nod. "You with us?"

"You know I am," she says.

Wini fires off two railgun rounds and shouts, "Let's chafe these assholes!"

"What?" I ask.

"Somebody's never gotten laid in the sand," she says.

"It's in the coupon book!" I shout, and I prepare to twist my throttle. Before I can, motion lifts my eyes to the sky, where Cassidy is flipping—*flipping*—from Mazzola's back. She lands on the front end of my ATV, crouching down in a Spider-Man squat. She stabs a fearless finger forward and shouts, "Chafe these assholes!"

I sigh, and throttle forward toward thousands of pale assholes, who are about to get royally chafed.

54

"Center mass!" Chuy shouts, and then she fires her railgun straight ahead.

What follows is a scene straight out of anime. The tungsten round bends light around itself as it tears through the air at roughly two miles per second. A shockwave of dust follows its path, transforming to red and purple mist as the round evaporates every living thing it touches. A miles long path through the oncoming army is carved out.

And not one of them saw it coming. Cassidy's plan is working. The confusion created by an unexpected attack from a force composed of advanced UFOs, grays whose inorganic minds can't be read, and empaths waging emotional warfare, resulted in the Neos in disarray—but they remain undeterred.

Something doesn't feel right, though. The Neo we encountered in Antarctica roiled with unfettered emotional and mental power. It dropped us to the ground in the same way our teenage empaths are doing to the Neo ranks now. So why aren't they able to resist? Or even fight back? They look like the creature we encountered in Antarctica, but they're different somehow.

Not as refined.

And ambivalent to what's happening to them.

The level of carnage unleashed by the railguns would make the average army reenact the Mt. Saint Helens eruption in their pants, turn tail, and beat feet the other way.

But the Neo-Cryptos keep coming, maybe because they're badasses. Maybe because the singular-minded Europhids attached to them are injectting adrenaline and dopamine into their brains, making them fearless.

Doesn't really matter which.

Before the bodies have hit the floor, the empty path fills in with new bodies, gnashing their teeth, baring their claws, bounding back and forth, making themselves harder targets.

"Widen the path!" I shout.

Delgado pulls up on one side. Hildy on the other.

All three railguns unleash streaks of death, widening the path ahead, which is now slick with blood-soaked stone coated in chunks of meat and bone that make the ride more than a little bumpy.

"Hang on tight!' I shout to Cassidy.

"I am!" she replies, poofy skirt flapping in my face, making it hard to see.

But I can still see above me, where a UFO is struck by some kind of energy weapon that tears it apart.

We might have caught the Neo-Cryptos and the reds off guard, but they're prepping for war. Won't be long before their counterattack turns us back or gets us all killed.

The UFO falls from the sky, crashing down a hundred feet straight ahead.

Instinct tells me to veer to the side, but I have absolute faith in Chuy.

She fires three railgun rounds. The first two shatter the UFO's sides. The last punches the middle into oblivion, sending shards of shrapnel out into the onrushing, never-ending horde.

At this rate we're going to run out of ammo before reaching the Europhids.

"Delgado," I say.

"Yeah?" he says, sounding a bit frazzled. Some people are built for solving mysteries, others for charging the gates of hell. But he's getting the job done.

"You can talk to the UFOs, right?"

"Yeah," he says, and I wonder if the intensity of our situation has reduced his vocabulary.

"Have them target that skyscraper's base. Bring it to the ground."

He weaves to the side for a moment, avoiding the top half of a twitching Neo-Crypto. Then he's right beside me again, Cowboy behind him, laying down a steady stream of accurate railgun fire. Like Wini, he's firing quickly. Unlike Wini, each shot he takes lays waste to a massive number of the enemy.

"I don't know," Delgado says. "Seems kind of 9-11."

9-11.

The worst attack on American soil since Pearl Harbor.

I wasn't around for it, so I can't comment on what it was like to live through it. The vision of those towers falling to the ground was etched on the permanent record of every American who watched the news on that day. It was old news by the time I saw the footage, and I still wept.

But this isn't the same.

"We're not terrorists," I tell him. "And that is not an office building full of innocent civilians. This is a forward operating base for an enemy that has Earth in its crosshairs."

"Not just Earth," he says.

He was connected to the Europhids, but unlike Drago, Chuy, and Cowboy, he retained his core self. Had access to everything they know and what they're planning.

"Give me the bullet list version," I say, swerving around a pair of legs.

"Their motivation isn't wrong," he says, wrestling with the words. "The danger they're sensing is real. But their reaction to it is extreme. They want to control the response to it so much that they'll conquer anyone with a different opinion. They faced the Neo-Cryptos first, but after the first forced union and the revelations that followed, the Neos agreed with the reds' assessment. With both controlling vast amounts of the universe, they were natural partners and an impressive alliance. After merging, they became hyper aggressive and obsessed with order."

Blood sprays from beneath my tires. "I. Said. Bullet list!" I lean to the right, twist to the left, and unleash a one-handed spray of railgun discs, shredding the Neo sailing over Delgado, on a collision course with me.

They're still focusing on me, seeing me as the primary threat despite the spanking being doled out by Delgado's crew.

And they're not wrong.

The discs twist and turn inside the creature's body, carving it up from the inside until it comes apart—and splashes down toward me, Cassidy, and Chuy, like a hellish version of the painting Under the Wave off Kanagawa.

"Masks!" I shout, and I yank the adaptive armor's mask over my head, just as the gore cascade splashes down. Chunks of who-knows-what cling to the ATV, but the rest slides away from the armor's non-stick surface faster than the grease from those pans peddled by the angry British chef.

When my vision clears, I see Cassidy in front of me, absolutely dripping in nastiness, no doubt regretting her decision to prioritize fashion over function. But she hides it well, clinging in place, attention straight ahead, on mission.

I glance up at Chuy and realize that while I shouted, "Masks!" I was the only one in a position to put one on. Chuy's armored body is clear of death fluids, but her face is streaked with blood. Chunks of gristle wriggle in her hair. Not that she's squeamish. The sight of it probably bothers me more than it does her.

I turn my attention back to Delgado. "Are they going to attack Earth?"

"Yes."

"Are they going to kill everyone? Or body-snatch them?"

"Yes."

"Then bring down those fucking buildings!"

I can tell he doesn't like it. War doesn't sit well with people whose moral compass is more sensitive than mine. But he doesn't have a choice ...and he knows it.

A moment later, the UFOs targeting the horde shift tactics, pounding the skyscraper's base. Explosions shake the battlefield, stumbling some of the Neos forward, right into Chuy's line of fire. They barely have time to think, 'Oops,' before being erased.

"How we doing, Blackbird?" I ask, knowing McCoy's still got a view of the battlefield.

"Line is holding," he says. "Enemy is bunching up in front of the kids. Can't approach without breaking down into tears. Grays are finishing the job, but ammo is running low."

"You and Mazzola pull the kids back and get them back home. The grays can cover your retreat. But Blackbird, I need you to close the gate once everyone is through."

"Close it?"

"We'll be okay," I insist. "But I need that gate closed."

"Copy that," he says. "Pulling back now."

"I'm out!" Wini shouts.

Hildy falls back and then falls in line behind us, following our narrowing path through the enemy ranks.

Ahead of us, the Neos are trying something new, all of them charging and leaping in waves. Moving vertically keeps the railgun rounds from impacting all of them, but I don't think that's the goal.

They're obscuring our view.

Keeping us from seeing what's coming.

"Incoming!" I shout. "Cowboy, make a mess."

At first, his shots seem random, but then I see the pattern, expertly punching holes in the mass of enemies, looking for the secret like a game of Battleship.

But he can't find it.

Because the waves ahead of us were a distraction.

We're in the shit now, completely surrounded by Neos. The attack comes from the sides.

A massive rygar emerges from the horde, its charge so mindless that it tramples Neos underfoot, thrashes more of them into the air, and even sucks up a few into its sphincter-like maw along the way.

Chuy swivels toward it, firing two railgun projectiles. The first goes wide, punching a hole straight through one of the smaller buildings. The second carves a trough in the rygar's side, but the creature doesn't even flinch. It's lost in bloodlust.

Until Cassidy screams.

I catch a whiff of the abject despair and horror she's projecting toward the oncoming beast, and it's nearly enough to undo me. The depths of her pain are something no one should have to endure. Breaks my heart that she has such a deep well of pain from which to draw negative energy. That she's peppy and loving is a testament to her fortitude.

But her raw, unleashed power?

The rygar doesn't stand a chance.

The pulse of soul-crushing emotion strikes the rygar and plunges an emotional knife into its will.

It folds in on itself, faceplanting in despair.

But it's still coming, sliding forward...until its flesh, currently being scoured away by the rough, stone terrain, catches on a boulder. All that forward momentum springs it up, catapulting the beast up and over us, its desperate wail dopplering away as the creature pinwheels in slow motion.

I watch its progress above us until the beast crashes back down on Delgado's left side, rolling into the oncoming troops. Then I turn forward, pushing the ATV to its limits just five hundred feet from our goal. Cassidy faces forward, unleashing her wave of empathic energy, emotionally shattering anything that isn't cut down by Chuy and Cowboy.

For a moment, I'm confident.

Then a new challenger enters the fray. I turn my eyes upward.

"What the happy hell is that?"

55

"Female of the species," Delgado says, somehow staying professional in the face of something that is dragging the teenage boy in me to the surface. I have so many things to say, but I manage to contain them, because: fate of the world and all that.

She stands fifty feet tall—on all fours. Would be a hundred feet if she reared up. But I don't think she's going to be doing that any time soon. Because she's popping out Neos like they're going out of style—oozing them out of pores on her sides that I really hope are not vaginas. The Neos fall to the ground, wrapped in translucent white sacks that burst on impact. After tearing free, the newborn-yet-fully-grown Neos don't rush into battle.

First, they satiate their thirst, running over to—*shit, I can't handle this*—running over to one of a few dozen twenty-foot-long teats hanging from a pair of swaying udders. The Neos join a gaggle of other newborns suckling away, shuffling toward the battle. As they drink, red Europhid buds appear on their backs, growing to full size in seconds.

I look up at the female again. Its back is littered with red Europhids. They've burrowed throughout her body, injecting her young with spores, taking control almost from the moment of birth—turning them into war machines.

The moment the young are satiated, they're ready to fight, and they join the horde's ranks.

The true horror of what I'm seeing settles in.

We're fighting babies.

Do they even know what they're doing?

Are they under full Europhid control, or are they intelligent and evil from the moment they're born?

No way to know. No way to ask. All we can do is press on and find good therapists.

"Target the big one," I say to Cowboy. "Put her down fast."

Stopping more young from being born is Step One. She's between us and the field of Europhids. No way through unless she's down.

Then Cowboy says, "Which one?"

I reassess the battlefield. The females were hidden behind the structures. There're a dozen of them total, spewing out a new army every few minutes. But his question has an obvious answer. I stab my finger straight ahead and shout, "That one!"

Cowboy swivels his railgun up and—hesitates. "Dark Horse…"

He's just figured out what I did. We're on some shaky moral ground here, but if we can't stop the Europhids here and now, the next army they create might be human toddlers strapped with C4.

"I know," I say. "We're out of options."

He frowns—and pulls the trigger.

The railgun disc cuts up through the air above the army being cut down by Chuy and repulsed by Cassidy. The air behind it bends, warping the female Neo's image, which is fine by me because I don't really want to see what comes next.

But I do.

And it's not what I expected.

The female leans her big, crested head to the side, easily avoiding the round.

The time between firing the weapon and the impact should have been only measurable by an atomic clock. But she dodged it like…

She knew it was coming.

Just like the Neo we encountered in Antarctica.

Is she a powerful psychic or—I spot him beyond the top of her forehead's crest, wedged into a depression that looks like it was made for…

Ugh. I've seen enough weird adaptations in my life as an exo-hunter to recognize them when I see them. The Neo is attached to the female, not quite at the hip. A little bit lower. Playing his biological role in the creation of this army. But he's also controlling her, lending his psychic mastery to her, keeping her alive. Keeping the army coming.

I focus on the male and see three familiar scars. This is the Neo that came for me. That took Chuy and the others. The Europhids might ultimately be calling the shots, but this asshole is a conduit for their influence. He needs to be taken out—if only to send a message—screw with my people, get a tungsten railgun round shot through your face.

The Neo's black eyes shift toward me. When we make eye contact, his head leans back, communicating something like, *YOU.* Then I feel his mind reaching out, trying to pry our plan from my head, rippling with horrific energy that fails to undo me the way it first did.

He's the key.

Maybe not to victory, but to surviving the next few minutes and doing what needs to be done with the Europhids.

Cowboy fires another round and fails to connect. "No use. Is predicting my shots."

"Not sure it's our biggest problem," Hildy shouts.

I glance back. Our path through the Neo-army has become a pocket. The moment we pass, the enemy ranks close in behind us. They're no longer rushing the hill. We're their primary focus—the seven of us against an army of alien babies fresh off the teat, controlled by a maniacal leader. Another horror I wish was unique to alien life, but child soldiers are common on Earth, now and throughout history, blindly following their elders to a violent death.

It's a universal evil.

When I realize I'm guilty of the same, I feel sick to my stomach. Here I am with Cassidy on the front of an ATV, plowing through the enemy ranks, supported by teenage empaths putting their lives on the line. Every single one of them could have been cut down by some unforeseen threat.

But sometimes war doesn't leave many choices.

We wouldn't have made it this far without them.

I'll live with the guilt if it keeps Earth from being conquered and used as fodder in an intergalactic conflict that isn't ours.

"Whatever you're doing," Wini shouts, "better do it quick! They're like an army of thirsty, middle-class, knee-high-boot-wearing, soccer moms chasing a pumpkin spice truck!"

An explosion to our left sends a shockwave through the Neo ranks. Those closest to it are sent sprawling through the air, probably considering their brief life choices before slamming back down. I'm rocked to the side, but I manage to stay upright.

I nearly fall over again when I see the wreckage of a UFO at the base of the skyscraper.

For a moment, I think the grays piloting it must have kamikazed into the building, but then the sky is full of ships with similar capabilities to the UFOs, but twice the size and with far greater numbers. Our UFO fleet kicked ass when it had the sky to itself. Now, they'll last just a few minutes. If that.

The crashed UFO did the trick though, reducing the skyscraper's structural integrity. The base crumples and for a moment, I think the whole thing will just compress and fall straight down. Instead, it jolts down, cants to the side, and slowly falls.

Straight toward the big female and the lead Neo.

They turn their heads skyward as the building's shadow falls over them. The energy flowing from the Neo shifts from 'I'm a big scary alien,' to something like, 'Holy shit balls,' and finally to panic. The female turns and runs, trampling her young around her and dragging some especially thirsty ones along for the ride, as they cling to her elastic udders.

She's big, but she's fast, easily bolting from the falling building's path.

"Dark Horse," McCoy says through the comms.

"I see it," I say.

"Kids are home safe."

Thank God.

"And in case you can't see it—"

"I see it." I look up at the descending skyscraper. Its vast size makes it look like its falling in slow motion, but it is absolutely cruising toward the ground. Where it will flatten a large swath of Europhids—but not nearly enough of them. "Gonna need that gate closed, pronto."

"Stepping through now, unless you need anything else."

"We're good." It's a lie, but I'm trying to convince myself that everything I'm about to attempt will 1) work, and 2) not get everyone I love killed.

"Closing gate in three, two..." His comm signal crackles and cuts out.

"Stay in the dust cloud, until you're clear. Maybe do a few donuts in the Europhid field. Then rotate the hell out of here."

"No way I can navigate back to Earth," Chuy says, "and there's no way Hildy can take us all."

"Won't need to," I say, and because I have absolute faith in my people, I look to the sky just in time to see the *Bitch'n* rotate into the airspace previously occupied by the skyscrapers. Her array of railguns, chain guns, rocket pods, and future weapons installed by Burnett unleash aerial wrath on the Neo air force and the enemy ranks on the ground.

"Am I late?" Burnett asks, sounding excited.

"Right on time," I say, swerving around an airborne Neo that's managed to avoid Chuy's rail discs and has gone limp thanks to Cassidy's empathic energy wave. "Keep them busy. The team is en route. If things get hairy, bug out."

"What about y—" I cut off the comms, reach forward, and tap Cassidy on the back. She looks back at me, her bluster and excitement gone. I think she's seen enough horrible things for a lifetime.

"Need you to take the wheel," I say.

Her eyes widen, a little bit of her energy returning. "Really?

Chuy fires a double shot, widening our path.

Beside us, Cowboy shouts, "Out!" and Delgado falls back, pulling up behind Hildy and Wini, our choo-choo train of death nearly out of ammo.

Cassidy climbs back, sliding into my seat and taking the controls, as I stand up behind her.

"Got it?"

She gives me a thumbs up with her left hand, keeping the right on the throttle.

"Know what you're doing?" I ask.

"Not a clue!" she says, laughing now. Chaos is her friend.

I turn my head up, looking at Chuy upside down. "Don't wait for me, okay?"

"What are you up to, cabrón?"

I smile at her. "Love you."

She frowns down at me. "Moses..."

I face forward and make eye contact with the Neo-Controller a moment before the skyscraper collides with the ground and kicks up a billowing wall of dust and grit.

"Predict this," I say, and I rotate away from the ATV.

56

I slip out of the fourth dimension two hundred feet in the air, looking down at the battlefield. The three ATVs are swallowed up by the expanding dust cloud rushing out across the landscape. If all goes right, they should rotate to safety inside *Bitch'n* any second now.

I look for the Neo-Controller and the big female as I begin falling, but they've been swallowed up.

A portion of the dust cloud rises as though ejected from a volcano, but it's actually being shoved up by the female's massive crest as she stands on her hind legs, cutting through the grit and rising above it. The Controller is still there, on his perch.

His black eyes make it hard to tell if he's pissed, but he must be. We've brought chaos to the Order's doorstep. This might only represent a small portion of their overall might—just one base amidst hundreds, maybe thousands, but the destruction wrought by our small force should make them think twice before trying to subjugate Earth.

And I'm not done yet.

After building up a little speed from falling, I rotate into the fourth dimension and exit a moment later, ten feet above the Controller. He senses my presence, but he only has time to whip his head toward me and widen those black eyes a bit.

I drive my heels into his forehead.

Were he human, the impact would have probably broken his neck, and the fight would have come to an anticlimactic but welcome end. Instead, I've struck one of the creature's most protected body parts. I all but bounce off the thick forehead and his armored crest.

He stumbles back a step, but I'm sent sprawling—and I no longer have my railgun.

The Controller has it.

He could gun me down with ease, but he doesn't even consider it. He crushes the weapon in one hand and tosses it away. Even with my enhanced strength and speed, I think he might be more than a match. But that's not how he's going to fight me.

The mental assault begins even before I've slid to a stop on the top of the female's snout. Her big black eyes focus on me for a moment. Then she snaps up on her hind legs and flings me through the air, straight toward her crest, which is now rushing at me with the destructive power of a runaway train.

I don't care how much stronger my merger with Garfunkel made me, the female is about to pulverize me.

I think about rotating.

Can see how to do it in my mind, but I'm cut off from my limbs.

The adaptive armor, detecting the impending impact, begins to inflate, but I don't think it will be enough.

The Controller is in my head, immobilizing me while his tag-team partner jumps from the top rope.

I close my eyes, focus for a moment, and let the part of me that is Garfunkel expunge the Controller's influence. Doesn't take long, but time is short.

Partially inflated, I rotate away just as I'm about to strike the female's crest. Had there not been a pocket of fourth dimension between us, I'd be doing a great impression of a bug on a windshield. Instead, I'm surrounded by endless white, watching a rectangular chunk of the female's crest spiral away into the void, where it will be lost forever. The armor deflates, conforming to my body's shape once more.

Then I'm back out, standing directly behind the Controller.

Reminded of the armor's bonus capabilities, I turn my body into a lamp and bump up the lumens as high as they can go. The Controller glances back, and quickly squints and shields his eyes, bathed in white light.

Catching him off guard, I shout "Ha!" and deliver a testes-destroying kick between his legs.

I shut off the light so I can watch him writhe in pain.

But he doesn't crumple to the ground in a vomitous fetal curl. He slow-turns until one of his eyes is locked on to me.

"Right," I say, "Undescended nards. Little dick. How can a..." I glance down at his micro-penis. "...man like you satisfy a woman like *this*." I motion to big-Bertha beneath us.

"Procreation is utility," he says, mind-to-mind.

"You're missing out," I tell him, and I throw a punch.

He sees it coming, as usual, leaning away from the strike. But I manage to graze his cheek. His skin feels like a shark's, rough and sandpapery. Pretty sure I just rubbed away a few layers.

He counters with a swipe of his clawed hand. I manage to duck it, not because I'm clairvoyant like him, but because I'm fucking good at this, and I prove it by kicking his kneecap while I'm down there.

The joint inverts for a moment, getting a howl of pain—and sprawling the big asshole straight toward me.

His fall turns into an attack. He stabs both hands down at me. I slide to the left, dodging the first hand. Then I slip back, but not quite far enough. One of his long claws punctures my shoulder.

But he's also dug the rest of his claw into the female's head. She howls in irritation, the volume of her voice nearly loud enough to shatter my ears. She also kicks off a massive emotional burst that has more of an effect on the Controller than it does on me. He yanks his finger from my shoulder, and despite having the advantage, he staggers back, clutching his head. He's wounded her, and she's giving him a mind full of shit for it. Time to make my move.

"Burnett," I say. "Status."

"All team members on board and accounted for. Ready to feel the burn?" he asks.

"What? God. No. Send me the data."

"That's what I meant. Starting data stream." A series of squeaks and clicks fill my ear. Means nothing to my conscious mind, but in theory, the Garfunkel in me can decipher the data, revealing a set of special coordinates and exactly how to move from here to there.

The moment we left Earth, Burnett began searching for our active slew drives. Once he had our location out among the stars, he just needed to wait for the gate to show up. Then the ship's slew drive did the rest, performing the rotation and navigation without human involvement. PSDs work differently, and without precise control, or a strong sense of intuition—how I operate compared to someone like Hildy—it can be a dangerous prospect.

But I'm no longer flying by the seat of my pants. My intellect has been expanded in ways I don't fully understand. I don't really feel like an Einstein. My sense of humor is still juvenile, and the idea of doing math makes me nauseous, but understanding things that should be impossible? Well, it's kind of a snap now.

The data stream stops, and all at once, I understand the precise ballet of movement required to get myself to my destination.

But it's more than that.

A lot more than that.

I back step, as the female's cry ends, and the Collector shakes it off. "Burn, how much celestial data did you send?"

"Just the ones you asked fo—wait. No. Oh, wow. How are you feeling?"

"What did you send?" I ask, time running short.

"Uhh, everything. All known celestial coordinates in the system. You don't have a headache or anything? That much data—"

"I feel fine, Burn," I say, glowering at the Collector with newfound confidence. "Out."

I crack my knuckles. "Last chance to surrender nicely and let me have a chat with your better-endowed counterparts." When he doesn't respond, I waggle a finger at the red Europhids covering the distant landscape. Everything around us is covered by the dust cloud.

"You do not understand what you are doing," he says, mind-to-mind.

"And you clearly don't know who you're screwing with," I say. "I've already saved the universe from a bunch of white assholes. I have no problem doing it again."

He sneers, baring his needle teeth.

But then the red Europhids on his back flare a little brighter, holding him back. "Show us..."

I can feel them probing at the fringe of my consciousness, knocking gently rather than trying to pry their way in. It's a dangerous gamble, but a chance to have a conversation, something this conflict has been sorely lacking. We're just reacting to their overreaction.

I open the door and take them someplace where they'll have no power.

"Hi Moses," Max says, looking down at me from the top of the swing set. He'd always talked about climbing up there and jumping off like Superfly Snuka, but he never worked up the courage to try. But this isn't Max. It's...

"Garfunkel?"

"Part of you now," he says. "Technically a manifestation of yourself, but you still feel a duality, so in here, we—are us. One, but plural."

"Cool," I say.

"Who are they?" he asks, pointing behind me.

I look back to find the Collector and the reds on his back transformed into the Roth twins: Fred and Fran. Both of them are eight years old, and they don't look like much trouble.

"Explain yourself," Fran says. She speaks for the Europhids.

Fred just kind of stalks around the yard, keeping an eye on me and getting used to his much smaller body.

"I'll show you," I say, and without much effort I unleash the memory of my time in the future.

Not all of it.

Just my meeting with the Europhids, the outcome of that meeting—Garfunkel's insertion into my consciousness—and the battle that ensued, where the reds and I worked hand-in-hand to kick our mutual enemy's ass.

"Could have been the same," I say, and I catch just a whiff of mental regret.

"Quiet, vermin," Fred says, his squeaky voice diffusing the threat.

So much of life is determined by who we meet and when we meet them. Under different circumstances, the reds trusted me to help defend their kind. Flash backward a thousand years, some kind of new universal threat—that didn't manifest in the Union timeline—and contact with Earth's previous tenants, led to genocide.

Fred stalks toward me like he's still big and intimidating. Maybe he's feeling all manly because little Fred's packing a little more downstairs than the Controller is accustomed to. "Witness for yourself."

A memory washes over me, propelling me to another world, where I experience horrors through the Controller's eyes.

57

In the night sky, a shadow looms, blotting out the stars. A massive starship, its shape hard to distinguish.

Experiencing the scene through the Controller, I feel confused and angry. But not afraid. I don't back down from a fight. Never have.

Power.

Order.

Perseverance.

Violence.

These are the forces that guide our society as they have since the millennia-long dark times, when my kind descended into madness. Out of that chaos came a few remaining bloodlines, the strongest of our kind, destined to remake the population in their image.

And anyone or anything that doesn't fit into that paradigm—blood and ashes.

Order is everything.

So, when I look up in the sky and I see the missing stars, I do not fear the unknown, I rage against it.

Reaching out with my mind, I summon the Guard—elite warriors who have spent a lifetime fending off decades of challengers, vying for command. They'll be airborne in moments, reducing the intruder to dust.

The city wakes and alarms blare, spotlights beam skyward, illuminating a black hull, tracing its outer contours. It's a long vessel, intersected by two forward facing arches. It's held aloft by some unknown technology, hovering in the air as though in orbit, despite its considerable size.

Not of this world, I think.

It's not really surprising. My people have been exploring the depths of space for eons. Life is abundant. But we rarely encounter intelligent species, and those that show promise are either easily subdued or happy to make peace while they war with each other. Odd that a new lifeform would discover us first, and without triggering the planetary defenses.

No matter.

All challengers will be destroyed.

I stand on the balcony, patiently waiting for explosions to wrack the intruder's hull. My residence is a hundred floors up—the highest in the city, displaying my prowess. It's an ancient tradition held over from when we were long-necked primitives with tails and simple lives.

"Report," I demand, but the Guard are silent.

Until I open my mind and allow the ambient city noise to filter in. While I'd normally hear the sounds of one-on-one combat, loud carousing, or nothing at all, tonight I hear...screaming.

Wailing.

And not just from my people.

We're being invaded, but the intruders sound like they're being tormented. In pain. Full of sorrow.

A slave army, I think, and I wonder for a moment if the Tenebris have broken our truce granting them farming rights to our alpha-planet.

I flinch when the pain and anguish billowing from both forces reaches me from the floor below. They're already in the citadel? How long have they been here, assaulting the city without raising alarms?

I rush for the hallway, pausing for a moment to consider arming myself. Our weaponry is advanced, but outside of aerial and space combat, the use of weapons on the body is considered reprehensible. I will not give in to temptation.

Instead, I charge into the hallway wielding the only weapons a true son of Chut'un requires. I extend my left hand, flexing my fingers, extending my claws. "Darmok! Awaken and cut down your enemies!" I repeat the action with my right hand. "Jalad! I infuse you with the power of our ancestral thirst for blood!"

My human self interjects for a moment with, "Oh my god. You *named your arms?*"

The memory presses on. I lunge into a hallway, crash into the far wall, and then charge for a sweeping stairwell that encircles the building's round interior, floor after floor all the way down to the bottom. There are faster ways to reach the ground floor, but instinct guides me to the nearest sound of battle—which is mostly screaming.

The claws on my feet screech, digging troughs in the hard floor as I slide to a stop at the top step and look down. The last of the Guard falls to—

What is it?

I recognize one of the species, but they shouldn't be here.

Shouldn't be a threat.

They're still primitive. Still thousands of years away from interstellar space travel. How did humans travel from Earth to Chut'un? I have no answer, but there they are, overwhelming the last of my warriors, not with superior fighting skills or weaponry, but with sheer numbers and a complete disregard for self-preservation.

They're mad.

Insatiable.

Even as my warrior cuts down three, four more take its place, gnawing on his flesh, desperate for a bite. And all the while, moaning pitifully. I don't know what they're saying, but their feeble cries make it sound like they are losing the fight, rather than winning.

But they are not alone.

Smaller creatures—bundles of brown hair—sprint past the feast as my warrior finally succumbs. Blood red eyes focus on me while their two-inch-long front teeth chatter madly, spraying foam.

I nearly throw myself down the steps to face my foe.

But a detail catches my attention. One of the four-legged creatures is wounded, its side opened up, entrails dragging behind it while a second creature follows close behind, devouring its partner. The wounded creature either doesn't care, can't feel it, or—

The wound heals around the exposed intestines, pinches the entrails tight and severs them from the body, leaving no trace of injury. The second creature, mouth full of its partner's guts, gives them a savage shake and swallows them down.

It has been a long time since I have felt revulsion, but it settles heavily in my gut.

My discomfort spirals downward when the humans cut down by
the warrior pick themselves up, slowly stitch back together, and turn
their hungry attention to me, wailing sadly.

Inner conflict roots me in place.

I do not run from battle!

I do not—

The nearest of the furry creatures springs toward me with surprising speed. I had no sense of its impending attack. Its mind is unreach-
able.

Long, flat teeth puncture the meat of my shoulder, burrowing deep
into muscle. As I flail back, it reaches up and rakes its claw-tipped paw
down my face, three times in rapid succession.

"Gah!" I shout, stumbling back. Darmok tears the creature away and
throws it into the wall with enough force to crush its bones and splatter
blood.

Red blood.

Earth blood.

As the others crest the top of the stairs, the slain creature begins
reassembling itself, drawing its spilled blood and organs back inside,
bones fusing back together. This beast will never know the endless death
that awaits all living things.

Seeing no path to victory, and no watching eyes, I do the unthink-
able.

I run.

I tear down the hallway for the saferoom at the end. The chamber
protects my clan's most prized possessions. It is capable of being sealed,
and in dire circumstances, launched into orbit.

Jalad swats away one of the hairy beasts, slamming it into the wall.
The rest are nearly upon me, the hungry human horde not far behind.
I slide to a stop inside the saferoom, spin around, and initiate a lock
down.

A heavy hatch drops and crashes into the floor, severing the lead
creature's head. It rolls to a stop at my feet, gurgling.

I'm about to grumble an insult to the severed head, but then it attempts to bite me, forcing me back a step. I glare at the thing as the door

is assaulted by dozens of scrabbling claws, none of them strong enough to breach the chamber.

But they might not need to. Moisture in the air condenses and collects around the bloody flesh.

Beyond all comprehension, the severed head begins to regrow a body.

If it reforms, I will have to fight it over and over again, forever, until I succumb to exhaustion.

They are the perfect weapon.

The Guard defeated, hiding in a vault, I feel no shame when I pick up an energy weapon captured from a now-in-ruins civilization, point it at the head, and fire, reducing the creature to ash.

Alone, I take a moment to breathe.

To settle my thoughts.

I must escape. Regroup with the Guard. Then we will discover who is behind this, spawn the greatest army the universe has ever seen, and make them pay. But first...steps must be taken. An...*alliance* must be forged.

I move to the chamber's core, admiring the collection of weapons and trophies taken from my enemies, both on Chut'un and on other worlds throughout the cosmos. I approach a glass case. Inside, clinging to a patch of soil, are two of the most prolific organisms in the universe— one red, one blue. They appear simple, bound for the dinner plate, but they are...immense.

With the push of a button, the protective barrier between us rises, allowing me to reach out with my mind and make a connection. I let them see all that I have seen, and to my surprise they recognize the threat. They have been awaiting its exposure.

But they do not agree on how to proceed. The blue wants to make peace with others. To forge alliances. To let go of the past and face the threat as a unified force.

The red wants to merge with the Chut'uni. To become one. To empower my people and give us the strength to overcome any threat and restore order—through glorious, savage violence.

I reach out, wrap my hand around the blue variation—and squeeze.

58

I snap out of the memory and back into Max's backyard.

"You know what they say about walking a mile in someone else's shoes?"

Fred squints at me. "No."

"Doesn't matter. They were wrong."

"You mock the fall of my citadel?" he asks.

"That...was horrible," I say, and I mean it. The Neos—the *Chut'uni*—have their own planet. Their own culture. Over the past 65 million years, since leaving Earth, they've become brutal and patriarchal in the extreme, but they're not human. I'm not going to judge them any more than I would a pride of lions. "But at the end—red or blue—you chose wrong."

"I chose strength." Fred flanks me, exuding menace. Fran just stands still, watching everything play out. But I know the reds. She might look calm on the exterior, but she is a swirling cauldron of reactionary emotion.

"You chose the illusion of strength. It's simple-minded and—"

Fred dashes forward, arms outstretched like he's still got claws.

I sidestep just enough so that he misses and faceplants into the swing set's upright support beam. He sprawls to the ground, spinning around like he's just been slain by the Holy Spirit.

"—easy to predict."

I back away from him, putting myself between the twins.

"There's nothing wrong with self-reliance," I say. "Henry Jones taught me that."

Fred glares at me, confused by the reference.

"*Indiana Jones and the Last Crusade?*" I throw my best Sean Connery at him. "Shelf Reliansh. Nothing? Chut'un doesn't pirate Earth movies? Missing out. *Last Crusade* was one of the last movies I saw before—"

Fred squeaks out a roar and charges again.

This time he doesn't even reach me.

Max double taps his elbow, lets out a "Duh-duh-daaa!" and leaps from the swing set's top beam. He slams down on Fred's back, driving him down into the grass. Max rolls away, gets to his feet, gives me a high five, and then stands by my side, hands on his hips, thick chest thrust out. Classic Max.

"Strongest thing in the universe is friends you can count on," I say. "What you all have going on? That's not friendship. Not even really an alliance."

"We have the strength to scour your world clean," Fred growls, pushing himself up.

"And yet, here we are, duking it out in a mental backyard from my childhood. Why do you think that is?" I thrust my hand out toward Fran. "Why do you think she's just watching?"

Fred's eyes flick to Fran, full of doubt.

"Because you chose wrong," I say, turning to face Fran. "And so did you."

"Lies," Fred leaps toward me and mixes things up, feigning a punch and driving a knee into my mid-section. It staggers me back a few steps, but his strength is gone here.

"Your great army was torn apart by a handful of my people, a bunch of weird automatons, UFOs created by one of your kind left behind on Earth, and a gaggle of teenagers—*teenagers*. Do you have any idea how hard it is to get a teenager to do anything? To focus? But pushing you back, cutting through your ranks? That was easy. Because you can't predict what we're going to do."

I prove it by kicking him square in the raisins.

Fred clutches his crotch, twists in agony, and drops to the ground, writhing in pain.

I stand over him. "FYI, real men have their testicles on the outside."

Fred groans.

"Hurts, doesn't it? Builds character, though. Makes every other kind of pain bearable in comparison."

"I will peel the skin from your bones," he says, fighting to stand again.

"Skin from my...bones?"

"Rwar!" Fred swipes at me. Had he been big and clawed, I might have been eviscerated. But I don't bother moving. His fingers just slide across my abdomen.

Max appears behind Fred, wrapping his thick arm around the smaller boy's neck, a perfect sleeper hold. "You chose wrong." He levels his gaze at Fran. "But there is still a chance for you to choose correctly."

Fran approaches, stoic. She looks from Fred to me, and finally to Max.

"It is possible..." She's fighting against emotion, reigning herself in. "...that we acted...rashly."

"You acted completely insane," I say, pushing it, but it needs to be said. "What you did... You made the chaos worse, and you nearly wiped out the one thing every military needs to win—a brain."

Fred seethes. "All that is needed is—"

I backhand him across the face. I'd never strike an actual child, but this is a five-hundred-pound asshole whose selfish actions might result in the destruction of life in the universe. "In case you missed it, the force that so easily overwhelmed your citadel and sent you scurrying to your hidey-hole came from Earth."

"Explain," Fran says.

"Those pitiful, violent people...were people. They were humans. Like me. I don't know how, but they were. Speaking English, too. And the little furry things with the big teeth? Those are capybara. Usually just really big and cuddly rodents. Looks like someone tinkered with their DNA a bit, but they all bled red, like me..." I motion to Fred. "Like him. And like most everything else from planet Earth...which is somehow at the center of whatever funky mumbo jumbo has you all riled up and OCD about galactic order.

"You need to think," I tell Fran. "You still can."

Fran mulls it over, and I'm not sure she's convinced, so I ice the cake in chocolate or whatever metaphorical spread the Europhids are fond of—algae or something. "I know where to find them, and how they're making the gates. The Lady in Red, too."

I open my memories just a sliver, letting Fran experience the fringe of my encounter with the moaning humans and the Lady in Red on

Command Central. But I hide the location from my thoughts. Leverage is key.

Fran's eyes flick to me. That got her attention. "Very well."

"What?" Fred says. Sounds almost hurt by the sudden shift.

"We were...overwhelmed..." Fran says. "We were...afraid." To me, she says, "Mistakes have been made, but they can be rectified."

"I know," I say, and I motion to Fred-Controller. "What about them?"

"We will take care of the Chut'uni," Fran says.

Fred rages. Struggles to reach her. But Max is as indomitable as ever. He holds on tight—until Fred simply vanishes.

Fran grasps my arm, eyes wide. "Wake!"

I'm back in the real world, just a few heartbeats away from the moment I left, still standing atop the female's head. Still facing off with the Controller—who is on his knees, Darmok and Jalad wrapped around his back. Claws extended, he drags his hands up over his spine, severing the red Europhids. He screams, not from the physical pain, but from the mental effort it takes to override the Europhid influence on him. It's a life and death struggle...and he wins.

The red Europhids fall away, turning to gel atop the female's head.

Free from the Europhids for the first time since his citadel fell, the Controller spreads his arms wide, opens his mouth, and unleashes a powerful roar coupled with a psychic fear tsunami. Wasn't long ago that it would have brought me to my knees.

But I'm not the same man I was then.

Not even sure you can classify me as a 'man' anymore.

I mean, physically, yeah, obviously. I got the goods. Just maybe not human.

I'm something...new. But still a dick to people who do me wrong. I mimic his posture and roar back in the most annoying, mocking way I can manage. "Blleeeeaaahhrrrgg."

He winces, which makes me laugh.

Enraged he leaps forward, knowing that here in the real world, I'm Fred and he's...

Well, he's about to be very surprised.

In the time it takes him to reach me, I activate the PSD on my hip, and position myself to receive his incoming weight. After ducking his swiped claw, I catch him around the waist and follow him in the white void of the fourth dimension.

Moments later, thanks to the copious amount of celestial coordinates Burnett packed into my mind, we emerge—twenty feet above Sea World's Dolphin Cove.

59

Falling toward fifteen-foot-deep water, I plant my feet against the Controller's chest and shove off, propelling myself away—and him a little farther out. As I arch back, I extend a middle finger, trigger my PSD again, slip into the white void, and reemerge on the shoreline in time to see him splash down.

"Time to learn the power of friendship," I say, and then I cringe. "Oh my god, I can't let Burnett show me any more anime."

After deciding to leave this bit out of my memoirs, I cup a hand to my mouth and call to the one...uh, *person...*who can help me now. "BigApe! I could use a hand. Or a flipper."

The Controller surfaces, slashing at the water like it's attacking him. For a moment, I think he can't swim, and that this will be easy. But he's just confused, raging at the water, hoping to strike me.

His attack slows, and then stops.

Treading water, his eyes just above the surface like a dang crocodile, he rotates around until he finds me on the shore.

"BigApe?"

"They're in the pens for grooming."

I turn around to find Laylah, the dolphin trainer, casually approaching with a smile on her face and a bucket in her hand. Nose scrunched. Eyes squinted against the sun. Hand to her forehead.

She's oblivious to the danger wading toward shore.

"Laylah, right?"

She smiles wider, happy to have her name remembered.

"You need to leave," I say, eyes on the water. "Now."

"There's some algae that needs scrub—"

I take hold of her chin and turn her attention to the water. "*Now.*"

"What the…" She backs away. "What the shit?"

"Do me a favor?" I ask.

Her panicked eyes dart to me.

"Let BigApe and the boys out."

She nods and bolts.

I approach the water, stepping into the shallows, fists clenched and ready to meet the enemy.

But I'm exhausted.

I might be better, faster, and stronger, but I still have limits. Been going all-out for a long time, without any sleep, with not much to eat, and I suddenly need to take a shit. Part alien. Still annoyingly human.

"C'mon," I say, "let's get this over with. You're either going to win and kill me, or I'm going to whup your ass and run to the bathroom. Either way, I'm emptying my bowels in about two minutes."

His feet reach the bottom in eight feet of water.

He rises from the depths, powerful like a shrunken down, two-armed Kraken, water sluicing off his crest.

His black eyes exude menace, but he's not trying to intimidate me or predict my moves with his mental abilities. I'm protected against them now. He won't need mental prowess to kick my ass, but I'm glad he's not trying…

…because he doesn't see what's coming.

A dolphin emerges from the water beside the Controller. It rises high into the air, a twinkle in its eye. BigApe.

He…or she…performs a magnificent flip, swinging her three-hundred-pound body up and around until, at the very last moment, she extends her tail and bitch-slaps the Controller, sending him sprawling back into deeper water.

In my mind, I hear BigApe's old catchphrase, spoken at the range, when shooting bad guys painted on metal sheets. "In da face!"

Enraged again, the Controller splashes toward shore.

But he doesn't make it far.

The first of BigApe's male protectors strikes hard and fast, approaching from the side like a torpedo, hammering the Controller's side. Before he can react, a second drills his back, knocking him forward.

They swarm him, hammering his body while dragging him back into the deep water. He attempts to fight back, but the alien is out of his element. Blood fills the water, frothing to the surface with a cascade of bubbles.

A moment later, the water settles.

The blood dissipates.

"Ho-lee porpoise shit," Laylah says, standing beside me. "Was that..."

"An alien," I say. "Yup."

Before she can ask any more questions, the water breaks, and BigApe launches skyward, twisting around in circles with a loud, happy squeak. Two males jump next, in opposite directions, passing each other in midair as they flip and splash down. Then three more are up on their tails, walking backward past us like dolphin Michael Jacksons.

While the males continue their joyful display, Big Ape slides into the shallows, squeaking at me.

I wave, smile, and say, "Thanks, man. Girl. Whatever. Appreciate the save."

He squeaks again, surges away, and joins the frolicking.

"Give her some extra fish?"

Laylah nods. "Yeah. Okay."

"One more thing," I ask, clenching. "Bathroom."

Three minutes later and a good pound lighter, I pull my adaptive armor back on, stretch from side to side, and rotate from a SeaWorld bathroom stall to the surface of another planet on the far side of the universe.

The dust has settled.

The battlefield is quiet.

Surveying the landscape, I find it covered with fallen Chut'uni, but not all of them are dead. Many of them appear to be unconscious, lulled to sleep by the Europhids on their backs—including the big female.

Motion pulls my eyes to the side. Two small figures walk toward me, battle scarred, but still upright.

I smile at them.

"Hans. Franz. You made it."

One of them gives me a thumbs up. Then they just wait to be told what to do.

I turn my eyes to the sky and find several UFOs hovering, no air force left to fight. But the *Bitch'n* is missing, already rotated back home.

Safe, thank god.

"Cover me," I tell the grays. "Anything moves...stare at it real hard."

I work my way through the maze of fallen Chut'uni, headed for the glowing red field beyond.

Each step feels like a mile, but I press on, not really eager for what comes next, but looking forward to getting it over with.

At least it won't be a fight.

I pause at the red field's periphery, scanning the innocent looking Europhids that are anything but. The human in me wants to wipe them out. Go all tit-for-tat on their assless little bodies. But that's not what I'm here for.

Because it's not the way I do things.

Because it's never been *our* way.

I peel the adaptive armor away from the top half of my body, letting it hang from my waist. Then I crouch down on one knee, reach out a bare hand and offer something undeserved, but required—

Redemption.

Little red tendrils snake out of the field, each tipped with a small hook. They snap out and puncture my flesh. But nothing else happens.

This isn't an attack.

It's a connection. It's unfettered access.

And I use it.

All at once, the entire history of the Europhid species, perceived and recorded by the blues, flows out of me. I grit my teeth from the intensity, but I maintain my position, transferring everything known by Garfunkel, from our time and a thousand years into an alternative future, in our dimension and several others. Then I add a little something else. Something human, binding everything together with the red's emotion, intensity, and passion.

Starting from my small connection, a change sweeps out across the field.

At first it illuminates just my face and the dust still lingering in the sky. Then it expands, farther and farther, stretching out over the landscape, around the planet, until the sky itself changes color.

To purple.

I turn around and watch as the same change flows out through the Chut'uni ranks. Enemies to allies, just like that. And maybe just in time. If what I saw in the Controller's memory ever makes it to Earth...in the immortal words of Private First Class, William L. Hudson, 'Game over, man.'

The connection breaks, and I stand, still the last blue Europhid, but witnessing the birth of something new.

Hopefully something better.

I sigh, looking out at the new view. "Man... I hate purple."

EPILOGUE

"So, how do we do this?" Chuy asks.

"You sit there," I say, "and listen."

It's Sunday.

Time for new music, but this time it's no longer a private affair for Hildy and me. We've been joined by Cowboy—no longer hiding in the shadows, Chuy, Delgado, Wini, Cassidy, and Burnett. Mazzola and McCoy were invited but are off chasing down a lead that might reveal what happened to the cryptoterrestrials on Earth, post-asteroid impact.

The rest of us, who are taking some R&R like normal people, are gathered outside our St. Augustine home, seated in lounge chairs, enjoying a little late-day sunshine, the air less humid after a booming thunderstorm.

"Who goes first?" Cassidy asks, licking a massive ice cream cone and kicking her legs up in the air, one at a time. Can't sit still, even while actually sitting. "Let's say youngest goes first."

Cassidy is on loan from Delgado Investigations. She's not officially part of team Dark Horse. It's more like an internship, helping Hildy with her duties and keeping all of us on our toes. They've become like sisters over the past few weeks, during which life has returned to something resembling normalcy...if you ignore my continuing contact with the Europhids and the Chut'uni, who have seen the error of their ways.

Plans are being drawn up. Contingencies. But mostly we're all just getting to know, and trust, each other. Whatever chaos is being sown throughout the universe, there doesn't seem to be a rush, or an apparent end game.

We'll be ready to fight when the time comes, but for now, life needs living.

Otherwise, what's the point?

"I go first," Hildy says, holding up a hand to stop Cassidy's complaints before they begin. "It's tradition."

"Can't mess with tradition," Delgado says. "Just wait your turn and prepare yourself for my dope jam."

"Dope jam," Cassidy says. "Is that spreadable? Sounds like something your mom fed you too much of as a kid."

Wini snickers. "I miss this kid." She reaches out, takes Cassidy's hand, and gives it a squeeze.

"You're not the only one," Delgado says, his tone indicating that he's not talking about himself.

Cassidy rolls her eyes. "Not going to happen. Tell your son, 'In his dreams.'"

"Oookay," Delgado says, apparently knowing otherwise. I wonder if Delgado's willingness to let Cassidy join us here was partially influenced by him keeping a pair of teenagers out of trouble. Glad I'm the one dealing with aliens. Teenagers are so much harder.

Since we're outside, Hildy uses our newly installed outdoor sound system, courtesy of Burnett. "Hey, Google. Play 'Top Songs' by Little Big."

"Top songs?" I ask.

She shrugs. "Only way I could actually get it to play."

"Playing Little Big on Pandora," the Google Nest system responds.

The sudden cry of a rooster makes me flinch, and I look for an enemy. I realize my mistake a skipped heartbeat later when a beat emerges from the cock-a-doodle-do. The melody is...different, but strangely catchy.

And apparently, the song isn't new to Cassidy, who leaps out of her chair, shouts, "Skibidi," and starts walking around, knees high, pumping her fists across her chest to the beat.

Cowboy lifts the Stetson covering his face. Think he might have been snoozing.

He's been different since getting back from Chut'un. We're all a little different. Hell, I'm not really human anymore. But his pain runs deep. He used to regale us with conspiracy theories and tales of his adventures in other dimensions, but now he's mostly quiet. I don't know if he just feels emasculated after being controlled and taken out of the fight, but it doesn't suit him, and I hope he can recover.

Delgado seems like his old self, not that I ever knew him well. But he's laughing, telling stories, corralling powered teenagers, and running a secret organization with a global reach. I'd say he's doing okay. Man on a mission. While he could take control of the world's military using his nanobot connection to all things electronic, he's being a little more responsible than I am. Instead of claiming the world's autonomous vehicles and nuclear arsenals for himself, he's using his vast power to rework the schedules of world leaders, inserting meetings during which he and I will blow their minds with the existence of hostile aliens, time travel, interstellar gates, and an impending attack of unknown origin, with the hopes of bringing the world together.

But he's more interested in the few people he can't find.

The ones with abilities beyond those of the hybrid teenagers, his nanobots, and my current state of inhumanity. Real heavy hitters. He believes they're essential to our cause, but despite Wini's trips around the world in search of new allies, the small group of people remains elusive.

Off planet, he thinks.

If anyone can find them, it's him and Wini, but I'm not counting on them showing up. I'm doing everything I can to prepare. Have spent more time communing with the Europhids and Chut'uni than I have with my people, learning about the universe, discussing who might ally themselves with us, and discovering that some of them have been wiped out already.

We can't ignore the threat.

At the same time, much as I'd like to, I can't poke it with a stick, either. Not yet.

So, I haven't returned to Command Central. Haven't gone looking for the Lady in Red.

That time will come, but I'm not sure when.

For all I know, it could be years.

And I'm fine with that. Because I'm putting in overtime with Chuy. We've been mostly inseparable. She joins me when I travel to other worlds, and we spend a lot of time actually cuddling, and 'cuddling'—in orbit, by the ocean, and in bed.

Cassidy stops in front of me as the music shifts into its chorus. She performs a series of dance moves that involves a lot of Vogue-like hand movements coupled with gyrations that make me uncomfortable. But the ultimate effect it has on me is laughter. It's so strange, and it seems the perfect theme song for the madness that has been my life as of late.

"Good choice," Hildy says, "right?"

Hildy, once the eager new recruit, is now an indispensable member of the team, without whom I'm not sure any of this would be possible. And it's not just her intellect. It's her unshakable hope and her positive outlook. We could all be glum right now, depressed by the impending conflict and exhausted by our preparations. Instead, we're here, gathered like we're at the end of a *Fast and Furious* movie, having a good time.

Which is about to get better.

As the song fades, and Cassidy continues dancing, Burnett runs toward us, crossing the wooden catwalk leading to the ocean. "They're coming!"

I climb to my feet and have a clear view of the water below, sparkling with sunlight. I've made peace with BigApe's fate, but I still felt bad about him being penned up. I convinced Laylah to help me stage a breakout, on account of Ape being a human intelligence. To my surprise, she agreed, and she suggested the harem also be freed. "I'm not in the business of separating lovers," she said.

That was yesterday. BigApe squeaked his thanks, but before he left, I made one last request—that he swim by the house today, and again once a year, to let us know he was okay.

Everyone on their feet, we watch as the six dolphins leap into view, swimming through the ocean, thrilled to be free. Despite that freedom, they take a moment to put on a show. Then with one last group flip, they turn and swim out to sea.

"Majestic," I say. "Live your life, buddy."

Feeling good, I turn my thoughts to the song I've picked out.

But someone breaks the rules.

Static fills the air, coming from the Nest speakers, but also from all around us. "Who's cheating?" I ask, and I see nothing but confused faces.

Through the static—music.

A chugging guitar and a solid beat. Takes just a moment for me to recognize the tune, originally released in 1976. But there's something different about it. The tone. It sounds distorted. Eerie. Like it's coming from the air all around us.

Delgado figures out why first. He pulls out his phone. "It's playing from all of our devices."

I pull out my phone, and sure enough, it's playing the song, the volume slowly increasing.

"Is message," Cowboy says, sounding ominous. "Is warning."

"It's a song," Wini says.

Delgado turns his eyes skyward, a habit of his when he's connecting to satellites. "I think he's right. The signal is everywhere. I can't pinpoint where it's coming from."

"Everywhere?" Hildy asks. "How is that possible?"

"I don't know," he says. "Shouldn't be. But—"

Without warning anyone, I activate my PSD and rotate myself to Chut'un, emerging in the quarters they've set aside for Earth delegations. The song is still playing, from my phone and from whatever the Chut'uni use for sound systems. It really *is* everywhere.

I rotate back, but I pause for a moment in the white—quiet—void.

Almost everywhere.

Then I step back out onto my patio, and I nod confirmation. "Everywhere."

"Everywhere in the *universe?*" Burnett asks, eyes wide.

I listen to the song, which under normal circumstances would get me charged up. *What the hell does it mean? And if it's a warning, who is it meant for?*

I side-eye Chuy and say, as though speaking to myself, "How does this song work into the Lady in Red's machinations?"

When I glance at her again, she's got an eyebrow raised in my direction. "How long have you been holding on to that big word?"

Damn.

"I love big words," I say, and I wave her off as the music shifts into the chorus. I recite the familiar lyrics in my head, and I realize it's not a warning, or a message. It's an introduction.

Hello Daddy.
Hello Mom.
I'm your Ch-ch-ch-ch-ch-ch...
Cherry Bomb.

AUTHOR'S NOTE

Writing a novel is intimidating. Even after publishing more than seventy. Writing a *crossover* novel bridging three standalone books published over the past six years? It's enough to make a writer metaphorically crap their pants. Capturing a vast array of character voices, personalities, and histories requires a boatload of memory, notes, and questions sent to Kane, editor supreme, who generally remembers (or can find) what I need. Then there is the story, which not only needs to merge elements from the previous novels, but also needs to point toward the big picture, the mother of all crossovers we're calling the 'Infinite Timeline.' Basically, we're bringing together eight standalone novels with three crossovers (THE ORDER, INFINITE2, KHAOS) and then merging those three crossovers in the ultimate monstrosity of a crossover novel:

SINGULARITY.

For details, including which books to read, visit: bit.ly/infinitetimeline.

When I started THE ORDER, the demon on my shoulder was performing a one-man musical about my impending failure. He called it *Robins-Doom: The Story of a Writer Whose Brain Exploded.* Now that I've finished, he's pouting on my clavicle and he doesn't have a whole lot to say. Because I'm thrilled with how it came out, and how the characters from disparate stories coalesced into a unified world.

Speaking of characters...I ultimately chose to tell the story from Dark Horse's perspective for a few reasons. I knew the story would be centered on him and on Garfunkel, not to mention on interstellar travel, but of the three protagonists from THE OTHERS, FLUX, and EXO-HUNTER, he was the most recent. His voice was still clear in my head. Jumping back into his relaxed tone was easy, and for me, a lot of fun to write.

And I wanted this book to be fun. While the core thread in the Infinite Timeline is serious, the stories binding everything together and propelling us forward are light-hearted, full of humor, and rife with twisted science fiction and action that cries out for a big screen adaptation. I think THE ORDER delivered all those things and hopefully a few that no one saw coming. I didn't outline this beast, so there's a lot I didn't see coming, either.

And now, because a novel following the exploits of Dark Horse wouldn't be complete without an epic soundtrack, visit...

bewareofmonsters.com/playlist

...to hear the complete list of songs "heard" in this novel, and to which I listened while writing it. This page also includes the playlist for *Exo-Hunter*, and in the future will feature playlists from my other novels as well.

If you're digging the Infinite Timeline and you want to help ensure we finish this thing in the most spectacular way possible, please consider posting a review at Audible, Amazon, and/or on Goodreads. In the days of analytics and automated book suggestions, reviews are king. Even short ones.

If you want to connect with me, and an awesome group of fellow fans, considering joining The Tribe at facebook.com/groups/JR.Tribe. We have a good time, we keep everyone updated on what's brewing in Hollywood, and we give away prizes every dang week. Hope to see you there, and thank you, *thank you* for reading THE ORDER.

Now...on to KHAOS!

—Jeremy Robinson

ACKNOWLEDGMENTS

Big thanks to R.C. Bray for making my writing sound better than it is, and to Podium Audio for all their support and awesome marketing. Thanks to Jeffrey Belkin and Jon Cassir, the team working on bringing my novels to screens of various sizes. Won't be long now! As always, thanks to Kane Gilmour for editing my books and for keeping me (mostly) sane, on task, and on schedule. Roger Brodeur, Dee Haddrill, Brandon Burnett, Becki Laurent, Kyle Mohr, Julie Carter, Liz Cooper, Heather Sowinski, Rian Martin, Dustin Dreyling, Micah Bell, Joseph Firoozmand, Donald Firl, Kevin Phelps, Adrian Brooke, Steven Newell, Jeff Sexton, Stephanie Maubach (who proofread from the hospital! Get well soon!), Reese Rayner, Morgan Contreras, Jon Fish, and John Shkor, you guys continue to make me look like I understand grammar and I know how to spell and type better than I do. Thanks for the awesome proofreading. Also, thank you to Rian Martin and Rene Ramirez, for once again ensuring my foul-mouthed Spanish-speaking characters get away with saying all the horrible things that I couldn't get away with in English. And finally, thanks to the real-life Dan Delgado, Brandon Burnett, BigApe (Alex Maddern), Laylah Martin, and Cassidy Rose Martin for enjoying that I use your names in my novels...even if I do horrible things to your characters.

—JR

ABOUT THE AUTHOR

Jeremy Robinson is the *New York Times* and #1 Audible bestselling author of over seventy novels and novellas, including *Infinite, The Others*, and *The Dark*, as well as the Jack Sigler thriller series, and *Project Nemesis*, the highest selling, original (non-licensed) kaiju novel of all time. He's known for mixing elements of science, history, and mythology, which has earned him the #1 spot in Science Fiction and Action-Adventure, and secured him as the top creature feature author. Many of his novels have been adapted into comic books, optioned for film and TV, and translated into fourteen languages. He lives in New Hampshire with his wife and three children.

Visit him at www.bewareofmonsters.com.